TRAPPED

Suddenly, Marcie thought of the phone and picked it up. Thank God there was a dial tone! She punched out 911 and shivered as she waited for someone to answer, knowing that if her stalker heard her, he might crash through the door and rip the phone out of the wall.

A woman's voice answered, but before Marcie could say a word, the line went dead. Instantly she knew something had been done to disconnect it. She glanced frantically around the room. She knew the lock on the bedroom door wouldn't stop him for long. But where could she run to? Where?

She rushed into the bathroom, where there was another lock. She clicked it shut and leaned against the door, trembling with fear. The walls were thin, and she could hear him pacing the floor like a caged animal outside the bedroom door.

How long would he wait before he broke down the doors to kill her?

Books by Joanne Fluke

Hannah Swensen Mysteries

CHOCOLATE CHIP COOKIE MURDER
STRAWBERRY SHORTCAKE MURDER
BLUEBERRY MUFFIN MURDER
LEMON MERINGUE PIE MURDER
FUDGE CUPCAKE MURDER
SUGAR COOKIE MURDER
PEACH COBBLER MURDER
CHERRY CHEESECAKE MURDER
KEY LIME PIE MURDER
CANDY CANE MURDER
CARROT CAKE MURDER
CREAM PUFF MURDER
PLUM PUDDING MURDER
APPLE TURNOVER MURDER
DEVIL'S FOOD CAKE MURDER
GINGERBREAD COOKIE MURDER
CINNAMON ROLL MURDER
RED VELVET CUPCAKE MURDER
BLACKBERRY PIE MURDER
DOUBLE FUDGE BROWNIE MURDER
JOANNE FLUKE'S LAKE EDEN COOKBOOK

Suspense Novels

VIDEO KILL
WINTER CHILL
DEAD GIVEAWAY
THE OTHER CHILD
COLD JUDGMENT
FATAL IDENTITY

Published by Kensington Publishing Corporation

FATAL
IDENTITY

JOANNE
FLUKE

KENSINGTON BOOKS

http://www.kensingtonbooks.com

KENSINGTON BOOKS are published by

Kensington Publishing Corp.
119 West 40th Street
New York, NY 10018

All Kensington titles, imprints and distributed lines are available at special quantity discounts for bulk purchases for sales promotion, premiums, fund-raising, educational or institutional use. Special book excerpts or customized printings can also be created to fit specific needs. For details, write or phone the office of the Kensington Special Sales Manager: Kensington Publishing Corp., 119 West 40th Street, New York, NY, 10018. Attn. Special Sales Department. Phone: 1-800-221-2647.

Kensington and the K logo Reg. U.S. Pat. & TM Off.

ISBN-13: 978-0-7582-9106-6
ISBN-10: 0-7582-9106-X
First Kensington Mass Market Edition: September 1993

eISBN-13: 978-0-7582-9107-3
eISBN-10: 0-7582-9107-8
First Kensington Electronic Edition: May 2015

10 9 8 7 6 5 4 3 2

Printed in the United States of America

PROLOGUE

He knew he'd lived in a house once, but it hadn't been as big as this mansion in Mandeville Canyon. Although he couldn't remember it, he'd had a mother and a father, and maybe even a dog. The Red Lady had told him that once, when she was having one of her good days.

He remembered that day very clearly. It had been the best day of his life. Miss Razel had given him a box of new pencils for his birthday, with his name stamped on them in gold letters. There were twelve pencils in pretty bright colors. Three orange, three green, three blue, and three yellow. He'd counted them out for Miss Razel and she'd said, *Very good, Jimmy.* And then she'd hugged him and told him that he was a very good student, the best she'd ever had in kindergarten.

The flat box of pencils had rattled under his shirt, and there had been an unaccustomed smile on his face as he'd run all the way back to the apartment building. He'd pulled open the door to the dark, cramped little lobby with its row of broken mailboxes, and his smile had abruptly disappeared. The Red Lady was waiting for him upstairs, and he had to be very careful. He never knew which one she'd be. The one who slept on the rumpled bed in the red room with her mouth slightly open to let out the snores, the one who sat at the table and smiled and told him how much she loved him, or the one who grabbed him roughly and made him do nasty things with one of the Uncles because he was a bad boy who needed to be punished.

As he tiptoed up the creaky wooden steps that led to the fourth floor, he put on the mask he wore for her. It was a good mask, and it had saved him from her punishment several times in the past. He wore it so she wouldn't learn how much she hurt him.

His eyes were downcast so she couldn't read his expression and call him a rude little bastard. His head was bowed in an attitude of respect. His expression was carefully blank, like the glass-eyed face of the teddy bear Miss Razel had on the shelf in their classroom. It was a look of impassive surrender to the things over which he had no control.

It was a lot like the reading contests in school. If you could read the word, Miss Razel let you go out for recess early. But if you missed your word, Miss Razel gave you another and another, until you got one right. It wasn't fair to compare her to Miss Razel, but he'd learned the whole thing was very similar. If he got the mask right, the Red Lady hit him once or twice, and then she gave up and let him go. But if he whimpered or started to cry, she hit him again and again, until he was perfectly quiet.

When he reached the second-floor landing, he stepped around an old drunk sleeping off the effects of the bottle in the brown paper bag he still clutched in his hand. The landing smelled bad, a combination of human waste and breath wheezing past rotten teeth. As he started up the stairs, they creaked loudly. The drunk woke up and reached out for him, but he was young and fast and he scrambled up the stairs as fast as he could.

There was garbage on the stairs, and he held his breath as he hurried past. Flies crawling over something that looked like dog food. The Red Lady had told him that some of the people who lived here ate dog food. It was cheap and it kept them alive.

As he came to the top of the stairs, he bent down to pick up a piece of ripped cloth that was caught on the banister. Then he took out his pencil box and stuffed in the cloth, so his pencils wouldn't rattle. If the Red Lady was having a bad day, she might break them all, especially if she guessed that he liked them. The first chance he got, he'd hide them under the loose board in the closet. The rats might find them, but that was better than watching her destroy the present Miss Razel had given him.

He stopped and felt his face to make sure his mask was in place. Then he took off the key he wore on a string around his neck, and opened the door very cautiously. She was up, sitting at the table, her back to him. Before he could say anything at all, she turned. There was a smile on her face, and she looked almost happy, but he still kept the mask in place. He'd seen her smile turn into a frown in the blink of an eye.

"Happy birthday!" Her smile was still in place. "Come over here, sweetie. I've got a present for you."

It still wasn't safe, so he approached very quietly in case she was having one of her bad days. But she hugged him and patted the chair next to her.

"Open it, sweetie." She handed him a heavy box

wrapped in silver paper with a big blue bow on top. "Uncle Bob picked out this present for you."

He couldn't help it. He started to smile. Uncle Bob was his favorite Uncle. He was older than the rest, and when he did the nasty thing in the red bedroom, he was always very gentle.

She held out her hand, and he took off the blue ribbon and handed it to her. She liked ribbons and she kept them. Then he loosened the tape and took off the paper, so she could use it again. There was a white box under the paper, and he was almost afraid to open it.

"Go ahead." She urged him. "Take off the cover."

The lid of the box was taped shut, and he slit the tape with his fingernail so it wouldn't tear. Then he lifted off the cover. His smile spread all the way across his face as he saw what was inside.

"Books!" He turned to her, almost afraid she'd say it was all a mistake and they weren't for him. But she just smiled.

"Uncle Bob thought you'd like them. They must be pretty old, because he said he read them all when he was a boy, and Uncle Bob's no spring chicken. Now listen to me, sweetie. You keep these books right here on the table. I want Uncle Bob to see you reading them."

He nodded. "I will. I promise."

"All right then." She smiled and opened one of the books. Her eyebrows lifted, and she started to frown as she handed him the open book. "These words are hard. Can you read them?"

"Sure." The moment he said it, he knew he'd made a big mistake, especially since she'd dropped out of school in the sixth grade, and she'd never learned to read very well. Now there was a frown on her face.

"Oh, yeah, Mr. Smarty Pants? You'd better watch it, because I'm starting to see red!"

He looked up at her with a worried frown on his face. He had to eat his words fast, or she'd start having a bad day and punish him.

"These really *are* big words!" He looked properly contrite. "Could I ask Uncle Bob if I don't know some? That way he'll know I'm reading his books."

It took her a minute, and then she clapped her hands and smiled again. "You're a smart little boy! Every time Uncle Bob is here, you ask him about a word. He used to be a teacher, you know. If he thinks he's helping you, he'll come to see us more often. And that'll mean more money for us."

"Okay." He nodded. "Shall I pick out a word right now?"

She shook her head. "No hurry. Uncle Bob isn't coming back until later, and then we're gonna have us a little party. Now open this."

He tore his eyes away from the box of wonderful books and took the small envelope she handed him. "What is it?"

"It came with you, and I saved it for you. I think it belonged to your mother."

His hands were shaking as he opened the envelope. Inside was a picture of a young woman, all dressed up in a long white dress. She had a halo of beautiful blond hair around her face, and her lips were curved up in a gentle smile. She was standing in front of a white house with green trim around the windows, and she was holding a bouquet of flowers. There was a dog at her feet, a small dog with a happy face, and he could see the shadow of the man taking the picture. His father?

"Is that . . . her?" His breath caught in a painful sob. She looked like an angel, and he wished she were here right now. His mother looked kind and sweet, almost like Miss Razel, except much prettier.

She shrugged. "I guess so. I told you, it came with you, so it's gotta be her. I bet you think she's pretty, huh?"

Something in the way she said it made the hair on the back of his neck bristle a warning. Careful. He had to be very careful. A line from a cop show he'd seen on Miss Gladys's television flew through his mind. *Anything you say can and will be used against you.*

"Her hair's white." He looked down at the picture again. "Was she real old?"

That made her laugh, and he breathed a sigh of relief. He'd done the right thing. He didn't know why, but she was jealous of that picture.

"No, she's young. Her hair's just bleached out real white. And see those flowers she's carrying? That must have been her wedding picture. And you see the shadow in front of her?"

He looked down at the picture again and nodded. "I see it."

"It's a man's shadow so maybe it's your father. Somebody had to take the picture, right?"

He nodded and did his best to look impressed. "That's right! I never thought of that!"

"I'd make a pretty good detective, huh?" She grinned at him as he nodded. "I think that was their house. You can almost make out the name on the mailbox. It's kind of fuzzy, but their last name starts with a B, and it's got seven letters, just like yours."

This time he really was impressed. "You know a lot, Aunt Neecie! I wish I could be as smart as you."

A quick smile spread over her face, and for just a moment, she looked almost pretty. She reached out to ruffle his hair, and he was careful not to flinch. This was a good day, not a bad day, and he wanted to keep it that way.

"Okay. So now you've got the picture. And don't go asking me questions. All I know is they found you in a basket in front of the place, and that picture was tucked inside your blanket. Now, why don't you . . ." She stopped suddenly, and reached in her pocket to pull out a flat, tissue-wrapped packet. "I almost forgot. Here's my present. It's old, but I can't afford to buy you new."

"Thank you, Aunt Neecie." He took the packet and unfolded the tissue paper. Inside was a thick silver chain. Why would she give him a silver chain? His mind sifted through the possibilities, but he couldn't come up with a thing.

"Well?"

She was frowning slightly, and he put on a delighted smile. "Wow! It's . . . it's wonderful, Aunt Neecie!"

"You bet it is!" She smiled. "Old Roy gave that to me when we got married. 'Course you don't remember your Uncle Roy, do you? He died when you were just a baby."

"I think I remember him." The truth was, he didn't remember Uncle Roy at all, but he said what she wanted to hear. According to her, Uncle Roy had been a saint. And since he'd lost a leg in a train accident, they'd had his disability check every month. When Uncle Roy died, the checks had stopped coming, and she'd sold everything to pay the bills. That was when they'd gone on welfare and moved to this old apartment building.

"You can keep your key on that chain." She smiled at him. "Then you can't lose it. Now you go pick out a couple of big words and write them down, so you can ask Uncle Bob. He's bringing Chink food for our party.

And after we eat, you'll make him feel real good about that present he gave you, won't you?"

He nodded. It was what she expected, and it wouldn't do any good to tell her that he didn't want to do the nasty thing in the red bedroom anymore.

"You like to help me with the Uncles, don't you, sweetie?"

He'd nodded again, because he'd learned that it was the smart choice. If he told her that he hated what the Uncles did to him, she'd beat him. And then she'd tie him to the bed in the red room, so Uncle Bob could do it anyway. But if he wore the mask and agreed with everything she said, he could avoid the beating. Of course, there was no way to prevent what the Uncles did to him. It was a part of his life, like breathing.

"I'm going out for a pack of smokes." She picked up her purse and headed for the door. "You stay right here and don't you make any noise, you hear?"

The moment she was gone, he picked up one of the books and started to read. It was all about two boys who lived in an orphanage. *Orphanage* was a good word to ask Uncle Bob. It was nine letters long, and no one would expect him to know it.

There was a smile on his face as his eyes skimmed the words, following the story. These books were old, but they were still good. He would be able to live in a wonderful, storybook world for as long as they lasted. And then he could start reading them all over again. It was very good of Uncle Bob to give him these books. Now he'd have something interesting to think about when he was alone in the red bedroom with the Uncles.

He came back to the present with a jolt as he heard the glass door to the patio slide open. He parted some of the dense leaves in the hedge bordering the side of the pool, and peered out anxiously. It was only the housekeeper. She had a broom in her hand and she was going to sweep off the patio, as she did every night.

He liked the housekeeper. She was always friendly, and she took good care of the children. She thought she knew him, but all she really knew was the mask. They thought they were locking him out with the new security system, but he could get inside the gates any-time he wished. And they'd never guessed that most of the time he was here already. It was like the Red Lady used to say, there was always a way around everything, if you used your head. Of course, she wasn't saying anything now. Now her mouth was closed forever.

He could feel the red mist threaten as he thought of that night, and he pushed it away. Not now. He had to be alert. The housekeeper was sweeping back and forth with hard, even strokes of the broom. It reminded him of something that made him shiver, but he pushed that out of his mind, too.

He felt the hair on the back of his neck prickle, as a voice called out from the house. Not one of her chil-dren. And not the husband, either. This was a different voice, a voice that made him ache inside with its haunt-ingly familiar tone.

And then he saw her, and his breath caught in his throat. She was wearing a white bathing suit, and she looked like a swan, all sleek and glossy and graceful. Or perhaps she was an angel. Her beauty was pure and immaculate. He felt his hands begin to tremble uncon-trollably as she stepped into the light by the pool. She was going to swim, and he loved to watch her swim.

The warm feeling rushed through him as she slipped into the water. Ah! How beautiful! How lovely her arms were as they rose up and down in the water, stark white columns of curving beauty that cut through the dark surface to emerge again for the next stroke. Her long, shapely neck arched out of the water, and her glorious blond hair gleamed in the moonlight, even though she'd piled it high on her head in a shining knot. She was supple and strong, like a young sapling, but as delicate as a piece of fine lace. She was Homer's Helen of Troy, and Poe's Lenore, and Sir Lancelot's Lady of the Lake. She was the only woman he had ever loved. She was Jimmy's lost mother, and he wouldn't let her leave him again.

But there was something wrong, a hateful red color spilling out from the garden just beyond the pool. Red blossoms like the blood that had bubbled and bloomed from Aunt Neecie's mouth. He had to stop it before it spilled out and covered him.

The red mist began to swirl around his feet, rising, rising. He had to move quickly, before it was too late. He stepped out very softly, very quietly, to do what had to be done. Around the pool, behind the hedge of lush green boxwoods without a rustle. Like a cat in the dead of night, he moved without hesitation. And then he dropped to his knees on the soft earth by the bubbling blossoms. And he whimpered as he plucked them off one by one, crushing the petals between his fingers and feeling them die.

Her head turned in his direction. It seemed as if she were looking directly at him with her beautiful green eyes. But he knew that was only an illusion. She saw only a shadow, heard only a faint rustle. A neighbor's cat in the garden, a fierce night prowler stalking his blood prey. Her head rose out of the water, watching, listening. But he was as still as death.

And then she began to swim again, her fears laid to

rest. As well they should be. He was here. And he would always protect her from the red.

Tears fell from his eyes, like warm spring rain. How he loved her! He had broken the rule to warn her, broken his vow of silence. He had chosen the words to tell her, cut them out of paper and pasted them to the letter he'd sent to her. *Red is the color of blood.*

He knew he had frightened her. And he was ashamed. But his words had done their work, and she had been wise enough to listen. She had changed her hateful red bedroom to a sea green place of beautiful peace.

The red mist was rising now, rising up to claim him. In a few moments it would reach his mind, and then there would be a merciful darkness. But there was work to be done before he could rest.

He dropped to the ground, shredding the petals into thin strips that blew away in the winter wind. They would shrivel and fade, buffeted by the air until they turned to a harmless brown. Earth, air, fire, and water. They were the ancient elements. They had the power to destroy the red, to send it away forever.

At last he was finished, and he smiled as he got to his feet. It was his job to keep her safe. He was her guardian, her lover, her unseen protector. Only he knew how to save her from the certain destruction of the red.

CHAPTER 1

Even though she'd had a grueling day, Mercedes Calder flashed the driver one of her famous, million-watt smiles as he helped her out of the studio limo. Her smile was totally genuine. Mercedes liked the new driver the studio had assigned to her. George never tried to make idle conversation on the twenty-minute trip to the studio when she had lines to learn; he didn't mind stopping at the school to pick up her twins on the days she finished shooting early; and he was unfailingly prompt. Even though George was well paid by the studio, Mercedes planned to give him a generous bonus when they wrapped her film.

"Six-thirty tomorrow morning, George? I have an early call."

"No problem, Miss Calder. I'll be here. Do you want me to check out the house for you?"

Mercedes shook her head. "That's not necessary, George. They finally finished installing the security system. But thanks for asking. That was very thoughtful."

George tipped his hat and slid back in, behind the wheel. He was a retired policeman who looked like a fullback, over six feet tall with the muscular body and lightning reflexes of a professional athlete. He'd told Mercedes he'd taken his early retirement option when he'd been shot chasing down a murder suspect. He'd known they were planning to kick him upstairs, and he hadn't liked the idea of sitting behind a desk all day. Early retirement pay wasn't all that much, and George had done private detective work for a year or two. Then he'd landed this job with the studio as a combination bodyguard and driver.

Although the studio had dismissed Mercedes's threatening letters as a crazy prank by an unstable fan, they'd immediately assigned George to be her driver. And it had worked, as far as Mercedes was concerned. She never worried when George was around. He was more than capable of defending her, and when she was with him, she felt safe. At least there hadn't been any threatening letters today. Mercedes had checked the mailbox at the end of the driveway, when they'd stopped at the gates. She hoped that her ordeal was over, that her crazy fan was locked up tight in some mental hospital or jail.

Mercedes still shivered when she thought about the letters that had come in the mail. The words had been cut out of magazines, and pasted on pieces of plain notebook paper. The whole thing had sounded like something you'd see in a bad B-movie, but the message had been chilling.

Most stars got an occasional letter from a crazy fan. It was so common, it was almost normal. Ashley Thorpe, her costar in *Summer Heat,* had told Mercedes about the proposal he'd received from a seventy-year-old widow who'd offered her life savings if he'd spend the night with her. And Sandra Shepard, the character actress who played her mother in the movie, had

mentioned a letter she'd received last year from a high
school student in Iowa, inviting her to be his date for
the senior prom.

Mercedes had been in the "biz" for over fifteen
years, and she'd shrugged off plenty of proposals and
propositions from crazy fans before. But the letters
she'd received two months ago were very different.
They'd come to her home, instead of the studio.

The first letter had arrived on a Saturday, and Mercedes had been alone in the house. She'd been out at
the pool, enjoying the warm rays of the sun, when
she'd heard the distinctive squeaking brakes of the
mailman's Jeep. Since she usually got a letter from
Marcie on Saturdays, she'd hopped into her car and
driven down the long, winding driveway to pick up the
mail.

Marcie's letter was there, and Mercedes had taken
the time to read it. Then she'd noticed another letter
marked "personal," with no return address, and she'd
opened that as well.

> *I am watching you. I will always be near. Do not*
> *try to hide. You can keep nothing from me. I am with*
> *you at night when you swim in the pool. I am with*
> *you when you go to bed in the red room. Please do not*
> *sleep in the red room. Red is the color of blood.*
> *The others will tell you lies about me, but I am not*
> *what they say. Do not try to escape me. I will not let*
> *you leave me again. You will be with me always, even*
> *in death.*
>
> *Jimmy*

Mercedes's hands had been shaking as she'd finished reading the letter. He knew her bedroom was
red! He really *was* watching her! She'd jumped back

into her car, locked all the doors, and peered out of the window in fright. The grounds seemed peaceful enough, but was he out there somewhere, taking vicious pleasure in her fear? Her instinct had been to race for the house, but she'd left it unlocked, and he could be waiting for her inside!

Pure panic had propelled her as she'd turned on the ignition and put her car in gear. She had to get away! But where should she go? What should she do? She'd made a quick U-turn, tires sliding on the gravel, and headed down Mandeville Canyon Road.

She'd glanced nervously in the rearview mirror, but no one had seemed to be following her. She was safe. For now. As she'd turned on Sunset Boulevard, she'd suddenly remembered the interview she'd done for a popular fan magazine. It had mentioned her exercise regime—twenty laps in the pool every night. And there had been several photos of her in her newly redecorated bedroom. If he'd seen a copy of that article, he would have known about the swimming and the color scheme of her bedroom. Perhaps he wasn't watching her after all.

With each mile Mercedes traveled away from the house, she'd felt a little calmer. She knew that most people who wrote threatening letters never dreamed of actually carrying out their threats. This man was probably nothing more than a harmless neurotic who got his kicks by scaring people. Still, it couldn't hurt to take a few precautions, like buying a handgun and learning how to use it. And while she was at it, she'd order a new security system. The one she had was over ten years old.

It turned out that buying a handgun in California was a frustrating experience. Although her life had been threatened, and she had a legitimate reason for wanting to arm herself, there was still a mandatory waiting period before she could take her new Lady Smith revolver home. Rules were rules in California, where the anti-gun lobby was strong. Crooks could buy guns immediately through illegal means, but honest citizens had to wait and hope that they'd still be alive at the end of the waiting period.

Mercedes had walked away from the gun store shaking her head. She was probably overreacting, but she had to take precautions, just in case. She'd stopped at a pay phone to call a home security service, and she'd hired an armed guard to patrol the grounds until her new state-of-the-art security system was installed. Then she'd arranged to have her room redecorated in a lovely shade of sea green. That would please Brad. Green was his favorite color. Brad hadn't liked her red bedroom. He'd said it was like sleeping inside a catsup bottle. She's laughed at his joke, but she'd been planning on changing the color scheme anyway.

That night, when Brad had come home and found the security guard, he'd told her he thought she'd done exactly the right thing. The letter *was* scary. And while it was true that Mercedes probably wouldn't hear from this particular man again, she was a big star and there were lots of crazy fans out there. Then he'd hugged her and told her he wished he could always be home to protect her. Unfortunately, his investment business demanded a lot of traveling. He'd certainly rest much easier after the new security system was installed. It would give him peace of mind, knowing that Mercedes and the twins were safe behind locked gates.

The second threatening letter had arrived a week later. Luckily, the security guard was on duty when Mercedes had taken it out of the envelope, and she hadn't panicked. Her crazy fan was still out there, but at least she now knew what he wanted.

I am still with you, watching and waiting. No one can protect you. You must do exactly as I say.

Give your husband twenty thousand dollars in a backpack. Tell him to go to the phone booth on the corner of Sunset and Gower at noon tomorrow. I will call him and tell him where to leave the money.

I love you. You belong to me. I have no wish to cause you pain.

Jimmy

When Brad had read the letter, he'd urged her to call the police. Naturally, Mercedes had refused. The police could do nothing, and there were bound to be leaks to the press. The studio wouldn't like that kind of publicity, and this whole thing was probably just a crazy prank.

Exactly a week later, the third letter had arrived. It was almost identical to the second, except that the sum of money had doubled, and there was one additional postscript after the signature. *Your security guard cannot protect you. If you continue to ignore me, perhaps your death will not be as merciful as I planned.*

When Brad read the letter, he was convinced that they had to take action. While he agreed that he didn't believe in giving way to threats, he'd suggested that perhaps they should pretend to do what the crazy fan wanted. He'd go to the phone booth, get the instructions, and deliver the money. And then he'd stake out the area and catch the nut case, when he came to pick it up.

Mercedes had vetoed that idea immediately. There was no way she'd let him do something that dangerous.

But Brad was insistent. He was her husband, and he wanted to protect her. There was no way he'd let a crazy fan get away with threatening his wife!

They'd argued about it long into the night, but Mercedes had been firm. She wouldn't let Brad put himself in danger, and she wouldn't even pretend to give way to blackmail. Brad knew how blackmail worked. If the crazy fan actually succeeded in getting the money, he'd keep right on sending threatening letters, demanding more and more cash. It was best to take a strong stand in the beginning, and not give in to this type of extortion.

Even though Mercedes had shrugged off the threats, she was concerned enough to take the letters with her to the studio the next morning. The studio hired experts to deal with crank letters from crazy fans, and Mercedes had asked their advice. They'd agreed that she had done all the right things to protect herself. They'd said not to worry, that they'd dealt with hundreds of extortion letters, and nothing had ever happened. It would have been an entirely different matter if someone had come up to her face-to-face and made these kinds of demands. But no one had, and chances were her crazy fan was already back in a mental institution or a jail cell.

Mercedes felt much better after she'd talked to the studio experts, especially since they'd assigned George to be her driver. George was armed and he was formidable. There was no way anyone would bother her while she was under his protection.

After she'd finished work for the day, Mercedes had asked George to drive her to the gun store. She'd picked up her revolver, and bought a gun safe that only opened if she pressed a series of coded buttons. George had installed it for her, and that weekend he'd driven her to a firearms safety class, where she'd learned how to use her Lady Smith with deadly accuracy.

Of course, Mercedes hadn't mentioned any of this to Brad. And she'd decided not to tell him if she got another threatening letter. Brad might do something brave and foolish, like trying to catch the blackmailer himself.

The letters had definitely changed Mercedes's life. Opening the mail had always been fun for her, but now she dreaded it. She held her breath every time she picked up the neat stack of letters her postman slipped in the box. It had been almost a month since the last threatening letter, and she was almost convinced that her crazy fan had given up. But even though their new security system was up and running, George had told her to carry her revolver from room to room, whenever she was alone in the house.

"Are you sure you're all right, Miss Calder?"

George looked concerned, and Mercedes nodded. "I'm fine. See you in the morning, George."

Mercedes waved as the limo drove off. The moment the gates had opened and closed again, she reactivated the alarm system. There was no way anyone could open the gates without the code. And if anyone tried to climb over the bars or force his way in, a patrol of armed security guards would be on the grounds in less than five minutes.

The alarm on the front door was set, and Mercedes punched in the code on the numbered panel. The advisor from the security company had cautioned her against using her birthday as a code. That was a matter of public record. Brad had suggested they use their anniversary instead, and he'd joked that it was one way to make sure she never forgot the date. As if she could!

As she opened the door and walked across the tile foyer, Mercedes caught sight of her reflection in the gold-framed, oval mirror on the wall. She'd never considered herself beautiful, although everyone else seemed to think she was. Green-eyed blondes weren't all that unusual in her home state of Minnesota.

When Mercedes had landed her first movie role, the studio publicity department had called her a cross between Doris Day and Marilyn Monroe. The comparison had made Mercedes laugh. Doris had been bubbly and innocent, while Marilyn had exuded sex from every pore. Mercedes knew she wasn't bubbly and innocent, or super-sexy. She was just an ordinary actress, who worked hard to learn to play any role she was offered.

At first Mercedes had played the fun-loving teenager, the cheerleader who fell in love with the quarterback on the football team. Then she'd graduated to college roles, playing the young freshman coed who fell in love with the professor. From there she'd played the young professional who fell in love with her boss. She was always falling in love and ending up happy, the essence of the female romantic lead. Finally, she was mature enough to play other, more demanding parts, but her latest role in *Summer Heat* was the biggest challenge she'd ever faced.

Summer Heat was a story of deception, of a marriage gone awry. Mercedes played the victim, a wife whose husband was slowly poisoning her, so that he could be free to marry his mistress. She had to be naively trusting and totally unsuspecting in the early part of the movie, a woman who was so in love with her new husband that she was completely blind to his faults. As the movie progressed, her character deepened and matured. The wife began to doubt her husband, and finally realized, in horror, that he was trying to kill her.

At the end, Mercedes had to play a woman so crazed by her husband's duplicity, she exacted a terrible revenge.

Her role in *Summer Heat* wouldn't have been all that difficult if it had been a play. Most plays were chronological, starting at the beginning and progressing in a straight line to their conclusion. But movies weren't like plays, although most people who weren't in the industry didn't realize that. Almost all of Mercedes's scenes were shot out of sequence.

The scene they'd done today had been near the end of the movie. Mercedes had played the vengeful wife, preparing to kill her husband and his mistress. Tomorrow they would shoot the park wedding at the very beginning of the movie, and that meant Mercedes had to jump back in time to play the trusting bride, meeting her husband's mistress for the first time, and being completely unaware of their relationship. It took mental preparation to jump back and forth like that, but it was more cost-effective. Scenes that took place in the same setting were shot on the same day, regardless of where they occurred in the movie. Mercedes reread the script every night, starting at the beginning and stopping at the scene they'd shoot the next day. That helped her to get into the right frame of mind for the morning's work.

"Rosa? I'm home!" Mercedes walked down the hall and peeked into the immaculately clean kitchen. Her housekeeper wasn't there. She walked through the beautifully decorated rooms on the ground floor, but Rosa and the children were nowhere to be found.

Since she was still uneasy when she was alone in the house, Mercedes got her Lady Smith from the gun safe and carried it upstairs to her pretty sea green bedroom, where she undressed and slipped into a robe. She loved the new color she'd picked for her bedroom: It was very calming and restful. Then she sat down at her white wicker dressing table and peered into the mirror to assess the damage after her long day of shooting. There were tiny lines at the corners of her eyes, but that wasn't surprising. She'd waited up for Brad to come home last night, despite her early call. Her green eyes were clear and bright, thanks to the eye drops her makeup artist had applied, but her pale blond hair was wet with perspiration.

Mercedes walked to the huge mirrored bathroom and turned on the shower. She'd feel much better once she washed her hair and used some conditioner. She took off her robe and surveyed her body critically. Her skin was still tight, and her breasts were high and firm with no signs of sagging. Another week of dieting, and she'd be in better shape than she'd ever been in before. And she needed to be in perfect shape, since she would wear a bikini in the honeymoon beach scene.

As she stepped under the hot stream of water, Mercedes gave a weary sigh. She really didn't feel like swimming laps tonight but she knew she should. Physical fitness and a proper diet had kept her looking like she was in her twenties, when she was actually thirty-four.

When Mercedes emerged from the shower, fifteen minutes later, she felt refreshed. She changed to a warm-up suit that had been especially designed for her. Then she towel-dried her hair-the ends were beginning to split from having it blow-dried too often-and carried her Lady Smith downstairs with her. Perhaps she was being a little too paranoid, since the new security system was armed, but it did make her feel much safer.

Her first stop was the den, where she poured herself a glass of perfectly chilled Chardonnay from her husband's new wine cooler. Brad was a wine connoisseur, and he had over two hundred labels in his temperature-controlled EuroCave. At least this hobby of his was useful, not like the racehorses that never won, or the antique cars that were stored in their specially designed warehouse garage.

The wine was delicious—a light, fruity vintage—and Mercedes smiled. A hundred and ten calories, she'd have to skimp on dinner, but it was worth it. Then she flopped down in the leather massage chair behind her husband's desk, and called the florist to order flowers for her hairdresser, who had just given birth to her first baby.

After five minutes in the massage chair, Mercedes felt rejuvenated. She took another sip of wine, picked up the phone again, and called the number for her voice mail.

The first message was from Brad. He wouldn't be home until late. There were harness races at the track tonight, and he wanted to check out some of their competition. By the time she got this message, he'd be at the stables with their horse trainer. Metro Golden Mare was having some problems, and they might have to scratch her in Sunday's race.

Mercedes frowned and tapped her pen on the message pad. Thoroughbreds were an expensive investment, and they weren't paying off. She'd wanted Brad to minimize their losses and sell out, but he'd convinced her to hang on for one more season. And now their prize racehorse was going to be scratched! When she'd married Brad two years ago, she'd thought that he was a shrewd businessman. But instead of increasing her capital, he'd reduced it considerably. It was a very good thing she'd met with Sam Abrams, her lawyer, on the set today. She knew Brad would be upset at first, but he'd understand when she explained exactly why she'd hired another investment firm to handle the bulk of her assets. If he continued to funnel her money into risky ventures, there'd be nothing left for her twins!

When Mercedes pressed the button for her next message, her hand was shaking. She took another sip of wine and got ready for more bad news. But this message was from her housekeeper, and Rosa always made her smile. Rosamunda Szechenyi Kossuth was a welcome addition to the family. Mercedes knew she'd always be grateful to her first husband for hiring Rosa to help out when the twins were born.

When Rosa had first come to work for them, there had been a language problem. Rosa spoke perfect English, but she had just emigrated from Hungary. Her accent was so thick, Mercedes had been unable to understand her. They'd solved the problem by calling in a friend, who made his living as a dialogue coach. After two months of speech lessons, three times a week, Rosa's accent had faded to only a faint trace.

Rosa had given Mercedes a worry-free decade. Mercedes's children were her children, and Rosa was a Super Mom. The twins would be ten years old next week, and Mercedes had planned a big party. What Rosa didn't know was that the twins had a surprise for her. Mercedes had taken Trish and Rick to an expensive jewelry store, and they'd picked out a beautiful watch to give to Rosa. Mercedes had assured them that Rosa would love it. Of course, Rosa would love anything "her babies" gave her. Rosa's room was decorated in what Mercedes called Early Twin, with crayon drawings, framed finger-paint handprints, and dried flowers they'd picked for her in the garden.

Mercedes laughed as she played Rosa's message. She could hear the twins in the background, urging her to please hurry. Rosa had left a message to say that she was taking the kids to an early movie, and they'd stop for a hamburger on the way home. Mr. Brad had insisted the kids needed a night out, and he'd given her money to spend. She'd prepared a chicken salad for Mercedes. It was in the refrigerator, along with a big pitcher of iced tea.

Mercedes sighed. Salad, again. A thinly sliced, skinless chicken breast on a bed of mixed greens with diet dressing. Three hundred and fifty boring calories, but she had to lose another four pounds before they shot the bikini scene.

Thirty-four was a rotten age for an actress. It was too old to play the ingénue and too young for "mature woman" roles. There weren't many parts written for actresses in their mid-thirties, and the competition was fierce. Her best hope for continued success was to stay in perfect shape.

Even though she tried not to think of it, Mercedes pictured Rosa and the twins in a green leather booth at Hamburger Hamlet, munching on thick, juicy burgers with crispy french fries. The twins would talk Rosa into ordering huge slices of chocolate cake with fudge sauce and ice cream for dessert. They always did. And Mercedes was stuck here with chicken salad! Of course, she couldn't have gone along, even if they'd waited for her to get home. She had script changes to memorize before tomorrow morning, and she couldn't afford to blow her diet.

Mercedes swallowed—her mouth was watering—and punched the button for her next message. It was a polite reminder from her dry cleaners, asking her to pay her last month's bill. She jotted down the information on a yellow sticky and placed it on the top of

Brad's desk. Since she was so busy with her career, Brad handled the bills for all of their household expenses.

The fourth message was also about an overdue bill, the landscaping service this time. Mercedes wrote out another yellow sticky and placed it next to the first. Brad had mentioned that they were having a slight cash-flow problem, but this was ridiculous! Perhaps he just hadn't gotten around to writing the checks yet.

The next message was a typical call from her sister. *"This is your twin sister, Marcie Calder, in Minnesota."*

Mercedes put the message on pause and laughed out loud. She only had one twin sister and she knew where Marcie lived. But Marcie was shy, and she felt so uncomfortable about leaving a recorded message that she always identified herself that way.

"I called to tell you that cousin Betty is getting married on Saturday. She's Aunt Bernice and Uncle Al's youngest daughter . . . the one who used to wet the bed when they came to visit? I'm not going. It's way up in Hibbing, and they're predicting snow for the weekend, but I'm sending a gift. I called to ask whether you want me to include your name on the card."

Mercedes frowned. She vaguely remembered their cousin Betty, and knew that anything that Marcie picked out would be fine. Her sister was an art teacher and she'd always had impeccable taste.

"I bought a beautiful pottery bowl at the college art sale, cerulean blue with pink and lavender blossoms that remind me of the ones in Cézanne's Vase of Flowers. *It was fifty-four dollars, which is a lot, but since it was the last day, the artist took ten dollars off. If I don't hear from you by tomorrow, I'll just add your name to the card and send it off."*

Mercedes grinned. Thank goodness one of them was organized! She remembered receiving Betty's wedding invitation last week, but she'd tossed it aside and forgotten all about it. How could twin sisters be so different? They looked alike, tall with blond hair, green eyes, and light complexions. If they dressed alike, no one would be able to tell them apart. But they had totally different temperaments. Marcie was solid, dependable, and sweetly naive, while Mercedes was exactly the opposite. The only thing they had in common was their disappointing luck with men.

Mercedes had married Mike Lang, the producer of her first picture, right after the film was completed. It was a May-December marriage, Mike was thirty years her senior, but both of them had wanted children. Mercedes had gotten pregnant almost immediately and delivered twin babies, a boy and a girl. They'd named them Patrick and Patricia, and they'd called them Rick and Trish. Both Mercedes and Mike had been delighted with their happy, healthy babies. But Mike had been a workaholic, and the stress of producing hit after hit had taken its toll. He died of a massive heart attack when the twins were only two years old.

At first, Mercedes had thought she'd never love again. Then she'd hired Brad James as her investment counselor, and everything had changed. She'd married him at the high point of their whirlwind Hollywood courtship, and she was beginning to wonder if the old adage was true. She'd married in haste, and she worried that she might repent in leisure. It seemed as if all the romance had gone out of their marriage. Brad was gone more often than he was home, and although she had no proof, she suspected that he was involved with someone else.

Marcie had suffered through a bout with a fickle lover, too. She'd fallen in love with a fellow art student when she was in college. Mercedes had met him. He was handsome and very talented, but she had been worried that he was only using Marcie, until someone else came along. As it turned out, she'd been right. The day after their graduation ceremony, Marcie's boyfriend had flown off to France with a wealthy widow, leaving Marcie with nothing but a note and a couple of his paintings.

"Oh, yes. I got the roundtrip airplane ticket, and I'll be there for the twins' birthday party. I can't believe they're ten years old already! But really, Mercy, I absolutely insist on reimbursing you. It makes me feel like a charity case when you pay for everything."

Mercedes grinned. Marcie was the only person who used her nickname. The Calder twins had been Mercy and Marcie all through high school, and Mercedes had hated it. Every time she'd complained, Marcie had told her she ought to be grateful their parents hadn't named them something even worse. They'd compiled a long list of names that made them shudder, names like Patrice and Caprice, Mabel and Sable, Clarissa and Marissa, Edwina and Bettina, and the very worst, the one that had made them collapse in gales of laughter, Drusilla and Ludmilla.

"Guess I don't have any other news. Curtis Benson spilled green poster paint all over the tan leather shoes you gave me, but it came right out with a little saddle soap.

Give the twins a kiss for me and keep one for yourself. Bye."

Mercedes was still grinning as she wrote another yellow sticky for Brad, telling him to send Marcie a check for twenty-two dollars, her half of the wedding gift. A call from Marcie always cheered her up, and having her here for the birthday party would be wonderful.

The last message made Mercedes frown. Her agent and business manager, Jerry Palmer, wanted to discuss her next project over lunch tomorrow. But there wouldn't be a next project for Jerry. She'd already talked to someone else, and she was planning to switch to them right after *Summer Heat* was completed.

When she'd broken the news to Brad last night, they'd had a nasty fight. Jerry was Brad's friend, and she'd hired him on Brad's recommendation. They'd argued for hours, but finally Brad had agreed that she needed to go with someone who had more clout with the big boys. And that brought up another problem, one she needed to solve immediately.

Mercedes picked up the telephone and called Sam Abrams. He'd been her lawyer for almost a dozen years, and he was practically a member of the family. That gave her certain privileges other clients didn't enjoy, such as access to his home telephone number.

It took only a moment to make sure that all her future earnings would go directly to Sam's office, and Mercedes was smiling as she hung up. By this time it was almost seven in the evening, and she was beginning to think much more kindly of Rosa's chicken salad. She'd swim twenty laps, treat herself to another glass of wine, and eat in the poolside cabana.

Since she'd already lost a total of ten pounds, none of her old bathing suits fit her new, svelte figure. She'd ordered more, twelve lovely, white suits that had been especially designed for her, but when she opened the drawer in the cabana, she found that the designer had made them in the wrong color. There were twelve new suits, but all of them were red.

Mercedes frowned as she remembered a line from the first threatening letter. *Red is the color of blood.* Her fingers trembled as she held up the suit, but she forced herself to remain calm. The crazy fan was long gone. And even if he wasn't gone, there was no way he could get past the sophisticated security system. She took another sip of wine to fortify herself, and slipped into the red bathing suit. She wasn't about to give up her exercise regime, because some looney objected to the color of her bathing suit!

There was a sound, and Mercedes froze. It sounded like the security gates were opening. Were they home already? She waited a moment, expecting to hear Rosa's car, but there was no crunch of tires on the crushed rock driveway.

It took no more than a second for Mercedes to pick up her revolver. The solid weight of the tempered steel was comforting, and she held it tightly as she listened for any other alarming sounds. But everything was perfectly quiet.

Since her security system was new, and she wasn't quite used to relying on it, it took Mercedes a moment to remember to check the closed-circuit monitor. There was one in every room, including the cabana. When she switched it on, the camera showed that the gates were firmly closed. The sound she'd heard must have come from the pool equipment, or perhaps her neighbor's gate had opened. Sound sometimes carried quite far in the canyon.

Mercedes felt a little prickle of fear as she stepped out of the cabana. Of course, there was no reason to be nervous. Her security system was armed. If anyone tried to get into the house, bells would clang, sirens would blare, and the police would be notified immediately. She was perfectly safe from any intruder.

She put her Lady Smith down at the side of the pool and tested the water with her toe. The pool was warm, just the way she liked it, and Mercedes slid into the water. She'd learned to swim at an early age, like most kids who grew up in Minnesota. The Land of Ten Thousand Lakes had several within biking distance, and Mercedes and Marcie had spent practically the whole summer in the water. But the swimming season was short in Minnesota, barely two months long. Mercedes was glad she lived in California, where she could use the pool year-round.

Mercedes used the Australian crawl for her first two laps. She was an excellent swimmer, and when they were teenagers, both she and Marcie had qualified as Red-Cross-certified Life Savers. When she'd moved to California, she'd actually taken a job as a lifeguard at Santa Monica Beach. It had paid for her acting lessons, and given her a great opportunity to get a tan. Then Mike had discovered her, and her dream had come true. She'd gone from her one-room, ramshackle apartment in Venice, to this gorgeous, twenty-room mansion in Mandeville Canyon.

She pushed off at the deep end and swam another lap, using the butterfly stroke. It was physically exhausting, lifting herself out of the water with her arms, and Mercedes was puffing by the time she finished. Time to change to something less rigorous, like the breaststroke. Two laps of that, and she switched to the sidestroke for another three laps.

Freestyle was next, and Mercedes alternated between her favorite strokes for five more laps. She was getting tired, but she was pleased at all the calories she must be burning. She chose a modified crawl for her last six laps. A total of twenty laps was a lot, but she knew she could do it.

The end was in sight, only one lap to go. Mercedes was running on pure determination, when she approached the deep end of the pool. She looked up and gasped as she saw a dark shape behind the palm tree by the diving board.

Suddenly, the pool lights went out, and she was

plunged into darkness. Mercedes opened her mouth to scream, but it ended in a sputter as strong arms pushed her head beneath the surface of the water. She kicked out desperately, trying to propel herself away, but her tired legs found only the slippery resistance of the water. There was nothing to kick, nothing to push, as her head was held under the water in a grasp of steel.

Her tortured mind screamed out for air. Her lungs were burning as her muscles began to spasm. She struggled to pry loose, but her frantically clawing fingers encountered padded gloves. It was no use. Her mouth and lungs were filling with deadly water. The last thing Mercedes Calder saw in the cold, blue moonlight before final blackness closed in, was the wavering image of her killer's familiar face above the surface of the water.

CHAPTER 2

It was seven-fifteen in the morning, when Marcie Calder stepped out of her apartment and prepared to perform the Minnesota Footwear Switch. She carried her shoes in a plastic shopping bag looped over her arm, and wore her boots. She needed boots to wade through the snow to the garage at the back of her building. Once inside, she would slip out of her boots and switch to her shoes to back the car out of the garage. Then she'd put on her boots again to get out and close the garage door. And then she'd switch back to her shoes for the drive to school because her snow boots were too bulky for driving. This was only part of the reason why Marcie never wore shoes that tied in the winter. The Minnesota Footwear Switch still had several more steps.

After parking her car in the faculty parking lot, she'd switch to her boots for the icy trek to the front entrance of the building. Once she was inside, she'd switch back to her shoes, and carry her boots to the rug in the closet of her classroom. This was Marcie's winter morning ritual. When school was dismissed for the day, she had to do the same thing, in reverse, until she was back in her apartment again.

Marcie sighed. Winter in Minnesota was exhausting. Just getting to work could be an ordeal. With her heavy wool coat, scarf, gloves, ski sweater, and moon boots, she carried around at least twenty extra pounds all winter long. No wonder every Minnesotan was delighted when spring finally rolled around. It was like finding a crash diet that worked overnight!

As Marcie walked down the carpeted hallway of her apartment building, she tried not to clump in her heavy boots. Her next-door neighbor worked the late shift at Franklin Manufacturing, and she didn't want to wake him. The Langers, in 103, were already up. Marcie could smell bacon frying, and she wondered how Bonnie Langer got the energy to cook breakfast every morning. She worked two jobs, and so did her husband, Tom. They were newlyweds, and they'd told her they were saving up to buy a house.

As Marcie passed the end apartment, she heard Sue Ellen Dubinski's baby crying. But no more than a second later, the crying abruptly ceased. Sue Ellen must have popped a bottle in his mouth. This was Sue Ellen's sixth baby, and she'd told Marcie that motherhood was easy, once you got the hang of it. She could heat a bottle, feed the baby, and get the older kids off to school without ever really waking up.

Marcie opened the door at the end of the hallway and went down three steps and across a small landing to the back door. Double doors were practically a necessity in Minnesota to keep out the winter cold.

There was a small window in the back door, and Marcie lifted the curtain to peer out at the world outside. It was dark, the sun wouldn't rise for another half hour, and the lights in the yard were still on. Icy snow pelted against the thermal windowpane, and Marcie shivered. It had snowed all night, and the winds were blowing even harder this morning. She was glad she lived only three and a half miles from Technical High School.

Marcie turned up the collar of her coat and tugged her red stocking cap down over her ears. Then she pulled on her gloves and opened the heavy back door of her apartment building. A blast of frigid wind almost knocked her off her feet as she struggled down the walkway to the garage. There was an outdoor thermometer mounted on the trunk of the elm tree, but Marcie didn't bother to look at the temperature. It was so cold her breath came out in white puffy clouds, and she knew the mercury would be huddled down near the base of the thermometer, too sluggish to peek out above zero.

The door to her one-car garage stall was stuck, and Marcie had to give several hard yanks on the handle to free it. The metal door creaked as it rose upward, protesting the bitter weather. The space inside seemed slightly warmer, but perhaps it was only because she was out of the wind. Marcie opened the door to her old VW Beetle, and performed the first switch of the day, from boots to shoes.

The old Bug started on the first try. It was a great car for the winters in Minnesota, heavy enough to plow through snowdrifts, and very stable on the icy roads. She backed carefully out of the garage, and groaned when she heard something snap. She'd forgotten to unplug the dipstick heater again.

Marcie opened the driver's door, switched to her boots, and got out to examine the heavy-duty electrical cord. She was lucky. The plug had pulled cleanly out of the socket, and the cord was still intact. She wrapped it around the bumper and pulled down the garage door. Then she switched to her shoes for the second time, turned on her windshield wipers to do battle with the blowing snow, and drove down the icy alley to the street.

Her radio was tuned to KCLD, a local St. Cloud station, and Marcie sighed as she listened to the weather report. Another two inches of snow predicted, accompanied by winds from the northeast at fifteen to twenty miles an hour. The temperature was expected to drop to minus sixteen, a record low for this date. The announcer sounded much too cheerful as he reminded the "good folks out there in KCLD land" that if you added in the wind chill factor, the total would be a frigid thirty-seven degrees below zero!

Marcie shivered and turned her heater on high. The Valentine's Dance was scheduled for tonight, and she was one of the faculty chaperones. It wouldn't be canceled. Minnesotans knew how to take bad weather in their stride, but the kids would be required to drive on the buddy system. Cars would team up, and if one driver got into trouble, the other would pick up the stranded passengers. Minnesota teenagers knew how lethal the freezing cold could be. With a wind chill factor of thirty-seven below, no one would take any foolish chances.

As Marcie turned onto the Tenth Street bridge, she mentally reviewed the contents of her trunk. She had a twenty-pound bag of kitty litter for ballast, an extra can of gasoline, a spare windshield scraper, two wool blankets, an old Army parka she'd picked up at a yard sale, and a pair of fur-lined gloves. There was also an empty three-pound coffee can, which contained a candle and a pouch of waterproof matches, an effective way to warm the interior of a stalled car until help arrived. It was a standard Minnesota survival kit that wise motorists carried throughout the winter. All those items definitely took up space, but the trunk wasn't used for much else in the winter months. If groceries were loaded into the trunk, soda cans would freeze and pop open, plastic milk cartons would expand and shatter, and a head of lettuce would shrivel up and turn as brown as a walnut.

"This tragedy just in on our newswire." The announcer no longer sounded cheerful. *"Local authorities have just recovered the body of a university coed who attempted to walk home from a party shortly after midnight last night. Preliminary medical reports indicate that her left ankle was broken in several places, and she was apparently unable to crawl for help. Her name will be released, pending notification of relatives in Arizona."*

Marcie pumped her brakes lightly and slowed to a careful stop, as the light on Fifth Avenue changed from green to yellow. Even though visitors from other states were cautioned about the severity of Minnesota winters, some of them disregarded those warnings. Just last winter, a businessman from Texas had suffered extreme frostbite while jogging in shorts in the early-morning cold. There were times when the temperature was very deceiving, especially when there was no wind. On a still, sunny day, fifteen below zero might feel almost the same as fifteen above. But there was a huge, thirty-degree difference. Any carelessly exposed patch of skin could be flash-frozen in seconds.

"Oh, for heaven's sakes!" Marcie spotted a familiar figure walking gingerly down a rut in the road, and rolled down her window. "Donna Hunstiger! Where are your boots?"

"I left them in my locker, Miss Calder."

Donna looked very sheepish, and Marcie did her

best not to laugh. Donna's mother would have had a coronary if she'd known her daughter was walking to school in tennis shoes. "Climb in, Donna. I'll give you a ride."

"Gee, thanks, Miss Calder." Donna slushed her way to the passenger door and got into the car. "I've got another pair of shoes in my locker, honest. These are my old ones."

"Don't worry, Donna. I won't squeal on you. Put your feet up by the heat vent." Marcie showed her where, and pulled out into the street again. "You got a ride home with Dennis yesterday, and it wasn't snowing then. You completely forgot you left your boots in your locker, until you got ready for school this morning."

"That's right! But . . . how did *you* know?"

Marcie laughed. "I did the same thing when I was in high school, but my sister saved me."

"Is that your *famous* sister, Miss Calder?"

"That's right." Marcie noticed the rapt expression on Donna's face, and she knew her story would be all over school by the end of first period. "Mercedes said I could use her boots, if I pulled her to school on the sled."

"Gee, Miss Calder! Mercedes sure was smart!"

Marcie nodded and pulled over to the curb to let Donna out at the entrance of the school. As she drove around to the faculty parking lot, she laughed out loud. Mercedes had been smart, much smarter than Marcie had realized at the time. Not only had she gotten a sled ride to school, she'd also made Marcie promise to do the dishes for a month!

By the time fourth period rolled around, Marcie was exhausted. Mr. Metcalf, the principal, had asked

Marcie's art classes to decorate the school gymnasium for the dance. Her first-period sophomore class had spent the entire hour making giant, poster board cutouts of hearts and cupids, and sticking them up on the walls. The freshmen in second period had strung ropes of red and white streamers to form a canopy over the dance floor, and her third-period juniors had set up the tables and decorated them somewhat artistically with bouquets of silver hearts and red candles that couldn't be lit because of fire regulations. Now Marcie's fourth-period seniors were decorating the platform where the Valentine King and Queen would hold court.

"Careful, Dennis!" Marcie winced as Dennis Berger almost sideswiped Tina Jensen with a six-foot-wide roll of silver paper. "Jim and Gary? Move the two thrones to the side. Now, Dennis . . . put the roll down right where the thrones go, and tape the end to the floor. Then trail it down the stairs, and let Tina and Debby tape it to the steps."

"You mean right here?"

Dennis looked confused and Marcie hurried over to help. She'd just finished helping him tape the end to the floor with a roll of gaffer's tape, when the loud-speaker crackled into life.

"Miss Calder?" It was Harriet Scharf's voice, Mr. Metcalf's secretary. "Please report to the principal's office immediately. There's a telephone call for you."

Marcie frowned. A telephone call? How odd. On the few occasions someone had called her at work, Harriet had always taken the number and informed the caller that she'd return the call during lunch or her free period.

"Donna?" Marcie motioned to Donna Huntstiger. "I have to go to the office, and I'm putting you in charge. Make sure Dennis doesn't tear that paper. It's our last roll. And when you finish the platform, start putting up the backdrops we painted last week."

Donna gave her a big smile. "Okay, Miss Calder. We know what to do. You don't have to worry."

"Right." Marcie walked to the door and turned back for one last look. Tina and Debby were tossing the roll of gaffer's tape back and forth, and the end was flapping. If one of them missed, which was almost a certainty, the strip of tape could land sticky side down and pull the silver backing off the paper. "Donna? There's another roll of tape under the basketball hoop. Give it to Debby so the girls each have one of their own."

The hallway was deserted with the exception of Tim Meister, who was hanging up his coat in his locker. He flashed her his excuse slip and tried to smile, but his grin was lopsided.

"You've been to the dentist?"

Tim nodded and mumbled something. Marcie managed to catch the words *Novocain* and *speech class*. She certainly hoped this wasn't Tim's day to give a speech!

As Marcie hurried down the corridor past a series of classrooms, she heard fragments of the class activities inside. Tom Jenkins, the math teacher, was demonstrating incomplete quadratic equations, and his whole class looked stumped. Next door, in American History, Dale Goetz was mapping out the path of the Confederate Army in the Civil War. The business class was typing, under the watchful eye of Shirley Whitford, and Lois Weick's English class was reading *Julius Caesar* aloud.

The blackout shade was pulled on the science lab door, and Marcie knew that Alvin Tideman was showing another movie. It sounded like *Our Mr. Sun*. Al had several standbys for the days when he couldn't face another lecture. *Our Mr. Sun*, directed by Frank Capra, was the best of them. There was also *Phun With Phylums, The Amazing Miss Molecule,* and *A Conversation With Your Pituitary.*

The principal's office was at the end of the corridor, and Marcie opened the glass door and stepped inside. Harriet Scharf was stationed at the long table next to the office Xerox machine, her tight gray curls bobbing as she stapled packets of papers together.

"Hello, Marcie." Harriet turned and gave her a nervous smile. "Use my desk. Your call's on line two. It's your sister's lawyer, and he said it was urgent."

"Thank you, Harriet." Marcie sat down behind Harriet's desk, and took a deep breath. Why would her sister's lawyer be calling her? She hoped nothing was wrong. Her hand was shaking slightly as she punched the blinking button for line two. "Hello. This is Marcella Calder."

Marcie listened carefully, but nothing he said seemed to make any sense. She felt dizzy and weak, and there were swirling black spots in front of her eyes. She gripped the receiver so tightly, her knuckles were white, but she couldn't seem to stop shaking. Sam Abrams. She remembered meeting him once, a tall man with brown hair thinning on top, and the voice of a nineteenth-century orator. But now his voice sounded faint and tinny, as if it had stretched thinner with each passing mile of telephone wire, until it arrived in St. Cloud, Minnesota, a mere shadow of its former self.

His voice asked a question, the same question over and over. But there was no way she could answer. She looked up at Harriet, who was staring at her, and held out the phone.

Dimly, she heard Harriet's responses. Yes, they'd make all the arrangements. Someone would drive her home and help her pack. They'd personally see to it that she got on the plane. It was the least they could do, under the circumstances.

And then the phone was back in its cradle, even though she hadn't seen Harriet place it there. And Mr. Metcalf was bringing her a cup of coffee, and awkwardly patting her shoulder. It had to be a dream. Principals didn't bring coffee to teachers. It just wasn't done.

Someone helped her into her coat and boots, and guided her across the parking lot. Not her car, and it felt like her boots were on the wrong feet, but none of that mattered. And then she was inside her apartment, sitting on the couch with Shirley Whitford, while Harriet packed her suitcases.

The two-hour drive to the airport seemed to take only seconds, and then the stewardess was buckling her seatbelt. Moments later, she heard the pilot announce that they were flying over the Grand Canyon. There was a dinner tray on the pull-down table with roast beef, a baked potato, and some vegetables she didn't recognize. The clear plastic glass of red wine looked like blood, and she was glad when the stewardess took it away.

And then she was walking down a carpeted ramp, and Sam Abrams was there to hug her tightly. Only then, as the tears poured down her cheeks, did she finally believe that Mercedes was dead.

CHAPTER 3

The restaurant in the center of the airport complex was beautifully decorated in her favorite colors, but Marcie barely noticed. She felt as if someone had wrapped her in a shroud of gauze, dulling every one of her senses. She'd nodded mutely when Sam Abrams had suggested they have a bite to eat while they waited for her luggage to arrive. His voice filtered through her cocoon of gauze, explaining that her bags had been delayed at the airport in Minneapolis, and they were coming in on a later flight. He'd taken her arm to guide her along the path to the restaurant, but she'd barely felt his touch. And when he'd commented on the heady scent of the night-blooming jasmine that bordered the steps, she'd caught only a faint, faraway scent. *Insulation was one of the defense mechanisms.* Marcie remembered that phrase from one of her college psychology classes. Withdrawal was one way of coping with things that were just too painful to accept.

Marcie watched as the waitress poured her coffee, a rich brown stream from a silver pot, filling the bone white cup. She wasn't sure why she'd ordered coffee, since she'd preferred tea, but it was the first thing that had popped into her mind when the waitress had come to take their order. Perhaps it was an unconscious wish to bring Mercedes back.

Mercedes had been a coffee drinker, even in high school. When they'd double-dated, she'd insisted they go to Perkins in the Pines, where the waitresses always left a full carafe on the table, and refilled it whenever it was empty. Mercedes had claimed that coffee was a gift of the gods, since it had no calories and lots of caffeine. And just a year ago, when Marcie had come out to visit, she'd noticed that Mercedes drank at least two pots a day, steaming hot and freshly made. Rosa, her housekeeper, bought a special kind of coffee bean, French roast or espresso, and ground it fresh for each pot she made.

Marcie took a sip of her coffee and sighed. She hadn't liked it when Mercedes was alive, and she wasn't sure she liked it any better now.

"It's terrible, isn't it?"

The smile on Sam's face was sympathetic, and Marcie nodded, even though she wasn't sure whether he was referring to the coffee, or what had happened to Mercedes. It didn't really matter. Everything was terrible, now that Mercedes was dead.

Her hand was shaking, and she set her cup down very carefully in its matching saucer. Then she raised her eyes to look at Sam. The layers of gauze were lifting, and she wasn't sure she wanted that to happen. With the return of reality, would come the pain of loss.

Sam reached out and took her hands, holding them in both of his. Warmth began to come back to her fingertips, and Marcie sighed. Everything was coming back into focus, and she could see him clearly now. He was tall, but not quite as thin as she'd remembered him, and his curly brown hair was beginning to recede.

Marcie wasn't certain how she knew, but she was sure that Sam's receding hairline didn't bother him in the slightest. He looked strong and capable, the image of a successful lawyer, a man that most people would immediately trust. And his eyes were the same brown as her coffee, deep and dark, with natural warmth.

"Better?"

Marcie nodded. Then she cleared her throat. She didn't want to know, but she had to ask. "How did . . . I mean, who was the one to . . . to . . ."

"Find her?"

Mercedes nodded gratefully as he finished the sentence for her. The question that had been hovering ominously in the back of her mind was out in the open now, where it could be answered. Not the twins! Anyone but the twins. It was horrifying to think of Trish and Rick finding their mother dead.

Sam seemed to read her mind, because he quickly set her fears to rest. "It's all right, Marcie. The twins didn't find her. When Rosa brought them home, she assumed that Mercedes was still at the studio. She put Trish and Rick to bed, and then she went out on the patio to sweep it. She did that every night. That's when she found Mercedes."

Marcie nodded, greatly relieved, and asked the other question. "How did it . . . uh . . . happen?"

"It was an accidental drowning. Mercedes was swimming laps in the pool."

"I know." Marcie nodded, blinking back tears. "She always said that swimming was the only thing that kept her in shape."

Sam squeezed her hands again. It was clear he didn't want to go on, but Marcie was looking at him expectantly. "Mercedes had been . . . drinking quite heavily. The police found an empty bottle of white wine on the cabana table. They think Mercedes got a cramp, and she wasn't alert enough to pull herself out of the water."

"But . . ." Marcie struggled to find the words. "I know Mercy didn't drink very much. She said liquor had too many calories. And she was a very good swimmer. How could she just . . . drown?"

"Mercedes had been dieting for a scene in *Summer Heat*. And she drank the wine on an empty stomach. Add a cramp to the mix, and even a strong swimmer might panic and go under."

Marcie nodded reluctantly. "I . . . I suppose you're right. Then, no one else was there?"

"No." Sam squeezed her hands again. He knew she was thinking about her sister, alone in the water, crying out for someone to help her. Ever since Brad had called him, he'd been imagining the same thing. And several times, during his uneasy sleep, he'd had nightmares about Mercedes's beautiful face, distorted by terror, when she realized she was helpless and drowning. "Don't think about it, Marcie. It won't do any good. Just think about how we can help the twins."

Marcie nodded and squared her shoulders. Dwelling on the terrible details of her sister's death wouldn't help to bring her back. The twins needed Marcie. She had to be strong for them. "You're right, Sam. I'm sorry. I just needed to know. How is Brad taking it?"

"Not very well." Sam shook his head. "I think he's blaming himself."

"But . . . why?"

"Because he wasn't home. He had a meeting with their horse trainer, and then he went to the racetrack. He told me he'd given Rosa some money to take the twins to a movie."

Marcie nodded. "I see. But he couldn't have known. I mean . . . it's not his fault no one was there."

"Of course not, but to top things off, he'd recommended the wine that Mercedes was drinking. He feels guilty about all those things. And I'm feeling guilty, too."

"You?" Marcie looked up at him in surprise. "Why do *you* feel guilty?"

"Because Mercedes called me earlier. And I didn't realize that she'd been drinking. If I had, I could have gone up to the house and taken care of her until Brad or Rosa got home."

"But that doesn't make any sense at all!" Marcie shook her head. "Mercedes was an actress. And I know she could act cold sober even when she wasn't. I remember one time in high school when we had warm gin at the lake and . . . but I shouldn't really talk about that."

Sam smiled. "Don't worry, Marcie. You're not telling tales out of school. Mercedes loved to tell me stories about when she was growing up with you in Minnesota. She remembered it as the happiest time in her life."

"Yes . . . it was." Marcie smiled through her tears. "I'm so sorry we drifted apart. She was out here with her career and everything, and I was back there. And then she got married and had the babies, and I only saw her once or twice a year. We talked on the phone every week or so, but that's not the same as actually seeing each other."

"You weren't close then?"

"That's just it." Marcie sighed deeply. "We *were* close. But we lived in different worlds. She was a glamorous star and I . . . I was just a high school art teacher."

Sam nodded. "I know exactly what you mean, Marcie. I used to be very close to my older brother, but we drifted apart, too. Now I only see him at the occasional family reunion."

There was a long moment of silence. Sam knew Marcie was feeling bad, so he deliberately broke into her reverie. "You were about to tell me about the warm gin at the lake?"

"Yes." Marcie smiled as she remembered that night so long ago. "Did Mercedes tell you we drank that gin with beer chasers?"

"Beer chasers?!"

Marcie actually laughed at the incredulous expression on Sam's face, but then she turned solemn. "Do you think it's right, talking about Mercedes like this? It feels almost disrespectful."

"It's not." Sam looked very serious. "I think talking about Mercedes is the very best thing we can do. It'll keep her alive in our hearts."

Marcie smiled through her tears. "Oh, Sam! That was beautiful! And I . . . I think you're right. It would certainly make me feel better to tell you all the old stories about her."

"So . . . ?" Sam smiled back. "Tell me about the gin with beer chasers. Mercedes didn't mention the beer."

"I think I can understand why she left that part out. It was pretty dreadful. But we were just kids back then, and we were experimenting. Mercedes had just finished reading a book about Denmark, and it mentioned that the Danes toasted with Akavit, followed by beer chasers. We didn't know what Akavit was but there was a picture, and we thought it looked like gin."

"And where did you get the gin?"

Marcie looked very guilty. "We found it in the back of our parents' liquor cabinet. To be perfectly honest, I was the one who suggested we pour out half, and fill the bottle up with water. We knew Mom and Dad never drank gin, and we figured their friends would never embarrass them by asking if it was watered."

"Ah ha!" Sam grinned at her. "Premeditated deception. How did you get the beer?"

"That was easy." Marcie smiled, lost in her memory of happier times. "Our neighbors used to have a barbecue every Wednesday night, and they kept the beer in a big tub of ice by the hedge. Mercy and I reached through the branches and pulled out bottles until we'd collected a six-pack."

"All the same brand?"

"Oh, no." Marcie looked shocked. "We were afraid they'd be missed if we took a whole six-pack of the same brand. We got two bottles of Hamms, two of Grain Belt, one North Star, and a Cold Spring Dark."

"Very smart. How did you get it out to the lake?"

"We hid the beer and gin in an old suitcase, and then we waited until we went out to our lake cabin. We stashed the bottles in an old bait bucket, and that night we sat out on the end of the dock and toasted everybody we could think of."

"How much did you drink?" Sam winced a little.

"I was a lightweight. I had two sips of gin and a bottle of beer. Then I stopped, because my head was spinning. But Mercedes kept right on drinking until the beer ran out."

"And your parents were waiting up for you?"

"That's right." Marcie smiled fondly. "Mercedes saved me. She told them I had to go straight to our room to put lotion on my mosquito bites."

"They believed it?"

"Of course. We have billions of mosquitos in Minnesota. The mosquito is practically the state bird."

Sam choked on his coffee, and Marcie glanced at him in surprise. She hadn't thought she was being funny. "Anyway, Mercedes talked to our parents for a good fifteen minutes. Then she came to bed and passed out cold in all her clothes."

"She must have been sick the next morning."

Marcie laughed. "Not a bit, but she couldn't remember anything after the second bottle of beer. Our parents never asked us whether we'd been drinking so I guess she pulled it off."

"She was remarkable, wasn't she?"

"She certainly was!" Marcie nodded. "What was she like when you met her, Sam? I was in college back then."

Sam told her about the first time he'd met Mercedes, right before she'd married Mike. Then Marcie told him about their senior play, and how Mercedes had stolen the show. They talked about Mercedes all through dinner, trading stories and actually laughing at the funny things they remembered. Marcie had just finished telling him about the time Mercedes had accepted two dates for the same night, and conned Marcie into pretending to be her so she could be two places at once, when she realized that Sam was staring at her in surprise. "What's the matter, Sam? Don't you believe me?"

"Of course, I believe you." Sam looked dubious as he stared at her. "Was it a blind date?"

Marcie laughed. "No, it wasn't a blind date. And he wasn't blind either, if that's what you mean. Mercedes and I are identical twins. We used to switch places and fool people all the time, even people who knew us well."

Marcie could tell that Sam still wasn't convinced, but she let it pass. She knew she didn't look like her twin now, not in the simply tailored blouse and skirt she'd worn to school. Mercedes had dressed in glamorous clothes, and her hair and makeup were always perfect.

A high school teacher in St. Cloud, Minnesota, couldn't look like a fashion plate. If she did, she'd be accused of putting on airs.

"I'm glad you enjoyed your dinner."

Sam was grinning, and Marcie looked down at her empty plate in surprise. She'd eaten every bite of her dinner, and she'd told Sam she wasn't hungry!

"I guess I was hungry, after all." Marcie gave a little shrug of apology. "Thank you, Sam. I'm so glad you met me at the airport."

They shared a smile as Marcie reached for another crusty French roll. She felt much better. Sam had been right. Talking about Mercedes had helped. She was very grateful to him for helping her through these first difficult hours.

They shared a sinfully rich chocolate dessert, which Marcie claimed she didn't need and Sam insisted she did. And then they went to pick up her suitcases at the baggage carousel. But Marcie's suitcases weren't there.

The baggage supervisor was very apologetic as he explained that Marcie's suitcases had been traced to Chicago. He'd called, and the supervisor at O'Hare had promised that they would be sent on the first available flight to Los Angeles. Unfortunately, that flight wouldn't land until three in the morning. No, Marcie didn't need to come back to the airport to pick up her luggage. The airline would send someone out to deliver it to her door the next day.

"It's a good thing Shirley Whitford packed a carry-on for me." Marcie sighed as Sam loaded the small bag in the trunk of his car. "At least I have the bare essentials, but I'm going to need a change of clothes for tomorrow. Do you think they'll deliver my suitcases early in the morning?"

"Maybe, if you're lucky."

"What do you mean?" Marcie gave him an anxious look as they got on the freeway and headed off toward the house in Mandeville Canyon.

"I lost a suitcase on my last trip from New York. They delivered it ten days later with tags from Washington, Texas, Nevada, and Hawaii."

"Oh, dear!" Marcie frowned. "But you did get it back, right?"

Sam nodded. "I did. And everything was inside, including the smoked whitefish I'd bought at Zabar's. It was a little worse for the wear, after its long vacation."

"Oh, no!" Marcie giggled. "Well, I don't have anything perishable in mine. Just some clothes and . . . Oh, they've put up lights!"

Marcie gasped as they stopped at the wrought-iron gates at the base of the winding driveway. The ten-foot walls surrounding her sister's estate were lit with bright floodlights . "They didn't have all these the last time I was here. It's lit up like a fairy-tale castle."

Sam nodded. "The lights are new. Mercedes had them installed with the security system. They're decorative, but they're also functional. Without the lights, you couldn't see who was coming up the driveway on the closed-circuit monitors."

"Closed-circuit monitors?" Marcie was puzzled. "That sounds very sophisticated."

Sam rolled down his window and picked up a telephone. "It's state-of-the-art. This telephone rings in the house. That lets Brad know we're here. He'll check the monitor to make sure it's us, and then he'll click us in."

There was a click and the gates rolled back. Sam replaced the phone and drove forward. As soon as his car had cleared the gates, they closed again.

"Good heavens!" Marcie was definitely impressed. "But I don't understand, Sam. Mercedes told me there was very little crime out here. Why did she need such a fancy system?"

Sam shrugged. "It's a big estate. And Mercedes was a very well-known actress. I don't think she was being overly cautious, especially since Brad was away on business so often."

"I suppose that's true." Marcie nodded, but she was still surprised. Mercedes had never mentioned being afraid to stay alone before. Had she sensed she was in some kind of danger? She'd have to ask Brad when the time was right.

Brad was waiting for them by the front door, and Marcie almost cried as she caught sight of his grief-stricken face. A wave of pity swept through her, and suddenly she was very glad she'd flown out to California to help. It was clear that Brad wasn't coping well, and the twins were probably devastated. Marcie wasn't sure what she could do to comfort them all, but she was determined to try.

The first time Marcie met Brad, she'd felt a twinge of uncharacteristic envy for her twin sister. Brad had dark wavy hair, and blue eyes so deep, they were almost purple. His skin was tanned to a rich copper color, and he had the body of a natural athlete. Mercedes had told her he worked out at a health club every morning, and the results were quite apparent. Although Brad was over six feet tall and very well-muscled, there wasn't an ounce of fat on him.

Brad and Mercedes had made a stunning couple, the perfect match in a Hollywood dream. When their wedding picture had appeared in the *Los Angeles Times,* one showbiz reporter had nicknamed them Cinderella and Prince Charming.

As soon as Sam stopped the car, Marcie got out and

ran to embrace Brad. There were tears in her eyes as she held him tightly.

"Marcie. I'm so glad you're here."

Brad's voice was shaking, and Marcie was sure he'd been crying. Poor Brad! What an awful tragedy!

"Are you all right, Marcie?"

Marcie nodded. Thanks to Sam, she was back in control. And not a moment too soon! "I'm fine. At least I'm as fine as I can be . . . under the circumstances."

"Here, I'll get that." Brad hurried to the back of the car, where Sam was unloading her carry-on bag. "Thanks, Sam. I just couldn't face a trip to the airport. You're a real friend."

"Hey . . . I'm always here to help." Sam handed over the bag with a smile. But Marcie noticed a flicker of emotion on Sam's face, and she instinctively knew that these two men weren't friends.

Brad didn't seem to notice. Either he was too upset to be observant, or she was imagining the whole thing. After all, they were walking toward her and both men were smiling.

"Come in for a drink, Sam?"

Sam looked ready to refuse, but then he glanced at Marcie. "Okay. But I can only stay for a couple of minutes. I've got an early meeting with a client tomorrow."

Brad opened the front door, and they all went inside. Marcie was ready to greet the twins, but they didn't run down the stairs to hug her, as they usually did. "Are the twins in bed already?"

Brad shook his head. "No, they're at Rosa's. I thought it might be best for tonight. I knew you'd be tired after your trip, and I wasn't sure what shape you'd be in . . . I mean the shock and all."

"But are *they* all right?"

Brad nodded. "They're doing better than we thought they would. And they wanted to stay with Rosa. She's like a second mother to them, you know."

Marcie nodded, even though she was disappointed. Brad was right. Rosa had taken care of the twins when they were babies, and Trish and Rick often stayed overnight with her. It was probably for the best, at least on this first night.

"Scotch?" Brad turned to Sam as they walked down the hall to the den.

Sam nodded. "That's fine."

"Marcie? You look like you could use a drink."

Marcie hesitated. She rarely drank, and when she did, it was one glass of white wine. Now that she knew what Mercedes had been drinking on the night she died, she didn't want to ask for the same thing.

"I have a very good bottle of Chardonnay. And an excellent Riesling. Or there's a very nice chilled Beaujolais."

"Well . . . all right. I'll have a glass of the Beaujolais." Marcie gave him a smile. It would be a breach of good taste to refuse, and a glass of wine might relax her and help her to get a good night's sleep. She'd need all her strength tomorrow, when the twins came home.

Marcie sat down on the leather couch and watched as Brad opened the EuroCave wine cooler Mercedes had told her about. Beaujolais was red wine, if she remembered correctly. She held her breath as he extracted the cork and gave a small sigh of relief as he poured it into a glass. It was red, thank goodness!

As Brad handed her the glass of Beaujolais, Marcie noticed that Sam was smiling at her approvingly. Had he guessed that she was avoiding white wine for Brad's sake? If so, he was very perceptive.

Brad poured Sam's scotch in a crystal tumbler and

handed it to him. "Here you go, buddy. Why don't you try my massage chair? It takes out all the kinks. I'll sit over here with Marcie."

Marcie glanced at the massage chair. It was another expensive purchase that Mercedes had told her about, a leather desk chair with remote-controlled rollers, designed to ease back pain while you were working.

Sam switched on the chair and leaned back with a smile on his face. "Very nice. My partner has one of these. It's a little expensive for my taste, though."

"Not really." Brad shook his head. "Especially when you consider what a good masseuse charges. I figure this chair paid for itself in the first month."

"Well . . . that might be true in your case, but I don't have a masseuse. Do you have back trouble, Brad?"

"Not anymore." Brad gave him a grin. Then he turned to Marcie. "How long can you stay, Marcie?"

Marcie frowned slightly. "I'm not really sure. As long as you need me, I guess. I'm sure the school will grant me a leave of absence."

"Good." Brad nodded. "I want you to feel that this is your second home, Marcie. Mercedes would have wanted it that way."

"Thank you." Marcie smiled at Brad. Then she turned to look at Sam. He was leaning back in Brad's massage chair, wearing a very startled expression. But before Marcie could ask him what the matter was, Brad took her hand.

"Another thing, Marcie, while we're on the subject. If you want any of Mercedes's things . . . as far as I'm concerned, they're yours."

Marcie took a sip of her wine and blinked back tears. Mercedes's things. She hadn't even thought about the task that lay ahead of her, going through all of her sister's possessions. It was bound to be painful, but that was why she was here. It would be cruel to ask Brad to do it alone.

"Thank you, Brad. That's very generous. Perhaps we could go through them together, and put some things away for the twins. When they get a little older, they'll want some of their . . ." Marcie cleared her throat and choked back a sob. ". . . their mother's things to remember her by."

"Of course." Brad nodded solemnly and squeezed her hand. "I was hoping you'd help me with that, Marcie. I wouldn't know what to save for them. Another drink, Sam?"

Sam looked very uncomfortable as he shook his head. "No, thanks. I really have to be going."

"Just a second. I'll open the gates for you." Brad stood up and went to a box on the wall with flashing red lights. He punched in a code and returned to shake Sam's hand. "Thanks, Sam. I appreciate all you've done for us."

"No problem." Sam nodded. "I can see myself out."

"Oh, I'll walk out with you!" Marcie jumped to her feet. "I'd like to check to make sure I didn't leave anything in your car."

Marcie hoped she hadn't been too transparent as Sam followed her to the front door. She knew she hadn't left anything in Sam's car, but she needed a private moment with him.

It was a beautifully clear California evening. The night breeze was gentle, barely moving the heavy palm fronds in the two tall trees that bordered the driveway, and Marcie could smell the scent of sweet flowers blooming as she walked Sam to his car. For one brief moment she thought about Minnesota and its icy cold winds and deep snowdrifts. Then she put the freezing temperatures firmly out of her mind. No wonder Mercedes had moved here! California was wonderful!

"Do you want me to open the trunk?" Sam took out his keys.

"No. I know I didn't leave anything. I just wanted to talk to you, alone."

"Are you all right?" Sam turned to her with concern.

Marcie nodded. "Yes, thanks to you. You made me feel much better, Sam, and I wanted to tell you how much I appreciate it. But I do have one question before you go."

Sam gave her a quizzical look, and Marcie took a deep breath. She might as well just blurt it out. "You looked so startled when Brad told me to regard this as my second home. Why?"

"Sorry, Marcie." Sam turned away from her slightly. "I really can't tell you right now. You'll have to be patient, okay?"

"Uh . . . okay." Marcie was still puzzled, but she put her arms around Sam and gave him a big hug. Sam had been her sister's friend, and she hoped he'd be hers, too. The hug felt good, especially when Sam put his arms around her and hugged her back. Sam made her feel safe, as if nothing bad could ever happen to her again.

"Marcie? Do you want me to drop by tomorrow, after my meeting? I can help you and Brad make all the arrangements."

The arrangements? For a moment Marcie was confused, but then she realized that Sam was referring to the funeral arrangements. "It's kind of you to offer, Sam. Everything will be a lot easier if you're here."

"Promise me you'll try to get some sleep?"

Marcie nodded. "I will."

Sam gave her another little hug, and then he opened

his car door. He reached inside, pulled out a card, and handed it to her. "This is my private home number. Call me anytime, day or night. If I'm not there, the service will find me for you."

"Thank you, Sam." Marcie gave a little wave as he slid behind the wheel. She stood and watched as he started the car and pulled out of the driveway, red taillights disappearing around a bend in the road. She wasn't sure why, but she felt a terrible sense of loss.

She heard the gates at the bottom of the driveway slide closed, and she knew that Sam was gone. Suddenly, the night felt chilly, as if Sam had taken all the warmth with him. Marcie shivered and turned to walk slowly back to the house. She wondered why Sam had told her to be patient. It didn't make any sense at all.

The only light in the house came from the husband's bedroom window. It cast a gold rectangle on the surface of the pool, and he shuddered. He couldn't think about her now. There was work to be done. The evil red was hiding somewhere here in the darkness, and it was his duty to ferret it out and destroy it.

No rest for the wicked. The Red Lady had told him that, and then she'd laughed. *And you're a very wicked boy, aren't you, Jimmy?* He'd nodded. That was what she expected. And then she'd laughed again. *That's why Uncle Gene came to see you. He adores wicked little boys.*

He shuddered again, pushing back the memory of sweat-soaked sheets and nasty sounds in the night. It was over. He was here. The Red Lady could no longer hurt him with the Uncles. That chapter in his life was closed. The final word had been written. The Red Lady was neutralized, and he would never be forced to endure another Uncle.

His ears were alert for any sound as his eyes searched the familiar shadows. There was no longer any red in the pool. It had been drained and filled with fresh water. But this red gave off an almost palpable scent, hot and angry and violent. It was here somewhere. He had to find it.

The bougainvillea was flowering but its blossoms were orange. There was no danger in orange. And the night-blooming jasmine had white flowers. No danger there, either. The rose garden was neutralized. He'd seen to that right after the housekeeper and the children had left, digging out the roots of the American Beauty Rose and tossing them in the Dumpster at the bottom of the hill.

Could his instincts be wrong? He wrinkled his nose and sniffed the air again. Damp and dark, with a hint of jasmine. And then he smelled it again, a faint trace of red that tickled his nostrils with a scorching, metallic odor.

He sniffed his way across the patio, to the potted palms at the end. And then he saw it, a shiny red matchbook left carelessly on the arm of the lounge chair. Who had left it there? Not the housekeeper. And certainly not the children. A repairman perhaps, or one of the gardening crew. It really didn't matter. He had found the red, and now he could neutralize it.

He approached slowly, stepping carefully over the red mist that rose around his ankles. His mind was filled with thoughts of destruction. Which method should he use? Which ancient element would give him the power to destroy the evil red?

Earth, air, fire, and water. He would use fire, of course. He pulled out the matches he carried in his pocket, the matches from her wedding. White matches with gold tips in a white satin box. The gold writing on the cover spelled out their names, Brad and Mercedes, September twentieth. Nine, two, zero. It was the combination for the gate, the one the husband had thought was so clever.

He glanced down at the matchbox and frowned. They had been kept in a large white basket on the bar at the reception. Although he didn't smoke, he'd taken several for just this purpose.

Even though the matches were over two years old, he was certain they would work. She had always bought quality goods. But the red mist was rising up toward his knees, and he had to hurry.

He used a towel that had been left on the chair to flick the red matchbook from its hateful resting place. Then he opened his pure white matchbox, took out a match, and struck it.

The flame was a bright flicker in the darkness as he dropped to his knees and brought the point of fire to the edge of the evil red matchbook. It was a bit like bringing coals to Newcastle, and he would have smiled if he'd been able.

The red matchbook smoldered, the cover was flame resistant. For a moment, he thought he might have to light a second white match, but just as he was about to strike the second match, it blazed brightly, almost leaping up to lick his face.

He stumbled back awkwardly, catching himself as he began to fall. Then he got to his feet by the flaming pyre, and glanced up toward the windows. A woman had come in the night. He'd seen her arrive with the lawyer, but it had been too dark to see her face. She was staying in his love's room, something he found disturbing, but perhaps she was only an overnight guest.

No light spilled from her window, and he breathed a deep sigh of relief. No one could know that he was here, inside the locked gates. His presence was a secret that had to be kept.

The fire was dying now, fading to a flicker and then to darkness. He stared down at the small pile of ashes the ancient element had left in its wake, and gave a shaky smile. No need to sweep the patio. The morning breeze would lift the ashes and bear them away. He would have time to get to a place of safety, before the blackness closed in and made him sleep.

CHAPTER 4

Marcie awoke to sunlight streaming through sheer sea green curtains. Very pretty. It was a lovely color that reminded her of spring, and tiny green shoots of early-blooming irises peeking up through the cold, white snow. But the curtains in her bedroom weren't green. They were harvest gold!

The shock made Marcie sit bolt-upright in bed. She blinked in confusion at the array of perfume bottles and jars of makeup on the white wicker dresser. She didn't wear makeup, and this wasn't her dresser. Her dresser was an antique oak piece she'd taken from her parents' house. She turned her head, blinked at the enormous walk-in closet, the white wicker chaise lounge in the corner with its peach and green cushions, and finally . . . the waving palm tree outside the window.

"Mercedes!" Marcie closed her eyes as the pain washed over her in a crashing wave. She was in her twin sister's bedroom. And Mercedes was dead.

Marcie sat there for a full minute, blinking back tears. But it was against her nature to dwell on tragedy. She had to get up and get busy. Rosa and the twins

would be home today, and they would need her. And
Brad would need her, too. She had to hurry and dress.

One glance at the clock on the white wicker bedside
table, and Marcie let out a groan of remorse. It was
almost ten in the morning. How could she have slept
so late? And so soundly? She'd expected her dreams to
be full of painful memories, perhaps even a nightmare
or two. But she'd slept very peacefully. The sheets
weren't twisted up in a ball as they usually were when
she was upset, and the blanket was still tucked in. She
felt almost guilty for sleeping so well on the night after
her sister's death.

Marcie stood up and stretched. She felt rested and
ready to cope with the day. Then she remembered that
she had nothing to wear. Had her suitcases arrived
while she was asleep?

She padded, barefooted, across the deep pile rug
and opened the door. The hallway was deserted. No
suitcases. She was sure Brad would have brought them
up if they'd been here when he'd left for his golf tournament. She remembered how apologetic Brad had
been last night, when he'd mentioned the tournament.
He'd told her he'd tried to cancel, but he hadn't been
able to find a replacement on such short notice. Marcie
had urged him to go. His partners were depending on
him, and the tournament was for charity. It would do
him good to get out of the house and be with his
friends. She'd promised him that she'd take care of
things on the home front so he needn't worry. Sam was
coming over to help with all the arrangements, but
they'd wait with any final decisions until Brad got
home.

Poor Brad. When she'd mentioned the arrangements, he'd confessed that he just couldn't face making
them. Anything she wanted was fine with him, as long

as it was private. Could Marcie please take care of it for him?

Of course, Marcie had agreed. Brad shouldn't worry. She would take care of everything. But in the cold light of morning, Marcie wondered exactly what she should do. How did one arrange a funeral in a city as large as Los Angeles? Thank goodness Sam was coming over this morning to help her. But he could be on his way right now, and she wasn't even dressed!

Marcie walked to the connecting door to Brad's room, and knocked. Perhaps he hadn't left yet. She needed to ask him if she could borrow some of Mercedes's clothes until the airline delivered hers. But there was no answer.

Marcie opened the door and peeked in. There were several crumpled towels on the floor, and she could smell the faint hint of his cologne in the air. She was too late. Brad was gone.

Even though she'd urged Brad to go to the golf tournament, Marcie still felt a bit deserted. But that was why she'd come, wasn't it? She was there to deal with the tragic details and spare Brad and the children. She just wished that Brad had knocked on her door to say something before he'd left.

Marcie hesitated in the doorway for a moment, and then she stepped in. Brad's room was done in dark green, with green and gold plaid on the overstuffed chairs on either side of the fireplace. Mercedes had mentioned that Brad's favorite color was green, and the room was obviously decorated to please him. There was a heavy mahogany bed with dark green sheets and a matching bedspread. It was flanked by two mahogany bed tables, with identical brass lamps on their tops. On the far wall was a huge mahogany dresser, six drawers high and four drawers wide. There was a life-size portrait of Mercedes in a brass frame hanging over the fireplace, and several Remington prints on the walls.

Even though she knew she shouldn't intrude on Brad's private quarters, Marcie couldn't resist walking over to examine the prints. She reached up to touch one, and gasped as she realized that they weren't prints. Four Remington originals! Marcie's mind boggled at what they must be worth. Then she saw the sculpture on the table between the two overstuffed chairs, and she gasped again. Another original Remington. It must have cost a fortune!

Marcie took a quick turn around the room, noticing the large walk-in closet filled with expensive clothing on wooden hangers, and the bathroom with its private sauna. This was a totally masculine room, the direct opposite of Mercedes's feminine boudoir.

Marcie had been shocked when she'd first learned about her sister's living arrangements. Wasn't there something wrong when a married couple chose to sleep in separate bedrooms? But then Mercedes had explained it, and it all made perfect sense. She often had early calls when she was working on a movie, and Brad was normally a late sleeper. Mercedes preferred to go to bed early, and Brad stayed up past midnight almost every night. *It's just that we have conflicting schedules,* Mercedes had said with a laugh. *It doesn't mean that we don't love each other. After all, we have a connecting door.*

Marcie walked back to Mercedes's room and shut the connecting door. She felt slightly guilty for examining Brad's room, but she couldn't help being interested in the handsome man her twin sister had married.

She still hadn't solved the problem of what to wear, but perhaps Rosa was here by now. Marcie picked up the telephone on her sister's night table, and pressed the intercom button. She really didn't want to wear the same clothes she'd worn yesterday. They were wrinkled from her long airplane flight. But she wasn't sure it was right to wear her sister's clothes. She'd ask Rosa what to do.

"Miss Marcie!" Rosa answered on the first ring. "I'll bring your tea right up."

Marcie frowned. For some strange reason, she didn't feel like tea this morning. "Rosa? I think I'd rather have coffee, if you don't mind."

"I don't mind." Rosa sounded amused. "Why should I mind? I think it's about time you stopped drinking that awful herb tea. I made a big pot of coffee for Mr. Brad so there's plenty left for you."

A moment later there was a knock on the door, and Rosa came bustling in. She set the tray down on the dressing table and rushed over to give Marcie a big hug. As Marcie hugged her back, she realized that there were tears in her eyes. She'd known the heavy-set Hungarian housekeeper for ten years, and Rosa had always treated her like one of the family.

"Oh, Rosa." Marcie stepped back to give her a teary smile. "I'm so sorry you had to be the one to . . . to . . ."

Rosa shook her head. "Don't worry, Miss Marcie. You should be glad it was me, and not the babies. I've seen a lot of tragedy in my life. And I know Miss Mercedes is happy with Mr. Mike in heaven now. He was her first and best love."

Marcie nodded. She certainly didn't want to start a philosophical discussion about the existence of a higher being right now, and she was glad that Rosa could draw comfort from her faith in the hereafter. "How are the twins taking it?"

Rosa smiled. "I think they'll be fine, Miss Marcie. They've got each other, and now they've got you."

"Where are they?"

"Oh, Mr. Brad told me to take them back to school this morning. He says the longer they wait, the harder it'll be."

Marcie frowned. "But did they want to go back this soon?"

"No, but I told them to call if they needed me, and I'd drive right over to bring them home. But they haven't called, so they must be all right."

"I suppose their friends will ask a lot of painful questions. Brad said there was a story in the paper."

"On the front page." Rosa nodded. "But if Trish and Rick don't want to answer those kinds of questions, they're going to say it makes them feel bad to talk about it. Their friends don't really want to hurt them. They're just kids, and they're naturally curious."

Marcie raised her eyebrows. Rosa knew more about human nature than anyone else she'd ever met. "You've got so much common sense, Rosa. How did you learn so much?"

"I'm fifty-two and I've raised four of my own." Rosa shrugged the compliment away. "You don't get to be my age without learning something."

"I suppose that's true. At least in your case. I'm not so sure about me."

Rosa laughed. "Don't be silly, Miss Marcie. You've got plenty of common sense. So where are your clothes? I'll hang them up for you."

"They're in my suitcases, and the airline sent them to Chicago by mistake. They're supposed to send a man out with them this morning, but Sam told me I'd better not count on it."

"Airlines!" Rosa snorted. "That's what happens when you deregulate things! My daughter lost a suitcase once, and they never did find it. And all they paid her was fifty dollars! She couldn't even replace her shoes for that! So you don't have any clothes?"

"Only what I wore to the airport."

"That's no problem. You can wear some of your sister's. She always said you should dress better."

"She did?" Marcie frowned slightly.

Rosa nodded. "But she didn't say it in the mean way. Miss Mercedes told me that you always tried to hide your beauty, even when you were just a little girl. I know that if she was standing here right now, she'd open up her closet and tell you to wear anything of hers you wanted."

"But how about the twins? Won't they be upset, if they see me wearing their mother's clothes?"

Rosa shook her head. "The twins love you. And they know their mother doesn't need clothes in heaven. I think they'd like seeing her pretty clothes on you."

"Well . . . perhaps." Marcie wasn't convinced. "But it might bother Brad."

Rosa shrugged. "Take it from me, he'd never know the difference. I don't think he ever noticed what Miss Mercedes was wearing. But if you want, I'll look for some new things that Miss Mercedes never wore. I know I can find something."

Marcie sat down at the dressing table and sipped her coffee. To her surprise, she was actually learning to like the taste. Rosa was a problem solver, no doubt about it. If she dressed in something new, no one would know it had belonged to Mercedes.

"I found some." Rosa carried an armload of clothing to the bed. "Here's a pretty new blouse. This royal blue would be a good color for you. And here's two pairs of shorts, the kind that look like little short skirts. And I found a brand-new jogging suit that Miss Mercedes bought last year, before she had those peach ones made. And here's a skirt to go with the blouse. A wraparound, see? And I even found a new pair of Italian sandals. Is that enough, Miss Marcie? Or do you want me to keep on looking?"

"That's enough. The skirt and blouse will be perfect for today, and maybe I'll have my suitcases by tonight. Thank you, Rosa. I really appreciate it."

"You'd better hurry, Miss Marcie." Rosa glanced at the clock on the bedside table. "Mr. Sam called twenty minutes ago, and he said he'd be here in an hour."

After Rosa had left, Marcie took a quick shower in her sister's bathroom. It was a huge, mirrored room with a large, glass-walled shower, a bathtub that could easily accommodate four people, and a full-sized Jacuzzi. Even though she told herself she was being overly sensitive, Marcie felt like a thief when she used Mercedes's perfumed soap and body lotion. It seemed almost like they were in high school again, and she was sneaking some of her sister's expensive perfume.

Marcie had just finished dressing when Rosa called to say that Sam had arrived. She slipped her feet into the new pair of sandals, and took the time to run a comb through her hair. Then she hurried down the stairs to greet the man she already thought of as a friend.

"Marcie." Sam gave her a little hug. "How are you this morning?"

"I'm fine, and my suitcases are having a wonderful vacation."

"I told you." Sam grinned at her. "There's something about American Tourister. Once it lands in Hawaii, it wants to stick around to get a suntan. Is there anything you need, Marcie? I can run out and get it."

Marcie smiled. "Nothing, Sam. Rosa found me some clothes, and I can wait for the rest."

"Are you sure?"

Marcie began to frown. Everything else could wait, but there were two things she'd remembered to ask Harriet Scharf to pack. A set of acrylic paints for Trish, and a collector album for Rick's baseball cards.

"What is it, Marcie?" Sam looked concerned.

"It's nothing really. I had some gifts for the twins, but I'm sure my suitcases will come, sooner or later. It's just that every time I fly out to California, I always bring them a little something."

"That's not an insurmountable problem. I'll take you down to the biggest mall in town right after we finish our business. Would you like to have lunch while we're out?"

Marcie hesitated. "That would be wonderful, but I want to be here when the twins get home from school. And I'm not sure if Rosa has . . ."

"I haven't," Rosa called out from the kitchen. She'd obviously been listening. "Mr. Sam told me not to, so I didn't."

Marcie grinned at Sam. "All right then. What do we do first, Sam?"

Sam turned very serious. "First we go to the den, where there's a desk with a telephone. And then you read this letter, and do what it says. Mercedes had everything planned, Marcie. She left instructions with me."

"But . . . how did she know that . . ." Marcie choked on the words. "I don't understand, Sam!"

Sam put an arm around her shoulders and led her into the den. "It's quite simple, really. Mercedes had a hard time when Mike died. She had no idea what sort of service he'd wanted, and she agonized over what to do. Right after his funeral, she brought me this letter. And she asked me to keep it for you."

Marcie nodded and sat down at the desk. Her hands trembled as she took the letter and opened it. As she read her sister's words, written so long ago, it was almost as if Mercedes were alive again.

Dear Marcie. Mercedes's writing was clear and even, much different from her usual hasty scrawl. Marcie knew this letter had been very important to Mercedes. She'd taken the time to write legibly.

> *I want to make this as easy as possible. Sam has all of my legal papers, including my will. Tell him I said you can trust him, even if he is a lawyer. He'll get a kick out of that. Even better, give him this letter to read, and let him help you carry out my wishes.*
>
> *Don't let anyone make a big production of my funeral. I don't want one at all. No funeral, got it? Just call one of those places like the Neptune Society, and have my ashes scattered at sea. No need to go along on the boat. I know you get seasick.*
>
> *The studio will probably want to hold a memorial service. Publicity and all that jazz. It's fine with me, but make sure the hoopla is all over within a week. It'll be easier for everyone that way. And don't ask Trish or Rick to attend unless they want to. Ask Rosa's advice on that. She's got more sense than any of us put together.*
>
> *One more thing. Don't feel you have to get up to speak about what a wonderful sister I was. I know how shy you are, and you'd be lying anyway. As I remember, I was a real pain when we were in high school.*
>
> *I love you, Marcie. We're cut from the same mold, except you're much nicer. Carry on, okay? I'm depending on you to make sure the twins are all right.*

*Sam will tell you about the bank account I set up for
Rosa. It's more than enough to pay her salary until
the twins are grown. And I want you to promise to
uphold the family tradition. One of us has to live to
be older than Great-Aunt Sarah.*

When Marcie finished reading the letter, there was
a smile on her face and tears in her eyes. She handed
it to Sam and cleared her throat. "Read it, Sam. She
wanted you to."

Marcie watched as Sam read the letter. He was
blinking back tears, too. When he finished, he folded
it carefully and replaced it in the envelope.

"Seventy-six." Marcie faced him with a smile, even
though she felt more like crying. She had to play out
her sister's joke.

"Great-Aunt Sarah?"

"Yes." Marcie nodded. "But that was twenty years
ago, when she married her eighth husband. She flew
off to his estate in England, and Mom and Dad got
Christmas cards every year until they died. Mercedes
and I always figured that Great-Aunt Sarah would live
forever."

Sam smiled. He could tell this was hard on Marcie,
and Mercedes had asked him to help her. "Why don't
you get me some coffee, Marcie? I'll make some calls
and take care of the details."

"Well . . . if you're sure . . ."

Marcie hesitated, but Sam waved her away. As a
lawyer, he was used to handling difficult situations like
this.

When Marcie had left, Sam squared his shoulders
and picked up the phone. Three short calls later, and
everything was done. There were advantages to being
a lawyer. All he had to do was identify himself by his

profession, and he got right through to someone who had the power to cut through the red tape.

Sam made a few notes that he could give to Marcie, and then he leaned back in the chair and relaxed. He was very glad Mercedes had written the letter. It made things easier, knowing exactly what she had wanted. He still remembered the day she'd come to his office and left the letter with him. She'd been wearing a navy blue Chanel suit, and her hair had looked like spun gold against the dark material. That was the moment he'd finally admitted to himself that he loved her.

He'd known that Mercedes had loved him, too. But not in the way he'd hoped. He'd been a fond family friend, and a sort of uncle to the twins. Sam had spent hours trying to think of a way to plead his case, to encourage Mercedes to think of him as more than a friend. In the beginning, after Mike had died, he hadn't wanted to rush her into a new relationship. He'd waited patiently for her to visualize him in a romantic role, but that had never happened. Sam had stayed in the background as her trusted friend and confidant for the past eight years. And then, right when he'd finally decided to ask her to marry him, she'd met Brad, and everything had changed.

When Mercedes had told him she wanted to marry again, Sam had seen red. Hadn't she guessed that he loved her? Or didn't she care? He'd been angry with her for one long, miserable week. And then he'd decided to forgive and forget. Mercedes had hurt him, but he had to believe it wasn't deliberate. It was his own fault for not declaring himself earlier. Perhaps it wasn't too late, even now.

Sam had driven to the house to see her, and urge her to wait with her wedding plans. It hadn't been entirely a selfish request on his part. Mercedes was a wealthy woman, and she'd only known Brad for six short months. But Mercedes had insisted that she wanted to marry Brad as soon as possible.

He'd done his best to dissuade her. She wanted what was best for the twins, didn't she? Was it fair to them to marry someone they barely knew? It was only right to wait a bit and give them a chance to build a good relationship with the man who would be their new father.

Mercedes had handled the rebuttal well. Of course, the twins didn't love Brad now, but she was sure they would in time. They loved her, and they would be delighted that she was happy. And Brad didn't want to be a father to the twins. He was perfectly content to be their friend, the way Sam was. Even though Sam had argued half the night with her, he'd only been able to convince Mercedes of one thing. She'd agreed to establish a trust fund for the children, and keep her inheritance from Mike in a separate account.

So Brad and Mercedes had married, despite Sam's objections. And Sam had to admit that things had gone well at first. Brad was a charming, personable man, and Mercedes had been deliriously happy. The first hint of trouble hadn't reared its ugly head until Mercedes had decided to let Brad handle her money. Perhaps Brad's intentions had been good. Sam was willing to give him the benefit of the doubt, even though he'd never really managed to get over his initial dislike, but Brad obviously had no head for investments. Sam was convinced that Mercedes might have ended up bankrupt if she'd allowed things to go on for much longer.

"Here's your coffee, Sam."

Sam looked up and smiled, as Marcie came in and set a tray down on the desk. Even though Mercedes and Marcie had been identical twins, they'd turned out to be very different people. Mercedes had been like a blazing comet, streaking through life on an erratic course that was dictated by her fiery beauty and her explosive talent. Marcie had never reached for the skies. She was calm and firmly grounded, like a graceful oak on an old family estate. He'd seen her at her weakest point last night, with tears streaming down her face. But this morning she was steady again, ready to do her duty and help her loved ones in any way she could.

"Is everything all right, Sam?"

Sam nodded. "The Neptune Society will handle all the arrangements. And the studio agreed to hold a memorial service on Friday afternoon at the Academy Theater."

"I want to be there. And I'll ask Rosa if she thinks the twins should go. Will you come with us, Sam?"

"Of course." Sam picked up his coffee cup and took a swallow. He'd slipped into the lawyer's trap for a moment, yearning to play God and set everything to rights. He'd caught himself wishing that Mercedes had inherited some of Marcie's qualities. She could have used a little of Marcie's patience and sweet humility. It would have added some tranquility to her life. And Marcie could have benefited from a dose of her twin sister's extreme self-confidence. From the things Mercedes had told him, Sam knew that Marcie was a loving, talented woman, who was sorely lacking in what his father had called *chutzpah.* Roughly translated, it meant guts, or courage, or belief in one's abilities. Marcie doubted she had anything worth offering, so she gratefully accepted the crumbs that other people put on her table. She wasn't aware that she could have the whole loaf if she just stood up and claimed it.

And now Marcie was here, and Mercedes had asked him to help her. Sam liked Marcie, and he was prepared to do his best, but he knew it wouldn't be easy.

Marcie was very naive, and Sam suspected she'd let Brad and the Hollywood crowd walk all over her. It was a damn good thing he was around to protect her interests. And there was no time like the present to start.

"Marcie?" Sam put down his coffee cup and leaned forward. "Do you think of me as a friend?"

Marcie looked slightly startled. "Of course. I know you were Mercedes's friend, and I was . . . well . . . I was hoping you'd be mine, too."

"Good. Then I'd like you to hire me as your lawyer."

"My lawyer?" Marcie frowned slightly. "I'd certainly hire you if I needed a lawyer. But why would I need a lawyer?"

Sam sighed. There was an issue of confidentiality at stake, and he knew he couldn't say too much. "There are a lot of details to be settled with your sister's estate. Take it from me. You're going to need some expert advice."

"Oh, dear." Marcie looked nervous. "Of course, I'd like you to represent me, Sam . . . but are you terribly expensive?"

Sam laughed. "Some say yes, some say no. But don't worry, Marcie. You'll be able to afford me. I personally guarantee it."

"All right then."

When Marcie walked over to the desk and held out her hand, Sam shook it. He held it a little longer than was necessary. Marcie was a sweet person, but she was much too trusting.

"Do you want me to sign a paper or something?" Marcie looked slightly worried.

"That's not necessary. A handshake is binding. Now, I want you to promise me not to sign *anything* unless I read it first. As your lawyer, it's my duty to protect you."

"It's a promise." Marcie nodded solemnly. "I won't even move unless you tell me it's all right."

"You don't have to go quite that far . . . especially since you're standing on my toe."

Marcie jumped back, and Sam laughed. "Just kidding, Marcie. You weren't anywhere close to my toe."

"That was rotten, Sam!" Marcie glared at him, and then she giggled. "I'm glad you're my friend, Sam. I know Mercedes trusted you, and I do, too. You can be my lawyer until the day I go back to my teaching job in Minnesota."

Sam smiled. He was almost certain that Marcie wouldn't be going back to Minnesota. Ever. But it would be premature of him to tell her that.

When she heard the gates open, Marcie jumped up from the couch. She rushed to the door and watched as the car rounded the bend, tires crunching on the crushed rock driveway. Rosa was back with the twins.

Even though she was nervous, Marcie put a smile on her face. The twins would be sad, perhaps even morose. It was her duty to comfort them, and help them get over their mother's death.

"Aunt Marcie!" Rick was the first to jump out of the car. He'd grown taller since the last time she'd seen him, and his hair, the same blond as his mother's, was bleached almost white with the California sun. Marcie noticed that there were tears in his eyes, but he blinked them back quickly as he ran to meet her. "We're so glad you came, Aunt Marcie!"

"I'm glad I came, too." Marcie blinked back her own tears as she reached out to hug him. Then Trish raced up to join in their embrace.

"Aunt Marcie! Rosa said you were here, and we could hardly wait to get home!"

"And I could hardly wait to see you." Marcie gave Trish another hug. "I like your hair, honey. Did Rosa braid it for you?"

Trish nodded, and her long, blond braids bounced. Rosa had mentioned that Trish was letting her hair grow, and Marcie was glad she'd picked up some barrettes and ponytail holders for her at the mall.

"They're hungry." Rosa shook her head as she herded the twins toward the house. "Trish says they had beef stew for lunch at school, and she couldn't find any beef."

Trish nodded. "It's true. Rick had one piece, but I didn't get any. It was awful, Aunt Marcie. Not like Rosa's at all. She's going to make us all grilled cheese sandwiches without any crusts."

Marcie smiled as she followed the twins inside. They were coping much better than she'd thought. And they'd certainly seemed glad to see her! Except for the tears that Rick had blinked back, they showed no outward signs of their grief.

"Miss Marcie?" Rosa gestured toward the kitchen table. "You're going to have a grilled cheese, aren't you?"

"Well . . ." Marcie frowned slightly. Sam had introduced her to Hungarian food at lunch, and she'd eaten a massive helping of something called Farmer's Goulash.

"Oh, come on, Aunt Marcie." Trish gave her a very adult look. "You don't have to watch your weight like Mom always did. You're nice and thin."

"So was Mom!" Rick glared at his twin sister. "She just had a real thing for chocolate, that's all. As long as we hid our candy bars, she was just fine. Do you like chocolate, Aunt Marcie? I can't remember from the last time."

"Of course, she does." Trish gave a disgruntled sigh. "Remember when we all went to Hampton's last year? Aunt Marcie ate almost a whole piece of Chocolate Death by herself."

Marcie raised her eyebrows as she joined the twins at the table. They were acting normal, almost too normal. They'd always been very sensitive, and it was possible they were putting on a cheerful act for her. Perhaps it was time to ask how they really felt.

"Are you guys okay?" Marcie faced them. "I mean, *really* okay?"

Rick shrugged. "Not really. We're just trying to cope."

"It's true." Trish nodded, and her lower lip quivered. "We're really sad, but we cried a lot before you came. Rosa says we should cry if we feel like it, and talk everything over so it won't hurt so bad. Are you all right, Aunt Marcie?"

Marcie sighed deeply. She had to be honest. "I think so. I still feel awful, though. I wish the whole thing was a bad dream, and I could wake up."

"That's how I feel!" Rick gave her a shaky smile. "When I went to bed last night, I thought maybe I'd wake up and Mom would be back. But then I woke up at Rosa's, and I knew Mom was really dead."

Trish nodded. "I did the same thing. I'm glad you came out here, Aunt Marcie. Now it'll be almost like normal. You're going to stay with us for a long time, aren't you?"

"I'll stay for as long as you need me." Marcie reached for the two bags of presents she'd picked up at the mall. "I brought you something from Minnesota, but my suitcases haven't come yet."

Rick smiled. "That's okay, Aunt Marcie. We can wait."

"But you don't have to." Marcie handed the bags to Trish and Rick. "Sam Abrams took me to the mall, and I bought you new presents."

"Do you like Sam?" Rick looked interested.

"Very much. Do you like him?"

"We adore him!" Trish spoke up. "Sam's practically one of the family. Even Mom used to say that."

Even Mom? Marcie frowned as she heard an undercurrent of wistfulness in Trish's voice. She had no idea what it meant, but she was sure she'd find out. The twins were very open about their feelings and they seldom kept secrets.

"These things for my hair are really neat." Trish reached across the table to hug her aunt. "Thank you, Aunt Marcie."

"You're welcome, honey." Marcie turned to Rick, who'd just unwrapped his book of baseball statistics. "I hope you don't have that book, Rick. I wasn't sure."

Rick shook his head. "I don't have it. And it's small enough to carry in my pocket. Thanks, Aunt Marcie."

"Here you go." Rosa set a plate of grilled cheese sandwiches on the table. "Eat these before they get cold."

"We will!"

Both twins spoke at once and Marcie smiled. But they didn't act as enthusiastic as they'd sounded. Trish picked up her sandwich and nibbled, and Rick chewed his much slower than usual. The twins were definitely subdued, but that was understandable. She was just beginning to get over the shock of Mercedes's death, and it was bound to take them much longer.

"I've got an idea." Marcie smiled at them. "You two

eat, and I'll tell you about the time your mother ate a whole chocolate pie."

"She didn't!" The corners of Rick's mouth turned up in a grin.

"Oh, yes, she did. I was right there when she ate it."

"All by herself?" Trish looked intrigued.

"Yes, and she was only ten years old, just like you two. And to make things even worse, that was the very pie your grandmother was planning to take to the church bake sale."

"Uh-oh! Tell us, Aunt Marcie . . . please?"

Both twins spoke at once, and Marcie grinned. Rick had taken another bite of his sandwich, and Trish was reaching for her milk.

"Grandma had set the pie out on the window ledge to cool." Marcie began her story. "And your mother came home from school and smelled it the minute she opened the door. Chocolate pie was her absolute favorite."

Trish was grinning. "Did she get into trouble with Grandma?"

"She would have been in really big trouble, if she hadn't come up with a plan. But maybe I shouldn't tell you about it. It might give you ideas."

"We've already got ideas." Rick laughed. "Come on, Aunt Marcie. We want to know more about Mom when she was young."

"Okay, then." Marcie smiled as she began to tell the story. Sam Abrams was right. Talking about Mercedes was the best way to keep her alive in their hearts.

CHAPTER 5

"Marcie?" Brad knocked on the connecting door. "Are you ready?"

"I'll be right out, Brad." Marcie took one last look in the mirror. She knew she'd never looked better in her life. Mercedes had been right to criticize her wardrobe. Although Marcie hadn't realized it before, she'd been wearing clothes that weren't very flattering.

Her suitcases had finally arrived, two days later than the baggage supervisor at the airport had promised, and they bore tags from five different airports. When Rosa had unpacked for her, Marcie had examined her clothing with a critical eye. Her things were serviceable, but they weren't very stylish. And there were several outfits she probably wouldn't have purchased at all, if they hadn't been on sale.

Trish and Rick had been in her bedroom when Rosa hung up her clothes. Marcie had noticed they'd exchanged meaningful glances. Then Trish had spoken up.

"Aunt Marcie?" Trish had looked a little nervous. "We don't want you to take this wrong, but . . ."

". . . but we think you should wear some of Mom's

clothes." Rick had finished the sentence for her. "We think they'd look really good on you, and we'd like you to have them."

They'd both looked up at her expectantly, and Marcie had smiled. They'd obviously been trying not to hurt her feelings, but it was clear they thought her clothes weren't right for California.

"Well . . . all right. But only if you're sure it won't bother you."

"It won't."

Both twins had spoken at once, and Marcie had smiled at them fondly. The twins often spoke together, or finished each other's sentences. From their earliest years, they'd seemed to know exactly which words the other would say. She'd been the same way with Mercedes. Trish and Rick had been confined together in their mother's womb, and perhaps they'd been able to communicate even then. And ever since their birth, they'd shared their own private world. Although they were no longer physically linked, there was perfect understanding between them.

Trish had marched to the closet and pulled out a lovely dark blue suit. "I think you should wear this when you go to Sam's office. Mom always said it was perfect for business meetings."

"It's beautiful." Marcie had reached out to touch the soft material. But would it upset Brad if she wore that outfit?

"It won't bother Brad." Rick had caught her hesitation. "He never . . ."

". . . even noticed what Mom wore." Trish had nodded.

Marcie had smiled at them. They were very perceptive, and they'd known exactly what she'd been thinking. "Okay, I'll wear it. But if you change your mind, all you have to do is—"

"We won't." Rick had returned her smile. "We talked about it last night, and we decided her things should stay in the family. And you're Mom's family."

Trish had nodded. "Mom had a lot of pretty clothes. And yours are . . . uh . . ."

"Pretty awful?"

"Well . . . no." Rick had looked very serious. "They're not exactly awful, Aunt Marcie. They're perfect for a schoolteacher in Minnesota. But out here . . ."

". . . people dress up more." Trish had jumped in. "Since Brad said he talked you into staying for at least a month, we think you should use Mom's clothes. I mean . . . you wear the same size, and you used to exchange things all the time when you were kids and . . ."

". . . and we know she would have wanted you to have them." Rick finished the thought.

The twins had stayed in her room for two solid hours, going through their mother's closet, and pointing out the things they thought would look especially good on her. They'd even urged her to try on a few outfits, and they hadn't seemed the least bit upset. Marcie had promised them she'd wear their mother's dark blue Chanel suit to the meeting in Sam's office this morning, for the reading of Mercedes's will.

Marcie smiled as she took one last look in the mirror. Quality clothing really made a difference. She felt much more self-confident as she walked down the stairs to join Brad and Rosa. They were the three principals, not counting the twins. Since the children were minors, they weren't required to be present. Sam was the executor, and he would look after their interests.

When Sam had told her that she was a principal, Marcie had wondered what her sister had left to her.

Then she remembered that they had divided their parents' valuables after their deaths. Mercedes had probably left her their father's pocket watch, and their mother's antique opal ring. If that was the case, Marcie planned to keep the ring for Trish and the pocket watch for Rick.

"Miss Marcie! You look wonderful!" Rosa gave her an approving smile. "Don't you think so, Mr. Brad?"

Brad nodded. "You certainly do. That's strange. I never noticed how much you looked like . . . I mean . . . you do look a lot like her, you know."

"I'm sure that's because I'm wearing one of her outfits. Does it bother you, Brad? I can always go up and change."

"No, it's fine." Brad slipped an arm around her shoulders and lowered his voice. "I like it, Marcie. It's almost like having her back with me again. I always loved the way Mercedes looked in that suit."

Marcie gave him a happy smile. The twins had been wrong, and so had Rosa. Brad *had* noticed what Mercedes had worn!

"I was hoping you could use some of her clothes." Brad opened the door and escorted her out. "I don't think I'd like it if a stranger wore them, but you're family."

Brad opened the rear door for Rosa, and then he turned to Marcie. "Sit up front with me, Marcie. You'll be able to see more of the sights that way."

Marcie sighed as she got into the passenger side of Brad's Jaguar. Such luxury! The supple leather upholstery seemed to cradle her softly, and she was beginning to understand why someone would spend a small fortune on a car. This was particularly true for Brad, who spent a lot of time in his car. Mercedes had told her that Brad logged over fifteen thousand miles a year, commuting to financial institutions and meetings as her investment counselor, and to the stables in Ojai where they kept their prize racehorses.

"You like it?" Brad smiled at her as he started the car and pulled out into the driveway.

"It's fabulous! And it's quite a change from my old Volkswagen. I hope my Beetle doesn't find out I've been unfaithful to her with other cars. If she suspects anything at all, she'll break down in the middle of a snowbank."

Brad laughed. "You call your car Miss Ladybug, right?"

"Yes." Marcie looked over at him in surprise. "How did you know that?"

"Mercedes told me. She said you always name things, and you were the one who named her sink disposal."

"It's true. When the twins were little, Mercedes wanted to make sure they didn't turn on the disposal. I told her to name it Chomp, and it worked."

"That's right." Rosa spoke up from the backseat. "They were into everything else, but they never touched the switch to the disposal. They were afraid Chomp would chomp them."

They rode in silence for a few minutes, watching the Los Angeles skyline pass by. Then Brad took the entrance to the Santa Monica Freeway, and Marcie gasped. "I can't believe all these cars! It's not rush hour, is it?"

"No, this is fairly light." Brad maneuvered his way to a faster lane. "During rush hour we wouldn't even try the freeway. It's a giant parking lot."

"Where are all these people going?" Marcie stared at the hundreds of cars that stretched out as far as she could see.

"All over the city. The rapid transit system here is such a joke, people almost have to drive. They've tried car pools, but they don't work very well, since there's really no central business district, and everyone has a different place to go."

Marcie nodded. "Los Angeles is awfully big, isn't it?"

"It's huge. And when it grew, it sprawled out in every direction it could. You've heard of the San Fernando Valley?"

"Mercedes was working at Universal Studios, the last time I came out for a visit. It's in the valley, isn't it?"

"That's a good example." Brad smiled at her. "It used to take her almost an hour to get to work. And the studio's only fifteen miles from our house. These freeways were built years ago, and they can't handle today's traffic. Everyone jokes about gridlock, but that's what we'll have if we keep on going the way we are."

For the rest of the ride, Marcie stared out the window as Brad pointed out landmarks. They passed the two triangular buildings in Century City, the Convention Center, which always reminded Marcie of an oversized field house, and the round, mirrored Bonaventure Hotel. Then Brad pulled up in front of a huge black marble building that must have been at least twenty stories high.

"Sam's office." Brad gestured toward the entrance.

Marcie was almost speechless as she stared at the huge building. "All this?"

"No." Brad laughed. "Sam has a suite on the seventeenth floor. The building's owned by the bank on the ground floor, and they lease out the rest."

A valet parker rushed up to open her door, and Marcie got out. Then Brad led them into the lobby where there were two banks of elevators.

"This side." He pressed a button on the left bank,

which had a plaque that identified it as the North Tower. "The ones on the right only go up to the tenth floor. These start at the tenth and go up to the twentieth."

Marcie nodded, but she didn't quite understand. If an elevator picked them up on the ground floor, how could it start on the tenth? She almost asked Brad, but she didn't want him to think she was a total hick. She'd ask Rosa later, when Brad wasn't around.

The elevator was paneled with wood and mirrors, and Marcie checked her appearance again. The twins had been right. This lovely blue suit was perfect for a business meeting and she thought she looked very cosmopolitan. If she didn't ask any stupid questions, everyone would think she belonged in a beautiful building like this.

Marcie stifled a gasp as the elevator rose swiftly upward. She felt as if she'd left her stomach on the ground floor. It reminded her of the "kiss-me-quicks" back in Minnesota. When she and Mercedes had been very small, their parents had taken them out on the road to Cold Spring, and they'd driven up sharp little hills their mother had called kiss-me-quicks. At the very top, right before the rapid descent, there was a moment of weightlessness. Marcie still remembered how they'd gasped and then giggled, clutching their stomachs as the car fairly flew down the hill. They'd asked why these hills were called kiss-me-quicks, and their mother had promised they'd experience that same, breathless feeling again, when they kissed the man they loved.

Marcie sighed. She'd never experienced that breathless feeling from a kiss. Perhaps it was just an old folk tale. Without really being aware of what she was doing, she glanced up at Brad, and wondered if his kisses could make her feel breathless.

"Something wrong, Marcie?" Brad smiled down at her.

Marcie blushed. She was ashamed of herself. She really shouldn't be thinking romantic thoughts about her sister's husband. "No. I just . . . uh . . . I've never been in an elevator that went this fast before. It's almost like a ride at an amusement park."

"That reminds me." Brad looked thoughtful. "We should take the twins to Disneyland before you go back. They've got a couple of new rides, and Mercedes was planning on taking them there for their birthday. What do you think, Rosa?"

Rosa nodded. "That's a good idea, Mr. Brad. Trish and Rick love Disneyland."

Just then the elevator beeped and slowed. Marcie felt the kiss-me-quick feeling as it stopped, and she resisted the urge to giggle as the doors slid open. Sam certainly didn't need to go to Disneyland, not when Sam's office was in a building like this. She almost envied him. Sam got to ride on the equivalent to a roller coaster every day he went to work.

"Oh, how beautiful!" Marcie stepped off the elevator and into a lobby with deep blue carpeting and two blue leather couches that were several shades lighter than the grass cloth on the walls. The end tables by the couches were made of rosewood, and each had a bouquet of dark red, silk lilies in a tall, navy blue ceramic vase. Although Marcie was sure that there were no natural flowers of that rich, deep red hue, she still reached out to touch a petal. The bouquets were so realistic, they had almost fooled her.

"This way." Brad led them through a door and down a wide corridor with the same carpeting and the same blue grass cloth on the walls. There was a double door at the end of the corridor and he opened it to usher them in.

"Good morning." A secretary with lovely, snow white hair greeted them. "Mr. Abrams will be with you in just a moment. Please follow me to the conference room."

As they entered the conference room, Marcie looked around in delight. Here the color scheme changed to a restful gray and mauve. The carpeting was a deep shade of gray, so dark it was almost black, and there were beautifully framed charcoal prints on the mauve-colored walls. The conference table dominated the center of the room, a shining oval of blond Philippine mahogany, with a floral centerpiece of freshly cut white daisies arranged in a low, wide crystal bowl. There were four gray leather swivel chairs arranged around the table, and on the tabletop, in front of each chair, was a pad of yellow legal paper and a pen.

"Please make yourselves comfortable. Mr. Abrams will be with you in just a moment." The white-haired secretary smiled at them. "Would you care for coffee or tea?"

"Black coffee for me." Brad turned to Rosa.

"Yes, me, too." Rosa nodded. "But with cream and no sugar. Miss Marcie?"

"Thank you. I'll have . . ." Marcie stopped in mid-sentence. She'd been about to ask for tea but she was really beginning to like the taste of coffee. "I'd like black coffee, please."

The secretary went to an alcove at one end of the room and opened the shuttered doors. Inside was a full coffee service. She arranged three delicate china cups and saucers on a wooden serving tray with a silver carafe of coffee. Then she filled a matching cream pitcher, and carried the tray to the table.

Marcie was impressed as the secretary served the

coffee. The whole procedure was very elegant, and it made her feel like a valuable client. She wished her parents' lawyer, in St. Cloud, Minnesota, could see how they did things in Los Angeles. When Marcie had met with him to settle her parents' estate, he'd given her instant tea in a Styrofoam cup.

"Good morning." Sam appeared in the doorway, carrying a mug of coffee. "Brad? Rosa? Marcie? It's good to see you."

They made polite conversation for a few moments, while the secretary refilled Sam's coffee mug. Marcie almost laughed out loud as she noticed the slogan on the side. In bright red letters it proclaimed, LAWYERS PREFER EXPENSIVE SUITS.

Sam caught Marcie's amused expression, and he smiled at her. "A gift from a client. I usually leave it in my private office, but it holds more coffee than those little china things. Are we ready to get down to business?"

They all nodded, and Sam opened the folder he'd placed on the desk. He took out three copies of stapled papers, and placed them on the table. "As executor, I'll read the will to you aloud. And then I'll answer any questions you may have. My secretary has prepared copies for each of you to take with you when you leave."

Sam looked very serious, especially when he glanced at her, and Marcie felt a strange sense of foreboding. As he began to read, she clasped her hands tightly together in her lap. Her hands were trembling, and she didn't know why.

The will was fairly short, and it took Sam only a few minutes to read it. The letter Mercedes left for her had mentioned the account she'd set up for Rosa. That was no surprise. But the rest of the will certainly was!

As one fateful word followed another, Marcie felt

dizzy. Then the conference room began to revolve around her, and she had to take several deep breaths to keep from fainting. Mercedes had left her almost everything, including custody of the twins!

"I know this has been a shock." Sam handed them copies of the will. "Do you have any questions?"

Marcie swallowed hard, and hoped she could find her voice. Sam was wrong. This was much more than a shock. It was unthinkable! "But why in the world . . . ? I mean . . . I can't believe how unfair this is to Brad! Don't community property laws apply?"

"Yes, they do." Sam nodded. "And this will isn't at all unfair to Brad. He's inherited all the property and material wealth Mercedes acquired after their marriage. The racehorses, the antique automobiles, the time-share condo in Hawaii, and any other investments he made for her."

Marcie nodded. That much was true. "But how about the house? Shouldn't Brad have the house?"

"It's not community property." Sam did his best to explain in layman's terms. "Mike Lang and Mercedes bought that house together. And when he died Mercedes inherited it, along with the rest of Mike's estate. Mike's assets were kept separate, so there were no commingled funds. And even though Brad is Mercedes's surviving husband, he has no legal right to any part of Mike Lang's estate."

Sam turned to Brad. "Do you have any questions, Brad? I know it's complicated."

"I understand." Brad's face was white. "But I thought Mercedes made out a new will last year."

Sam looked a little uncomfortable. "She mentioned it to me, but she never followed up on it. I'm sorry, Brad. But you did inherit everything you purchased jointly since your marriage. I'd estimate that to be worth a couple of million, at least."

"Mr. Sam?" Rosa spoke up. "I don't understand that account Miss Mercedes left for me. What does it mean?"

"It means you have an income for life, Rosa. Mercedes made sure she put away the money for your yearly salary, with a five percent raise every year. And when the twins turn eighteen, you'll get a lump sum payment that will be more than enough for your retirement."

"But what if Miss Marcie goes back to Minnesota?" Rosa looked worried. "My babies'll go with her, and then I won't have a job."

Marcie smiled at the worried housekeeper. "Oh, yes, you will. The twins can't get along without you, Rosa. You'd move back there with us, wouldn't you?"

"I'd love to, Miss Marcie." Rosa gave a deep sigh of relief. "I just wanted you to ask me, that's all. I'm willing to go anywhere with my babies."

"That's it then, except for one thing. Brad? I hate to be the bearer of bad news, but right before she died, Mercedes hired another investment firm to handle her money."

"Mercedes fired me?" Brad looked shocked.

"No, of course not." Sam patted him on the shoulder. "You'll still be handling the profits from the joint investments you made with Mercedes, except you'll be your own boss now. And the stable of racehorses and the antique cars belong solely to you. Mercedes didn't fire you, Brad. It's quite the opposite. Under the terms of Mercedes's will, you have enough money to be totally independent."

"That's . . . uh . . . that's great!" Brad still looked

upset as he gathered up his papers. "That was very . . . kind of her."

Sam nodded. "I want you to remember that Mercedes was very much in love with you when she made up that will. She told me she wanted to be fair to everyone, including her children. Perhaps, if she'd drawn up a later will, she would have given you custody. But you were newly married, and I don't think she wanted to burden you with her responsibilities."

"Of course."

Brad still looked upset, and Marcie gave him a sympathetic smile. "I'm sure things would have been different if she'd written a new will, Brad."

"Okay. We're finished." Sam stood up. "How about some lunch? There's a new place on Wilshire, and I'm buying."

Brad shook his head. "I've got a couple of appointments I have to keep. Another time, Sam?"

"And I have to get back to the house." Rosa stood up. "They're coming to check the sprinklers again this afternoon."

"Again?" Marcie looked puzzled.

"It's the fourth time this week, and they still don't work right." Rosa gave a sigh. "Maybe I should offer them room and board. They come out to check them almost every day."

Sam turned to Marcie. "How about it, Marcie? We have more business to discuss, and I'll give you a ride home after lunch."

"Well, if you're sure you don't need me . . ." Marcie hesitated and looked at Rosa.

"You go on and have lunch with Mr. Sam." Rosa gave her a nod. "It'll do you good to go out to a fancy place and have some fun."

* * *

"This is wonderful, Sam." Marcie finished the last of her Peking duck, and looked up at Sam with a smile. "I'm afraid I'm developing expensive tastes. I'll never be satisfied with our little Chinese restaurant in St. Cloud, now that I've tasted food like this."

"You don't have to be satisfied with things back there, Marcie. You're a rich woman now. You can give up teaching and stay out here."

"Just how . . . uh . . . how rich am I, Sam?" Marcie looked concerned.

"Your net worth is about seven million dollars, less a thousand or two. And that'll increase, now that you have a new investment firm."

"Seven million dollars?" Marcie looked dazed. "But . . . most of that's for the twins, isn't it, Sam?"

"No, that's yours. The twins have a separate trust account. You don't have to work anymore, Marcie. You have more than enough money for the rest of your life."

"But . . . what will I do if I don't work?" Marcie frowned deeply.

Sam smiled at her. "You'll stay here and be a mother to Trish and Rick. And if you feel you need some outside interest, there's always charity work."

"You mean like giving parties for people who support diseases?"

Sam threw back his head and laughed. "They don't support diseases, Marcie. They support the cures for diseases. But you've got the general idea."

"Okay, I stand corrected." Marcie sighed. "And I know somebody has to do things like that, but I'd make a terrible hostess."

"How about painting? Mercedes told me you always

wanted to be free to paint, but you couldn't afford to take the time off."

"Oh, that would be wonderful!" Marcie looked wistful. "There're so many projects I've wanted to do, but I've never had the time . . . or the money."

Sam reached out to take her hand. "You have it now, Marcie. And maybe that's what Mercedes had in mind. She wanted you to be free to pursue your talents."

"But, Sam . . . I'm not sure I have any real talents."

Sam shrugged. "You'll never know if you don't try. Your sister made sure you'd have the means. Why don't you give it a whirl?"

Sam's words were still ringing in her hears as Marcie walked up to her sister's bedroom. She passed the open door to Brad's room, and stopped in surprise as she saw he was there.

"Hi, Brad." Marcie gave a little wave. Then she noticed the suitcases on the bed. "Are you going on a business trip?"

Brad looked upset as he answered her. "No. I'm moving. It's your house now, and I didn't think it was right for me to stay here."

Marcie's mouth fell open. She couldn't believe her ears. "But, Brad . . . do you *want* to move?"

"No. Of course, I don't want to move. I just didn't think you'd want me to stay."

"Oh, Brad!" Marcie hurried to take his arm. "Don't be silly. Of course, I want you to stay. The twins would be terribly upset if you left . . . and . . . and so would I."

Brad looked uncertain. "Really? I wasn't sure how you'd feel. I didn't want to leave the twins, but . . ."

"Of course, you don't have to leave the twins!"

Marcie shook her head. "I want you to unpack right now, and never even think of leaving again!"

Brad looked hopeful. "Does that mean you're staying here in California? It would mean a lot to me, Marcie. I know I'm not their real father, but I think I'd die if I couldn't see the twins again."

"I give you my solemn promise that you can see the twins anytime you want to." Marcie smiled at him kindly. "I'm not sure I'll stay in California, but I promise I'll give it some serious thought. Now call Rosa to unpack your bags. As far as I'm concerned, this house is as much yours as it is mine."

Brad caught her as she was about to leave the room, and he gave her a big hug. "Marcie, you're wonderful. Please stay here. I'm beginning to feel . . . uh . . . very close to you."

Marcie didn't say anything. She wasn't sure what would be proper. But when she closed the door to her own room behind her, she was smiling. She was glad she'd been able to talk Brad into staying. What she'd said about the twins was true. She was convinced they'd miss Brad if he suddenly moved out. But there was another reason she wanted him to stay. Brad had said he was beginning to feel very close to her. Marcie wasn't sure exactly what he'd meant, but she had her hopes. She'd liked Brad as a brother-in-law, and she liked him even more now. She was beginning to feel very close to him, too.

CHAPTER 6

Even though the Academy Theater was huge, every seat was taken. Marcie was in the front row next to Brad, who had the seat on the aisle. The twins were on her other side, Trish next to her, and Rick one seat down. Sam was next, because Rick had insisted he wanted to sit by him, and then Rosa. The rest of the row was empty, and tied off with a maroon velvet rope. The studio had reserved it for Mercedes's immediate family.

The service was due to start any moment. Marcie tried not to be too obvious, but she looked around with awe as she recognized some very famous faces.

"Aunt Marcie?" Trish moved closer to whisper in her ear. "That's Robert Redford on the other side, two rows from the front. And Barbra Streisand is in back of us, five rows behind Sam. I know you're terrible at recognizing stars, so I thought I should tell you."

Marcie nodded. "Thanks, Trish. Who's the man directly behind Rosa? He looks just like O.J. Simpson."

Trish clamped her hand over her mouth and poked at Rick, who leaned over her to explain. "That's George Williams. He was Mom's driver. But you've got the right sport, Aunt Marcie. George used to play football in the police league."

"Your mother's driver was a policeman?" Marcie was surprised.

"A retired policeman." Trish corrected her. "George got shot chasing a killer. He showed us the scar on his leg."

Before Marcie could ask any more questions, the curtains opened, and a short, distinguished-looking man took his place behind the podium.

"Mr. Cox." Rick leaned over his sister to whisper. "He's a veep at the studio."

Marcie looked puzzled, and Trish explained. "Veep stands for vice president. There's a bunch of them, but he's the most important one. I guess Mom was a really big star, or they would have sent one of the others."

Marcie nodded and reached out to squeeze Trish's hand. The twins were adjusting, but it would take a while. When they'd come home from school that first day, they'd clung to Marcie, almost afraid to let her out of their sight. And they'd been clinging to her ever since. Marcie knew it was because they were fearful that something bad would happen to her, too.

Even though she hadn't thought so at the time, Brad had been right in sending them back to school. Being with their friends had helped a bit. But their teachers said the twins had been unusually silent and withdrawn, and their test scores had dropped considerably.

When Marcie had discussed the problem with the school counselor, he'd advised her to spend as much time with the twins as she could. He'd also suggested starting a new hobby activity, anything to spark their interest. Since her suitcase had finally arrived, Marcie had tried painting with Trish, and organizing baseball cards in the collector's album with Rick. They'd been polite and thanked her for the gifts, but they hadn't really responded with any enthusiasm. Sam had arrived one night with a couple of new video games, but that hadn't worked either. And when they'd taken the twins roller skating, one of their favorite pastimes, they'd just skated around the rink listlessly. Seeing them so morose was terribly sad. Marcie was sure they'd snap out of their depression eventually, but she wished she could think of some way to speed up the process.

Brad shifted slightly in his seat, and Marcie turned to look at him. He was staring down at the note cards he'd prepared, going over his speech. He'd told Marcie he'd felt that someone in the family should give a eulogy to Mercedes, and he'd volunteered to do it.

Mr. Cox wasn't a very good public speaker. His voice was flat with very little inflection, almost a monotone. Marcie did her best to concentrate as he praised Mercedes, but it was an impossible task. She thought, instead, of how she should have offered to say something personal about her twin sister. She could have told these people how Mercedes had supported her all through college, and even paid her way through graduate school. Of course, she'd paid back every cent but the money had been there when she'd needed it.

Her twin sister's generosity was something these people should know. Marcie doubted that Mercedes had told anyone about the scholarship she'd funded for one of Marcie's best art students, or the big contribution she'd made to establish the school's film library, or the way she'd picked up most of the expenses when their parents' best friends had lost everything they'd owned in a fire. She wished she had the nerve to march right up to the podium and tell everyone about the new animal shelter Mercedes had founded, when

Marcie'd told her that the city had condemned the old building where they'd gotten their first puppy. And about their cousin's children who'd had their teeth straightened, thanks to Mercedes. And their former third-grade teacher with asthma, who'd been hired by Mercedes to take care of her condo in Arizona where the air was dry and much better for her health. Miss Mielke had no idea that Mercedes had purchased the condo in response to one of Marcie's weekly letters.

Marcie sighed. Mercedes had helped so many people. The local community theater was thriving, thanks to her sister's contributions. And so was old Mr. Hansen's drugstore, where they'd sat in polished wooden booths and ordered Black Cows, her sister's favorite soda with root beer and chocolate ice cream. The drugstore was back on its feet because Mercedes had arranged a small business loan out of her own bank account.

Mr. Cox was winding up his speech now, and Marcie took a deep breath. Maybe it was about time she stopped being so shy. So what if she stumbled for words, or broke down in tears? She owed it to her sister's memory to try.

Her hands were shaking as she tapped Brad on the shoulder. She knew that he was the next scheduled speaker, but her tribute to Mercedes wouldn't take long.

Brad leaned over so she could whisper in his ear, and Marcie's courage almost failed her. Then she remembered what Rosa had said this morning, about how happy Mercedes would be when she looked down from heaven and heard the wonderful things everyone would say about her. Marcie wasn't sure there was a heaven, but she liked the idea of Mercedes knowing that she'd conquered her shyness, for the moment at least. If Mercedes weren't already dead, she surely would have died of shock if she saw Marcie getting up to speak in front of all these important people!

"What is it, Marcie?" Brad frowned slightly. There were tears in Marcie's eyes, but she looked almost amused.

"Could I have two minutes, right before your tribute? I . . . I want to say something, after all."

"Of course." Brad tried not to look surprised. Mercedes had once told him Marcie had no self-confidence, but perhaps she'd been wrong. Marcie certainly looked determined, and it took a lot of courage to get up in front of all these people and give a speech.

Marcie felt her hands grow damp as Mr. Cox finished. It was too late to back out now. She had to do it. And then she was behind the podium, standing on legs that shook so hard, she had to grip the wooden stand with both hands. Why had she done this? It was insane! She'd never been so scared in her life!

But Brad and Sam and Rosa were smiling. And the twins were staring at her with rapt faces. They knew how shy she was, and what an effort it had taken to simply walk up here. Marcie drew a deep breath and pretended she was back in St. Cloud, Minnesota, talking to her class of art students.

"Most of you don't know me. I'm Marcie Calder, Mercedes's twin sister. My sister wrote me a letter eight years ago, telling me exactly what she wanted. She knew the studio would want to hold a memorial service. And she also knew how shy I am, so she told me I didn't have to get up here and speak."

There wasn't a rustle in the big theater, and Marcie took another deep breath. "Mercedes was right. I *am* shy. But I'm the only one who knows just how generous my sister was, and I want to tell you."

Once she'd started, it wasn't as hard as she'd thought. Marcie told them about the money for college. And the braces for her cousin's children. She mentioned the art scholarship, and the school film library, and the condo in Arizona for their third-grade teacher. The list of contributions Mercedes had made was lengthy, but Marcie didn't leave anything out. And when she was finished, she gave a big sigh of relief.

"That's all. I don't need to tell you how much I loved her, because everyone loved Mercedes. And I don't need to tell you about how beautiful and talented she was. She was a loving mother, and a good wife, and a wonderful sister. I'm going to miss her terribly, and I know all of you will, too."

Somehow, without even being aware of how she'd gotten there, Marcie was back in her seat. As Brad got up to take his place at the podium, Trish reached out to hug her. There were tears in her eyes.

"Thanks, Aunt Marcie." Trish spoke very softly. "Mom would have loved it."

Rick leaned over his sister to whisper in Marcie's ear. There were tears in his eyes, too, although he quickly blinked them back. "Mom would have been surprised, too. I don't think she figured you had the guts to do it."

Brad started speaking, and the twins leaned back in their seats to listen. He told everyone how grateful he was for the two years he'd had with Mercedes, how much he'd loved her, and how very much he would miss her. It was a touching speech, and Marcie could feel the tears running down her cheeks. It was clear that Brad was suffering. His voice cracked several times as he told a particularly poignant story, and Marcie looked over at the twins through a haze of tears. But neither Trish nor Rick was crying. They were just staring at Brad with carefully composed faces.

After Brad had finished speaking, Sam got up and gave his tribute. This time the twins cried right along with Marcie, and she reached over to hold their hands. Then Sam told several funny stories about the client who'd also been his friend, and the twins ended up smiling through their tears.

The remainder of the service went fast. The studio showed several clips from the movies Mercedes had made, including the one that had earned her an Academy Award nomination. And then Ashley Thorpe, Mercedes's costar, got up to introduce a scene from *Summer Heat*. A final word from the head of the studio, and the service was over.

When they walked out of the theater, the sun was beginning to lower in the sky. They stood in a tight family circle at the top of the steps, as several dozen people came over to offer their condolences. The twins stood on either side of Marcie, taking turns telling her who the people were. Sandra Shepard, a supporting actress in *Summer Heat*. Jolene Edwards, their mother's personal assistant. Elena Garvey, the costume designer. Beau LeTeure, her makeup artist. Reuben Lowe, the head cameraman. Tom Porter, the lighting supervisor. David Edward Allen, her director. There were so many names that Marcie knew she'd never be able to keep them all straight.

"Lovely speech, Miss Calder." A short, stocky man with a reddish beard rushed over to shake Marcie's hand. Then he turned to the twins. "Hi, guys. Are you making out okay?"

Trish and Rick nodded. Then Rick spoke up. "We're fine, Mr. Buchannan, now that Aunt Marcie's here."

"Aunt Marcie?" Trish tapped her on the arm. "This

is Mr. Ralph Buchannan, Mom's producer in *Summer Heat*."

Marcie nodded. "I'm glad to meet you, Mr. Buchannan."

"Not as glad as I am to meet *you*." Ralph Buchannan smiled. "I couldn't believe it when I heard that Mercedes had an identical twin."

Marcie smiled and sneaked a glance at Sam. "That's not surprising. Most people have trouble believing it, since we look so different now."

"But you don't! That's just the point. Dave and I were just talking about that. Same bone structure, same coloring, same smile. And I bet him that you and Mercedes used to switch places to try to fool people. Am I right?"

"Yes, you are." Marcie nodded.

"Did it work?"

"It worked almost too well. I remember one time when we were staying with my aunt. Mercedes got grounded, but I was allowed to go out, so I borrowed her new blue sweater. When I got home, Aunt Becky thought I was Mercedes, and it took me an hour to convince her that she was mistaken."

"Just as I thought!" Ralph Buchannan smiled in satisfaction. "With the right hairstyle and the right makeup, no one could tell you weren't your sister!"

Ralph Buchannan was beaming at her like she'd won first prize in a pie-baking contest, and Marcie was puzzled. "Well . . . it's kind of you to say so, but I'm not so sure about that."

"Why don't we find out? I promised the twins they could see the last batch of dailies. Bring them to the studio tomorrow, and we'll shoot a test film."

"But isn't that rather silly? I mean . . . just to settle a bet with your director?"

"Oh, that's not it." He lowered his voice and leaned a little closer. "You see, we've got a real problem with *Summer Heat*. There are a dozen critical scenes left to shoot, and now that Mercedes is . . . uh . . . gone, we'll have to can the whole thing. There's no way we can write our way out of it with script changes. Believe me, we've tried."

Trish's mouth dropped open, and she let out a little gasp. "Wow! You want Aunt Marcie to double for Mom?"

"Precisely." Ralph Buchannan beamed at her. "I can tell you inherited your mother's intelligence. And she loved *Summer Heat,* didn't she, guys?"

Rick nodded. "She told us it was the best movie she'd ever done. And the dailies really looked super! I think she would have won an Oscar."

"Maybe it's not too late for that . . . if your aunt Marcie will agree to a screen test."

"Please, Mr. Buchannan." Marcie was embarrassed. "I'm very flattered but I'm certainly no actress. I've only been in one play in my life, and that was in second grade, when I played a stalk of corn in the Thanksgiving pageant."

Trish nodded sagely. "That's method acting, Aunt Marcie. Mom told us about this class she took once, when she had to be a car. She was trying for a Ferrari, but everybody thought she was an old station wagon."

"I think you should do it, Aunt Marcie." Rick spoke up. "If you're lousy, it doesn't matter. They have to ditch the film anyway. But maybe you'll be good. And . . . well . . . if Mom's watching over us, like Rosa says, I know she'd be really happy if you helped to finish her movie."

Marcie could feel herself beginning to waver. The whole thing was ridiculous, but the twins really wanted her to do it. And it seemed to have snapped them out of their depression, at least momentarily.

"But really, Mr. Buchannan . . . I wouldn't know the first thing to do!"

"That's why you have a director," Trish explained. "He tells you exactly what to do. Why don't you try it, Aunt Marcie? Rick and I will help you learn your lines and everything."

Rick looked excited. "Come on, Aunt Marcie. It'll be fun. And if you're in the picture, we'll come to the studio every day after school and help you."

"You're going to show her some of Mom's dailies, aren't you, Mr. Buchannan?" Trish looked concerned. "It's not fair to make Aunt Marcie read cold."

Ralph Buchannan patted her on the back. "Right you are, young lady. We'll watch some scenes that are already in the can, and then your aunt Marcie can test for the part."

"You're going to do it, aren't you, Aunt Marcie?" Rick looked up at her hopefully.

"Well . . . I'm willing, but you'll have to get my lawyer's permission." Marcie motioned to Sam. "He told me I shouldn't agree to anything, unless I consult him first."

While Sam and Ralph Buchannan discussed it, the twins told Marcie all about their mother's role in *Summer Heat.* Marcie was amazed at how much they knew, and how involved they'd been in the whole process. The school guidance counselor had advised her to get them involved in some outside interest, and this seemed to fit the bill. If she hadn't been convinced to take Mr. Buchannan's screen test before, she certainly was now. Trish's eyes were shining with excitement, and Rick was just as enthusiastic as his twin sister.

"It's just a screen test," Marcie cautioned them. "I don't want you to be too upset if it doesn't work out."

Trish nodded. "We won't be, I promise. Right, Rick?"

"That's right." Rick nodded, too. "We're just excited about going to the studio again, Aunt Marcie. And if you bomb, we'll understand. Mom didn't get every part she tested for, either."

"What's going on?" Brad came up to join them.

Rick nudged his sister and Trish explained, "Mr. Buchannan said there were too many scenes left in *Summer Heat,* and they'd have to drop it if they couldn't find someone to double for Mom. He asked Aunt Marcie to test for the part, since they look so much alike."

"That's great!" Brad smiled at Marcie. "You're going to do it, aren't you?"

Marcie smiled back. "I guess so. The twins promised to help me if I get the part."

"I'll help you, too." Brad nodded. "We can make this a family project. Isn't that right, kids?"

Trish and Rick nodded, but Marcie noticed that they looked slightly subdued again. They seemed to be a bit uncomfortable around Brad. Perhaps they thought he was intruding on their project with her?

"Okay. It's all set." Sam came over to join them. "The studio will send a driver to pick you all up at eight tomorrow morning. Ralph's going back to his office right now, and he'll send a messenger over with the scene they want Marcie to do. That'll give you time to study it tonight."

Brad nodded. "You're going to need an agent, Marcie. I'll go find Jerry Palmer. He was Mercedes's agent."

"I don't really need an agent, do I, Sam?" Marcie turned him for advice. "I mean . . . it's not exactly the start of a career or anything like that. And even if I get the part, I'll just be filling in for Mercedes."

"I agree. I don't think you need an agent . . . at least not yet. Let's hold off on that until we see the results of the screen test. Okay, Brad?"

Brad nodded, but he looked disappointed. "Sure. Anything you say, Sam. You're her lawyer."

"You'll be there tomorrow, won't you, Sam?" Marcie turned to him anxiously.

Sam hesitated. He had a ton of work to do tomorrow, but he couldn't resist the appeal in Marcie's eyes. And the twins were looking at him apprehensively. It was clear that they wanted him there, too.

"I'll be there." Sam smiled at them, and then he turned to Marcie. "You told me you used to switch places with Mercedes, and I had trouble believing it. This is your chance to prove it. I wouldn't miss it for the world!"

A sound from the pool area made him jump, and he hurried to the window. His love was there. A lovely angel in a white flowing robe.

Carefully, quietly, he crept out the door. His feet were soundless on the well-watered earth, as he made his cautious way around the hedge. He parted the leaves and peered out, only inches from his lovely angel.

He watched for a breathless moment, drinking in her incredible beauty. And then his eyes widened, and an expression of terror replaced his startled demeanor. The red haze rose like a cloying mist, choking his mind and beginning to drive out all rational thought. But he fought it back with all his strength.

This could not be! It was impossible! He'd felt her wrist and found no pulse. He'd looked into her eyes, empty with death. He'd put his lips to her cold, dead lips, and he'd felt no answering breath. It was impossible to conceive the reality of what he saw. He'd watched her die. He knew he had! But now she was back, alive!

And then the red mist swirled up to claim him, invading every cell of his body, snaking its insidious way into the deepest recesses of his mind. And he slumped to the ground, his body curling into a tight fetal ball, whimpering until the image of her beautiful face faded into merciful blackness.

CHAPTER 7

"Look, Aunt Marcie. They sent George!" Trish raced for the door, and Marcie hastily pushed the series of buttons to cancel the automatic alarm. The twins weren't used to the new security system, and they'd set it off twice since she'd been here. Luckily, the security people checked up with a telephone call before they sent anyone out. Marcie had been able to cancel the alarm by repeating their personal code.

Marcie caught Rick as he was about to dash out after his sister. "Ask George to come in for a quick cup of coffee. Rosa just brewed a fresh pot."

The twins grabbed George's arms and practically pulled him out of the car, but Marcie noticed that he was grinning. A moment later he was standing in the doorway, smiling at her.

"I'm pleased to meet you, Miss Calder." George reached out to shake her hand. "I hope everything works out fine for you today."

Marcie smiled at him. "So do I! And I'm very glad you're driving us to the studio."

While George went into the kitchen with the twins, Marcie gathered up the things the twins had told her she'd need. There was a jar of her sister's special cream to remove her makeup. A soft towel for her hair, the cotton cape Mercedes had worn to protect her costume, the scene Mr. Buchannan had sent over by messenger, and her sister's personal copy of the script, with scrawled notes in the margins that the twins had helped her decipher. Marcie sighed as she zipped up the small bag Mercedes had always carried to the studio. She hoped she knew her lines. There would be no time to study on the trip to the studio, since Brad and the twins were going along.

Just then Brad came down the stairs, and Marcie turned to smile at him. He'd been very helpful last night, reading her cues and checking to make sure she didn't miss any lines.

"All ready?" Brad smiled back.

"I think so. The studio sent George to drive us. He's in the kitchen with Rosa and the twins."

Brad raised his eyebrows. "You invited him in?"

"Yes." Marcie was puzzled. "That's all right, isn't it? The twins said their mother always gave George a cup of coffee if they weren't running late."

Brad shrugged. "Sure. That's fine. I was just surprised that's all. Most people aren't quite that friendly to the people who work for them."

"Well, we always do that in Minnesota. If somebody comes in to help you clean your house, or do home repairs, you always give them coffee.

"Minnesota hospitality, huh?" Brad grinned at her. "So that's where Mercedes got it! But you do have to be a little more careful out here, Marcie."

"Why is that?"

Brad slipped his arm around her shoulders and gave her a friendly squeeze. "You probably knew almost everyone who worked for you. Or if you didn't know them personally, you'd heard of their families."

"That's true." Marcie nodded. "Almost everybody is related back there. They say that's why we have such a high percentage of birth defects in Stearns County. Cousins marrying cousins, and that sort of thing."

Brad looked curious. "Did you have a kissing cousin, Marcie?"

"Oh, yes. Mercedes and I had plenty of kissing cousins but they weren't interested in kissing us. They were all married by the time we graduated from grade school. Mercedes and I were the babies in the family. When we were born, we already had four cousins who were parents."

Brad smiled at her. "Big family, huh?"

"Very big. When we held a family reunion, we always had a picnic at the lake. Nobody's house was large enough to hold us all."

"So you knew almost everybody and everybody knew you. Is that right?"

Marcie nodded. "That's right. Especially in St. Cloud. That's where everyone settled."

"Well, it's not like that out here. Los Angeles has a lot of transients, and some of them aren't very trustworthy. That's why you can't invite everyone in for a cup of coffee. You never know who might come back a week later, and steal everything you own."

"That's awful!" Marcie looked genuinely shocked. "But why would you hire someone to work for you, if you didn't trust them?"

"That's just it. You don't hire them. You hire a service. And the service hires the personnel they need to do the job. We've had the same gardening service for two years now, but almost every time they come, it's a different crew."

Marcie drew a deep breath and nodded. "I understand, Brad. I won't let anyone in the house unless I know them. It was all right with George, wasn't it? I mean . . . he's a retired policeman and all."

"He is?" Brad looked surprised. "I didn't know that. But it was fine, Marcie. I'm sure George is perfectly trustworthy. I just wanted to warn you to be careful in the future."

Marcie nodded. "Oh, I will be. You can count on it."

"Okay, then." Brad gave her a little squeeze and propelled her toward the kitchen. "Let's get George to drive us to the studio. I told Jerry to meet us there at eight."

"Jerry Palmer?"

"Right. I know Sam doesn't think you need an agent, but Jerry agreed to come unofficially, as a favor to me. I just want to make sure that no one tries to take advantage of you."

"Oh." Marcie nodded. "That was nice of you, Brad. But Sam's going to be there, too. I'm sure he can protect my interests."

Brad didn't look convinced. "I know he'll do his best, but Sam's a layer. He's a fish out of water as far as show business is concerned. Jerry's an agent, and he has lots of experience dealing with studio contracts and negotiations."

"You mean you don't think Sam is qualified?"

"I don't mean that at all. Sam's an excellent lawyer. We may not need Jerry, but I'd like him to be there . . . just in case Sam needs to ask any questions from an expert in the field."

"I see." Marcie gave him a grateful smile. "Thanks,

Brad. This is a brand-new world for me, and I'm glad you're here to help."

Brad hugged her again and reached out to open the kitchen door. "Anytime, Marcie. I want you to know I'll always be there for you, just like I was for Mercedes."

Marcie was mesmerized as she sat in a comfortable chair in the screening room and watched the flickering images on the screen. She'd seen every one of her sister's movies, and there was no doubt in Marcie's mind that the part Mercedes had played in *Summer Heat* was her best performance. It was ridiculous to even consider doubling for her sister in her finest role!

The screen went dark, and Trish leaned over to whisper as they changed to another scene. "She was good, wasn't she, Aunt Marcie?"

"Good?" Rick leaned in from the other side. "Mom was fantastic!"

"Yes, she was," Marcie agreed. "This was her very best role."

The screen lit up again, and they leaned back to watch. There was a sick, sinking feeling in the pit of Marcie's stomach. Too good. Perhaps she might have been able to pull it off, if Mercedes had walked through the part, but she'd given *Summer Heat* her all. Mr. Buchannan was wasting his time and his money testing Marcie for the part. There was no way she could do it, no way at all. She might as well back out now and save herself the embarrassment of trying.

Marcie's mind was in turmoil as they watched one of her sister's best scenes, the one that immediately preceded the lines that Mr. Buchannan had asked her to study. Mercedes was playing a wife who was beginning

to have doubts about her husband. It was there as a
flicker in the depths of her dark green eyes, there in
the slight trembling of her fingers as he handed her a
drink, there in her reluctance to put the glass to her
lips. She didn't yet know what was wrong, but the audience could sense the general mistrust that invaded her
whole being.

"What's the matter, darling? Did I make it too strong?"
Ashley Thorpe had just the right blend of sincerity with
a hint of menace. Everyone who watched the film
would immediately know that he was too nice, too
loving, too concerned to be real.

Mercedes's character felt it, too. And Mercedes let
the audience know through her body language. She sat
just a bit too stiffly on the living room couch, and she
hesitated just a little too long before she responded. It
was clear to anyone who saw it that she was being very
cautious and extremely alert.

"I'm not really in the mood for scotch tonight." Her voice
quivered slightly, almost imperceptibly. *"I think I'd rather
have . . . a glass of wine."*

The screen went dark and Marcie sighed. The clip
she'd just watched had run less than thirty seconds.
And even though there were only four lines of dialogue, it had told the audience volumes about the
story. How could she hope to finish this scene as well
as Mercedes had started it? It was as ridiculous as trying
to teach a pig to fly!

The lights came up and Marcie blinked. Mr. Buchannan was looking at her expectantly. "Are you ready for
makeup, Marcie?"

Marcie was about to tell him to forget the whole
thing, that he'd only be wasting his time. Then she
caught sight of the twins' anxious faces, and she nodded.

"Your sister's P.A. is waiting to show you the way. I think you met her yesterday. Jolene Edwards?"

"Oh, yes." Marcie picked up her bag and followed him to the door. Trish had told her that Jolene was her mother's personal assistant. That must be what P.A. meant.

Jolene was waiting right outside the door. She was a petite redhead in her mid-twenties, with gray-blue eyes, a smattering of freckles, and an impish smile.

"Hi, Miss Calder." Jolene reached out to shake Marcie's hand. "Beau LeTeure is here to do your makeup."

Marcie nodded. She remembered the thin man with dark hair that Rick had introduced as his mother's makeup artist.

"And Rhea Delaney is back to do your hair! Isn't that wonderful?" Marcie looked puzzled, and Jolene quickly apologized. "I'm sorry. Of course, you wouldn't know. Rhea was your sister's favorite hairdresser, and she's been on maternity leave. She just came home from the hospital a couple of days ago, but she called in and said she wanted to do your hair for the screen test."

Marcie smiled. "That's very nice of her! Especially with a new baby at home."

As they walked across the studio lot to the sound-stage, Marcie tried not to stare as she spotted several celebrities. Her first impulse was to rush right up and ask for an autograph, but Mercedes had told her about the people she called star gazers, who waylaid any star they saw. Although her sister had always been very polite about signing autographs and shaking hands, she'd told Marcie that it was sometimes a nuisance.

"There's the commissary." Jolene pointed to a low brick building in the center of the lot. "And . . . uh-oh! There's a tour group. When Miss Calder . . .

I mean, the *other* Miss Calder, spotted a tour group, she usually took a detour. They can hold you up for quite a while, with autographs and questions."

Marcie smiled at the friendly redhead. "I don't think that's necessary in my case, do you?"

"You can never tell." Jolene grinned back at her. "But if you want to, we'll take the chance."

The busload of studio tourists pulled up in front of the commissary, just as Jolene and Marcie walked by. Most of the tourists passed them without paying much attention, but Marcie noticed that a heavyset lady in a hideous green and purple flowered dress was staring at her intently.

"Uh-oh." Jolene grabbed Marcie's arm. "Don't look now, but I think we've been spotted."

The woman looked uncertain for a moment, and then she hurried through the crowd to hand Marcie a sheet of paper. "Excuse me. Are you somebody?"

Marcie couldn't help it. She started to laugh. "I'm somebody, but I'm not who you think I am."

"You're not a star?" The woman looked very disappointed. "You look just like Mercedes Calder, but I bet you hear that all the time. She's my son's favorite actress, and I promised him I'd ask for her autograph if I saw her. Are you an actress?"

"No, I'm not." Marcie gave her a kind smile. "I'm visiting here, just like you."

The woman looked very embarrassed and Marcie began to feel sorry for her as she began to speak again. "I'm so sorry I bothered you. But you really look a lot like . . . oh, dear! Of course, you couldn't be! Mercedes died in a swimming accident. I read it in the paper."

The rest of the tour group had moved into the restaurant, and the woman turned to follow them. Marcie reached out to stop her. "Please don't tell any of the others, but I'm Marcie Calder. Mercedes's twin sister. And I'd be happy to give you an autograph, if that would please your son."

"Oh! My goodness! That's really nice of you!" The woman handed over her paper. "Thank you so much! And . . . I'm really sorry about your sister. All the magazines said she was wonderful person. Will we get to see the movie she was making?"

Marcie looked to Jolene for help, and her sister's P.A. took over the conversation smoothly. "We're not sure yet. It all depends on the screen test Marcie is taking this afternoon. We're hoping she can double for her sister and finish the film."

"Oh, that's wonderful!" The woman was clearly delighted. "My son will be thrilled. I can tell him, can't I?"

Jolene nodded. "Of course, you can, but please don't mention it to anyone else."

"I won't." The woman took the paper with Marcie's autograph and smiled at her. "Good luck, Miss Calder."

As they walked away, Marcie turned to Jolene anxiously. "Did I make a mistake by telling her I was Mercedes's sister?"

"Of course not." Jolene shook her head. "I thought you handled the whole thing very well. When that lady gets home, I'm sure she'll tell everyone how nice you are. It's important to keep your fans happy."

Marcie nodded, but she was a little confused. "My fans? I don't have any fans."

"But you will. I'm absolutely positive your screen test will be a huge success. It'll be the start of a new career for you."

Marcie almost opened her mouth to say she didn't want a new career. She was only here to finish what Mercedes had started, and nothing else. But Jolene looked so hopeful, Marcie didn't have the heart to disappoint her. And it was very nice to have someone believe so firmly in her abilities.

"Here we are." Jolene motioned to a huge, ware-house-type building. The sign on the side identified it as SOUNDSTAGE 23. "That's where they're going to shoot your screen test. And this is your sister's personal trailer."

Marcie eyed the large Winnebago that was parked by the side of the building. "Her personal trailer? What does that mean?"

"It's where she went to relax between scenes. There's a kitchen, a master bedroom, a full bath, and a living room where she took meetings with Mr. Allen and Mr. Buchannan. And that's your sister's private makeup trailer." Jolene pointed to a smaller trailer that was parked behind the motor home. "Beau came in early, so he could set up for you."

Marcie nodded, even though she was surprised. She hadn't known that the studio provided a motor home and a makeup trailer just for her sister. It was a whole new world.

"We'd better hurry." Jolene glanced at her watch. "Beau's a perfectionist, and he'll want you to look just like your sister."

Jolene opened the door to the makeup trailer and ushered her inside. Beau LeTeure was waiting at the long makeup table with a lighted mirror.

"Miss Calder." He smiled and shook her hand. "It's nice to see you again under happier circumstances. Please have a seat in front of the mirror."

Marcie sat in the swivel chair, and returned his smile. "It's very nice of you to help me like this. Thank you, Mr. LeTeure."

"You can call me Beau."

Marcie nodded. "Then I'm Marcie. Did my sister call you Beau?"

"Not after she went on her diet." Beau chuckled. "Then she started calling me B.L.T."

Marcie laughed. "I think I'd better stick with Beau. B.L.T. means bacon, lettuce, and tomato sandwich to me."

"It did to her, too. Mercedes absolutely adored them, and they were at the top of her list of forbidden foods. She said she was hoping to defuse the urge by calling me that."

Marcie noticed that he was gazing at her critically, and there was a slight frown on his face. "Is something wrong?"

"No. Something's right. This is going to be a lot easier than I thought. Same bone structure. Same coloring. Same features. I think your lips are slightly fuller, but we can hide that. And you have incredibly lovely skin! You don't wear makeup very often, do you?"

Marcie shook her head. "Just a little lipstick for special occasions, and a skin conditioner every day in the winter, so I don't chap. It's very dry in Minnesota."

"Just lean back, Marcie. And close your eyes and relax. We'll have you ready in no time at all."

Marcie did exactly as he'd asked, except for the part about relaxing. There was no way she could relax when the fate of Mercedes's movie was at stake. As Beau wrapped her hair in a turban, she thought about the scene she had to do. Perhaps she could have taken her sister's place in an easier scene, one that didn't demand so much acting ability. But Mr. Buchannan had given her a very difficult passage for her screen test.

Beau smiled as he worked with an array of jars

and tubes and sponges and brushes. Doing Marcie's makeup was much easier than he'd expected, and he was finished in less than twenty minutes. When he was entirely convinced that no one could tell she wasn't Mercedes, he stepped back and patted her shoulder. "You can open your eyes now, Marcie."

Marcie was so shocked, she almost cried out as she saw her reflection in the lighted mirror. She was Mercedes!

"Startling, isn't it?" Beau smiled proudly.

Marcie blinked, but the image didn't change. Her sister was alive again, through Beau LeTeure's magic. "You're incredible, Beau! I can hardly believe my eyes. When I look in the mirror, I feel exactly like Mercedes!"

"Perhaps it'll help with your screen test. If you know you look like your sister, it should be easier for you to play your sister. Remember, we're all pulling for you, Marcie."

"Why, thank you!" Marcie gave him a big smile. "I suppose I shouldn't ask this, but do you have any tips for me? I've never done anything like this before, and I'm very nervous."

Beau looked surprised, and Marcie wondered if she should have asked. Perhaps it was a breach of etiquette to ask her sister's makeup man for advice. But then he smiled, and that put her fears to rest.

"This is the first time a star has ever asked *me* for advice!"

"That's just the point." Marcie laughed. "I'm not a star. My sister was a star, and I'm just pretending to be her. I know how much Mercedes loved this film, and I really want to finish it for her."

Beau nodded. He was very pleased by her answer.

"Well . . . there is one thing I noticed when I was on the set. Mercedes had a way of tipping her head to the side when she was thoughtful. That might be a good thing to do, when you're waiting for your third cue."

"Like this?"

Beau nodded as Marcie tipped her head to the side. "That's it. You look exactly like her when you do that. Now come with me, and I'll take you to hairdressing."

Marcie followed him out one door and through another, where a pretty dark-haired woman was sitting in a chair, reading a magazine. She was so engrossed in the article, she didn't hear them come in.

Beau cleared his throat to get her attention, and then he turned to Marcie. "This is Rhea Delaney, your hairdresser. Rhea? I'd like you to meet Miss Calder."

The woman's mouth dropped open, and she jumped up from the chair as if she'd been shot from a cannon. Her face turned white, and she leaned against the counter heavily for support. "Beau! You . . . I can't believe . . . oh, Lord!"

"Sit down and take a deep breath, Rhea." Beau grinned at her. "And please don't faint until you finish Miss Calder's hair. I take it you approve?"

The woman sank back down in the chair. "Oh, dear! I'm sorry. I guess I made an awful fool of myself, but . . . I still can't believe it!"

"You thought you were seeing a ghost?" Beau laughed.

"That's exactly what I thought. And I don't even believe in ghosts! Please accept my apology, Miss Calder. They told me you looked like your sister, but it's almost uncanny."

Marcie laughed. "You can thank Beau for that. I'm afraid I didn't look that much like her at first."

"All right, Rhea, it's your turn." Beau turned to go. "Are you going to do natural, or wig?"

Rhea Delaney stood up and took a deep breath. Marcie was relieved to see that the color was coming back to her face. She gestured to the chair in front of the mirror, and Marcie sat down.

"I'm going with the wig. Reuben sent me over some stills from the scene, and I've restyled the one Miss Calder—I mean, the *other* Miss Calder—wore. Don't worry, Beau. I won't spoil your illusion. I'll even bring her over for your approval when I'm through."

"Beau?" Marcie called him back. "Will you be there when they shoot my screen test?"

Beau shook his head. "I'd like to be, but it's a closed set. Mr. Buchannan thought you'd be more comfortable that way."

"But that's not true." Marcie shook her head. "I always do better when I'm surrounded by friends. I'll ask him if you can come. And you, too, Mrs. Delaney. If you'd like to, that is."

Rhea Delaney smiled. "I'd love to! And please call me Rhea. Every time someone calls me Mrs. Delaney, I look around for my mother-in-law. Now let's see if that wig I styled is right for you."

It took only a few minutes, and Rhea Delaney was finished. She told Marcie she was perfect, took her to Beau, who agreed, and then she escorted Marcie back to her personal trailer where Elena Garvey, the costume designer, put the final touches on her costume.

After everyone had left, Marcie sat down on the couch and tried her best to relax. She was very impressed with everyone she'd met. The members of the crew were courteous and very friendly. And when she'd asked, every one of them had given her tips on how to do the scene. Now the only person left to meet before her screen test was the director, David Edward Allen. He would give her his final instructions, and then she'd rehearse with Ashley Thorpe.

Marcie was too nervous to sit for long, so she got up and paced. She looked like Mercedes, down to the finest detail, but could she actually *be* Mercedes?

There was a knock on the door, and Marcie got up to answer it. David Edward Allen was here. She opened the door to invite him in, but the director stepped back so quickly, he almost fell down the step. Marcie stared at him in surprise, and he gave a sheepish grin.

"Sorry. For a minute there, I thought . . ."

"You were seeing a ghost?" Marcie smiled sympathetically. "That's what Rhea said when she saw Beau's makeup. And Elena thought the same thing. I'm sorry I startled you. Please come in, Mr. Allen."

The director stepped into the trailer. "Call me Dave. My full name's too much of a mouthful. I only use it because there's another David Allen in the biz. Let's stick with Dave and Marcie, all right?"

"That's fine with me." Marcie nodded.

"You know, Marcie . . . the resemblance is really remarkable." Dave took a seat on the sofa. "If you can just act, we're home free."

Marcie nodded. "I'll try, but I've never had any training. I promise I'll do my best, Mr. Allen . . . I mean, Dave. Just tell me what to do, and I'll do it."

"Your attitude's good, especially since you're willing to take direction. You have no idea how many prima donnas there are out here. Let's rehearse it one time, and see how you do. I'll read your cues."

They rehearsed it, and after the scene was finished, Marcie sighed. She knew she hadn't done her best. She was just too nervous. Then Dave gave her some instructions on body language and explained the motivation, and she tried it again. When she finished, he smiled.

"That was a hundred percent better. No one's expecting you to be perfect, Marcie. If we can keep you focused, you'll do just fine."

"Maybe." Marcie looked slightly dubious. "But I'm really nervous about the closed set. I know I'd do a lot better if I could have some friends watching me."

Dave looked surprised, and then he nodded. "I should have guessed it. Your sister was the same way. She always performed better in front of an audience."

"Then I can ask some people to come?"

"Ask anyone you want. But they'll have to get here fast. We're shooting in twenty minutes."

"Oh, they're already here."

"They are?" Dave frowned. "You're really not supposed to bring anyone onto the lot without permission, Marcie. It's a matter of security."

"Oh, I didn't bring them. They work here. Beau LeTeure said he'd come if you'd let him. And Rhea Delaney, and Jolene Edwards, and Elena Garvey. They've been so nice to me, Dave! I just can't believe how much they want me to succeed!"

"That's good, Marcie." Dave picked up his script and headed for the door. "I'll tell Jolene to invite them. You stay here and try to relax, and she'll come to get you when it's time."

Dave was grinning as he walked onto the soundstage. Marcie was charming. It was clear she had no idea what was at stake for the cast and crew of *Summer Heat*. Naturally, everyone was anxious for the picture to be completed. As the director, he was no exception. If they had to ditch *Summer Heat*, there would be no screen credits. And good screen credits were very important. They led to new and better jobs. For a moment, he'd almost blown it and told her that, but it was better to let her think that everyone was pulling for her because they liked her.

"Yes, Mr. Allen?" Jolene hurried up when he beckoned to her.

"Miss Calder wants you on the set during her test. You must have made a good impression."

"Oh, great!" Jolene looked excited. "She's really nice, Mr. Allen. I'll do anything I can to help her, if she gets the job."

Dave smiled. "We all will. Those screen credits are important. Right, Jolene?"

"Yes, they are, Mr. Allen." Jolene frowned slightly. "But that's not the only reason. I really like her. The other Miss Calder was great, but I like this one even better. She treats me like I'm a real person."

"You're not a real person?" Dave laughed.

"Well, sure I am. But you know what I mean, don't you, Mr. Allen?"

"I think I do." Dave nodded. He could tell that Jolene was utterly sincere. "I want you to round up Elena Garvey, Rhea Delaney, and Beau LeTeure. She specifically asked that they be there."

Jolene gave him a huge smile. "I just knew she'd like them! Remember how the other Miss Calder used to invite us all to the set? It'll be just like old times, if she makes it. I probably shouldn't ask this, but do you think she will?"

Dave shrugged, and resisted the urge to cross his fingers for luck. He hadn't done that since he was a kid, but he felt the need to do it now. "I hope so, Jolene. I really like her, too."

CHAPTER 8

When Jolene knocked on the trailer door, Marcie almost jumped out of her skin, she was so nervous. She'd tried every technique she'd ever heard of, to try to relax. She'd stretched out on the bed and imagined gentle waves washing up on a sandy beach. That hadn't worked at all, except to make her slightly seasick. Next she'd conjured up an image of her mother's face, telling her that everything was going to turn out fine. But her mother had *always* told her everything would be fine, even when she knew it wouldn't be.

Marcie had moved from the bed to the couch, and visualized her sister's face. But Mercedes's image seemed to be pleading with her to do a good job, and that made Marcie even more nervous. So she'd thought about Brad, instead.

When she'd left the screening room with Jolene, Brad had smiled at her in approval. But how would he react when he saw her in Mercedes's makeup, and Mercedes's wig, and Mercedes's costume? Brad was just beginning to adjust to a life without the woman he'd loved. Would he experience the pain of loss all over again, when he saw her looking exactly like Mercedes?

Switching her thoughts to the twins hadn't helped much. Marcie knew how disappointed they'd be if she didn't finish their mother's film. If she flubbed her screen test, they would be very upset. They might even slip back into their depression again, and that would be awful!

There was no sense worrying about it. Marcie had begun to pace the floor. Then she'd thought about Sam, and she'd smiled for the first time. Sam had absolutely no expectations, nothing to gain and nothing to lose. He said he liked her, and Marcie knew it was true. And she knew he'd still like her whether she landed the part, or not.

But how about her job in Minnesota? How long could she expect the school board to wait for her return? There was a provision in her contract for compassionate leave, but was completing her sister's movie an act of compassion that the school board would accept? Assuming she landed the part, how many days would it take? The length of time was very important, and she hadn't even asked!

That brought up another important question. Did she really want to go back to teaching? Now that she was a wealthy woman, her choices had broadened. She could paint, or sculpt, or do anything she wanted, and she'd never have to worry about money. It was a freedom she'd never expected, and she wasn't quite sure how to handle it.

It was at that point in her train of disjoined thoughts that Jolene had knocked. Marcie hurried to open the door.

"They're ready for you, Miss Calder."

Marcie nodded. Her throat was too dry to speak, and she wondered whether she'd lost her voice. They were ready for her. But was she ready for them?

Jolene sensed her fear, and she tried to put Marcie at ease. "It'll be easy, Miss Calder. I just know you'll be fantastic."

Marcie took a deep breath and marched down the steps of the trailer. She wanted to break away and run for the studio gates, but she couldn't. She'd promised everyone, and she had to try.

The first person she saw when she walked onto the set was Brad. He was standing in back of the row of directors' chairs, talking to a man she'd seen at the memorial service. Marcie frowned slightly. She'd met so many people it was difficult to remember, but she was sure that the twins had identified him as Jerry Palmer, their mother's agent.

Jerry had a round, boyish face, clear, sparkling eyes, and a totally guileless smile. If he'd worn a velvet suit and a lace collar, he would have looked like Gainsborough's *Blue Boy*. Mercedes had once commented on her agent's boyish charm. Jerry Palmer was Brad's age. They'd been classmates in college, but he looked much younger.

"Marcie?" Brad called her over. "I'd like you to meet Jerry Palmer. He was Mercedes's agent. Jerry, this is Marcie Calder."

It happened again. Jerry Palmer's face turned pale, and he looked as if he were seeing a ghost. But he recovered quickly, and reached out to take her hand.

"Miss Calder. You look exactly like Mercedes."

"That seems to be everyone's reaction." Marcie gave him a quick smile. "I'm glad to meet you, Mr. Palmer. I saw you at the memorial service, but we didn't get the chance to talk."

Just then Sam motioned to her from the side of the set. "Marcie? Could I speak to you for a moment?"

Marcie resisted the urge to give Jerry Palmer a pat

on the head. He looked as innocent and nice as a puppy. "Sorry, I have to go. I hope you enjoy the screen test, Mr. Palmer. I'm not entirely sure I will."

Jerry Palmer laughed, and Marcie felt herself warm toward him. He seemed like a very nice man. She'd heard all the quips about Hollywood agents, that their hearts were calculators adding up the percentages, but Jerry Palmer seemed to be an exception. At the same time, there was something about him that seemed terribly sad, and she found herself feeling sorry for him without knowing why. Perhaps she'd ask Brad more about him. Mercedes had told her that Brad and Jerry had been close for years.

"Yes, Sam?" Marcie hurried over to his side.

"I just wanted to say good luck, and tell you you'd won."

Marcie was puzzled. "What did I win?"

"That bet we didn't quite get around to making. You look exactly like Mercedes."

Marcie smiled. "That's the magic of Hollywood. Rosa would look like Mercedes if they'd spent as much time fixing her up."

"That's doubtful. I noticed it *before* Hollywood worked its magic. When you came to my office, wearing her blue Chanel suit, you looked just like her."

Just then Jolene rushed up and tapped Marcie on the shoulder. "Miss Calder? They're ready for a lighting check. And then I'll take you to meet Ashley Thorpe for a final rehearsal."

Marcie was smiling as she went with Jolene. Sam had recognized the blue suit she'd borrowed from Mercedes. She'd been right in thinking that he was a very observant man.

The lighting check didn't take long. Tom Porter, the lighting supervisor, had Marcie sit on the couch in the exact position Mercedes had occupied in the film clip they'd seen. He'd taken one look, beamed from ear to ear, and declared that the original lighting worked. Reuben Lowe, the head cameraman, had agreed with him, and both men had wished her luck.

"That wasn't so bad, was it?" Jolene led her off the set and out to another huge Winnebago parked at the other side of the soundstage. "Mr. Thorpe thought you'd be more comfortable if you rehearsed your scene in his trailer. He's really nice. Not like a big star at all. I just know you'll like him."

Jolene tapped on the door, and the butterflies in Marcie's stomach did a little dance as Ashley Thorpe answered her knock.

"My God!" He stepped back in surprise. "They told me you looked like Mercedes, but you could be her clone!"

Marcie smiled at him. "I am, in a way. I'm her identical twin. And the makeup, costume, and wig help a lot."

"They certainly do! Come in and have a seat on the couch." Ashley Thorpe led her into the trailer. "You can leave us, Jolene. I'll bring Miss Calder to the set when we're ready."

As Marcie followed him to the couch, she was thoroughly awed. Ashley Thorpe was even more handsome in person than he was on the screen. He was tall, with the body of an athlete. Muscles rippled under the light blue shirt he wore for their scene. His hair was the color of a field of wheat in the autumn sun, and it fell in a natural wave over his forehead. His light blue eyes were startling in a face tanned golden by the sun, and Marcie had all she could do not to giggle as she imagined her students' reactions if they knew she was alone in a motor home with America's favorite leading man.

"Just relax, Marcie. This won't be difficult at all. Did they show you the beginning of the scene?"

Marcie nodded. "I saw it, Mr. Thorpe."

"Lee. That's my real name. The publicity department tacked on the Ash. They decided Ashley would make me sound more romantic. So, what did you think of our scene?"

Marcie sighed. "I thought you were wonderful. And so was Mercedes. I'm not an actress, Lee. I really don't know how I can be my sister in the rest of that scene."

"That's the key." Ashley Thorpe smiled at her. "Just pretend you're Mercedes. Think of what she'd do, and do it. Let's go through it once, and see what happens."

Marcie took a deep breath. "I'll try."

As they rehearsed the scene, Marcie did her best to act like Mercedes. And when they were finished, she was much more satisfied with her performance.

"I think it'll work." Lee Thorpe smiled at her. "Remember, you love me, and you're just beginning to suspect that I'm trying to kill you. You want to trust me completely, but you can't quite do it. The doubts have been planted, and they're there in the back of your mind, coloring every word you say, every action you take. But you know you could be imagining the whole thing. And you desperately don't want me to know that you're thinking these disloyal thoughts about me."

Lee took her through the scene once more, and this time Marcie knew she was better. His advice had helped. When they'd finished, Lee grinned at her.

"Much better! You can do it, Marcie. You've convinced me, and I'm a hard case."

"Thank you, Lee." Marcie smiled at him. "You really helped me a lot."

"Just remember to stay in character, and I'll do my best to make you look good. Nobody expects you to be perfect, Marcie. You just have to convince them that you have a little raw talent. If you get the part, they'll hire a whole army of coaches to help you."

Marcie nodded. And then she asked the question that had been bothering her. "Everybody I've met says they want me to get the part. And they're all so helpful. Why is everyone being so nice to me, Lee?"

"Mercedes told me you were the innocent type." Lee grinned at her. "And she definitely had you pegged. Now, don't get me wrong here. I'm sure everyone wishes you well. But there's more than that at stake."

Marcie listened carefully as Lee explained how good screen credits led to future work, and how a good performance could lead to a nomination for an award. When he'd finished, Marcie sighed deeply.

"I understand now. And Mercedes was right. I'm terribly innocent. I really thought people were being so nice because they liked me."

"That's part of it." Lee smiled at her. "Four people knocked at my door to tell me how nice you were. They like you already, Marcie. And they'll absolutely adore you, if you get the part. Now let's get out there and give it our best shot."

Marcie nodded and Lee led her out the door. As they walked to the soundstage and onto the set, she was in a state of near hysteria. How could she relax and give it her best shot, when people's careers depended on her performance? It was impossible!

Marcie knew she looked nervous as she sat down on the couch with Lee. As they waited for their cue to start the scene, Lee put his arm around Marcie and gave her a little hug. "Are you nervous?"

"Scared is more like it." Marcie took a deep breath. "I just hope I can do it, Lee."

"You'll be fine. Just let your stage fright work for

you. Throw yourself into the scene and let your fear give you extra energy. Remember you *are* Mercedes."

Marcie nodded and repeated it in her mind. She was her twin sister. She was Mercedes. If she could fool her Aunt Becky, she could certainly fool the people who didn't know her well. And then the cameras were rolling, and Lee was giving her the first cue.

Somehow she got through her first line. It was almost as if Mercedes had come back to take over her voice, and her body, and her actions. Marcie wasn't playing this scene. It was Mercedes.

He felt his mouth drop open, and he closed it quickly. He had to be careful not to be noticed, but it was hard to hide the joy that bubbled through his veins. She was back! His lost love was back. In a slightly different body, of course, but there she was, so close he could almost touch her.

The night he'd seen her at the pool had been a dreadful shock. At first he'd been sure that his love had risen from the grave. Now he knew that it had only been an illusion. They were identical twins, and he had been fooled! Identical twins often looked and sounded very much alike, but there were subtle differences.

When she'd walked onto the soundstage, everyone had gasped. They'd dressed her in his love's costume, done her makeup, and styled her hair as his love had worn it. The resemblance was uncanny, but it was only a resemblance. Then she'd taken her place on the couch, the cameras had started to roll, and she'd spoken her first line. That was the moment he'd known that he was witnessing a miracle.

He blinked once, twice. Put a smile on his face. He couldn't let the others around him know that he had been so deeply affected. He was in love again. Or perhaps he was *still* in love? It was a question for a philosopher, not for a man like him.

He watched and listened, his smile firmly in place. And he tried to keep the fear from rising and showing on his face. Somehow he had to protect her from the red that would surely destroy her, if the Fates had their way.

But could he succeed this time? He had failed his former love when the red plague had invaded her body. He had fought with all his might but in the end, he'd been forced to kill her. Now the evil red would try to invade his new love's body. That was the way of the red. He just hoped that he wouldn't be forced to kill her, too.

The scene was finished, and Marcie gave a deep sigh. Then everyone on the set broke into spontaneous applause, and she looked up at Lee apprehensively. "Was I all right?"

"You were fantastic." Lee pulled her into his arms for a hug. "For a moment, I truly believed that you were Mercedes."

"Oh, thank you!" Marcie smiled at him happily. But before she could say more, Dave Allen and Ralph Buchannan were rushing over to shake her hand.

"I knew you could do it!" Ralph beamed down at her. "What did I tell you, Dave?"

The director nodded. "You were right, R.B. She'll be perfect."

"Does that mean you want me to do it?" Marcie held her breath, and let it out in a sigh of relief as they nodded. "Thank you! I promise I'll do my absolute best."

And then Brad was congratulating her and the twins

were hugging her, and everyone else was telling her how good she was. She had the job! She could finish her sister's picture. But one person was missing. Where was Sam?

Marcie slipped out of the happy group to look for him. She found him still sitting in his chair, looking dazed.

"Hi, Sam." Marcie tapped him on the shoulder, and he jumped. "What did you think?"

Sam blinked several times, and then he got up to hug her. "You did a fantastic job, Marcie. I still can't believe it. You *were* Mercedes!"

"Thank you, Sam." Marcie hugged him back. "Did you hear? They want me to finish the movie."

Sam nodded. "Good for you, Marcie. Mercedes would be very proud. I guess I'd better have a talk with Ralph Buchannan to hammer out the details."

"Marcie?" Dave Allen called her over to his side. Then he turned to the rest of the group. "Let's have a toast to the woman who's going to pull our collective fat out of the fire. Right, gang?"

Everyone applauded as a man dressed in white rolled in a cart with champagne and glasses. Marcie noticed that there was even a bottle of sparkling apple cider for the twins. While corks popped and glasses were filled, another man wheeled in a second cart of hors d'oeuvres.

"Dave?" Marcie looked up at him in surprise. "What would you have done if I'd *failed* my screen test?"

The director grinned at her. "The same thing. We would have given you a little party to thank you for trying. But we wouldn't have had such a good time."

There was a toast to Marcie. And another to the success of *Summer Heat*. It was an impromptu party, and Marcie was the center of attention.

Marcie smiled as she accepted congratulations. And she made sure to give credit to the people who had helped her. At last the party started breaking up, and she spotted Sam at the side of the set, talking to the producer and the director.

There was a slight frown on Marcie's face as she watched Sam. He looked perfectly normal now. When she'd gone over to see him after the screen test, he'd hugged her and told her that she'd been fantastic. But Marcie was sure she'd seen tears in his eyes. She didn't understand why Sam had blinked back tears, when the scene she'd done hadn't been the least bit sad.

CHAPTER 9

Marcie was smiling as she turned on Mandeville Canyon Road. For the first time since she'd come to California, things were looking up. The twins had been delighted by her performance yesterday, and this morning they'd asked to join their friends for a trip to the zoo. Naturally, Marcie had agreed. She'd dropped them off at their friend's house, and she'd promised to pick them up at the end of the day. Things were returning to normal, and it wasn't a moment too soon.

Even Brad had perked up today, and he'd taken one of his antique cars to a show. He'd asked her to come along, but Marcie had declined. She was happy to stay home and relax. Tomorrow would be another stressful day when she arrived at the studio to film her first scene.

But today wasn't the time to worry about anything. It was a picture-perfect day in Southern California. The temperature was in the low eighties, the air was clear, and the sun was shining brightly. Marcie smiled as she passed colorful landscaping, gently waving palms, and expensive homes that cost more than she'd ever dreamed of earning in her whole lifetime. Driving her sister's white convertible was wonderful, and she could scarcely believe that it was actually hers to keep.

Naturally, Mercedes had driven a Mercedes. She'd purchased it right before she'd married Brad, and according to the terms of her will, that meant it now belonged to Marcie. It was a beautiful car, and Marcie loved the built-in music system, the white leather upholstery, and all the glamorous little touches of a luxury car. It was a far cry from her mode of transportation back in Minnesota.

Marcie thought about her old, reliable Volkswagen Bug as she zipped around the curves in the road. She felt a bit disloyal to the car that had served her so faithfully for the past ten years. She couldn't face the thought of selling it, but perhaps she'd give it to Shirley Whitford. Shirley's husband had to get up an hour early every day to drive his wife to school. And Shirley had to wait in her classroom for an hour and a half, so he could pick her up after he finished his shift at Fingerhut Manufacturing. Even though they both worked, the Whitfords couldn't afford two cars. Shirley's mother was in a nursing home, and that was very expensive. But could they afford the insurance and upkeep on a second car? Marcie just wasn't sure.

Suddenly a solution occurred to her, and Marcie's smile grew even wider. She'd call Shirley tonight and ask her to use Miss Ladybug as a favor. Everyone knew that cars shouldn't sit too long in the harsh Minnesota winter, and she'd be here in California for at least another month. A simple phone call to her insurance agent, and Shirley's name would be added to her policy as a secondary driver. It would all work out perfectly.

Marcie approached the gates and stopped to punch in the security code. She had to remember to ask Brad to change it. The numbers were Brad and Mercedes's wedding anniversary, and it was bound to bother him. She'd just tell him that she had trouble remembering the code, and they'd think of another. It was one of the little ways she could help him get over his loss.

As she rounded the bend in the driveway, Marcie noticed a black Nissan parked in front of the house. Rosa must have buzzed the driver in. It was probably the television repairman. They'd been having some trouble with the big screen set in the living room. But wasn't it odd for a repairman to work on a Sunday?

Marcie put the car in the garage, let herself in through the connecting door, and headed straight for the kitchen. She was surprised to find Rosa sitting at the table, having coffee with George Williams.

"Oh, good. You're home." Rosa jumped up. "I was just keeping George company until you got here. I have to run to the store for the asparagus Mr. Brad wants tonight."

"Asparagus? I thought the twins hated asparagus."

Rosa nodded. "They do. I'm fixing corn for them. Is there anything special you'd like?"

"Not really. Anything you make is delicious." Marcie smiled as Rosa hurried out the door. Then she turned to George. "Hello, George. What are you doing here?"

"I came to tell you that I'm going to be your driver. I hope you don't mind, Miss Calder."

"It's Marcie. You don't have to call me Miss Calder, George. I'm not a big star like my sister. And I'm very glad you'll be my driver. But isn't that a little unusual? I thought only big stars rated a driver."

"That's generally true, but I twisted their arms a little. I told them that since you weren't familiar with the area, you might have trouble getting to the studio on time. And then I suggested myself for the job."

Marcie laughed. "Good for you! I hope you'll be my

friend, George. I'm going to need a lot of help getting used to this movie business."

"You can bet on it, Miss . . . Marcie."

Marcie poured herself a cup of coffee and sat down at the table. "What time do I start, George? The studio didn't tell me."

"I pick you up at eight tomorrow morning. That'll give us plenty of time. You don't have to be in makeup until eight forty-five. I'll pick up the twins after school, and bring them to the set if you want me to."

"Wonderful!" Marcie smiled at him. "No wonder Mercedes told me that you were the best driver she'd ever had. You think of everything!"

George looked a little uncomfortable at the unexpected praise. "I try, Miss . . . I mean, Marcie. Actually . . . there's another reason I drove out here today. I need to talk to you about something personal."

George looked very serious, and Marcie felt her pulse begin to race. She had a premonition she wasn't going to like what George had to say. "What is it, George?"

"It's about your sister. If you don't mind, I'd like to ask you a couple of questions."

Marcie sighed in relief. George was probably curious about how Mercedes had died. "Of course, George. Go ahead."

"In your estimation, would you say your sister was a strong swimmer?"

Marcie's mouth dropped open in surprise. George sounded just like a detective. Of course, he had been on the police force. The twins had told her that.

George was waiting patiently for an answer, and Marcie nodded. "Yes, George. Mercedes was an excellent swimmer. Before she became an actress, she worked as a lifeguard at the Santa Monica Beach. And she swam twenty laps every night to keep in shape."

"Would you say your sister was a heavy drinker?"

Marcie frowned slightly. She didn't really want to discuss her sister's personal life with George, but she supposed it really didn't matter, now that Mercedes was dead. "No, Mercedes didn't drink often. She said alcohol had too many calories and she couldn't afford to drink too much when she had to look her best in the morning."

"Did you know that the officers at the scene found an empty bottle of wine?"

Marcie nodded. "Yes. Sam Abrams told me."

"Didn't that strike you as odd?"

"Well . . . yes, now that you mention it. I can't imagine Mercedes drinking that much. Especially when Rosa told me she had an early call in the morning."

"Did your sister ever mention anything about receiving threatening letters?"

"No." Marcie gazed at George in shock. "Are you telling me that someone was threatening Mercedes?"

"I'm afraid so. She received three threatening letters in the month preceding her death."

"Wait a minute." Marcie took a deep, calming breath. "How do *you* know about it?"

"The studio told me. And they showed me the letters. That's why they assigned me to be her driver. I've done bodyguard work, and they wanted to make sure that she was protected."

Suddenly, Marcie thought she understood. George felt guilty because Mercedes had died while he was assigned to protect her. But that was ridiculous!

"Please don't feel guilty, George. It wasn't your fault that she died. The police said Mercedes drowned accidentally, and there was no way you could have prevented it."

"That's not it." George faced her squarely. "I read the police report. I've still got friends on the force, and I can call in a favor once in a while."

Marcie frowned. "I don't understand."

"Look, Marcie . . . I've got a hunch, and my hunches are usually right. That's why I asked the studio to let me be your diver. I'm going to protect you, and this time I'm going to be a lot more careful. Do you trust me?"

"I . . . I . . . of course!" Marcie looked up at him with startled eyes. "But I still don't understand. Do you think I'm in danger?"

George looked at her with concern. "I honestly don't know. But you look exactly like your sister, you're living in your sister's house, and you're acting in your sister's movie. Your sister got three threatening letters from a real nutcase. And he may still be out there."

"But . . . but nothing happened!" Marcie felt her heart hammer hard in her chest. "I mean, it's not like somebody actually tried to kill Mercedes!"

George just looked at her, and Marcie began to harbor a terrible suspicion. She didn't even want to ask, but she had to know. "You believe what happened to Mercedes was an accident, don't you, George?"

"No, Marcie. I can't believe it was accidental, at least not on the strength of the police report. I don't know why, or how, or who, but . . ." George paused and gave her a sober look. "I'm convinced your sister was murdered."

CHAPTER 10

Of course, it would have been a lot more comfortable inside the house, but the guest cottage they used for storage was a nice place to live. He'd covered the window so they couldn't see any light from the house, and he'd stacked the boxes in high, even rows to make a labyrinth of tunnels. Sometimes he pretended he was a priest, leading a sacrifice to the Minotaur. Other times he pretended that the boxes were hedges, and he was hiding in an English garden maze. The furniture he'd uncovered was in a secret spot in the center of the tunnels, and that was where he lived. No one ever came here to see the boxes of things that had belonged to her first husband, so it was safe.

The guest cottage was a lot nicer than the Family Services Home, where they'd taken him after the Red Lady had died. He'd lived there for almost a year, and he'd hated every day he'd spent inside its damp, brick walls. They'd called it a Home, but it wasn't.

There was a big room they'd called a dormitory, with gray metal cots placed along the walls. They had given him the fourth from the door, right next to the boy who cried all night long in his sleep. Of course, he hadn't cried, not even when the big boy who was called the monitor had taken him off to the laundry room to do the nasty thing. He'd learned to be silent from the Red Lady.

Just as he'd done with Uncle Bob, he'd turned the monitor into a friend. All he'd had to do was to say what the monitor wanted him to say, and do what the monitor wanted him to do. The Red Lady had given him plenty of tips on how to please the Uncles, and the monitor was nothing but an Uncle in training.

Before the end of the first month, the monitor had started to do favors for him, like finding a metal foot-locker for his books, and giving him permission to go to the Home library anytime he wanted. There was only one thing the monitor couldn't do for him, and that was to get him adopted.

On Sundays, they brought in prospective parents to meet the children. The kids got all dressed up in their best clothes, and sat quietly on chairs while the hopeful couples looked them over. The kids were supposed to smile and look cute, but they weren't allowed to talk unless one of the adults asked them a question. The whole thing reminded him of the pets in cages at the pound.

Naturally, the little kids were picked first. Every couple wanted a sweet, cuddly baby or a round-faced toddler. The puppies went first at the pound, too. No one wanted an older dog with bad habits, just like nobody wanted a ten-year-old boy with emotional scars. The monitor said he didn't have a chance in hell of being adopted, but he knew better. All he had to do was look for an Uncle, and he'd get adopted right away.

But he'd soon realized that there weren't many

Uncles who came to the Home. And the few he spotted didn't come to their wing. They chose younger children who couldn't talk yet. It made perfect sense. The Uncles didn't want to get in trouble with Family Services.

He'd been at the Home for almost a year, when the first Uncle came into their wing. At first he didn't think the nice, older man was an Uncle at all. Perhaps he didn't even know it himself. He was sure the Uncle's wife didn't know. If she had, she wouldn't have wanted to adopt a child.

He put on his best smile, and the innocent, loving mask he'd worn with the Uncles. It was a look that said, *I'm yours, and I'll let you do anything with me.* And this Uncle stopped and looked at him for a moment, and then he smiled back. It was a friendly smile with just the barest hint of dark yearning.

The Uncle's wife looked worried. They'd agreed that they would choose a younger child. But he could tell that the Uncle wanted him, instead. All he had to do was convince the Uncle's wife.

He smiled at her, too. A big, happy smile that said, *I'm a good boy. I'm the best boy you'll ever find.* Then he pretended he was a pet in a cage, waiting to be adopted. If he'd had a tail, he would have wagged it. And then he would have licked her hand. Of course, he wasn't a dog in the pound, so he did the next best thing. He broke the Home rule and sighed. And then he whispered, "Oh! How pretty!"

"What's pretty, honey?"

She took a step closer, and he made the tears well up in his eyes. "I'm sorry, ma'am. We're not supposed to talk, unless you talk to us first. But . . . you look just like the picture of my mother!"

He pulled out his precious picture to show her. For

favors rendered, the monitor had given him a little plastic sleeve so he could carry it in his pocket. "Here she is, ma'am. See?"

She glanced down at the picture, and he could tell she was surprised. She didn't look anything like his mother. His mother was beautiful, and she was just a plain-looking woman with a long, thin face.

"That's very sweet, honey. But your mother was blond, and I have brown hair."

"I know." He nodded, looking up at her with wistful, puppy eyes. "But you have the same smile. It's an angel smile, just like hers."

"Why, thank you, honey!"

She blinked back tears as she smiled at him, and he knew he'd won. The Uncle was looking at her hopefully, and she nodded. It was done. They'd chosen him. He'd be a good boy for her, and a nice, nasty boy for the Uncle. It would all work out just fine.

He smiled at the pleasant memory. It *had* worked out just fine. They'd filed the papers to adopt him, and he'd gone home with them a month later to a pretty little condo in the San Fernando Valley. His room had been white with a blue bedspread and blue curtains. And theirs had been a pale, sunshine yellow. There had been no red rooms, and that had made him feel very good. When he'd asked, she'd told him she'd never liked colors that bright.

She had loved him from the start, and the Uncle had loved him, too . . . in a very different way. Luckily, she'd never found out about that. They had been very careful. At first the Uncle had only come to his room when she went out to her Bible study class, or her weekly bridge club. He'd been a good boy when she was with them, polite and happy, a regular kid. But when he'd been alone with the Uncle, he'd turned into another person.

After a while, he'd felt the two boys grow apart, even though they'd occupied the same body. And that was when the trouble had started. The Uncle's boy was crafty and smart, and more than a little nasty. Her good, studious boy didn't like the Uncle's boy at all.

She'd been a librarian, and there had been fascinating books on shelves all over the house. She'd loved to see him read, and he'd spent every Saturday in the library with her, devouring the books she'd recommended. By the time he'd finished sixth grade, he'd read his way through most of the classics. That was when she'd introduced him to poetry and plays.

Junior high had been next, and during those years she'd concentrated heavily on nonfiction. He'd read his way through the Dewey Decimal system from General Works to Geography and History.

When he'd entered high school, the Uncle had decided he was old enough to learn about business and he'd spent an hour every night analyzing data and predicting trends. He'd even gone on several business trips with the Uncle, and stayed in fancy hotels all over the country.

Her good boy had loved words, gobbling them up from the printed page and relishing the beauty of a perfectly concise paragraph. The Uncle's boy had loved numbers, and he'd learned to figure out complicated equations in his head. Both loves had paid off. He'd been awarded a full scholarship to the college of his choice in the University of California system.

He'd decided he wanted to live with them and go to UCLA, and he'd really enjoyed the first half year. The class work hadn't been all that difficult for him. Naturally, there had been a lot of reading, but she'd taught him good study habits. And his math classes had been simple, mostly because the Uncle had trained him to figure out percentages, and probabilities, and margins of profit. Before he'd known it, the Christmas season had rolled around, and the Uncle's boss had invited them to a huge Christmas party at his home in Beverly Hills. If he'd known, he would have kept them away somehow. But nine years of safety, of being her good boy, had almost erased the memory of the bad thing that had happened in the red room. The memory hadn't surfaced until he'd seen the new dress she'd bought for the party.

"Are you almost ready?" He knocked softly on their bedroom door. "It's seven-thirty."

The Uncle opened the door and stepped out. "It'll take her just a minute. She's still fussing with her hair."

"Do you want me to back the car out of the garage?"

The Uncle smiled and nodded. "Good idea. We'll meet you out front."

He waited in the driveway with the motor idling, and a minute or so later they came out the front door. The Uncle looked handsome in a dark suit, white shirt, and tie. She was wearing her black dress coat with the gold Christmas tree pin he'd given her last year, and her hair was swept up in a cascade of curls. She looked almost beautiful, and he was glad. He'd made an appointment for her with the best hairstylist in the Valley as an early Christmas present.

Even though it was Friday night, it didn't take long to drive to Beverly Hills. She was in a party mood, and she chattered gaily all the way there. And she and the Uncle oohed and aahed over the lavishly decorated homes on Camden Way.

"Oh, my!" she gasped, as they pulled up in front of the house. There were giant candy canes stuck at two-foot intervals on either side of the driveway. The roof sported a lighted Santa's sleigh with eight reindeer, and there were evergreen garlands and wreaths on all doors and windows. Even though it was a dark night, the whole area was as bright as day. Every tree and shrub in the front yard was strung with thousands of colored light bulbs.

"His power bill must look like the national debt." The Uncle turned to him with a twinkle in his eye. "Of course, he can afford it. He probably writes it off as a business expense."

Then they were ushered inside by a maid in a black uniform. Her only concession to the season was a small sprig of holly pinned to her apron.

"The party's out on the patio."

The maid gestured toward the French doors in the living room that led to the patio, and they went out to greet their host and hostess. He lingered behind when he spotted a familiar face in a group of new arrivals. It was one of his professors, and he wanted to say hello.

The professor was talkative, and several minutes passed before he could break away and head for the patio to join them. He went out through the French doors and found himself in a huge tent that had been erected on the back lawn. The pool had been covered with wood, and it now held dozens of tables set with crystal and silver, all ready for the buffet dinner that would be served in the living room. Each table had six chairs, and there were gas patio heaters to take the chill from the air. The tent was so massive, it easily accommodated a giant Christmas tree, a string quartet playing an arrangement of Christmas carols, and over a hundred people.

He stared at the sight for a moment, ladies dressed in their finest and men in well-cut suits, all displaying their best party manners. Waiters and waitresses wove their way through the crowd with trays of appetizers and crystal glasses of champagne. Again, there were garlands of evergreen and holly everywhere, held in place by shiny gold ribbons.

He didn't spot them at first, so he went to the bar and ordered a Coke. Since he was driving, he wouldn't drink. It turned out that the bartender was also a UCLA student, so they talked about school for a while.

"There you are!" The Uncle came up and patted him on the shoulder. "We thought we'd lost you for sure in this crowd. She's waiting for us over there."

He went with the Uncle around the huge Christmas tree. And then he saw her, sitting at a table alone. Someone had taken her coat, and now he could see the new dress she'd bought for the party. The cut was perfect. The style suited her beautifully. But it was red!

"Is something wrong?" She looked alarmed as she saw his horrified face. "What is it, Jimmy?"

He sank down in a chair next to her, and clenched his fists so his hands wouldn't tremble. "Uh . . . nothing. Everything's fine."

But it wasn't. The horrible red mist was starting to swirl around his feet, and he fought to keep it down. It was the same red mist that had risen to choke his mind the night the Red Lady had died. It was difficult to fight something so intangible, so utterly unsubstantial, but this time he tried.

"How do you like my new dress? It's Christmassy, isn't it?"

He nodded and forced a smile. She had no idea what was wrong, and he wasn't going to tell her. This was something he'd have to fight on his own.

He remembered the class he'd taken in clinical psychology, how coming face-to-face with an irrational fear sometimes rendered it harmless. But his fear wasn't irrational, it was real. Red was the color of blood, and nothing but the ancient elements could disarm its potency.

"Champagne?" A waitress was smiling down at him, and he realized that they'd taken their glasses, and now they were looking at him. He wanted to tell the waitress to leave him alone, so he could fight the red mist, but he couldn't seem to find his voice. Perhaps it was a good thing. The words would have frightened them. It was much easier to smile and nod, as she took a glass from the tray and handed it to him.

"To our son! You've made us very proud."

The Uncle raised his glass, and she raised hers, too. And for a brief moment, the red mist thinned. Gratefully, he raised his glass and clinked it against both of theirs. Their love had made the red mist disappear. Now he had to make sure it didn't come back.

"Excuse me for just a minute?" He pushed back his chair and stood up. "I have to get something."

He watched his feet as he headed back toward the house. No red mist swirled up to threaten. It took a few moments, but he found the place where they'd hung the coats. Hers was easy to recognize, since it had his gold, Christmas tree pin on the collar. He grabbed it and hurried back to the tent, handing it to her with a flourish.

"How thoughtful!" She smiled as she took the coat. "Did you think I was cold?"

He nodded. "It's drafty in here, and you're just getting over a cold. You'd better put it on."

"Oh, I'm just fine." She draped the coat over the back of her chair. "It's not chilly with all these heaters."

His heart pounded with terror, as he realized that she wasn't going to wear it. His plan to cover the red had failed. Then he looked down and saw that the red mist was swirling again, around his ankles. It was *her* fault for buying the red dress. Didn't she know that red was dangerous? It was the color of blood!

Even though he tried his best to make it disappear again, the red mist rose and grew. It was hot in the tent, so hot that the whole room turned red. He jumped to his feet to turn down the heater, but the red mist knocked it over on top of her, and there was a terrible explosion.

People screamed as the Christmas tree caught fire. And then the sides of the tent began to turn fiery red. He saw her face, ugly with terror, as the Uncle tried to free her. But her red dress was caught on the heavy metal heater, and then the Uncle began to turn red, too.

He tried to help them, tried to free them, tried to lift and tug and pull, but someone shoved him, and then he was caught up in the stream of people fleeing the blazing tent. He felt the cool grass of the lawn on his scorched feet and then there was only a deep blackness.

He remembered the ride to the hospital, sirens wailing. And someone in white, with the face of an angel, who'd wheeled him down the hall to the operating room. Shock, they'd said. Shock and minor burns on his hands, and a shattered ankle. They'd used new technology to replace the shattered bones so he could walk again.

They'd held the funeral on the third day. A double casualty. Both of them were gone. He hadn't been allowed to leave the hospital, but the Uncle's boss had come to tell him it had been a beautiful service. He'd called him a hero for trying to rescue them from the inferno of the tent, and said he'd already filed a suit against the company that had catered the party. It would only be a matter of time.

The Uncle's boss had been right. The company had settled very quickly. A million dollars. That, plus his inheritance, had made him a wealthy young man.

That had been years ago. Now he looked back down at his ankle; it was as good as new, perhaps better. And the scars on his hands were long gone. Of course, the emotional scars would never heal. That was what the doctors had told him.

He knew now that the doctors had been wrong. The emotional scars had healed completely. He was fine, perfectly normal, as long as he didn't think about the red.

CHAPTER 11

Sam was having fun. He'd never been in the executive dining room at the studio before, and he was glad Marcie had invited him to join her for lunch. The restaurant looked like an upscale bistro, nicely decorated with green walls covered with white latticework, and lots of potted and hanging plants. There were white-linen-covered tables, fine china and silver, and attentive but unobtrusive waiters. The wine list was impressive, the menu was innovative, and the cuisine was on a scale with some of the best restaurants in town.

"You're gawking, Sam."

Marcie grinned at him, and Sam looked properly abashed. "Sorry about that. But isn't that Robert DeNiro over there near that potted fuchsia?"

Marcie turned to look and then she giggled. "Don't ask me. I'm terrible at recognizing the stars. Meryl Streep stopped by the set last week to say hello, and I didn't know who she was until Jolene clued me in."

"So, Marcie . . ." Sam turned serious. "You said you had something important to discuss?"

Marcie nodded. "I'm afraid I do. You see, Mercedes's former chauffeur is my driver now, and he has a theory about how Mercedes died. I don't know what to think, Sam. And I wanted to run it past you."

Marcie's hands were shaking as she told Sam everything George had said. When she finished, she realized that Sam was looking at her incredulously.

"It's true, Sam. George is convinced that Mercedes's death was no accident. He told me that he's sure she was murdered."

"Murdered!?"

Marcie held a warning finger to her lips. They were sitting at a table in the center of the restaurant, and she didn't want anyone to overhear their conversation. Jolene had warned her that everyone in the executive dining room kept an ear out for interesting tidbits. "George asked me not to mention it to anyone else except you."

"I'm glad you told me!" Sam reached out to pat her hand. "I don't want you to take all this too seriously. Whenever anyone dies alone, there's the possibility of foul play. That's why the police came out and investigated. They brought in experts to examine the scene, and they all agreed that your sister's death was accidental. It's right there in the police report."

Marcie nodded. "I know that. But George read a copy of the file, and he doesn't agree."

"Calm down, Marcie." Sam patted her hand again. "You're getting alarmed over nothing. I sincerely doubt that George has seen the police report. You can't just go down to police headquarters and ask to read a confidential file."

"But George has contacts on the force. And he wouldn't lie to me, Sam."

"Wait a minute." Sam frowned slightly. "Exactly what kind of contacts does George have?"

"Good ones. His partner's a senior detective now. He got promoted to George's old job."

"Your driver was a senior detective?" Sam's frown deepened as Marcie nodded. "What's his name?"

"George Williams. He was in the—"

"Devonshire Division." Sam's frown changed to a look of respect. "That puts a different light on this whole thing, Marcie. Detective Williams is a legend. The guys still talk about the wild hunch he had that led to the capture of the Doorbell Killer."

Marcie shuddered. "I remember reading about that. The killer rang the doorbell, and when people looked out through the peephole, he shot them right through the door. They caught him just as he was about to do it again, but the poor officer who arrested him was almost—oh, Sam! That's how George got his bad leg. He told me he was chasing down a murderer, but I never dreamed he was talking about the Doorbell Killer!"

"And Detective Williams says he's got a hunch about Mercedes's death?"

Marcie nodded. "Do you think he could be right?"

"Unless he's lost his touch, and that's pretty unlikely, I'm afraid he could be."

"Oh, dear!" Marcie shivered slightly. "George asked me to bring you over to my trailer after we finish our lunch. He wants to ask you some questions. He needs more information, and he said that sometimes people tell their lawyers some very confidential things."

Same nodded. "That's true. Some people do confide in their lawyers. But, Marcie . . . your sister was a very private person. I really don't know that much about her personal life."

"Then she didn't tell you about the threatening letters she got in the mail?"

Sam looked thoroughly bewildered. "What letters?"

"I'll let George tell you. He's got copies the studio gave him. I . . . I read them, Sam. And they scared me half to death!"

George and Sam were seated at the table in Marcie's Winnebago, sipping cups of coffee that Jolene had brewed for them before she'd left to join Marcie on the set. Classical music was playing softly on the stereo system, and the curtains were drawn for privacy. The air conditioner hummed softly, circulating fresh, chilled air, and although the atmosphere was cool and comfortable, Sam felt beads of sweat break out on his forehead as he finished reading the first letter.

George handed him the second, and Sam read that, too. And then the third. He looked up at George several times, but the ex-detective's face was impassive

"Well?" George faced him squarely. "Do you think I'm crazy?"

"No. But I think whoever wrote these letters is."

"Agreed." George gave a slight smile, acknowledging the joke.

"Of course, these letters could be nothing more than the ravings of a harmless psychotic."

George nodded. "That's true, too. But do you know what Mercedes was wearing the night she died?"

"She'd been swimming her laps, so I assume it was a bathing suit."

"A *red* bathing suit."

"I didn't know that!" Sam frowned, and reached for the first letter again. "*Red is the color of blood*'?"

"You got it. Still, that might not figure into it at all. We'd have to assume that the crazy fan was there to see her in her red bathing suit. And that means he had to get in the gates and out again without setting off the alarm. I talked to the security company. They swear that's impossible."

"Of course, they do." Sam nodded. "They don't want to open the door to any future lawsuits. But are they right?"

"No one makes a security system that's impenetrable, but this one comes close. And we know the system was armed when Rosa and the twins came home. She remembers she let Rick punch in the code at the gate."

"Then the crazy fan's not a suspect?"

"Wrong." George gave a tight little smile. "He's still on my list. For all we know, he could have come in before the security system was installed, and holed up somewhere on the grounds. Or he could have sneaked in with the gardening crew, or the bottled water man, or someone making a delivery. It's even possible he came in when Brad or Rosa drove out. Rosa told me she didn't check her rearview mirror when she drove through the gates."

Sam nodded. "You said you have a list of suspects. Do you think someone else might have killed Mercedes?"

"It's possible, and that's why I wanted to talk to you. As Mercedes's lawyer, you have some valuable information. Who had the most to gain financially from Mercedes's death?"

Sam drew a deep breath and considered it. "Marcie. She inherited the bulk of her sister's estate. And then the twins, but that money's in a trust fund, and they don't get any actual cash until they reach twenty-one."

"Okay." George jotted the information down in his notebook. "Let's forget about the twins for the moment. Who inherited the most after Marcie?"

"Brad. He got everything covered under the community property laws."

George wrote that down. "That includes the house?"

"No. The house is Marcie's. It was part of Mercedes's inheritance from Mike Lang. Since the funds were never commingled, Marcie got everything Mercedes inherited from Mike."

"I see. And how about Rosa? Did Mercedes leave anything to her?"

"She set up a trust fund for Rosa, to pay her salary until the twins are of age. And after that, there's a lump sum settlement for her retirement."

George jotted that down. "Rosa didn't know about the fund Mercedes had set up for her?"

"I'm sure she didn't. She told me she thought she'd be out of a job if Marcie took the twins back to Minnesota."

"Okay. Let's concentrate on Brad. How much did he inherit?"

Sam hesitated. He knew George wasn't asking for personal reasons, but there was an issue of confidentiality at stake. George was no longer a policeman. He was a private citizen with no authority to request that kind of information.

"Come on, Sam." George fixed him with a level gaze. "I know it's confidential, but it might make a real difference. How much?"

Sam thought it over for a moment, and then nodded. "At least two million, probably more like three. Of course, that's not in cash. Brad would have to sell off the time-share condo, the thoroughbreds, and the antique cars to liquefy his assets."

"Could he do that?"

Sam frowned. "Not without taking a beating. Mercedes wanted him to sell their thoroughbreds last year, but Brad said they were running so far in the red, and they'd only realize a fraction of what they'd invested.

He convinced her to give him one more year to make a profit."

"And she went along with it?"

"Yes. I advised against it, but Brad had just bought Metro Golden Mare, and he was sure she'd finish in the money and turn everything around." George looked at him expectantly, and Sam shook his head. "Unfortunately, the mare is having some physical problems, and she hasn't run at all this year. Mercedes gave me the bad news when she called on the night she died. I'm sure that's one of the reasons she decided to move the bulk of her assets to another investment firm."

"Marcie told me that Brad was shocked when he heard what she'd done."

"Yes." Sam nodded. "He seemed to think Mercedes had fired him. But she hadn't, not really. She set it up so that he'd still handle the investments they'd made together."

"The thoroughbreds and the antique cars?"

"That's correct. She moved everything else to another firm."

George looked thoughtful. "Thoroughbreds are a risky investment, aren't they?"

"Definitely, especially if the owners bet on their own horses. That's why I advised Mercedes to cut her losses and get out of the business."

"Do you think Brad's a gambler?"

Sam shrugged. "I really can't say one way or the other. He's always struck me as the type, but Mercedes never mentioned it."

"Maybe she didn't know." George jotted down a note on his pad. "How about the antique cars? They're a safe investment, aren't they?"

Sam shook his head. "Not really. Prices fluctuate,

and the maintenance costs are high. The cars have to be stored in a temperature-controlled warehouse, and places like that don't come cheap. And Brad didn't buy the cars and restore them. He purchased them at premium prices, and waited for them to appreciate. That hasn't happened yet."

"So Brad had plenty of assets, but he couldn't cash out without taking a loss. Is that what you're telling me?"

"That's it, in a nutshell." Sam nodded. "Mercedes told me that Brad wanted to hold on until the market went up, but he needed more operating capital. And that's something he was short on."

"You just painted me a picture of a desperate man. Do you think he was desperate enough to kill Mercedes, to get his hands on her money?"

Sam shook his head. "Absolutely not. Brad's much smarter than that. Killing Mercedes would have been like killing the goose that laid the golden egg. Her earnings were keeping his investments going. He had nothing to gain by killing her. As a matter of fact, her death put him in an even more desperate position, since the will left the bulk of her assets to Marcie."

"Brad *knew* that Marcie would inherit the bulk of Mercedes's estate?"

"Actually . . ." Sam stopped short. "No. He didn't. Brad seemed very surprised when I read the will. He said Mercedes had told him that she'd made out a new will, leaving everything to him. I know she intended to do that. We discussed it almost a year ago. I drew up a new will, but she never came in to sign it."

"So Brad thought he was going to inherit everything. That's motive in my book. Thanks, Sam. You've been a big help."

"But Brad couldn't have killed Mercedes. He was at the track that night. You told me that yourself."

George nodded. "That's true. But he could have slipped away, and returned before anyone missed him. The track's only twenty minutes or so from the house."

"I don't believe it!" Sam shook his head. "Look, George . . . it's no secret I never liked the guy, but he's not a killer. And to do something violent, like drowning his wife? That's way out of character."

"True. But if I've learned one thing from my years on the force, it's that a desperate man is totally unpredictable."

"You think Brad killed Mercedes!?" Sam was clearly shocked.

"No. I don't think he's got the balls to do something like that. But it's possible he hired someone else to do it. It's not that hard to arrange a hit. All it takes is money. And you're a lawyer. You know that makes him every bit as guilty, in the eyes of the law, as the person who actually killed Mercedes."

"That's true." Sam nodded. He felt sick inside. While he'd been unable to visualize Brad actually drowning Mercedes, he found he could easily imagine him on the phone, arranging for her death.

"That's enough for now. Let's go join Marcie on the set. I promised her we'd drop in after our talk." George stood up to shake Sam's hand. "Thanks, Sam. That makes three suspects with motives."

Sam clicked them off on his fingers. "There's the crazy fan. He could have done it. And it's possible Brad arranged a hit for money he thought he'd inherit. But who's the third suspect?"

"It's obvious." George opened the door, and they stepped out into the sunlight. "The third person is the one who actually inherited. Marcie Calder."

CHAPTER 12

It was Marcie's first real day off in over two weeks. No dialogue coaches, no acting lessons, no rehearsals. And when Brad had suggested they all spend the day at the racetrack watching one of his thoroughbreds make his debut, she'd jumped at the chance to do something different.

Brad's excitement was contagious, and Marcie felt her spirits soar as they parked in the special section for owners and walked past the beautiful garden area near the entrance to the track. Everyone they passed was smiling, and the whole crowd seemed to be in a holiday mood. She turned to Brad and asked, "Why is everyone smiling?"

"They're happy. Watching the races is a lot of fun."

When Brad went up to the window to show his season pass and collect their box tickets, Trish leaned close to Marcie. "I know why they're smiling, Aunt Marcie. Everybody comes here to gamble, and they all think they're going to win. And the races haven't started yet, so . . ."

". . . so they haven't lost any money yet." Rick finished the thought for her. "Mom told us that, the last time we came here. She said all the people on the plane to Vegas are happy, too. But on the way home, the only people smiling are . . ."

". . . the newlyweds!" Trish giggled. "Mom didn't approve of gambling. She said it was . . ."

". . . a disease. And we should be very careful never to catch it." Rick reached out to take Marcie's hand. "Do you think she'd be mad, if she knew Brad was letting us bet on the races?"

Marcie shook her head. "I don't think so. I'm sure she'd say it was a learning experience."

"But what are we going to learn, Aunt Marcie?"

Brad came up just in time to hear her question, and he winked at Marcie. "I can answer that. You're going to learn to put your money in a savings account, and not take it with you to the track."

Trish and Rick burst into laughter, and so did Marcie. Then they all linked arms and rode up the huge escalator to find their box seats. They had a box built for six, and as soon as they were seated, Brad handed each of them a program, a pencil, and a copy of the racing form. "Okay. You read about the first race and pick your horse. And when you've decided, I'll place your bets."

Marcie listened as the twins discussed the pros and cons of the horses in the first race. Trish wanted horse number three, because the jockey was wearing blue, and Rick preferred number seven, because he liked the name. Finally, they'd marked their choices, and Brad turned to Marcie. "Which horse do you want?"

Marcie looked down at the program. She'd been so busy listening to the twins, she hadn't picked a horse. "Uh . . . I'll take number two."

"Number two?" Brad's eyebrows shot up. "But,

Marcie . . . number two's never finished in the money. And look at the odds. Eighty-seven to one!"

Marcie nodded. "That's why I picked him. If I win, I'll collect a lot of money. And if I lose, it's only two dollars."

"Okay. Number two it is." Brad jotted it down in his book. "Now, how are you betting? Win, place, or show?"

Marcie looked confused and Brad explained, "If you bet a horse to win, he's got to come in first. If you bet to place, he can come in first or second. And if you bet him to show, he can come in first, second, or third. Just remember, if you bet him to show and he ends up winning, you don't earn as much money."

Marcie nodded. "Then I'll bet him to win."

"You're not going to hedge your bet, huh?" Brad sighed as Marcie shook her head. "Okay. You're the boss. Number two to win."

Rick and Trish exchanged meaningful looks. Then Rick spoke up. "We'd like to change our bets. We're going with the number two horse, the same as Aunt Marcie."

"You're kidding!" Brad turned toward them in surprise. "Are you sure? I saw him run last week, and he finished dead last."

Trish nodded. "That's okay. We want to bet on him anyway. He's probably embarrassed because he finished last, so he'll be trying even harder today."

"Okay." Brad turned away, but Marcie saw the corners of his mouth turn up in a grin. "I'll be back in a flash with your tickets."

While Brad was gone, they talked about the horses for the next race. And when they'd picked their next choices, Marcie decided the time was right to ask a question. "Do you guys like Brad?"

Rick shrugged. "He's okay. Actually, he's been . . ."

". . . a lot better lately." Trish finished the sentence for him. "He talks to us now, and he never used to. I think he knows he won't get . . ."

". . . anywhere with you, if he's not nice to us." Rick turned to give Marcie a serious look.

Marcie felt her pulse race, but she managed to keep her face composed. "You think Brad's trying to get somewhere with me?"

"Oh, sure." Trish nodded. "He wants to stay in the house. He likes it. And the only way you'll let him stay is if you like him."

Marcie frowned slightly. The twins were very cynical, and she wondered what had made them that way. "Well . . . maybe he just likes me. And maybe he just likes you. Did you ever think about that?"

"Well . . . maybe."

Rick didn't sound convinced, and Marcie was trying to think of a suitable reply, when she saw Brad climbing the steps to the box. He was carrying a bag and several tickets.

"Here you go." He handed out the tickets, and then he dropped the bag on the table. "Two orders of nachos. I didn't want anybody to starve before the race started."

Rick was smiling as he reached in the bag for the snacks, but Trish just stared at Brad with a puzzled look on her face. "Maybe Aunt Marcie's right . . . and you really do like us?"

Brad was clearly shocked. "Of course, I like you! Whatever gave you the idea I didn't?"

"Oh, nothing." Trish's face turned pink, and Marcie knew she wanted to eat her words. But she recovered quickly. "I think we're just experiencing temporary feelings of insecurity, because of the trauma of our loss. At least that's what the school shrink says."

"Right." Rick chimed in to save his twin from further

embarrassment. "We're in transition now, but we ought to be making an adjustment to our crisis quite soon. It's just a good thing we're not prepubescent. Then we'd have to deal with the instability caused by hormonal changes at the same time."

"What?!" Marcie looked at them with alarm. "Who told you all that?"

Rick looked slightly embarrassed. "Oh, no one actually told us. We just . . . uh . . ."

". . . read it in the file, when the school counselor got called to the office." Trish winced a little. "Well, it was *our* file, and we figured we had . . ."

". . . a perfect right to read it." Rick drew a deep breath. "You're not mad at us, are you, Aunt Marcie?"

Marcie shook her head, but there was no way she could maintain a sober expression. She started to laugh and Brad joined in. Soon all four of them were laughing, and the tense moment was forgotten.

"What are they doing over there?" Trish pointed to the group of emergency vehicles that were parked at the far end of the track.

"They're getting into position, in case there's an accident."

"I see the ambulance." Rick nodded. "That must be for the jockeys. But what's that big truck?"

"It's an ambulance for the horses. There's a team of doctors on duty inside, in case one of the horses gets hurt."

Trish looked interested. "Doctors? You mean like . . ."

". . . veterinarians?" Rick finished the sentence for her.

"Exactly right." Brad smiled at them. "It's a regular horse hospital inside. Would you guys like to see it?"

Rick jumped up. "Could we? That'd be great! I want to see what kind of equipment they have. I still don't see how they can get a horse . . ."

". . . on a stretcher." Trish interrupted him. "Come on, let's go!"

Brad turned to smile at Marcie. "Would you like to come along?"

Marcie considered it for a moment, and then she shook her head. She was interested, but it was good for Brad to be alone with the twins. "I think I'll just sit here and relax. You can tell me all about it when you get back."

"Could we see the paddock, too?" Trish looked hopeful. "I'd like to see if . . ."

". . . number two looks nervous. Can we, please?"

Brad turned to Rick. "You guys are really something! Trish starts to say something and you finish it. And if you start first, she says the last word. How do you do it?"

"It's easy."

Both twins spoke at once, and Brad laughed. Then he looked at Marcie. "Can you finish their sentences, too?"

"No." Marcie smiled, but she didn't say what she was thinking. When they'd been growing up in Minnesota, she'd often finished Mercedes's thoughts, and Mercedes had finished hers.

Brad turned back to the twins. "Something like that would come in really handy at board meetings. Could you guys teach me how to do it?"

"I don't think we can." Trish shook her head. "You see, you almost have to be . . ."

". . . a twin." Rick finished the sentence with a laugh.

"Okay, okay." Brad held out his hands. "Let's go look at the horse hospital. And then I'll take you down to the paddock and you can pick the horses you like for the next race. I suppose you'll want a—"

". . . hot dog on the way back." Marcie finished

Brad's thought, and the twins started to laugh. "See? You don't *have* to be a twin to do it."

When they walked away, the twins were still laughing. Marcie was pleased to see they were walking on either side of Brad, holding his hands. Coming to the track this afternoon had been a marvelous idea. The twins were beginning to develop a closer relationship with Brad, and that was very good. All it took was a little time together, and they'd think of him as part of their family.

But how did *she* think of Brad? Marcie frowned slightly as she considered it. She liked him. A lot. Perhaps too much for a brother-in-law. She didn't want to leave him to go back to Minnesota.

Marcie slipped off the lovely blue sweater she'd found in her sister's closet, and sighed as she looked out over the track. Thinking about Brad always made her feel warm, and a little uncomfortable. And she'd thought about Brad a lot in the past few weeks. What would happen to him when she left? *If* she left?

When she'd called Mr. Metcalf to request a leave of absence, he'd told her not to worry, that she was entitled to eight weeks with full pay and an additional four weeks with half-pay. If she added in the sick days she'd never used, it would take her to the end of the school year. Then it would be time for a contract renewal, and she had to make a career decision. Did she want to go back to teaching? Or would she rather move to California, and let another teacher have her job?

Sam had pointed out that she was now a rich woman. She could pursue her own interests, and never have to worry about money again. That was a big factor. Was it fair to go back to her job in Minnesota, when there were so many other teachers who really needed the position?

Marcie sighed. She remembered a seminar she'd attended last year, sponsored by a local women's group. The topic had been self-esteem, and the speaker had asked them to introduce themselves, and tell the group one additional fact about their lives. Shirley Whitford had given her name, and then she'd said, "I'm married to a wonderful man, and we have two children." Harriet Scharf had been next, and after she'd given her name, she'd announced, "I love to bake cookies, and someday I'd like to write a cookbook."

Marcie's heart had hammered hard as she'd waited for her turn. Then she'd said, "My name is Marcie Calder, and I'm a teacher."

When everyone had finished, the speaker had explained that the second part of the introduction had been a personality test. If you said something personal, as Harriet Scharf had, it meant you were comfortable with your life, and you had high self-esteem. And everyone had said something personal except Marcie, who'd defined herself by her profession.

Driving home in the inky blackness of a Minnesota night, Marcie had realized that she had no hobbies, no outside interests, no personal life outside the school. Teaching was her whole life. And perhaps that was why she was so reluctant to give it up now, even when she was free to do so. It meant taking a long, hard look at herself, and redefining what she really wanted to do with her life. Of course, she wanted to be a mother to the twins, but she was wise enough to know that it was dangerous to make them her whole purpose for living. She'd known mothers who'd done that, and they had been devastated when their children had grown up and left home.

What would she miss if she gave up her job and moved out here to California? Marcie thought it over carefully. She'd enjoyed teaching for the first few years, but it had turned into a ritual of boredom lately. She had no real control over the curriculum, and she'd been required to teach the same projects, over and over, with each new class of students. Every year the routine was the same. She taught a drawing class, a painting class, a crafts class, and a design class. How many macramé plant hangers could you make before you never wanted to see a ball of twine again?

But would she miss her roots in Minnesota? Marcie had thought it over carefully, and she'd decided she wouldn't. The nuclear family had gone with the death of her parents, and she'd sold the family home. She still exchanged the occasional letter or card with uncles, aunts, and cousins, but the only time she saw them was at their annual family reunion. She could always fly back for that, and take the twins with her. It would be good to give them a sense of family. And the family reunion was always held in the summer, thank goodness!

Marcie had called Shirley Whitford the night before, and asked her to give Miss Ladybug a good home. Shirley had been very grateful, and she'd admitted that she thought that Marcie would be foolish to come back before winter was over. The wind chill factor had been minus forty, and Marcie had heard the howling winds rattling against the windows in Shirley's living room. Shirley was right. There was no way she'd miss the hardships of Minnesota winters.

The first month of snow was wonderful. Marcie loved the soft white blanket of snow that shrouded the familiar landscape and turned it into a fairyland of glittering icicles and snug houses capped with gleaming white roofs. Towering trees with bare branches that resembled stark black fingers stretched up toward the pale winter sun, and children dressed in brightly colored parka frolicked in a sparkling white world. But the novelty wore off very quickly, when the snow became an obstacle.

Tons of dirty snow were piled in banks by the sides of the road, so motorists could inch their way down icy thoroughfares. Wet boots left muddy tracks on every floor. Wool coats smelled like wet dogs until they dried. And anyone who hadn't lived in snow country couldn't believe how heavy and awkward a snow-filled shovel could be. And then there was the cold.

When the temperature was below zero, even taking out the garbage called for survival gear. Lips chapped, lungs hurt with the freezing air, and fingers were unwieldy in heavy gloves. Just last week, when Sam had asked her what winter was like in Minnesota, she'd told him to try wearing oven mitts to unlock his door, and he'd get the general idea. No, she wouldn't miss Minnesota winters at all. Not one little bit.

Marcie laughed. She'd just done an excellent job of persuading herself to stay in California. The twins would be delighted. They loved their school and their friends, and she knew they didn't want to leave. Rosa would be delighted, too. She was used to life in California, and although she'd agreed to go anywhere with her babies, Marcie knew she'd rather stay right here in a familiar setting.

Sam would be happy. He loved the twins, and he'd told her he didn't want them to move away. And she was sure that Brad would be very relieved to know she was staying. But should she make such a big decision on the spur of the moment?

As always, caution won out. Marcie sighed and shook her head. She was ninety-nine percent positive she wanted to stay in California, but she'd give herself another week to mull over the possibilities. Brad was leaving on a business trip tonight, and she'd wait until he came home to make her final decision. Perhaps she'd ask Rosa to fix something special for dinner on Friday evening when Brad came home—a standing rib roast, or rack of lamb. And then, after the twins were tucked in bed, she'd invite him to join her on the patio, and she'd tell him.

Just anticipating that moment made Marcie's eyes sparkle. She was sure Brad would open a bottle of champagne to celebrate. And then he'd hug her, and tell her how pleased he was. He might say more about how close he was beginning to feel toward her. And then, perhaps, he'd even kiss her.

Marcie's face turned pink, and then bright red. It was happening again, that warm, breathless feeling that always rushed through her whenever she imagined Brad's kisses. But she was being ridiculous, indulging in a fantasy that was terribly adolescent. Brad had told her that he was beginning to feel very close to her, but that was only normal. She was here, she looked like Mercedes, and she was living in her sister's house and finishing her sister's work. She was Bad's closest link to Mercedes. They were all in transition, just like the school psychologist had said.

Marcie drew a deep breath and nodded. She had to be very careful not to let her emotions run away with her. Brad was a handsome man, a nice man, a loving man, and it was only natural to feel affection for him. Soon things would be settled, and everything would return to normal. And when it did, she was sure she'd get over the foolish notion that she was falling in love with her dead sister's husband.

CHAPTER 13

Marcie tiptoed down the hallway, the revolver in her hand. They were there, in her bed, the two people she'd trusted most in the world, the two people she'd loved with all her heart. But her love had turned to hatred, when she'd learned how they had betrayed her, and now her beautiful face was contorted with rage. She would exorcise them like demons, drive them out of her life and send them scuttling back to the depths of hell. She was an avenging angel, and they were sinful worms she would crush beneath her heel.

Slowly, very slowly, she inched open the door. Her hands were steady. Her eyes gleamed with the same cold steel that she held in her hand, the killing instrument, the weapon of death that she would turn on them without mercy.

Her lips parted and she made a sound, a hiss of wrath that ended in a subhuman growl. They looked up, and she took a dark pleasure in their startled confusion, at the way their fingers scrabbled for the blankets in a futile attempt to cover their shame. And then her pleasure heightened as their fear bloomed and spread to abject, cowering terror. Their time had come. Revenge would be both hot and sweet.

She raised the gun, bringing the luster of the cold blue metal to the burning glow of malice deep in her eyes. And then, quite deliberately, she pulled the trigger.

The gunshots bounced and echoed for a moment. Then they faded away to silence. She watched, eyes blazing with fervor, as the life fled from their blood-spattered faces.

Then, almost imperceptibly, her expression began to change. She blinked in confusion, as if she were waking from a nightmare. Then she looked down at the gun she still clutched in her hand. Puzzled. Why did she have it? And then as realization began to dawn, she glanced toward the bed again.

Now her expressions changed like wildfire. Shock. My God! And horror. What had she done!? She shuddered, and let the revolver drop from her nerveless fingers. And then her mouth opened and released a keening wail that ended only when she crumpled to the floor and curled her body into a whimpering circle of unending pain.

"Cut!" Dave Allen's voice was shaking, and he swallowed hard. Everyone on the set burst into spontaneous applause, and Dave and Jolene rushed to help Marcie up.

Marcie blinked, and then she smiled. "Was that all right?"

"All right!" Dave threw back his head and laughed. "Jesus, Marcie! That was fucking incredible!"

"We don't have to do it over?"

Dave shook his head. "Nope. It doesn't get any better than that! You've got the rest of the day off, kiddo. See you bright and early Monday morning."

Twenty minutes later, Marcie was sitting in front of the mirror while Rhea Delaney styled her hair. She was dressed in jeans and a blouse, her usual attire for trips to and from the studio.

"Very sexy." Rhea smiled as she brushed Marcie's hair up and back, securing it with a gold barrette. "What's the occasion?"

"Uh . . . well . . . I'm not sure."

"A man." Rhea answered her own question. "It's always a man when a woman's eyes sparkle like yours. So he's finally getting serious, huh?"

"Who?" Marcie felt her face grow hot, and since she was facing the mirror, she could actually see the blush rising to color her cheeks.

"Brad. We all figure it's only a matter of time before he begs you not to leave him."

Marcie whirled around in the chair to look at Rhea in surprise. "Do you really think so?"

"Absolutely. Beau noticed it first. Of course, he's always had his eye on Brad."

"Uh . . . his eye?"

Rhea laughed. "I'm sure he'd like to have more than that, but Beau's not doing any more than looking right now. He just broke up with the guy he'd been living with for ten years, and it'll take him a while to get over it."

"Beau is gay?"

Rhea nodded. "Does that bother you?"

"Not at all. But why does Beau think Brad is interested in me?"

"It's a lot of little things, and they all add up. Brad sent you flowers, and he never sent them to Mercedes. And he always hugs you after you finish a tough scene.

And he comes to take you out to lunch at least twice a week."

"That's true." Marcie nodded. "But Brad's just being supportive. He wants me to finish this picture for Mercedes."

"That's what I thought. At first I was sure that Beau was imagining things, but then I saw the way Brad looked at you the last few times he's been here. He never came to watch Mercedes, you know. And then Jolene noticed, and so did Tom and Reuben. And just the other day, Lee commented on it."

"I guess everyone noticed but me." Marcie gave a little self-conscious laugh. "But really . . . I think Brad just likes me because we're related. And don't forget that I look exactly like Mercedes when I'm on the set."

"That's true, but I don't think Brad is looking for another Mercedes."

"Why not?"

Rhea looked very uncomfortable. "Let's just forget I opened my big mouth, okay?"

"No way." Marcie shook her head. "I want to know what you mean."

"Well . . . I know they were having problems at home. Mercedes said something that made me think they were getting ready to break up."

Marcie looked shocked. "What did she say?"

"I'm not sure I should tell you. Mercedes didn't exactly confide in me. It was just a slip of the tongue."

"Come on, Rhea. You've told me this much. You can't stop now."

"Well . . . two months ago she came in looking like death warmed over. Beau and I worked on her for over an hour, but she still looked terrible. She told us she'd been up all night, and she couldn't keep anything down."

"The flu?"

Rhea raised her eyebrows. "That's what Beau thought. But then I remembered that she'd been gaining weight lately, and I wondered out loud if she was pregnant."

"What did she say to that?"

"She laughed. And then she said it was impossible, unless we'd seen a star in the East."

It took Marcie a moment to get it, and then she sighed. "Oh, dear!"

"Hey . . ." Rhea patted her shoulder. "I don't know whether she lost interest in him, or he lost interest in her. But I do know their marriage wasn't working. Mercedes told us she hadn't slept with Brad in over six months."

The twins were in bed, and Marcie and Brad were lingering at the table on the patio, sipping coffee. Marcie felt wonderful. Her part in *Summer Heat* was almost complete, and soon she could get on with her life. Before she'd left the studio this afternoon, Dave Allen had given her a copy of his newest script. If the studio liked the final print of *Summer Heat*, Ralph Buchannan was sure he'd be able to get the project funded. Dave wanted Marcie to play the lead, opposite Lee Thorpe. But Marcie wasn't sure she wanted to do it. Finishing *Summer Heat* had been fun, but acting was a full-time profession. She wanted to have more time to spend with the twins, and she was still considering what Sam had said about pursuing her art.

"That was a great dinner, Marcie!" Brad smiled at her.

Marcie smiled back and her heart beat a bit faster. Brad looked incredibly handsome. "Thanks, but I didn't make it. Rosa did."

"Then I'll have to tell her." Brad cupped his hands toward the kitchen. "Great dinner, Rosa!"

Rosa's voice floated out of the open door. "Thanks, but I didn't plan it. Miss Marcie did. Do you want dessert on the patio?"

Brad turned to Marcie, and she shook her head. "No, thanks. I'm stuffed."

"We'll wait until later, Rosa," Brad called out. Then he turned to smile at Marcie again. "How about a quick swim? I need to burn off some of that dinner."

Marcie hesitated. She hadn't been in the pool at all, even though it had looked very inviting. She wasn't sure she'd ever feel right about using the pool again, after what had happened to Mercedes.

"I'm sorry, Marcie. I just didn't think." Brad looked embarrassed as he realized the reason for her hesitation. "But I think all of us have to get over our fear of the pool. That's why I took the twins swimming last Friday, before you came home from the studio."

"The twins went swimming in the pool?" Marcie looked up at him, startled.

"Yes, and we had a wonderful time. Even Rosa went in, and she hates to swim."

"You're right, Brad." Marcie sighed deeply. "I know it's silly to avoid the pool, but . . . I just can't help thinking . . ."

"I know." Brad reached across the table to clasp her hand. "Just remember that it was an accident, a tragic accident. And now we have to get on with our lives."

Marcie opened her mouth to say that perhaps it hadn't been an accident, that George believed Mercedes was murdered. But George could be wrong. There was no proof. Why upset Brad needlessly?

"What's wrong, Marcie?"

Marcie realized that Brad was frowning, and she quickly shook her head. "Nothing, Brad. And you're absolutely right. It's not rational to be afraid of the pool."

"I've got an idea." Brad gave her hand a little squeeze. "It's pretty cold for swimming, so let's use the Jacuzzi instead. And while you're changing, I'll get us both a snifter of Grand Marnier. Would you like that?"

Marcie nodded quickly. "It sounds wonderful, Brad. But won't the Jacuzzi take some time to warm up?"

"I turned it on when I came home. I thought maybe you'd like to relax after your long day at work."

Marcie smiled as Brad got up and hurried toward the house. Sitting in the Jacuzzi would be nice, and it had been very thoughtful of Brad to turn it on for her. Luckily, she'd left her bathing suit in the cabana, when she'd sunbathed last weekend. She supposed Brad was right about the pool. It was silly not to use it. She'd force herself to go in one of these days, and get past that initial hurdle.

The white bathing suit was right where she'd left it, hanging on a hook next to the mirror. Marcie undressed and slipped it on quickly, giving her reflection an approving glance. She was losing that alabaster skin tone most Minnesotans wore all winter, and she could see the effects of her weekend tanning session. If she spent more time in the sun, it wouldn't take long for her to look like a native Californian.

Marcie gathered up a white silk robe and several fluffy beach towels. Brad was right. The air was nippy tonight, and they'd be cold when they got out of the Jacuzzi. Then she hurried out to the patio again, and climbed into the Jacuzzi.

She gave a sigh as she stepped into the tub and felt the hot water caress her body. What luxury! She'd always wanted to have an outside Jacuzzi, but it had been impossible in Minnesota. Now here she was, immersed up to her neck in lovely warmth, while steamy vapor rose toward a dark sky that was studded brightly with stars. March in a tropical climate was truly wonderful. If the other teachers could see her now, they'd be green with envy.

Since the house was isolated, there were no drapes on the downstairs windows. Marcie could see Rosa bustling around the kitchen, giving the counters a final wipe. Then the kitchen light went out, and Rosa disappeared from view. It was almost ten o'clock, so she'd probably gone to her room to watch the news on her private television.

There he was! Marcie's heart beat faster as she watched Brad come down the spiral staircase. He was dressed in a robe, but he wasn't carrying a towel. It was a good thing she'd brought one out here for him. He walked through the living room and went into the den, where he opened the doors to the liquor cabinet. She saw him take out a bottle and pour amber liquid into two crystal snifters. That must be the Grand Marnier he'd mentioned. Marcie had never tasted it, but Brad had seemed pleased when she'd agreed to try it.

Marcie slid over a bit and positioned herself so the stream of bubbles massaged her back. It felt wonderful, but she wasn't relaxed yet. She wouldn't be, until she told Brad about her decision to stay in California. She was terribly nervous about his reaction, but she wasn't sure why. He'd told her he wanted her to stay. And he'd encouraged her to give up her teaching job. But would he be as delighted as she *wanted* him to be?

Everyone at the studio seemed to think that Brad

was falling in love with her, but Marcie didn't see how that could be true. She wasn't as beautiful or as talented as Mercedes had been, and she was a novice in Brad's high-powered world. How could she ever hope to fit into his lifestyle?

She smiled as she remembered the first formal banquet she'd attended with Mercedes, and how nervous she'd been because she hadn't known a fish fork from a salad fork. She wasn't much more sophisticated now. She knew zero about fashion, zilch about foods with foreign names, and zip about how to make small talk with the rich and famous. Wouldn't Brad prefer a woman who was as socially correct and sophisticated as Mercedes had been? Then she remembered what Rhea Delaney had told her, and she frowned slightly. Had her sister's marriage really been in trouble? Or was that just studio gossip? And was it true that Brad and Mercedes hadn't been sleeping together?

Marcie sighed. It was really none of her business. There were lots of reasons why a married couple might not sleep together, and Mercedes had explained that they had conflicting schedules. That was why they'd had separate bedrooms. She was sure Brad hadn't lost interest in Mercedes. That seemed quite impossible. Perhaps Mercedes had been trying some kooky religion that encouraged celibacy. Or a strange, new health kick. She'd always been big on pop fads. Or perhaps she'd merely been in one of her outrageous moods, and Rhea had taken her seriously. Mercedes had always loved to shock people.

But what if it was really true? Marcie sighed deeply. If Mercedes had refused to sleep with Brad, he could have been desperate enough to turn to another woman. And now that Mercedes was dead, that other woman might still be in the picture. Perhaps that was why Brad took so many business trips. He could be seeing the other woman.

Marcie felt a pang of jealousy so intense, it made her gasp. But she had no reason to be jealous. Brad had promised her nothing. What Beau and Rhea had assumed was interest, might be simple kindness on Brad's part. Of course he liked her. Marcie knew that. But his affection for her could be simply as a sister-in-law.

"Marcie?"

Marcie jumped as Brad appeared next to her. Color rose to her cheeks, and she was glad it was dark so he couldn't see her blush. "Brad! I . . . you startled me!"

"I'm sorry." Brad set down the tray he'd been carrying, and Marcie noticed it held two brandy snifters, a bottle, and a plate of assorted cheeses and crackers. "You looked so serious. Were you solving the world's problems?"

Marcie smiled back. "Not really. I was just trying to remember how to turn on the lights in the Jacuzzi."

"I'll do it." Brad hurried to a redwood bench by the side of the Jacuzzi, and opened the hinged top. When he came back, he was carrying a remote control. "It's all electronic. Number seven controls the lights."

Marcie smiled as Brad pressed the button, and the lights in the pool and the Jacuzzi came on. Then he pressed another series of buttons and suddenly the area twinkled with lights. "What do the other buttons do?"

"There's a diagram tacked up on the inside cover of the bench. Number one turns on the Jacuzzi, two starts the jets, three controls the spots on the palm trees, four lights up the deck, five turns on the speaker system, six is for the rose garden, and seven turns on all the underwater lighting."

Marcie nodded. "It's a good thing there's a crib sheet. I'll never be able to remember all that."

"I wouldn't either, but Mercedes hated electronic gadgets, and she always asked me to do it. Are you in the mood for some music?"

"Sure." Marcie nodded. "That's button number five?"

"Right. There's also a switch for radio, CD player, or satellite. And there's a little radio dial on the bottom, so you can choose which station you want."

"Don't confuse me," Marcie warned him. "Just put on something nice and relaxing."

"I'll switch it to CD. I programmed some classical music before I came out here."

Marcie raised her eyebrows, as Brad turned on the speaker system and strains of Tchaikovsky floated out of the speakers. It was very romantic to sit in the Jacuzzi and sip a liqueur while listening to classical music. It was the perfect setting for a seduction. Or was that only wishful thinking on her part?

Brad put the remote control down on the apron of the Jacuzzi. "Have you ever had Grand Marnier before, Marcie?"

"Uh . . . no. I haven't."

Brad handed her a snifter, took the other one himself, and slid into the Jacuzzi opposite her. "Take a sip. I know you're going to love it."

Marcie brought the snifter to her lips and took a sip. It was delicious and she smiled. "I like it, Brad! It tastes like oranges."

"That's right. But be careful how much you drink. It's orange-flavored brandy, and it packs a wallop."

"Thanks for the warning." Marcie couldn't help feeling somewhat disappointed as she took another sip. She'd obviously been wrong about the evening Brad had planned for them. If he'd wanted to seduce her, he would have encouraged her to get a little tipsy.

"You don't work tomorrow, do you?"

Brad was looking at her expectantly, and Marcie shook her head. "No. I'm off until Monday."

"Great! What do you say we give Rosa the day off and take the twins to Disneyland?"

"Well . . . sure. That would be wonderful. But I thought we were taking them there next weekend, for a birthday celebration?"

"I don't think that's a good idea, Marcie." Brad looked very serious. "You see, that's what Mercedes had planned. And they know it. If we follow her plans precisely, the twins might start missing her even more. I thought we'd do Disneyland tomorrow with a couple of their friends, and then we'd plan some kind of surprise for their actual birthday. Since they've always wanted to learn how to ski, I thought maybe we'd take them to Aspen for the weekend. If you don't have to work, that is."

Marcie nodded. "That makes a lot of sense. And I don't have to work next weekend. Dave says I'll be through with all my scenes by Friday, and then there's only dubbing to do."

"Great!" Brad took another sip of his brandy and put the glass down. "Give me your feet, Marcie. I'll massage them."

Marcie was puzzled. "My feet? But . . . why?"

"I used to always do that for Mercedes. The cement floor on the soundstage used to make her feet ache. Of course, maybe that sort of thing doesn't bother you like it used to bother Mercedes."

Marcie laughed. "I don't know if it's the power of

suggestion, but now that you mention it, my feet are killing me."

"Ah ha!" Brad reached out to grab them. "Take another sip of brandy, and lean back and relax. You're going to love this. Just wait and see."

Marcie sighed as Brad propped her feet on his lap and began to massage them. She'd never had a foot massage before, and it was heavenly. "Maybe you should go into the massage business. That feels wonderful!"

"I'm even better with backs, but that's hard to do in a Jacuzzi. You really have to be stretched out flat on a bed."

Marcie took another sip of brandy to keep from saying the wrong thing. Did he want her to stretch out flat on a bed? And if she did, would he do more than massage her back?

"What do you think, Marcie? Should I take the Daimler or the Silver Ghost to Disneyland? Or do you think the kids would be more comfortable in a regular car?"

Marcie raised her eyebrows. "You mean you'd take one of your antique cars on the road?"

"Why not? We won't get there as fast, but it might be fun. Maybe I should use the 1927 Rolls-Royce limo. Then the twins could take two friends apiece."

Marcie took another sip of brandy, and wondered if she was losing her mind. She remembered Mercedes telling her that Brad never used his antique cars. "But, Brad . . . Mercedes said you never drove her anywhere in your antique cars."

"That's true, but only because she didn't want to ride in them. When they held the premiere for *Torch* last year, I wanted to take her in the Silver Ghost, but she said she'd rather ride in the studio limo."

"Oh." Marcie nodded, and reached out to refill their glasses. This was wonderful brandy, and she was beginning to relax for the first time tonight. "But you offered to take her?"

"Several times. Mercedes really didn't care for antique cars. I remember the first time I showed her the Daimler. I drove it to the studio so she could see it." Brad sighed, and then he smiled. "It's beautiful, Marcie. And I bought it in mint condition. I was so proud to own something that exquisite!"

Marcie nodded. "Wasn't that the royal family car? I seem to remember something about the Windsors always having a Daimler."

"That's right!" Brad beamed. "A Daimler was the finest automobile that money could buy back then."

"Mercedes was impressed?" Marcie asked the question, even though she thought she already knew the answer. It would have taken more than an antique car to impress Mercedes.

"She said, 'That's very nice, dear.' She had a two-hour break for lunch, so I suggested we drive to one of her favorite restaurants for lunch. But she said she'd rather stay on the lot, and not go anywhere at all."

"She didn't want to go for a drive?" Marcie felt very sorry for Brad. Even if Mercedes hadn't felt like going for lunch, she could have let him drive her around the block.

Brad shook his head. "She wasn't interested at all. And then I asked her to sit in the driver's seat so I could take a picture, but she wouldn't get in."

"Why not?"

"She said it smelled old and musty inside, like somebody's cellar."

"I see." Marcie nodded and took another sip of her brandy. That just proved there were two sides to every

story. While it was true that Brad had never taken
Mercedes for a ride in one of his antique cars, it was
only because she'd refused to go. And that made
Marcie wonder if there were also two sides to the gossip
Rhea had told her today. Of course, it wouldn't be
right to ask Brad something that personal, but she
was simply dying to know.

"What's the matter, Marcie? Don't you believe me?"

"Oh, I believe you." Marcie took another sip of her
brandy. "I know Mercedes never liked antiques. When
our parents died, I practically had to twist her arm to
get her to take Mother's ring and Dad's pocket watch.
She took them for the twins, but she didn't want anything for herself."

"Why not?"

Brad looked curious, and Marcie did her best to
explain. "I think it all started when we were kids. We
had a huge family of aunts and uncles and cousins, and
they all passed things around. It was a way of saving
money. If you had a baby, you borrowed the crib, and
the bassinet, and all the things you need once and
never need again. Buying new clothes is a big expense,
and kids outgrow them before they're worn out. Our
family passed them on from child to child, until they
finally did wear out."

"That makes sense." Brad nodded. "Go on."

"I never minded wearing hand-me-downs, but Mercedes hated it when she got older. I remember once,
when she was a high school freshman, she got invited
to the senior prom. Cousin Mary had a perfectly nice
prom dress she'd worn only once, but Mercedes really
didn't want to borrow it."

"Did she?"

"Mom made her. We couldn't afford a new dress for
her. Mercedes went to the prom, but she didn't have a

good time, and she blamed it on the dress. When she came home, she told me she'd never allow herself to be saddled with someone else's possessions again. That same night she vowed to make so much money, she could afford to buy everything new. It was an obsession with her, Brad. She hated secondhand things, and antiques were secondhand things to her, even if they were historic or valuable."

Brad sighed. "That explains a lot. Thanks for telling me, Marcie. Now I know why Mercedes wasn't thrilled when I bought her an antique diamond necklace for our last anniversary."

They sat in companionable silence for a moment, sipping their brandy. And then Brad smiled at her. "I'm sorry I didn't get back in time to see your big scene today, Marcie. How did it go?"

"Fine. Dave said we got it on the first take. He seems to be satisfied with my work, Brad. Now let's just hope that Ralph thinks it's good, when they screen it tomorrow."

"Everything I saw you do was perfect. You're a natural, Marcie. And I'm glad you're doing the earlier scenes in the movie. You're much more believable than Mercedes was."

"I am?" Marcie was clearly shocked. "But I'm not an actress. And Mercedes was."

"That's why you're more believable. Mercedes had to play an innocent, trusting wife, and that was very difficult for her, because it was totally out of character. You *are* innocent, and it comes across on the screen."

"But I'm not!" Marcie felt herself blushing. "I may be innocent about some things, but I'm not totally naive!"

Brad laughed. "I didn't mean that as an insult, Marcie. I just meant that you're very naive about men."

"Well, you're wrong!" Marcie jerked her feet away,

and sat up straight. "You might not know it, but I lived with a man when I was in college. And I can tell you, I learned a lot!"

"Did you, now?"

Brad was grinning at her in a very infuriating way, and Marcie felt her temper rise to the boiling point. "Look here! I'm tired of being treated like some poor innocent little hick from the country. Rosa babies me, and you tease me, and all the people at the studio think I'm Miss Goody Two-shoes. Well, I'm not! Everybody seems to think I'd curl right up and have an attack of the vapors, if a man so much as kissed me. And I can assure you, I wouldn't!"

"You wouldn't?"

"Of course not! I've been kissed before, and it's no big deal."

He was still grinning, and Marcie had the urge to dunk him under the water. But before she could give way to her impulse, he said something that made her stop cold.

"But you haven't been kissed by me."

Marcie's mouth opened and then closed again. This was absurd! It was so absurd, it took her a moment to gather her wits to reply.

"You've really got an inflated ego, Brad James! Just because you swept my sister off her feet, doesn't mean you could do the same thing with—"

Marcie's protest ended in shocked silence as Brad covered the distance between them in one step. Her heart was beating so fast she was afraid it would burst in her chest. He caught her in his arms and tipped her head to the side. And then his lips came down on hers, even though she tried to push him away. This wasn't a romantic kiss. It was a challenge!

She fought the urge to go limp in his arms, to open

her lips and taste the warm thrust of his tongue. She felt as if she were falling down swiftly; her breath caught in her throat, and it was impossible to breathe. The sensation was exactly the same as the kiss-me-quicks her father had driven over so long ago, and she felt the identical soaring, sinking feeling that made her toes tingle and her blood race singing through her veins.

And then quite suddenly she *was* falling. Literally. She gasped as they toppled into the center of the swirling, foaming water, arms and legs tangling, heads dipping down under the bubbles. Marcie came up laughing and sputtering at the same time. At least she'd managed to knock him off the ledge, and it was no less than he deserved.

"Okay, you win." Brad grinned at her as he lifted her back up to the ledge and draped a friendly arm around her shoulders. "I didn't sweep you off your feet. You knocked me off mine!"

Marcie giggled. "Told you so!"

"Are you cold?"

Brad seemed concerned, and Marcie laughed. "How could I be cold in a hundred-and-ten-degree Jacuzzi?"

"You've got a point. Maybe we should just stay here forever."

"I don't think that's terribly practical." Marcie giggled again. "But I don't want to get out. Do you?"

"No. Not yet. But let's fortify ourselves for later." Brad reached over to get their brandy snifters and re-filled them. "But go easy on this stuff, Marcie . . . or I might try to take advantage of you."

Marcie took the glass from his hand, and swirled it around the way Mercedes had done in her last movie. She felt very sexy and more than a little tipsy. "You really don't have to worry about that, Brad."

Brad turned to look at her, and Marcie sighed. His eyes were so deep, and they promised so much. Why not take a chance and say what she really felt, for the first time in her life? What did she have to lose?

Marcie set her glass down carefully. Then she turned so her breasts were brushing up against his chest. "You can't take advantage of me, Brad. That assumes an unwilling partner. And I'm definitely willing."

CHAPTER 14

There was one brief moment when she wondered if she was doing the right thing. And then the moment passed and his arms were around her, lifting her up from the water, carrying her up the staircase. She felt lighter than air, and she watched from the height of his strong arms as the stairs disappeared under his bare feet. The carpet had a lovely paisley pattern she'd never noticed before. Perhaps she would paint it someday. But then, why bother, since it already existed right there on the stairs?

No towels. She'd left them on the edge of the Jacuzzi. And no robes. They were still draped over the redwood box, the sleeves as empty as cornhusks after the corn had been carried off to the kitchen.

But they weren't going to the kitchen. They were going to her bedroom. No, she was wrong. They were going to his. How sensitive he was! She didn't want anything to remind her of Mercedes tonight, and he had read her mind.

But they'd left the brandy glasses out on the patio, and she wanted another sip. Just one, so she could wash away the bitter taste of sleeping with her sister's husband. It was a good thing she didn't mind hand-me-downs, because he was secondhand from Mercedes. But she wouldn't think about that. She'd never minded hand-me-downs before, and he was brand-new to her.

The Jacuzzi was probably lonely, bubbling away without them. But then, his bed might be lonely, too, and she sighed as he placed her there. Wet bathing suit on the sheet. Too bad they didn't have towels. But then he was stripping the bathing suit from her glowing, tingling body and she lost the train of her thoughts.

His lips were hot. Hot lips. Like the character on *M*A*S*H*. But Hot Lips had never felt like this with Frank Burns. She'd stake her life on that! His tongue was hot, too. She heard a gasp that came from her own throat.

A thought flashed through her mind. She couldn't remember if there was a danger. But it wouldn't be a danger. It would be a blessing. A baby to love. A baby of her own to take the place of the sister she'd lost.

And then that thought faded into a warm soft glow as she ran her fingers through his hair. Substantial, like a heavy fur coat brushing against her body.

She must have made a sound because he covered her mouth with kisses, whispered pretty things in her ear, told her to relax, to let him take care of her. Yes, she wanted that. She wanted someone to take care of her. Always. Forever.

Her legs were spread like two pillars of alabaster. The Song of Solomon. She remembered that from Bible school. But she shouldn't be thinking about that now. It was terribly sacri . . . sacri . . . fice. She was his sacrifice. He was her god. And he would consume her with his fire.

There was something heavy over her face. A pillow?

And then the fire swept down, and she felt the warm wetness of surrender. Total giving in a cantata of lust. A lyric of passion. A blaze of pure, sweet brilliance, so intense it drew her breath away. And then the patterns sang, and danced, and cavorted behind her eyes. If she could only paint the swirling, bursts of neon joy, she would be Michelangelo!

She reached out blindly to grasp something solid, something real. But she was floating in a cloud of desire. Nothing was real. Emotions were never concrete. And all that mattered was finding release.

And then the breath left her body in a sudden burst of blinding fluorescence, and her mind floated free. At last. At last. At last she could rest.

It might have been hours, it might have been minutes. She was too contented to care. But his voice called her back from that peaceful place, and she turned her head to look at him.

"Marcie? Are you all right?"

He was covering her with a soft blanket and tucking the pillow under her head. And then his arms were around her, and she was resting her head on his shoulder.

"Oh, yes. I'm wonderful!"

"You certainly are." He laughed, a nice rumbling sound she felt against her cheek. "Get some sleep, honey. We've got a big day tomorrow."

Time had no meaning, and she opened her eyes as he lifted her and carried her into the room. And then the blankets were around her again, and she snuggled into their warmth. She made a soft sound of protest as she heard the connecting door close. He had left. She was alone. But she was too tired. And too sleepy. And too happy to care.

* * *

"Come on, Aunt Marcie . . . it'll be fun!"

Rick grinned and grabbed her hand. And then Trish grabbed the other. Before Marcie had the presence of mind to object, she was in line at Space Mountain.

Marcie turned to look at Brad, who was bringing up the rear of their little group. Trish had brought two friends, a redhead with freckles named Megan, and Kumiko, a pretty dark-haired Japanese girl. Rick's friends were Mike, a husky boy who looked like he'd grow up to be a football player, and a very thin, aesthetic-looking boy with glasses, who'd told Marcie his real name was Arthur, but all his friends called him Doc.

"What's the matter, Marcie?" Brad grinned at her.

"Uh . . . nothing. Is this a roller coaster?"

"Sure is. Do you want to prove what a chicken you are, and bail out now?"

"I'm not a chicken!" Marcie glared at him. "I just . . . uh . . . I'm not all that fond of roller coasters. And my feet hurt. Maybe I'll just sit over there on that bench, and wait for you guys to—"

"No, Aunt Marcie!" Trish gripped her hand again. "You promised to go on any rides we wanted today. And after we get off the roller coaster, Brad will massage your feet like he used to do for Mom. Right, Brad?"

"Good idea, Trish. I'd be happy to massage your Aunt Marcie's feet."

Brad gave Marcie a devilish grin, and Marcie knew she was blushing. "Yes . . . well . . . thank you, Brad. But they don't hurt quite as much as they did a while ago."

"You're going then?"

Rick looked pleased, and Marcie didn't have the heart to disappoint him. "Yes. Of course, I'll go. If you really want—"

"We do!"

Trish and Rick spoke at the same time, and then they all laughed. Marcie sighed and accepted the fact that she was cornered. There was no way she could back out now.

"Who wants to go in the front?" Brad herded them all up the ramp.

"We'll go!" Rick motioned for his two friends to join him at the front of their group. "Trish and Kumiko and Megan can ride behind us. And then Aunt Marcie and Brad can take the next one, okay?"

Brad nodded. "Come back here, Marcie. And don't worry about a thing. They've only had one accident at Space Mountain. And that was the . . . let me see . . . It was a party of eight—six kids and two adults. Isn't that right, kids?"

"But none of the kids got hurt." Kumiko giggled as she took up the story.

"That's right." Doc nodded solemnly. "I remember reading about that."

Mike grinned as he turned to look at Marcie. "The man was fine. Only the lady fell out. But they fixed the roller coaster after that happened."

"Thanks a lot." Marcie joined in the laughter, but she could feel her knees starting to shake. She'd told the kids that she wasn't fond of roller coasters. That was the truth, but it was also a gross understatement. She was terrified of them.

The children started kidding one another as they entered the building, but Marcie shuddered. It had been designed to be eerie inside, with dim blue lights glowing in the half-darkness. As they approached the ramp, an employee asked them if anyone wanted to bail out now, before they actually climbed the ramp. Marcie was tempted, but she wasn't about to give way to her fear. She told herself that it wouldn't be so bad.

She'd shut her eyes and pretend she was somewhere else, somewhere safe, and she wouldn't open them until the car stopped.

"Marcie? Are you all right?" Brad slipped an arm around her shoulders and tipped her head up so she had to look at him.

"Yes. I'm perfectly fine."

"You don't look so fine to me." Brad looked very concerned. "In fact, you look suspiciously green around the gills."

"It must be the lighting."

Marcie drew in a deep breath, and let it out again in a shuddering sigh. She was glad they were in semi-darkness so Brad couldn't see how frightened she really was.

"Look, Marcie . . . I know we railroaded you, but you really don't have to do this. See those men over there in the white space suits? I can ask one of them to take you back outside."

Marcie shook her head. "No, Brad. I'm fine, really. And the ride doesn't last that long . . . does it?"

"I think they said it was a minute and a half."

"That long?" Marcie swallowed hard. "I thought it was only . . . uh . . . a couple of seconds. But I won't back out, Brad. I promised to go on this ride, and I will!"

Brad grinned at her. "That's the spirit! Actually, this roller coaster is rather tame. It doesn't do a loop, like the one at Magic Mountain. I don't think we go upside down at all."

"Oh. Good."

Marcie swallowed again. She could hear screaming in the distance, and she felt like screaming, too. Actually, she'd felt like screaming all morning, even on the drive to Disneyland. She wanted to scream at herself for being such a fool.

She'd managed to avoid Brad at the breakfast table by coming down late, after a cup of coffee in her room. She was terribly embarrassed about what had happened last night, and she really hadn't wanted to face Brad. She knew she'd thrown herself at him, practically forced him to make love to her, and she wouldn't blame him if he didn't have an ounce of respect left for her.

Thank goodness, Brad was a gentleman! He'd been his usual kind, courteous self, when he'd driven up in the beautiful Rolls limousine. It was as if last night had never happened. But she knew it had. And the tension inside her had been building all day. She felt guilty. And embarrassed. And terribly nervous, as she anticipated the awkward encounter that would eventually occur between them. That was why she'd been avoiding Brad. She wanted to delay that encounter until she could find exactly the right words to explain her unacceptable behavior.

Naturally, she'd insisted that the twins ride in the front seat of the limo with Brad. She'd said it was part of their birthday treat, and they had been thrilled. And when they'd arrived at Disneyland, she'd surrounded herself with the twins and their friends, so she wouldn't be alone with Brad. She'd managed to hide behind a protective wall of children all day, but that was about to change. When they climbed into the roller coaster, she would be alone in a seat with Brad.

Marcie wished she were more liberal. It was true that she'd lived with her boyfriend in college. And they had certainly been lovers. But it had been more of a trial marriage between two people who had thought they might make their relationship permanent someday. Last night hadn't been like that at all. She'd taken advantage of Brad's grief and thrown herself at him. And he was probably just as sorry it had happened as she was.

The screams got much louder as they neared the top of the ramp, and Marcie did her best to ignore them. Trish and her friends had turned around to talk to Brad, and she was very grateful she didn't have to take part in their conversation. It was difficult to act as if nothing were wrong, when her whole system of values was in jeopardy.

She caught a glimpse of the roller coaster as it sped by overhead. The girl in the front seat was laughing, her hair whipping from side to side, as the car hurtled around a hairpin turn. She didn't look at all frightened, and she reminded Marcie of Mercedes.

Mercedes had always been a thrill-seeker. Even in grade school, she'd been the one to try daredevil stunts on her bicycle while Marcie had watched helplessly from the sidelines, wringing her hands and praying that nothing would go wrong. And here she was, trying to take her sister's place. She was wearing Mercedes's clothes, acting in Mercedes's movie, and sleeping with Mercedes's husband.

Marcie sighed as the line moved forward. If Mercedes had spent a passionate night in a lover's bed, she would have given him a morning kiss, thanked him for a wonderful time, and gone on with her life without the slightest feeling of guilt. Marcie just couldn't do that. She wasn't Mercedes, and she didn't have her sister's ability to take things in stride. Somehow, she had to find the courage to apologize to Brad for acting like a desperate middle-aged woman, tell him that she was thoroughly ashamed of herself, and promise him that it wouldn't happen again.

"Isn't this exciting? We're almost there, Aunt Marcie!" Trish stepped back to grab Marcie's arm. "I counted off the people in line, and you and Uncle Brad are going to be the first ones in the next car!"

"Wonderful." Marcie forced a smile.

"Let me tell you what to do, Aunt Marcie." Rick broke away from his group to join them. "When you get on, put your hands up above your head. And leave them that way for the whole ride. It makes you feel like you're going to . . ."

". . . fall right out." Trish finished the sentence for him. "It's even scarier that way."

Marcie gave a shaky laugh. "Thanks for the tip, guys. I'm sure it's a lot more fun, if you think you're going to fall out."

"Better get in line, kids. You're almost up." Brad came back to take Marcie's arm. He lowered his voice as he asked, "Are you sure you want to go through with this? You're shaking."

"I'm positive. As a matter of fact, I can hardly wait."

Marcie gave him a grin that was meant to be cheerful, but it turned out to be more of a grimace. Brad slipped his arm around her shoulders again, and he gave her a little hug. "Okay, let's go."

"This is it?" Marcie stared at the roller coaster that had stopped at the top of the ramp. "It looks like a rocket!"

Trish turned around to grin at her. "That's why it's called Space Mountain. Watch, Aunt Marcie. The whole side comes open to let you in. And then they close it again."

A man in a white space suit pulled a lever and the

side of the rocket opened up. The people ahead of them in line began to file in, two adults or three children for each seat.

"See you at the bottom, Aunt Marcie!" Rick and his friends got in the second to the last seat. "Don't worry. We were only kidding about falling out."

Trish waved, and her group got in the last seat. And then the rocket began to move slowly along the track, until it disappeared around a curve. Marcie heard a chorus of screams, and she knew the children had started their descent.

Brad gave a little bow as their rocket stopped at the top of the ramp, and the man in the white space suit opened the side. "After you."

"No, you go first." Marcie pulled back. "I want to be by the escape hatch."

"It's not an escape hatch. It locks from the outside." Brad grinned as he got into the rocket, and pulled her in beside him.

Marcie closed her eyes the moment she sat down. But she was too curious to keep them closed for long. "It's like a cage in here. I feel like a trapped squirrel."

"No problem." Brad gave her a big grin. "I'll act like a nut."

Marcie burst into laughter, and she laughed so hard, she barely noticed when the roller coaster began to move. It started off slowly at first, moving smoothly along the rail.

"Hang on, Marcie. Here we go." Brad slipped his arm around her shoulders.

"Why, this isn't so bad!" Marcie gave a big sigh of relief as the rocket went smoothly around a curve. "I wonder why the twins were scream—"

Marcie stopped in midsentence and gripped Brad's

hands. Since they were in the first seat, she could see the rail stretch out in from of them, lit dimly by the blue lights. But the track abruptly ended in what Marcie quickly realized was a steep drop. "We're not actually going to go-oh, no!"

They reached the top of the incline, and Marcie bit back a scream. The roller coaster hesitated for a brief moment and then plunged ahead, dropping so steeply her hair lifted up off her neck.

Marcie screamed and threw her arms around Brad. Her eyes snapped shut. She couldn't bear to look. And then, suddenly, they were lurching and barreling around a series of hairpin turns that made her gasp and cry out in terror.

They slowed again, and Brad laughed as he held her tightly. "Hey . . . it's not that bad. I've been on faster roller coasters than this."

"That's . . . easy for you to say!" Marcie gasped and buried her face in Brad's chest, peeking out at the rail. Now they were climbing smoothly again, but she knew the ride wasn't over. "This is really . . . oh, no! Not again!"

The roller coaster hesitated on the brink of another steep decline. Marcie risked a glance at Brad, and saw he was anticipating the drop with pleasure. "How can you possibly enjoy something like . . . Ooooooh!"

Marcie clutched at him again, and Brad laughed. "I've got to remember to thank the twins. Space Mountain was a great idea. There's no way you can avoid me in a roller coaster."

"Avoid you?" Their speed was slowing again, and Marcie did her best to look innocent.

"That's right. You've barely looked at me all day."

"I . . . uh . . . I know." Marcie dipped her head in

acknowledgment. "I'm terribly embarrassed. I don't want you to think I'm that kind of . . ."

"I don't." Brad interrupted her.

"But I practically—"

Brad broke in again. "No, you didn't. And don't forget that I encouraged you every way I could."

"Well . . . maybe. I tried to tell myself that it was just the—"

"It wasn't. You didn't have *that* much. Actually, I think we ought to keep a bottle right by the bed after we're . . . uh-oh!"

Marcie hardly noticed as the roller coaster hurtled down the decline. She just looked up at Brad in shock. "After we're *what*?"

"Married." Brad's voice was shaky, as the roller coaster barreled around another steep turn. "You'll marry me, won't you, Marcie?"

Suddenly, Marcie wasn't a bit nervous about the roller coaster anymore. The ride was tame, compared to the emotions that were flowing through her at Brad's proposal.

"I . . . I . . . Are you sure that you really . . ."

"Yes, I love you." Brad grinned down at her. "Even with your hair standing up on end like that. And it's not because you're Mercedes's twin, and you look just like her. I love *you* Marcie."

Marcie snuggled a little closer in his arms. "But how about the twins? Do you think that they'll . . ."

"It'll take a little time, but I'm sure they'll adjust." Brad interrupted her again. "And we don't have to get married right away. We can give them some time to get used to the idea . . . say, a week or two at the most. How about it, Marcie? Will you marry me?"

Marcie giggled and opened her mouth to tell him yes. But just then the roller coaster went into its grand finale of screeching turns and hurtling descents, and she screamed instead, at the top of her lungs.

"Is that a yes?" Brad shouted in her ear.

"It's a YESSSSSSSSS!" Marcie laughed as the rush of air hurtling past their rocket took her words away, and sent them echoing against the walls of the building. And then Brad was kissing her. Her. Not the ghost of Mercedes. And she knew that she'd never been this happy before in her whole life!

CHAPTER 15

"Would you like lunch on the patio, Miss Marcie?"

"I guess so." Marcie roused herself from her lethargy and nodded. "Why don't you join me, Rosa? There's something I'd like to discuss with you."

While Rosa busied herself in the kitchen, preparing their lunch, Marcie gazed out at the beautiful grounds with a frown on her face. Even though there was no reason, she felt deserted. The twins were spending the day with friends, Brad had left early this morning on another business trip, and it was turning into a boring Sunday. Of course, there were a million things she *should* do. She should study her scene for tomorrow, shop for new school clothes for the twins, go through the things in Mercedes's closet, write a letter to the school board telling them she was resigning, make some calls to her friends in Minnesota to ask if they'd pack up her personal possessions and send them out to California, and contact Sam to find out the legal ramifications of her impending marriage. This would be a good day to accomplish all that, but Marcie didn't feel like doing anything at all. Perhaps the excitement of yesterday had been too much for her. She felt so lethargic, she just wanted to crawl into bed, pull the covers up over her head, and sleep until tomorrow morning.

Marcie sighed. She was definitely depressed, and there was absolutely no reason for it. Everything was going exactly the way she'd hoped. She owned a lovely mansion, the twins were adjusting beautifully to their new situation, everyone said she was doing an excellent job of finishing Mercedes's movie, and she would soon be marrying a wonderful man who loved her every bit as much as she loved him. How could she be depressed?

Perhaps her problem was the weather. It was a gray day in Southern California, and the air was still and muggy. The temperature was warm for March, seventy-eight degrees, and the sun was hiding behind a thick curtain of clouds. It didn't feel like rain, and now that Marcie considered it, she almost wished the clouds would gather, roiling over her head, and sheets of rain would pour down to soak the earth. Any kind of dramatic change would be welcome. She hated the gray limbo of the sky that stretched out as far as the eye could see.

Just then the patio door opened, and Rosa came out, carrying a tray with thick roast beef sandwiches. It was exactly what she'd asked for, and the sandwiches looked delicious, but Marcie couldn't seem to work up any enthusiasm as Rosa set down the plates.

"What's the matter, Miss Marcie?" Rosa looked concerned as Marcie took a small bite of her sandwich. "Aren't you hungry?"

Marcie shook her head. "They're delicious, Rosa, but I guess I had too many snacks at Disneyland yesterday."

"That doesn't surprise me a bit." Rosa smiled at her. "The twins wouldn't eat their breakfast, either. They said Mr. Brad bought them everything they asked for. It's a wonder they didn't get sick."

"It's true." Marcie laughed, remembering how they'd stuffed down hot dogs, and pretzels, and ice cream bars. "I think we stopped at every food cart on Main Street. They even ate hamburgers right after we got off the roller coaster at Space Mountain."

"So why the glum face, Miss Marcie? Are you missing your friends in Minnesota?"

"No. Not really. And that's why I wanted to talk to you, Rosa. I've decided to move out here permanently. I think it would be better if I didn't uproot the twins."

"Oh, good!" Rosa smiled broadly. "You're right, Miss Marcie. Trish and Rick just love it out here, and it'd be a shame to take them away from their friends. And you like it too, don't you?"

Marcie nodded. "Yes, I do. And now I've got another reason for staying here. Brad has . . . well . . . he asked me to marry him."

"You're going to marry Mr. Brad?" At first Rosa looked dismayed, but she quickly put on a smile. "Congratulations, Miss Marcie. Or am I supposed to congratulate Mr. Brad? I always forget which way it goes."

Marcie smiled. "I think you're supposed to give me your best wishes and congratulate him, but it really doesn't matter. Are you happy for me?"

"Of course, I am. I want whatever makes you happy, Miss Marcie. But . . ." Rosa stopped, and gave Marcie an anxious look.

"But what?"

"Maybe I shouldn't say this, but do you think you should jump right into something this important? I mean . . . it's only been a month since Miss Mercedes's accident, and people might talk."

"I'm sure they'll talk. And what they'll say won't be

very nice." Marcie gave a wry little smile. "That's why I told Brad we have to wait at least six months. I think that'll be better for everyone concerned."

Rosa looked relieved. "That's very smart, Miss Marcie. It'll give the twins time to adjust, and you won't have to rush to plan the wedding. And there's that old saying, '*Marry in haste, repent in leisure.*' You and Mr. Brad'll have lots of time to think about it and be sure."

Marcie opened her mouth to tell Rosa that they were already sure, but she was interrupted by a loud buzz from the security system beeper. "Somebody's at the gate. I'd better see who it is."

"I'll do it, Miss Marcie. You just sit there and enjoy your lunch."

Rosa got up and went into the kitchen to check the monitor. When she came back a moment later, she was smiling.

"It's Mr. Sam. I told him to come up and have some lunch. That was all right, wasn't it?"

"Of course." As Rosa scurried back to the kitchen to prepare another sandwich, Marcie smiled her first genuine smile of the day. She hadn't seen Sam in over a week, and she could hardly wait to tell him her wonderful news. She picked up her sandwich and took another bite. Her appetite had returned with a rush. And then the clouds parted and the sun came out, bathing the patio with warm golden rays.

"Hi, Marcie." Sam opened the patio doors and stuck his head out. "Nice day, isn't it?"

Marcie nodded. "It is now. You brought the sun with you."

"Anything I can do to please a client." Sam grinned at her. "Would you like blue skies? Puffy little white clouds? Maybe a rainbow or two?"

"Thanks, but I wouldn't want to wear you out. Just the sun will do. Is Rosa making you a sandwich?"

"Yes, and she asked me to carry this out." Sam stepped out with a tray. "Red wine, glasses, and some cheese and crackers to perk up your appetite."

"I think it's already perked." Marcie glanced down at the huge bite she'd taken out of her sandwich.

"So I see. But we mustn't disappoint her. Cooks of genius are exceedingly rare. Right, Rosa?"

"Right, Mr. Sam." Rosa waved at them from the open kitchen window. "Miss Marcie? Why don't you tell Mr. Sam your happy news?"

"The picture's going well?" Sam guessed, as he picked up the corkscrew and opened the wine.

Marcie nodded. "Yes, it is. But that's not the happy news."

"You're staying out here for good?"

"That's right." Marcie laughed. "But that's not all of it."

"You won the California State Lottery?"

"No. That's hard to do if you don't buy a ticket. It's even better than that, Sam. I'm getting married."

Sam's eyebrows shot up, and his hand trembled slightly as he poured the wine. "Anybody I know?"

"Oh, yes." Marcie gave him a happy smile. "It's Brad. He proposed to me yesterday, when we took the twins to Disneyland. And I accepted."

Sam handed her a glass. "Well . . . I guess this calls for a toast. Good luck, Marcie."

"Good luck?" Marcie hesitated, her glass extended. Then she drew it back and frowned. "What's that supposed to mean?"

"Nothing. It's just a figure of speech. You should know I wish you all the best. When's the happy occasion?"

"Not for six months. I wanted to give the twins time to adjust."

"Good thinking." Sam gave her an approving nod. "They've been through a lot in the past few weeks."

"That's exactly what I told Brad. He wanted to get married right away, but I really don't think that would be fair to Trish and Rick. They need time to get used to the idea."

"Have you told them yet?"

"No." Marcie frowned again. "I'm not sure exactly what to say. But I think I should tell them as early as possible, perhaps tonight."

"Do you want me to tell them?"

Marcie shook her head. "No, I'll do it."

"Alone?"

"Well . . . yes." Marcie took a sip of her wine, and nodded. "Brad's out of town until Friday night. He said he didn't want to go, but he's had this business trip planned for months, and he couldn't cancel at the last minute."

"Of course not. You don't want to wait until he gets home, so you can tell the twins together?"

"I really don't think that's necessary. It's not like their lives will be changing in any way. Brad's still living here, just like he always has. And everything will be just the same, except . . ." Marcie stopped and smiled. "Actually, things *will* be different. And I know it'll be a change for the better. Brad told me he wants to be a real father to the twins. He said Mercedes didn't want him to assume a parental role when they got married, but Brad's always wanted to have a closer relationship with Trish and Rick."

Sam nodded. "I see. Well . . . I'm glad you're not rushing into anything. Marcie. There are a lot of details we'll have to work out, with your inheritance from

Mercedes, and the trust fund Mike left for the twins. I assume you don't want to change the plans Mercedes made for her children."

Marcie felt a little uncomfortable. She really hadn't discussed that with Brad. "No. I don't want to change anything Mercedes already set up. That wouldn't be right."

"Good." Sam nodded. "We'll be very careful not to commingle any funds. And I'll draw up a prenuptial agreement for Brad to sign."

"But why?"

"It'll protect the assets you inherited from Mercedes. Anything you earn after your marriage, you'll share with Brad."

"Wait a minute." Marcie began to frown. "I want everything to be set up by the terms of Mercedes's new will."

"The one she never signed?"

Marcie nodded. "Yes. You still have a copy of that, don't you?"

"I do. But Marcie . . . perhaps there was a good reason why Mercedes never signed her new will."

"If there was, I don't know about it. And neither do you. And neither does Brad. I just want to do what my sister would have done, if she'd had the chance to do it."

"Okay." Sam nodded. "Don't spend time worrying about it now, Marcie. We'll work it all out."

Rosa opened the patio door and came out with another tray. "Here's your sandwich, Mr. Sam. And I fixed a few things to go with it."

"I guess you did! You've outdone yourself, Rosa. Potato salad, coleslaw, pickles, olives, and . . ." Sam laughed as he saw the final item on the tray. "Chopped liver? Rosa . . . I think I love you!"

Rosa laughed. "I know you love my chopped liver. It's your mother's recipe."

"But you make it better than she ever did." Sam grinned at Rosa, and then he turned to wink at Marcie. "If Marcie ever decides she can get along without you. I want you to come straight to me."

Marcie gave a sigh of relief. She was glad that Rosa had broken the tension that had grown between them from the moment she'd announced that she was going to marry Brad. Now she winked back at Sam and pretended to be outraged.

"You're a snake, Sam Abrams! I'll never be able to get along without Rosa, and you know it. I know your tricks. You're just trying to lure her away from me. And there's no way I'll let her go!"

"But Rosa loves me . . . don't you, Rosa?"

Rosa giggled as she nodded. "Yes, I do, Mr. Sam."

"But she loves me more." Marcie glared at Sam. "Don't you, Rosa?"

"I love both of you." Rosa declared with a laugh. "But there's no way I can work for two people . . . unless they get married to each other, of course."

Sam nodded. "Well, that does it! We'll just tell Brad that he's out in the cold. I have to marry Marcie for Rosa's chopped liver."

Before Marcie could say a word, the twins rushed out on the patio. They'd been so busy laughing, they hadn't even heard the kids come home.

"You're going to marry Sam?" Trish jumped up and down in excitement.

Rick was a step behind her, and he threw his arms around Marcie. "That's great, Aunt Marcie! We always wanted Sam for a father!"

There was a shocked silence as Marcie and Sam

exchanged glances. Then Sam nodded to Marcie. "I think you'd better handle this."

"Uh-oh." Trish gave a deep sigh. "You were just kidding around, right?"

"That's right." Marcie reached out to hug her.

Rick looked disappointed for a moment, and then he shrugged. "Oh, well. I knew it was too good to be true. Do you guys want to see the baseball cards Jimmy's dad gave me?"

"We'd love to!" Marcie jumped at the opportunity. "Go get the collector's album I gave you, Rick, and we'll file them in the right place."

It was bedtime for the twins, and Marcie held out her arms as Rosa brought them in after their baths. "Come on over here, guys. I've got something to discuss with you."

"Did we do something wrong?" Trish looked a little nervous as she sat on the couch beside Marcie.

"Not a thing," Marcie reassured her. "Remember how excited you were when you thought I was getting married?"

"Uh-huh." Rick sat down on the other side of her. "But that was just a joke, right?"

Marcie frowned slightly. "Yes. And no. I *am* getting married, but not to Sam."

The twins exchanged glances, and then Trish nodded. "Okay. Who are you marrying, Aunt Marcie?"

"Brad. He proposed to me yesterday when we went to Disneyland."

"Space Mountain." Rick gave a deep sigh. "We knew something was up, because you were . . ."

". . . laughing when you got off." Trish finished the thought for him. "But I told Rick you were just . . ."

". . . relieved the ride was over." Rick nodded.

Marcie hugged them both. "That was true, but it was a little more than that. And now I want to know how you feel about it."

"If we don't like it, will you tell Uncle Brad you won't marry him?" Trish looked anxious.

"No. I want to marry him. But I'd like you to be happy about it. You were very happy when you thought I was going to marry Sam."

"That's different," Rick tried to explain. "We love Sam."

"And you don't love Brad?"

"I wouldn't put it quite that way." Trish looked very adult. "Brad's okay, but he never paid much attention to us before. He was always too busy, or gone, or something. We don't really know him that well, Aunt Marcie."

"I know that." Marcie gave her another hug. "And that's why I told Brad we'd have to wait a while before we got married. I want you two to get to know him better."

"Then you're not getting married right away?" Rick looked hopeful.

"No."

"Good!" Trish smiled. "I think it would be a mistake to rush into things. That's what Mom did."

Rick nodded. "She rushed to get married, and she didn't even give Sam a chance to tell her he loved her. That was a big mistake."

"Sam loved your mother?" Marcie looked at them in astonishment. "I didn't know that!"

Trish shot Rick an angry look. "That's because it was supposed to be a secret. And my bonehead brother is terrible about keeping secrets."

"I'm not," Rick protested.

"Yes, you are!"

"Says who?"

Marcie tuned out as the twins began to squabble. They'd work it out. They always did. And while they were working it out, she'd do her best to digest this startling news. So Sam had been in love with Mercedes! It did make sense. She knew how devastated Sam had been when he'd met her at the airport. And it explained Sam's strange reaction when he saw her dressed and acting like Mercedes at the screen test.

Marcie sighed. Although Sam had plenty of confidence when it came to his legal profession, he might have been too shy to declare his love to Mercedes. And she could certainly understand why the twins loved Sam. He was a very likeable guy, and he inspired confidence. And he was very good with them, taking them to baseball games and picnics and amusement parks.

Just knowing that the twins had wanted their mother to marry Sam explained a host of things. Marcie was sure it was why they'd never let themselves get close to Brad. They regarded him as temporary, as the husband they hoped would be replaced. Now that they knew she was going to marry Brad and not Sam, they'd come around. They'd grow to love Brad once they were all together as a family. Marcie was sure of it. It might take some time, but she'd convince the kids to give Brad a chance to be a real father to them.

"No, you blew it." Trish was still arguing with Rick. "It can't be a secret, if Aunt Marcie knows it. Can it, Aunt Marcie?"

Marcie slipped her arm around Rick. "I think it can. I won't tell anyone, I promise. I certainly won't mention it to Sam, so you don't have to worry about that. But how did you kids find out that Sam loved your mother?"

Rick hesitated and then he spoke up. "Sam told us.

But he didn't get a chance to tell Mom, and she went ahead and married Brad."

"That's right." Trish nodded. "We really hoped Mom would wise up and divorce Brad so she could marry Sam, but she didn't."

"Wise up? What does that mean?"

Rick and Trish exchanged glances, and then Rick took over the conversation. "Brad's okay, I guess. I mean, he's nice to us and everything, but . . ."

". . . but we always got the feeling we were in the way." Trish nodded emphatically. "Brad didn't really want us. He wanted Mom. And Sam would have been a real father to us, not just . . ."

". . . Mom's husband," Rick broke in.

"I see." Marcie nodded. "As a matter of fact, Brad talked about that with me. He said he was sorry he never got a chance to get closer to you. And now he'd like to."

"Really?" Trish still looked dubious. "Are you sure?"

"That's what he said. It was his idea to take you to Disneyland in the Rolls, you know. And maybe I shouldn't spoil the surprise, but he's planning to take all of us skiing for your birthday."

"Wow!" Rick began to smile. "I always wanted to learn to ski! Do you know where we're going?"

"Aspen. Brad made the travel arrangements before he left on his business trip."

"Is Rosa going, too?" Trish looked concerned.

"Absolutely. I heard him order six tickets."

"Six?" Rick counted them off. "Brad, and you, and us, and Rosa. That's only five."

"I know. Jerry Palmer's going along. Brad says he used to live in Aspen, so he'll show us around. They've got a couple of business meetings planned, but they'll spend the rest of the time with us on the slopes. Do you mind?"

Trish shook her head. "We don't mind. We like Jerry. He's nice, and he really likes us. We think Jerry should get married and . . ."

". . . have kids of his own," Rick jumped in. "We felt really bad when Mom fired him."

"Your mother fired Jerry Palmer?"

"Well . . . not exactly." Trish gave Rick a warning glance. "She terminated their relationship because she needed to go with a bigger agency. Jerry's small-time, and she needed an agent with more juice."

"Juice?" Marcie looked puzzled and the twins laughed.

"Clout." Rick explained the word. "She needed someone with more power, to get her better deals. That's how they do things out here."

"I see. And how did you know all this? Did your mother tell you?"

Trish shot Rick a warning glance, and then she replied, "No. Mom didn't exactly tell us. But we . . ."

". . . kind of overheard it." Rick jumped in. "You know how it is, Aunt Marcie. If kids are really quiet, they get to hear a lot. The adults just forget they're around."

Marcie bit back a giggle. She was sure the twins had used that tactic quite often.

"Brad was pretty upset when Mom decided to go with someone else." Trish volunteered more of the story. "We heard them discussing it from all the way upstairs."

Rick nodded. "They were pretty loud at first, but then Mom talked him around. She was really good at getting people to see things her way."

"I know she was." This time Marcie had to laugh. She was well acquainted with Mercedes's powers of persuasion. "Did I ever tell you guys about the time your mother talked me into pulling her to school on the sled? Or how she got me to pretend to be her, when she had made two dates for the same night?"

"No." Both twins spoke at once. "Tell us!"

"Okay. But first you have to ask Rosa to make me a cup of hot chocolate. And while you're at it, ask her to make some for you, too."

"It's a done deal!" Rick jumped up. "Come on, Trish."

Trish let Rick pull her to her feet. "How about popcorn, Aunt Marcie?"

"Popcorn right before bedtime?"

"Why not?" Rich countered. "Popcorn goes really well . . ."

". . . with hot chocolate." Rick finished the sentence for his sister.

"You're absolutely right." Marcie smiled at them. "I'll sit right here and wait. And if you ask me very nicely, maybe I'll even tell you about the time your mother flunked a history test, and talked the teacher into giving her an A anyway."

He could see her in the living room with the children. She looked like a mother as they sat on the couch in a tight family circle. Even the housekeeper was there, and they were all laughing at something she said. He wished he could hear her, but he couldn't risk going inside the house. They couldn't know he was here. No one could ever know.

He'd heard her say that the husband had gone on another business trip. He'd hidden in the rose garden, behind a flowering bush of White Masterpiece Tea Roses, to the left of the Sutter's Gold they'd planted to replace the red American Beauty. He'd learned a lot about roses since he'd come to live with her. The gardeners had left the tags on, and since he was a compulsive reader, he'd gone from bush to bush, reading about their care and lineage. Directly in back of him was Blue Girl, a lavender hybrid tea rose, Latin name *Rosaceae* . It would reach almost six feet in height, if it was properly fertilized, watered, and pruned, and its flowers were large and shapely, generally one to a stem. Not that he cared. He'd never liked roses anyway.

From his vantage point in the rose garden, he'd heard everything she had said earlier, including the news about marrying the husband. That frightened him. She shouldn't marry the husband. It was a terrible mistake. Never mind that it was almost like incest, although technically, it was not. The fault did not lie with her, or her lovely twin sister. It was the husband. He should not marry again.

He sighed like the wind that swept down the hills and into the canyon. It was a sigh of knowing, and a sigh of regret. He was the only one who understood that the husband was mortally flawed. He was like a cog without teeth, or a wheel that was out-of-round. He could wreak terrible damage on an innocent and trusting wife.

What a happy family picture, a mother with two children gathered close, and a trusted family retainer smiling fondly at them all. How peaceful. How charming. It was a scene worthy of an expensive greeting card. Inside it would say, *May the peace and serenity of love touch your heart and bring you everlasting joy*. But how different this scene would be if the husband were standing behind her, his hand resting lightly on her shoulder. Then the message would read, *What is wrong with this picture?* And he would be the only one who could answer.

She turned then, toward the window, and his heart jumped up to lodge in his throat. She was so lovely, the image of his beautiful, dead mother. Could he save her? Was it too late?

He looked around with eyes that blazed, in a holy crusade to search for the red, ferret it out, and annihilate it before it claimed him in an agony of painful memories. It was here somewhere. He could smell it on the breeze, taste it on the tip of his tongue, feel its presence invading every cell of his body. But where?

The red roses were neutralized; he'd shredded the petals and let the air cleanse them. And her red bathing suit had disappeared, taken away on her poor drowned body by the men in the white coats. But there! He saw it! A taunting, grinning bundle of red on the table by the pool. And then the red mist began to swirl and rise, licking at his ankles like a hungry wolf. And he knew he had to destroy his old enemy before it had a chance to consume her.

There was one brief moment of clarity as he scuttled across the patio and snatched the red in his shaking fingers. A book. He could not destroy a book. His adoptive mother, the librarian, had taught him that it was a sin. But the inside could be removed, plucked from the womb of the red covers to stand alone and viable. For while it was certainly a mortal sin to destroy a book, it was only a venial transgression to neutralize its covers.

He placed the word child back on the table, and wrapped it carefully in the swaddling cloth of a towel that had been tossed on a chair. There. Soon it would be safe from the evil red. He would destroy the evil so that it could not threaten again.

Earth, air, fire, and water. The ancient elements. But which should he use? They might see the fire from the house, and come out to extinguish it before his merciful deed was accomplished. And the water was also a risk. The pool was clear and clean. They could see the red in its depths, and lift it out before the liquid destroyer had worked its healing magic. The air was here, all around him, but it would take days to destroy the sturdy leather covers. He would use the soft, dark, concealing earth. It would receive his red burden and hide it, until it was rendered harmless.

He took up the shovel and began to dig in the well-moistened earth. There was very little time left. The red mist was creeping up his legs, and it was fast approaching his groin. To keep from thinking about the awful consequences, he began to recite a nursery rhyme Miss Razel had taught him. One, two, buckle my shoe. Three, four, close the door. Five, six, pick up sticks. Seven, eight, lift the gate. Nine, ten, a big fat hen. He'd always giggled when she'd come to that part, imagining the Red Lady as a big, fat hen.

Now the hole was deep enough. He grabbed the despised red and dropped it in. Now he had to keep the shovel moving, and fill the hole perfectly, so the gardener wouldn't notice. Another rhyme, and he would be finished. Only then could he give way to the compelling red mist.

There was pain mixed with pure determination on his face as he scooped up a shovel of the dirt and tossed it back into the hole. One, two . . . *Shame on you! You're an ungrateful little boy, and you deserve to be punished!*

No. He couldn't give way. He had to concentrate on the rhyme to keep the shovel moving. Three, four, open the door. The door to the red room. *Open it! He's waiting for you! Now get on that bed and stop crying!*

The shovel wavered in his shaking hands, but he forced himself to dump the dirt in. He couldn't think about that now. It drove him crazy. The rhyme. Miss Razel's rhyme would save him. Five, six, pick up sticks. Seven, eight . . . *You're late! I told you to come home right after school! Uncle Stan has been here for an hour, waiting for you!* Nine, ten, a big fat . . . Ben. Uncle Ben, the worst of them all. *Come here, little boy. You know what I want, don't you? That's a good boy. You be nice and still, and I won't have to tie you down, hmmm? Now turn over. Ah, yes . . . and get ready. 'Cause here comes . . . Papa!*

No! Never again! The red mist covered his shoulders, but he fought it back as he stomped down the earth, the way he'd stomped Uncle Ben, before he'd run away to hide with the rats in the alley. Never again. He'd seen to that. Uncle Ben was gone. And so was the Red Lady. And the red room was destroyed by the ancient elements. Now he was the powerful one, the one everyone respected—the Uncle!

He opened his mouth to shout his triumph, and the red mist crawled in, filling his nostrils, his lungs, and his mind. But that didn't matter. He'd buried his prey, covered the evil red thing with layer upon layer of deep, dark earth, so that it could never again see the light of day. The red evil was dead, and he was alive. He was a survivor despite the tremendous odds.

Had he finally done it right this time? Would he be able to keep his mind and destroy the red mist inside him? It would happen one day. His adoptive mother, the librarian, had taught him that. It was the story of human initiative. From pauper to millionaire. From humble beginnings to president of the United States. It was the American Dream, and he was an American. If he tried and tried, over and over again, he would finally succeed.

For a moment, he thought he was going to win his final triumph. Right here. Right now. With his love inside the window, looking out into the darkness, where he protected her. But that was not to be. Not this time. He felt his mind start to shrivel and burn, and he cringed as the red fingers tightened. His mind was in a vise, caught firmly as the red fingers plucked, and tore, and squeezed out his essence, replacing his soul with a deep, black void.

CHAPTER 16

It had been one of those mornings when everything had gone wrong, and Marcie had trouble forcing a smile as she got into the studio limo. Rick had left his baseball card album out on the patio table, and when he'd gone out first thing in the morning to pick it up, he'd discovered that the cover was missing. The baseball cards were still intact, and Marcie had promised to buy him a new album, but it was disturbing. The only explanation Rosa and Marcie had been able to formulate was that a small animal, like a fox or a rat, had come into their yard through the security bars and dragged the leather cover off to eat it.

"What's the matter, Marcie?" George turned to look at her as he stopped the limo just outside the gates, and watched to make sure they closed properly.

Marcie shrugged. "Nothing, really. It's just been one of those weekends when everything goes wrong. The coffee grinder broke this morning, so I had to have instant, some animal ate the cover off Rick's baseball card album and I don't know where to get another one just like it, I set my alarm clock wrong, so I had to rush, and Brad's gone on a business trip, and I wanted to ask him about some wedding plans."

"Wedding plans?" George glanced at her. "Whose wedding plans?"

"Mine. I mean . . . ours. Brad and I are getting married."

"You're getting married to *him?*" George's hands tightened so hard on the wheel, his knuckles were white.

"Yes." Marcie gave him a happy smile. Talking about her wedding made her feel much better. "Everything is going to be so perfect, George. I'm staying right here in California, and we'll be a real family. Naturally, we'll keep the house. The school psychologist agrees that the twins need a sense of continuity, and I'd want to keep it anyway. It's a beautiful place to live."

George frowned and took his eyes off the road for a moment to glance at her. "Aren't you . . . rushing into things?"

"I don't think so. And we're not getting married for at least six months. We want to give the twins plenty of time to adjust to the idea."

"Okay." George gave a brief nod. "Have you told the twins yet?"

"Yes. And they said they were happy for me. Of course, they're not as delighted as they will be when they think it over, but they weren't against it. Oh, George! Isn't it wonderful?"

"Yes. It's very exciting for you."

George's hands gripped the wheel even tighter, and Marcie could tell he was upset. "What's the matter, George? Don't you approve?"

"It's not my business to approve or disapprove. I'm just your driver. But Marcie . . . I think it's only fair to tell you that Brad is a suspect in your sister's murder."

"What murder?" Marcie gave a deep sigh. "You're the only one who thinks that Mercedes was murdered. The police still say that it was an accident."

They were nearing the studio, and George pulled out of traffic and parked at the curb. Then he turned to face her. "Look, Marcie. I know I don't have anything concrete, but those threatening letters exist. I didn't make them up out of thin air. And I'm positive your sister was murdered. I want you to be very cautious until I can prove it."

"I *am* being cautious. I've got you to protect me, and I'm living in a house with a state-of-the-art security system. But I refuse to be paranoid, and I think you're going overboard with this suspect list of yours. Brad didn't have anything to do with Mercedes's accident. You know that as well as I do. You only suspect him because he inherited money from her."

"That's true." George nodded. "But don't forget that he had the means, and he had a motive. He had the code to the security system, and he needed money for those thoroughbreds of his. Don't forget that he assumed he'd inherit everything from Mercedes."

"But he didn't. I did!"

"That's right. And now he wants to marry you. Doesn't that strike you as slightly suspicious?"

Marcie glared at him. "No. It doesn't. Brad loves me and I love him. And I refuse to listen to any more!"

"Okay." George nodded. "I won't mention it again. It was my duty to warn you, and I did. But I wish you'd take my warning seriously."

"How can I be serious about that suspect list, when I'm on it myself?" Marcie faced him angrily. "You know that's absolutely ridiculous!"

"Of course, I do. But you did have a motive. And Mercedes might have told you the security code. I can't knock suspects off the list, just because I like them. That isn't good police work."

"But I was in Minnesota! There's no way I could have murdered my sister!"

"Sure there is." George looked very serious. "You could have arranged a hit on Mercedes. Life is cheap. A couple thousand would have done it. And then you waltz out here as the grief-stricken sister."

"How could a murderer be grief-stricken?"

George shrugged. "That wouldn't be difficult. Everyone at the studio says you're an extremely good actress. And after you convince everyone you're truly inconsolable, you inherit everything and marry your sister's husband."

"That's sickening! I loved my sister! How can you even think that I would . . ."

"I don't." George reached out to take her arm. "I don't think for one moment that you did it, Marcie. I'm just showing you the way cops think."

Marcie was silent for a moment, and then she nodded. "You're right, George. Cops *do* think that way. And that's why I wouldn't make a good cop."

"That's probably true. You're very trusting, Marcie. There are times when I wish I could be that trusting. But cops tend to be cynical, and you don't have a cynical bone in your body."

"Well . . . maybe one." Marcie giggled. Her good spirits restored. It was a relief to know that George didn't really suspect her. "My left elbow's been feeling a bit cynical lately."

George laughed, and Marcie could tell that he was relieved. "We're still friends then?"

"Always."

"Good." George put the car in gear and pulled out

from the curb. "I hope you still feel that way when I prove that Mercedes was murdered."

"Of course, I will. Why wouldn't I?"

"I'm afraid you'll be on the suspect list. And so will Brad. The police will come around to ask you a lot of questions."

Marcie shrugged and leaned back in her seat. "We can handle it. And as long as there's no law about two suspects falling in love and getting married, it won't bother us a bit."

Marcie stood in the reception line, dressed in a lovely white bridal gown. Her smile was radiant as she greeted the people who had come to celebrate their wedding day. Her handsome husband stood at her side, his arm possessively around her shoulders. Every once in a while, he gave her shoulder a loving squeeze.

"I'm so glad to meet you." Marcie looked up at her husband's mistress with the eyes of a trusting spaniel. "We're having a little house-warming party when we get back from our honeymoon. I really hope you'll come."

The beautiful redheaded woman looked shocked for a beat, and then she smiled. "Why, thank you! I'd love to. So nice of you to invite me."

"Who was that?" Marcie's mother tapped her on the shoulder. She looked upset as the beautiful redhead made her graceful way through the milling crowd to join the party in the other room.

"Craig's secretary. Isn't she pretty?"

"Yes." Marcie's mother stared off toward the spot where the secretary had disappeared. "Do you know much about her, dear?"

"Not really. But Craig says he can't get along without her. She practically runs his whole office."

"Let's hope that's all she runs."

Marcie turned to look at her mother. "What do you mean, Mom?" She seemed to be a very nice person."

"I'm sure she is, dear. *Very* nice."

Marcie looked into the camera with a slightly puzzled expression. It was clear she didn't understand her mother's implication. There was a beat of silence, and then Dave yelled, "Cut! Very good, Marcie."

"Thanks, Dave." Marcie slipped out from beneath Ashley Thorpe's arm. "Okay, Lee. You can move now."

"Thank God! My arm was starting to cramp. Where did you get that innocent expression? It's incredibly effective."

"Mercedes and I had a cocker spaniel when we were kids, and Cookie always gave us that look when she wanted us to pet her. We always did, so it must have worked."

"Well, it was perfect!" Sandra Shepard patted Marcie on the back. "I really believed you were totally naive, and I wanted to pull you away for a nice, long, mother-daughter talk."

"She's right, Marcie." Dave Allen came up to join them. "Your take is wonderful. I think it's because you're so naturally trusting."

Marcie laughed. "Thanks . . . I think. Do you really think I look that innocent?"

"Absolutely!" Rhea Delaney nodded. "It's all in the hairstyle. Loose and fluffy. So natural it looks like you set it in curlers yourself."

Beau LeTeure shook his head. "The hairstyle's nice, but I made her up to *look* innocent. It's that primrose blusher I put on her cheeks."

"Don't forget the costume." Elena Garvey turned to smile at Marcie. "I designed a beautiful fairy-tale wedding gown. All you have to do is look at her, and you know she thinks she'll live happily ever after."

Marcie looked down at the gown and nodded. "It's gorgeous, Elena. Maybe I should borrow it for my wedding."

"Your wedding?" Dave looked shocked. "You're getting married?"

Marcie nodded. She hadn't meant to break the news of her engagement quite yet, but now the cat was out of the bag.

There was shocked silence on the set for a moment, and then Ashley Thorpe threw his arms around Marcie and gave her a hug. "Congratulations, sweetheart. I knew Sam would get up the nerve to ask you sooner or later."

Marcie winced. Sam again. "It's not Sam. Brad proposed to me on Saturday. And I accepted."

"Well . . . that's great, honey!" Sandra put on a big smile. "When's the happy day?"

"Not for at least six months. We wanted to give the twins time to adjust to the idea."

"That's wise." Elena nodded. "And, of course, you can borrow the gown . . . can't she, Dave?"

Dave smiled. "Naturally. Send it out for cleaning, Elena, and then have it delivered to Marcie's home."

"Are you going to invite us? I didn't get to go to your—" Jolene stopped and looked embarrassed. "I mean . . . I haven't been to a wedding in ages, and I just love weddings!"

Marcie smiled at her. "We haven't really made any plans yet, but, of course, you're all invited. I thought we should keep it small, because of . . . the circumstances and all."

There was another uncomfortable silence, and then everyone began to congratulate Marcie at once. Reuben

Lowe, the head cameraman, came on the set to promise her he'd do a video of her wedding, and Tom Porter climbed down from the catwalk where he was adjusting the lights, to hug her. Dave called Ralph Buchannan, who said he wanted to host an engagement party, and the actress who played the mistress started to make arrangements for a studio bridal shower.

After about five minutes, Ashley Thorpe came up to Marcie and slipped an arm around her shoulders. "Come on, blushing bride. You just promised to love and obey me, so I'm ordering you to come to my trailer to rehearse our next scene."

"Careful, Marcie." Dave Allen laughed. "Don't forget that scene we just shot."

Marcie looked puzzled. "The wedding scene?"

"Right. And we're doing the honeymoon next. I think it's only fair to warn you that Lee's a method actor."

Marcie was still laughing as she stepped inside Lee's trailer, but she quickly sobered when she saw his face. "What's wrong, Lee?"

"Look, Marcie. I know I'm about to jump in where angels fear to tread, but I think you ought to think very carefully about marrying Brad."

"But why?" Marcie felt a sense of dread as she looked up into Lee's unyielding face.

"Sit down." Lee motioned toward the couch. "And then listen carefully. I'm going to tell you something in the strictest confidence. I want you to promise you'll keep my secret."

Marcie sighed. Another secret to keep. But Lee looked so serious, she had to agree. "All right, Lee. I promise. What is it?"

"Your sister and I got to be very good friends on this picture. Do you understand what I mean?"

"I . . . I think so." Marcie clasped her hands in her lap to keep them from trembling. Mercedes had been a beautiful woman. And Lee was a handsome man. They'd been thrown together constantly on long work days, in and out of each other's trailers, rehearsing romantic scenes. "Are you trying to tell me that you and Mercedes had an affair?"

Lee nodded. "That's right. But even more important than that, we were very good friends. And good friends who are also lovers discuss some very personal details."

"But . . . I thought you had a happy marriage."

"I do. I've never had an affair before, and I doubt I'll ever have another. Mercedes was the exception. I love my wife. And I loved Mercedes. She knew that, Marcie, and neither of us had any plans to continue our affair after the picture was over."

"Then why did you . . ." Marcie stopped, unsure of how to phrase her question.

"Because Mercedes was in trouble, and she needed me. Don't get me wrong. I'm not a noble man, and I didn't walk into an affair with your lovely sister for purely altruistic reasons. We had a wonderful time in bed, but that wasn't all we had. I'd like to think I helped Mercedes get through some very trying times in her marriage."

Even though she was upset, Marcie managed to nod calmly. She'd taken enough psychology classes in college to suspect that Lee was rationalizing his affair with Mercedes. Of course, there was no way she'd accuse him of that. What good would it do, now that her sister was dead? If it made him feel less guilty to think he'd helped Mercedes, she'd let him hang on to his delusion.

"You said that Mercedes was in trouble. And then you mentioned trying times. Wasn't Mercedes happy with Brad?"

"No, she wasn't. No one else knew that, Marcie. Your sister was very careful to maintain appearances. She wanted everyone to think that she was content with Brad. I think I was the only person who knew how truly miserable she was."

"But why did she pretend things were fine, when they weren't?"

Lee sighed. "She felt she had to keep up the illusion of a happy marriage for the twins. They hadn't wanted her to marry Brad in the first place, and she didn't want to upset them with a divorce. Part of it was pride. Mercedes didn't want to admit that her marriage had failed. And when I asked, she admitted that the situation wasn't actually *that* bad. Brad didn't abuse her or embarrass her in public. And he was always good to the children."

"What was wrong then?"

"When they were first married, Brad made some bad investments. Mercedes resented the fact that she had to bail him out. She said she was worried about her children's future, if Brad continued to spend money like it was water."

Marcie frowned. "But there was a lot of money left. I know. I inherited it. Why didn't she just tell him he couldn't invest any more of her money?"

"Mercedes hated confrontations. I'm not sure she even mentioned the problem to him."

Marcie nodded. "Then Brad didn't know she was upset?"

"I doubt it. Mercedes hardly saw him, you know. She complained that he was always out of town on business."

Marcie took a moment to digest that information. If

Mercedes had been worried about their finances, she should have discussed it with Brad. Marcie knew her sister had never been very knowledgeable about business. Marcie had always been the one to balance her checkbook when they were in high school, and warn her sister against signing up for something on a time-payment plan. Perhaps Brad had explained his investments to Mercedes, and she hadn't understood that some ventures took longer to pay off than others.

Mercedes's second complaint was legitimate. Brad *did* go out of town quite frequently. But he had a business to run, and he'd explained to Marcie that he never invested in a company unless he'd personally gone over the books and discussed the operating procedures with the management. Had Mercedes expected Brad to spend twenty-four hours a day with her, the way Mike Lang had done?

If that was the case, Mercedes had wanted the impossible. After all, she and Mike had been in the same business. Mercedes had worked in every picture Mike had produced after they married, and they'd been together on the set and then at home. She certainly couldn't have expected Brad to do the same. Could she?

Marcie sighed. That was probably exactly what Mercedes had expected. Even as a child, Mercedes had never been happy unless she'd been the center of attention. Marcie had always been content to step back and let her sister bask in the limelight. It was one of the reasons Marcie was so shy. And obviously Brad hadn't given Mercedes all the attention she'd thought she deserved.

Now, as Marcie considered it, her sister's complaints seemed rather trivial to her. And they were certainly no reason to break up a marriage. She turned to Lee with a frown on her face. "That's all that was wrong?"

Lee looked very uncomfortable. "There's more. Mercedes told me that Brad just wasn't the kind of loving husband she thought he'd be, when she married him."

"I see." Marcie nodded, although she was puzzled. Why had Mercedes lied about Brad? She'd obviously convinced Lee that Brad wasn't a good lover, and Marcie knew from personal experience that it just wasn't true. "And that's why you don't want me to marry Brad?"

"It's not that I don't want you to marry him. I just want you to know exactly what you're getting into."

Marcie sighed and forced a smile. "Thank you, Lee. I appreciate how honest you've been with me. And I'll certainly think about what you've said. Shall we rehearse the scene now? We don't have much time left."

Just then there was a knock on the door. Jolene was here to take them to the set.

"Uh-oh." Lee turned to Marcie with dismay. "Sounds like we don't have *any* time left. Shall I ask Dave for five more minutes?"

"No. I'm ready, if you are." Marcie stood up and followed Lee to the door. He was a nice man, an honest man. But he'd been misled by Mercedes, and he had the wrong opinion of Brad. It wasn't her place to correct that opinion. Not yet. But when she was Brad's wife, she'd make a point of setting the record straight, by letting everyone know what a wonderful man Brad was!

CHAPTER 17

Rosa and Marcie sat in the lounge at the ski lodge, watching the twins take their afternoon lesson from the private instructor Brad had hired for them.

"More coffee, Miss Marcie?" Rosa picked up the silver pot the waiter had left on their table, and prepared to pour.

"I guess so." Marcie frowned as Rosa filled her cup. "It's not as good as yours, though."

Rosa beamed at the compliment. "That's because we have the beans shipped in from a gourmet shop. Mr. Brad orders them special, and . . ." Rosa leaned close to Marcie's ear, ". . . they cost a fortune!"

"Whatever they cost, it's worth it. Your coffee is the best I've ever tasted. Oh, look! Rick is doing much better this afternoon. I think he's almost ready to go down the beginners' slope."

"I knew he'd be good at skiing." Rosa smiled as she watched through the plate glass window. "He's always been more athletic than Trish."

Marcie sighed. "It was the same way with Mercedes and me. When we were in school, she was the athlete, and I was the spectator. I never could hit a ball or run very fast. I was always the last one picked for the girls' softball games."

"Maybe you just didn't bother to learn, because you wanted your sister to be best. Miss Mercedes always said you had plenty of natural abilities you'd never used."

"Well . . . maybe," Marcie conceded. "But being an athlete wasn't one of them."

"You looked fine this morning, when you went out on the slopes with the men. You didn't fall down at all."

Marcie laughed. "That's only because Brad was holding me up on one side, and Jerry was on the other. They wouldn't *let* me fall."

"What do you think of Mr. Jerry? Do you like him?"

Marcie thought it over for a moment, and then she nodded. "Yes, I do. He's been very nice to me, and he's great with the twins. They told me they think he ought to get married and have kids of his own."

"I don't think that's going to happen." Rosa looked very serious. "You know about Mr. Jerry, don't you?"

"Know what?" Marcie looked puzzled.

"Mr. Jerry's not interested in women."

"He's not interested in—?' Marcie stopped as realization dawned. "Oh. I understand. Are you sure?"

"I'm positive. Miss Mercedes said so. The man who did her makeup told her. He saw Mr. Jerry at some kind of meeting."

Marcie nodded. "Beau LeTeure. I guess it's true then. But that doesn't necessarily mean Jerry can't have children. A lot of gay couples are adopting now."

Rosa looked surprised for a moment, and then she nodded. "Why not? All children need is someone to love them. Two gay people who want to be parents are a lot better than a mother and father who don't. Oh, look! They're all going to the beginners' slope."

"Let's just hope that Trish doesn't break something." Marcie gave a sympathetic smile as she spotted her niece. Trish was struggling along gamely, with the instructor on one side of her and his assistant on the other.

Rosa nodded. "I'd better order a pot of hot chocolate. The twins'll be chilled to the bone when they come in. You're right, Miss Marcie."

"About what?"

"Rick takes after his mother, and Trish takes after you. Trish would fall flat on her face if she didn't have two strong men to hold her up."

They'd had dinner at a wonderful little restaurant Jerry had shown them, and then they'd all taken in a movie. The twins had been so tired from the exercise and fresh, crisp air, they'd gone straight to their room the moment they'd come back to the ski lodge. Rosa had stayed in the lounge for one drink, and then she'd gone up to bed, too. Jerry, Marcie, and Brad had lingered over one more hot buttered rum, and then they'd retired to rest up for skiing the next day.

When they were sure that everyone was tucked in for the night, Brad had come to Marcie's room. And they'd spent a wonderful hour together, making love and talking about their future. Marcie sighed happily as she rolled over and nestled her head in the crook of Brad's arm. She could hardly wait until they were married, and they could sleep together without worrying that someone might find out.

"We're going to have a good life. You know that, don't you, Marcie?"

"Mmmm. I do." Marcie kissed his bare chest. "But I'm not sure about those separate bedrooms. I want to sleep with you every night."

Brad laughed. "Then we'll take down the door. Or maybe we'll do some remodeling. Whatever you like."

"I like this." Marcie nuzzled him and traced wet patterns down his chest with her tongue.

"Hey! You'd better stop that, or we'll never get any sleep. I think you have a problem, Marcie. You're insatiable."

"I'm just trying to make up for lost time. What's the matter? Are you tired of me already?"

"Impossible." Brad chuckled and reached out to ruffle her hair. "You might put me in a wheelchair if you keep this up, but I'll never get tired of you."

"Did you get tired of Mercedes?" The moment she'd asked the question, Marcie regretted it. "Forget it, Brad. I really don't want to know."

"Now, why would you ask something like that?" Brad sat up and clicked on the bedside lamp.

"I'm sorry. I shouldn't have mentioned it. It's just . . . never mind."

Brad looked very serious. "No, Marcie. I want to know why you asked me that question. You have to trust me enough to tell me if something's bothering you."

"I just . . . well . . . I heard a rumor at the studio. I know I shouldn't believe rumors, but . . ."

"What was it?"

Marcie sighed deeply. She'd opened a can of worms, and now she had to tell him. "Someone told me that you and Mercedes were having problems with your marriage."

"Well, it wasn't all roses, but we loved each other, and we were working things out. What did you hear?"

"That Mercedes was worried about the way you were handling her investments."

Brad nodded. "That's true. Mercedes didn't have a head for business. She thought everything should pay off right away. And she wanted me to put all her money in something safe, like municipal bonds."

"It's a good thing she didn't ask you to invest in the city of New York!"

"Precisely!" Brad laughed and patted her again. "But the New York situation was unusual, Marcie. Generally speaking, munis are very safe investments."

Marcie nodded. "They're safe, but they don't yield very much."

"True. And that's exactly what I told Mercedes. I suggested a mixed portfolio. She had a base of munis, just to be on the safe side, some medium-yield stocks to bring in a higher rate, and a small portion of high-risk ventures that we hoped would pay off."

"That sounds reasonable." Marcie smiled at him. "Of course, I don't know that much about investments, but that's what I'd want."

"It worked out great the first year. The risks really paid off, and she made a bundle. But then the interest rates started to drop, and she got worried. She wanted me to sell off all her high-risk stocks and reinvest the cash in Certified Deposits."

"Certified Deposits?" Marcie looked puzzled. "But why did she want to do that? She still had a safe base of munis, didn't she?"

Brad nodded. "You bet! I explained that CD's were

at an all-time low, and it would be foolish to buy them right then. But she panicked. And we fought over it."

"Who won?"

Brad sighed. "We both lost. She agreed I could keep the thoroughbreds, since they were a long-term investment, and we couldn't get out without taking a loss. The same for the antique cars. It costs a lot to store them properly, but they're bound to go up in value, if I hang on for a couple of years. But she insisted I sell off all her high-computer stocks at a loss. That was four months before they split and went through the roof."

"Oh, no!" Marcie groaned. "I think I understand now, Brad. Mercedes always was a little paranoid about money. She didn't feel safe unless it was stuck in a savings account. And I know that's not the way to make money."

"Good girl. You sound knowledgeable enough to put together your own portfolio."

"Oh, no!" Marcie shook her head. "I'm sure I'd make some awful mistakes. You'll handle it for me, won't you?"

"Of course . . . if you're sure you want me to."

Marcie turned to kiss him. "I do. I trust you completely, Brad. I just wish my sister had trusted you more."

"So do I." Brad sighed. "Is that the only thing you heard, Marcie? That Mercedes and I fought about money?"

"Well . . . I did hear something else. But I'm sure it's just idle gossip."

"Look, Marcie . . . I don't want anything you heard bothering you. Let's talk about it right now."

Marcie sighed, and then she repeated what Lee had told her. "Mercedes resented the fact that you had to go out of town on business so often. She felt you were ignoring her."

"That *was* a big problem." Brad slipped his arm around Marcie again, and gave her a little hug. "She never really understood how I operate my business. I don't think it's fair to advise anyone to invest in a company unless I personally check it out."

"That's a very sound business practice. Didn't Mercedes understand that?"

"No. We made a big mistake, Marcie. We should have talked about how often I'd be gone *before* we were married. When Mercedes asked me to stop traveling, I told her I couldn't do that. I promised to cut my business trips down to a minimum, and I did. But that wasn't enough for Mercedes. She asked me to give up my business so I could stay at home with her."

"But you couldn't do that?"

Brad shook his head. "I really couldn't. You have to understand the situation from my point of view, Marcie. I was doing well, bringing money into our family. If I'd given up my business, I would have been nothing but a gigolo, living off Mercedes's earnings."

"Of course." Marcie nodded. "I understand perfectly. I don't like the fact that you'll be gone so often, either. But I'll never ask you to give up your business."

Brad pulled Marcie into his arms and kissed her. "You're wonderful, Marcie. And I promise I won't travel any more than I absolutely have to. What else did you hear? I have the feeling you're saving the worst for last."

"You're right. There's one other thing, and I really have no right to ask you. But I heard that you weren't sleeping with Mercedes anymore."

"I'm afraid that's true." Brad looked very embarrassed. "Mercedes just wasn't interested in sex the last few months. She told me it was the movie, that she was too exhausted to do anything but study her lines and sleep, when she got home from the studio. And she promised me that things would change as soon as the picture wrapped, that we'd go away for a romantic vacation and rekindle the fires."

Marcie winced. After the picture wrapped. That was the time limit Mercedes had set on her affair with Lee. She hated to ask but she had to know. "Do you think she . . . uh . . . had someone else?"

"No. I'm almost certain she didn't. Mercedes always went through a real upheaval when she worked on a film. And her part in *Summer Heat* was emotionally exhausting. I'm sure she was telling me the truth, that she honestly didn't have any extra energy to spare. That's why I'm hoping you decide not to do another picture. I want you to have plenty of time and energy for us."

"Then I'll turn down Dave's offer." Marcie snuggled close to him. "Being with you is much more important than being a movie star."

As Brad lowered his head to kiss her, Marcie made up her mind. Lee would never tell anyone about his affair. And Mercedes had taken her secret with her to the grave. Sometimes you had to be strong enough to protect the person you loved from things that would hurt them needlessly. And because she loved Brad with all her heart, Mercedes's secret was safe with her.

Jerry woke up as he heard a soft tap on his door. He sat up in bed to switch on the light, and then he hurried to open it. His lover had promised to come, but he'd broken similar promises in the past.

"Is it too late for you? Or shall I come in?"

"It's never too late." Jerry felt the color rise to his

cheeks. He always blushed like a schoolboy when he was aroused. "Come in. Would you like a drink?"

"No. What I'd like is you."

Strong arms reached out to surround him. Firm lips pressed against his. Jerry felt the blood pound through his veins, as his heart raced faster and faster. It had been a long time since they'd been together. Too long for any social niceties, like *I love you,* or even *I've missed you.* They were too greedy, and the fierce hunger they shared had to be satisfied.

And then they were on the bed, clothes strewn carelessly on the chair, on the rug, tossed wildly in a corner. And their bodies were welded to each other with mutual longing, tongues licking, lips pressing here and there and everywhere to give the most pleasure, knowing each other's bodies as well as they knew their own.

"Now?" Jerry's voice trembled.

"Now."

"Do you want—?"

"No. I know you haven't been with anyone except me."

There was pain. Jerry muffled his startled cry in the depths of his pillow. And then there was the blinding pleasure that drove all conscious thought from his mind. He'd yearned for this feeling, every nerve end pulsing, every cell crying out for the glorious release.

But then it changed, slowly at first, so subtly he had no warning. Harder. Rougher. Until the pleasure faded, and he cried out for it to be finished. This was more like a rape than a loving encounter. What had happened since the last time they'd been together? And why was his lover punishing him? He didn't dare to ask. He'd seen his lover fly into a rage before, and that was something he didn't want to experience again.

Jerry buried his head in the pillow and endured his

punishment. If he objected, he could be risking another long separation. His lover might even decide never to meet him like this again.

At last it was over, and his lover kissed him gently, sweetly. "Sorry, Jer. I guess I got a little carried away. It's been so long."

"Yes." Jerry nodded gratefully, basking in the kindness. "I know what you mean."

But later, after his lover had left, and he'd bathed his bruised body, and had a stiff shot of brandy, Jerry wondered if love was worth this kind of pain. Wouldn't it be better to find someone new, someone who really cared about him as a person? He was nothing more than a whipping boy, a pawn for his lover's games. There was a nice man he'd met at one of the meetings. Beau LeTeure. He'd been Mercedes's makeup man. Beau was handsome, and he was kind. And he'd just broken up with the man he'd lived with for ten years. Beau liked Jerry, and they were on the same wavelength. His lover had abused him, too.

A billboard T-shirt he'd seen in a shop in Westwood suddenly flashed through his mind. It had read *MY NEXT LOVER WILL BE NORMAL*. It would be wonderful having a normal lover.

Jerry pulled the covers up to his chin and stared up at the dark ceiling. He knew he should break off this relationship, but he couldn't seem to gather the strength. It would be like killing off part of himself, a vital part of his history. They'd been together for too many years to separate now.

Marcie limped into the lounge and sank down in a chair. To her chagrin, she'd twisted her ankle on the beginners' slope. Two paramedics had taped it and carried her down the slope on a stretcher. Her injury wasn't terribly painful, but everyone had stared at her, and it had been a very embarrassing experience.

"Marcie!" A familiar voice called out from the bar. "What are *you* doing here?"

"Sam? What are *you* doing here?"

"You first." Sam smiled as he carried his drink over to her table. Then he saw the tape on her ankle, and his smile changed to a frown. "Are you badly hurt?"

Marcie laughed. "The only thing that's badly hurt is my pride. It's just a slightly sprained ankle, Sam. I was showing off for the twins, and I fell down the slope."

"That answers part of my initial question. You're here with Trish and Rick?"

"Yes. And Rosa, and Brad, and Jerry Palmer. It's a birthday skiing trip for the twins. But what brings you to Aspen? I didn't know you skied."

"I don't. I'm here on business. One of my clients owns this ski lodge, and I'm up here a couple of times a year."

"Mr. Sam!" Rosa bustled up to the table. "My goodness! This is a real family gathering!"

"It certainly is. Can I get you girls a drink?"

Rosa shook her head. "Not for me, Mr. Sam. I just came in to check on Miss Marcie, but now that you're here, I won't worry. I promised the twins I'd come right back out and watch them practice their turns."

"Nice outfit." Sam grinned as Rosa hurried back out the door. "Where in the world did she get a yellow parka with purple and blue flowers on it?"

"The ski shop at the mall. We all went shopping together, and she picked it out. She said it reminded her of a blanket someone sent her from the old country."

Sam laughed. "That pattern wouldn't be bad on a blanket, especially if you covered it up with a bedspread.

How about a hot buttered rum, Marcie? They're very good here."

"I really don't think I'd better . . ." Marcie stopped and reconsidered. She wasn't going back out on the slopes. The paramedics had told her to stay off her ankle for the entire afternoon. "On second thought, that sounds lovely, Sam. If you've got time, we can watch the twins from the window."

Sam nodded. "I've got time. I'm here until tomorrow evening. And now that I know you're here, I hope you'll all join me for dinner. There's an excellent Yugoslavian place about a mile from here. The owner's another client."

"You have two clients in Aspen?" Marcie was surprised. Aspen was a long way from Los Angeles.

"I have ten clients in Aspen. I used to live here before I moved to California. Excuse me, Marcie. I'll be right back with our drinks."

Marcie watched as Sam walked toward the bar. It was a strange coincidence, running into Sam in Aspen. But it was a nice coincidence, especially since she couldn't go back to join everyone else outside. She was glad Sam was here. Now she'd have someone to talk to while the others skied.

Sam was back in a moment, holding two steaming cups. "Here you are, Marcie. The specialty of the house."

"Thank you." Marcie took her cup and set it down on the table. Then she smiled at him. ""I'm really glad you're here, Sam."

Sam smiled back as he sat down across from her. "So am I, Marcie. You'll join me for dinner, then?"

"Well . . ." Marcie frowned as she glanced down at her ankle. "I'm willing, but you may have to carry me."

Sam stood up and bowed. "My pleasure."

Before she could do more than gasp, Sam scooped

her up in his arms and was carrying her to the window so they could watch the slopes. Marcie was slightly embarrassed. People were staring at them. But she had to admit that being in Sam's arms made her feel comfortable and safe.

"Miss Marcie?" Rosa came rushing in. "The twins want us to watch them . . . oh my!"

Marcie felt a blush rise to her cheeks, and she tried to act as if being in Sam's arms was the most natural thing in the world. "Yes, Rosa? The twins want us to watch them do something?"

"Uh . . . yes. They're going to ski right past the window and practice their turns."

Marcie frowned as Rosa turned on her heel and started for the door. "Rosa? Where are you going?"

"Outside." Rosa gave her a big smile. "You don't need me, Miss Marcie. You're in good hands now."

He caught a glimpse of her face, radiant as she watched the children. For one brief moment, he experienced a pang of horrible jealousy. He wanted to be there at her side, to have her turn and look up at him with the same trusting love and blind devotion. But then he decided that such emotion was entirely unsuitable for a man in his position. He knew he couldn't have her, not really, and certainly not in the way he dreamed. It was clearly impossible.

He spotted the housekeeper near a pine tree by the edge of the slopes, watching the children. She was a good woman, an excellent caretaker for the family. And his love was a perfect mother. Perhaps that was why she wanted to marry the husband, to form another complete family. Mother, father, two children, and housekeeper. It was neat and tidy, the perfect family circle. But the family that she dreamed of would be fatally flawed with the husband at its head.

He wished that there were some way to tell her, to appear at her side and warn her of the folly of marrying the husband. But he could not risk exposure. He'd risked enough by leaving his sanctuary to come here to Aspen.

He took one last look at her beautiful face, and then he forced himself to turn away. He could do nothing but pray that she would recognize the danger without his guiding hand. There was still time for her to escape the horrible fate that clearly awaited her, a fate that would be administered by his hand. The last thing he desired was to hurt her, but the battle of the red had definite rules. He could resist, and he could delay the inevitable. But eventually he would have to obey.

CHAPTER 18

A week had passed since their skiing trip, and Brad was gone again. This time he had meetings in Chicago that would last for five days.

Marcie had spent a restless night. Things weren't the same when Brad wasn't home. Just knowing that he was next door, behind the connecting door, made her feel safe and loved.

She had slept late, and she was just getting dressed when Rosa knocked on the door. "Miss Marcie? The head gardener's here, and he says the crew can't start unless you give him the money for last month."

"Last month?" Marcie frowned as she slipped into a pair of jeans, and searched through the closet for a suitable blouse. "Brad's handling all the household accounts, just like he did for Mercedes. Didn't he pay the gardening bill?"

"I don't think so, Miss Marcie. At least, he didn't ask me to mail any checks."

Marcie sighed. Since Brad was gone, she'd have to deal with it. Perhaps he'd just been too busy to make out the checks.

"All right, Rosa. Give the head gardener a cup of . . ."

Marcie stopped in mid-sentence, remembering Brad's caution about inviting people inside the house. "Do you know him? I mean, personally?"

"Not personally, Miss Marcie, but he's been working for us for over six years."

"Okay. Invite him in for a cup of coffee, and tell him I'm just getting dressed, and I'll be down in a minute."

Marcie pulled out a red blouse and was just preparing to put it on, when a line from one of the threatening letters flashed through her mind. *Red is the color of blood.* No one had heard from the crazy fan since Mercedes had died, but Marcie put it back on the hanger and pushed it to the very back of the closet. She'd wear the green blouse with the white collar. Everyone seemed sure that the crazy fan was gone, but she was still nervous about wearing red.

The head gardener was sitting at the table chatting with Rosa about his grandchildren when Marcie came down. He was an older Japanese man, and he seemed very nice when Rosa introduced them.

"Please sit down and finish your coffee." Marcie smiled at him. "I'm sorry you didn't get paid last month. My fiancé takes care of all the bills, and he's out of town on business right now. If you wait just a moment, I'll get the checkbook and write you a check."

The gardener looked very distressed as he shook his head. "I'm sorry, but I can't take a check, Miss Calder."

"Why not? Isn't that how we usually pay?"

"Yes." The gardener nodded. "But the bank returned your last check. They said there were insufficient funds."

Marcie frowned. "Oh, dear! I guess I'd better have a talk with the bank. I do have some cash, though. How much is the bill?"

The gardener handed her the bill, and Marcie

frowned. She had enough cash to pay it, but that would leave her with very little money, and Brad would be gone until the end of the week. Unfortunately, she had no choice. The gardening had to be done, and that meant the bill had to be paid. When Brad got back, she'd have a talk with him about putting more money in the household account, so something like this wouldn't happen again.

"Thank you, Miss Calder." The gardener was all smiles as she counted out the cash. "I'll tell my men to start now."

After the gardener had left, Marcie sank down in a chair. "I think I need some coffee. And then I'd better call the bank."

Rosa placed a cup of coffee and a tray of croissants on the table. "Here, Miss Marcie. Why don't you have some breakfast? And then you can go down to the bank and straighten everything out. That's what Miss Mercedes always did."

"This has happened before?"

"Oh, yes. It used to drive Miss Mercedes crazy when Mr. Brad didn't pay the bills. Everyone called her, and she didn't want to be bothered."

"All right then." Marcie nodded. "I'll go down to the bank right after I finish my breakfast. I need to get more cash anyway. And while I'm down there, it might be a good idea to transfer some funds and open another account in my name."

Marcie smiled as she got out of the Mercedes and turned it over to the valet parker. Valet service at the bank! She could imagine what her friends in Minnesota would say if she told them about this!

Since Marcie had signed authorization cards in Sam's office, there had been no need to actually go into the bank. Marcie assumed she'd have to show identification and introduce herself, but the young man who greeted her at the door seemed to know who she was.

"Miss Calder. How nice to see you! Please follow me."

Marcie was surprised as he led her through the bank. There were no lines and no tellers, just a beautifully decorated waiting room with leather chairs and tables for writing.

"Could I get you some coffee?"

Marcie nodded. "Yes. That would be wonderful. But I need to talk to someone about my accounts."

"Of course." The young man smiled. "Please have a seat, and I'll bring you your coffee. And then I'll come to get you as soon as one of our account executives is free."

A moment later, Marcie was sipping excellent coffee from a china cup. She could hardly wait to call Shirley Whitford and tell her how they did banking in Southern California! Coffee, leather chairs, and account executives. There were even telephones on every table, and she noticed a copier and several computers attached to a printer at a large workstation against the wall.

A few minutes passed as Marcie admired her surroundings. Then the young man came back into the room and motioned to her. "Please follow me, Miss Calder. Mrs. Marcusso is available now."

Marcie smiled as the young man led her to a door. He opened it and motioned her inside. An older woman in a business suit waited behind a desk. A small gold sign on the desk identified her as Adrienne Marcusso.

Mrs. Marcusso stood up as Marcie entered. "I'm

glad to meet you, Miss Calder. Please make yourself comfortable."

Marcie sat down in another leather chair in front of the desk, and pulled out her checkbook. "Thank you. This is a beautiful bank. I've never seen anything like it."

"It's lovely, isn't it?" Mrs. Marcusso smiled. "Let's see . . . you're from Minnesota, aren't you?"

"Why, yes! How did you know?"

"Mr. Abrams mentioned it when he brought us your signature cards. It's nice of you to drop by to see us, Miss Calder. We like to know all of our clients personally."

Marcie nodded. "You knew my sister?"

"Yes, I did. We were very sorry to hear about her accident." Mrs. Marcusso gave her a sympathetic smile. "Which account balance would you like to examine first?"

Marcie handed over her checkbook. "This one, I guess. The gardener mentioned that there was a problem with a check we sent him last month."

"I'll have the balance in just a moment." Mrs. Marcusso typed a series of numbers on a computer keyboard. Then she jotted down a figure on a piece of paper and handed it to Marcie.

Marcie was shocked as she read the figure. "There's only three hundred dollars in this account?"

"Yes. There was a substantial withdrawal last Friday. You'll find that figure at the bottom of the paper."

"Oh." Marcie frowned slightly as she glanced at the paper. Brad had withdrawn five thousand dollars.

"There's really no problem, Miss Calder." Mrs. Marcusso smiled at her. "One of your sister's treasury bonds just came due, and we'll be happy to transfer the funds to this account."

"You can do that?"

"Of course. We've done that many times in the past. Shall I make the transaction for you?"

Marcie frowned. "I'm not sure. I think I'd better check with Mr. Abrams. I wouldn't want to do anything that could cause a problem later."

"That's always wise." Mrs. Marcusso smiled. "Would you like me to get him on the phone for you?"

Marcie looked surprised. "That would be nice, but I can call him from the other room. I don't want to take up too much of your time."

"That's no problem, Miss Calder. That's why we're here, to serve all your banking needs. I'll place the call, and then I'll make a trip to the main computer area to get a printout of all your account balances."

Mrs. Marcusso picked up the phone and dialed. She obviously knew Sam's number, because she had his secretary on the phone almost immediately. "This is Mrs. Marcusso from Trans-World Mercantile. Miss Calder is here with me, and she'd like to speak to Mr. Abrams on a matter of some urgency. Yes, certainly we'll hold."

Marcie took the phone and smiled at Mrs. Marcusso. "Thank you."

"I'll get those printouts now. Just press the buzzer on my desk if you need me."

It took only a moment, and Sam came on the line. "Marcie? What's wrong?"

"I'm not sure if there's anything wrong. But you told me to check with you before I made any decisions. Mrs. Marcusso says one of Mercedes's treasury bonds just came due. Should I ask her to transfer the money to the household account?"

"Not unless the balance is low. That's not an inter-est-bearing account."

"It's very low." Marcie frowned as she glanced at

the paper again. "The balance is only three hundred dollars, and I had to use all my cash to pay the gardener before he'd start work. He wouldn't take a check, because the last one bounced."

"That's odd. There was a balance of over twelve thousand dollars in that account when I had you sign the signature card."

"That's what I thought." Marcie's frown deepened. "Our bills must have been enormous."

"Have you made any large withdrawals?"

"No. But Brad took out five thousand before he left on his business trip."

There was a long silence, and then Sam spoke again. "I'll drive right over. Don't do anything until I get there, Marcie. I want to check all the withdrawals before we transfer any funds."

"Thanks, Sam. I'll wait for you."

Marcie hung up the phone and pressed the buzzer for Mrs. Marcusso. If Rosa was right and Brad hadn't paid the bills, where had the money gone? She wished she could ask Brad, but he wouldn't call her until tomorrow evening, and he hadn't mentioned the name of his hotel. There was probably a very simple explanation, but she had no idea what it was. Thank goodness Sam was coming down to help her straighten everything out!

Marcie was still frowning as she drove back to the house. What Sam had discovered at the bank wasn't good news. During the past month, sixty thousand dollars had been transferred to the joint household account, and now there was only three hundred left. Marcie had followed Sam's advice and taken her name off the joint account. Then she'd opened another account in her name. No more treasury bills could be transferred without her approval, but that still didn't solve the mystery of where the money had gone. Marcie was sure that Brad had used it to pay some of Mercedes's bills, and Sam had agreed to meet her back at the house to go over the household ledger.

When Marcie pulled up the driveway, she spotted Sam's car parked near the palm tree by the front door. The problem must be serious. He certainly hadn't wasted any time getting here!

"What's the matter, Miss Marcie?" Rosa looked worried when Marcie came into the house. "You're as white as a sheet!"

Marcie gave her a reassuring smile. There was no sense in upsetting Rosa. "It's just a little banking problem. Where's Sam?"

"In the den. I fixed a tray of sandwiches. He said you'd be working through lunch. And George Williams called. He said he'd be joining you."

"George is coming here?" Marcie was puzzled.

"Yes. Mr. Sam said he called him from his car phone, and I'm supposed to buzz him in when he gets here. I fixed enough lunch for all three of you."

"Thank you, Rosa." Marcie drew a deep breath. "I guess I'd better get in there and help Sam with the books."

When Marcie opened the door to the den, Sam was sitting behind the desk, going through a ledger. He looked up and smiled. "Hi, Marcie. Is this the only household ledger?"

"I think so." Marcie frowned slightly. "I know that's the one Brad uses. I've seen him writing in it."

"And you keep the unpaid bills here?" Sam motioned toward one of the pigeonholes in the desk.

"Yes. If a bill comes in the mail, I stick it in there.

Then Brad writes the total in the ledger, and pays it at the beginning of the month."

"Brad writes all the checks?"

Marcie nodded. "I asked him to keep on doing it. He paid all the bills for Mercedes, and he promised me he'd take care of everything after we were married. It seemed silly to switch back and forth for such a short time."

"Of course. A perfectly rational decision, under the circumstances. But the bills haven't been paid this month."

"Are you sure?" Marcie glanced at the ledger. All the amounts were written in next to the creditors' names.

"Look at this." Sam flipped back to the previous month and showed her the little green check marks after the amounts. "When Brad paid a bill, he checked it off. These are paid."

Marcie frowned as Sam turned the page to the current month. "There aren't any check marks."

"Right. That means he didn't pay them." Sam patted the stack of bank statements on the corner of the desk. "If he'd written the checks on the first of the month, some of them would have cleared by now."

Marcie nodded. "But there may have been other bills that aren't in the ledger. These are just running expenses, like the power bill, and the telephone, and things like that."

"True. That's why I'm looking for another ledger, or even a check register. Do you know if Brad took his checkbook with him?"

"If it's not in his center desk drawer, he did. That's where he keeps it."

Sam pulled open the drawer, but there was no checkbook inside. "Can you think of any large expense you may have had last month? A one-time expenditure, like a decorator, or a big repair, or a catered party?"

"No. Nothing like that." Marcie shook her head. "Sam? Why did you ask George to join us?"

"He asked me to notify him if I discovered anything unusual about Mercedes's estate, and a withdrawal of over fifty-nine thousand dollars in less than two months is definitely unusual."

"I guess it is." Marcie sighed. "Fifty-nine thousand dollars is a lot of money, Sam. It's my yearly salary as a teacher! But I'm sure there's an explanation. Brad must have used it to pay off a very large bill."

"Perhaps." Sam didn't look convinced. "You have the number of the hotel where Brad's staying, don't you?"

Marcie shook her head. "He said he'd call me tomorrow night, and I have no idea which hotel he's using. I'm afraid our questions will have to wait until then."

There was a knock at the door, and George came in. He looked very grim. "Hello, Marcie. Sam."

"Hi, George." Marcie put on a smile even though she was upset. "Coffee?"

"I'll get it." George went over to the tray on the credenza and poured himself a cup. Then he pulled up a chair to the desk and sat down. "Did you find anything yet?"

Sam shook his head. "Nothing. And Brad won't call in until tomorrow night."

"Okay." George nodded, and then he turned to Marcie. "Are the twins home?"

"No. They're spending the day with friends, but Rosa's going to pick them up before dinner. We were planning on going out for pizza."

"Good idea." George nodded. "I think Sam and I should take you and the twins to Anna's."

Marcie smiled. "That would be nice. Where's Anna's?"

"It's on Pico, a block past the Westwood Mall. Anna's has the best pizza in town, and it's also a very good place to have a private conversation. I need to ask the twins some questions."

Marcie began to feel nervous as she stared at George. He looked very serious. "Questions about what?"

"About Brad. And about his relationship with their mother. I have a hunch the twins know much more than they're telling us."

CHAPTER 19

Marcie had to admit that Anna's was a fine Italian restaurant. It was everything that George had promised. The pizza was superb. She'd tasted a piece of the twins' pizza and found it delicious. And she'd certainly enjoyed the gorgonzola and pasta dish the owner had prepared for her at tableside. If George hadn't been planning to ask the twins questions, she would have thoroughly enjoyed their meal. But she knew that George's probing might be painful, and she couldn't help being terribly anxious.

"How about some chocolate gelato for dessert?" George turned to the twins. "Or some of those little pastries brushed with apricot?"

"Could we have some of each?" Rick spoke up. "That way we could split."

George nodded and gave their order to the waiter. "And while we're waiting, I'm working on a case and I need to ask you guys some questions."

"A murder case?" Rick's eyes widened as George nodded. "Wow! Trish and I watch every single . . ."

". . . detective show on television." Trish finished the sentence for him. "And we always know . . ."

". . . the murderer before the detective does." Rick nodded.

"That's what I was counting on." George smiled at them. "But this case is very unusual. We're not even sure it was a murder."

Rick nodded. "I bet it looked like an accident. That's the way they do it on television. But there's always a smart cop that gets . . ."

". . . suspicious and figures it out." Trish smiled. "Give us the facts, George. We'll help you."

George looked very serious. "You'll have to try to be very impartial. You see, this case involves your mother."

"You think Mom was murdered?" Rick's eyebrows shot up.

"Maybe. What's your opinion?"

"I think she was." Trish frowned slightly. "I don't believe she just drowned. Mom was a *great* swimmer."

George smiled. "Precisely. Now what do they do on television, when they think it's murder but they can't prove it?"

"They look for evidence." Rick jumped in. "And if they can't find any, they look for someone with a motive."

"A good motive," Trish added. "You want us to think of who had a motive to kill Mom, right?"

"That's right."

The twins were silent for a moment, and then they both spoke at once. "Brad."

"He had a motive," Rick said.

"And he could get in the gates," Trish offered. "We had the combination, but we were out with Rosa. That means we're not suspects because . . ."

". . . we have an airtight alibi." Rick grinned. "So

does Rosa, since she was with us. And Aunt Marcie was . . ."

". . . back at her apartment in Minnesota." Both twins finished up at once.

Just then the waiter arrived with their desserts. Marcie picked up her fork; her ricotta cheesecake looked delicious, but she couldn't eat it now. She waited until the waiter had poured their coffee and left, and then she objected. "You're all forgetting that Brad had an alibi. He was with the horse trainer, and then he went to the track."

"That's not a very good alibi." Rick corrected her. "He could have slipped away from the track without anyone noticing. And then he could have come back afterward."

Trish nodded. "He could have picked up some of those betting tickets from the ground, to prove he was there. You remember what happened when we were there, Aunt Marcie. If people lose they just throw them away."

"Very good!" George gave Marcie a look that made her resume her silence. Then he turned to smile at the twins. "But do you really think Brad had a motive?"

Rick's eyes narrowed. "Sure, he did. He needed Mom's money. And Mom was getting ready to cut him off."

"How do you know that?" This time Sam broke in. "Did you overhear something?"

Rick and Trish exchanged guilty glances. Then Rick spoke up. "Uh . . . not exactly. We got it from . . ."

". . . another source." Trish looked very nervous. "A confidential source."

George raised his eyebrows. "Can you tell us who it

is? I won't question your source unless it's absolutely necessary."

"You can't." Trish looked very upset. "You see, our source is . . . well . . . it's . . ."

". . . it's Mom." Rick frowned.

George nodded. "She told you that?"

Rick and Trish exchanged glances again. Then Rick spoke. "In a way, she did. You see she . . . uh . . ."

"You might as well tell them." Trish sighed deeply. "George is a smart cop. He's going to find out anyway."

Rick nodded. "I guess so. Mom kept a diary. And we took it out of her room after she died, because we . . ."

". . . didn't want Brad to read it." Trish swallowed hard. "Did we do something wrong?"

George shook his head. "You didn't do anything wrong at all. Your mother's diary was private. Brad had no right to read it."

"I guess you're right." Rick sighed in relief. "But *we* didn't have the right to read it, either."

Trish nodded. "You see, we never would have done it while Mom was alive. We knew it was private. But after she died, we just . . . well . . ."

"We got curious, that's all." Rick finished the difficult sentence for his sister. "Maybe we shouldn't have read it, but we did. And Mom wrote some not very nice stuff about Brad."

George nodded. "It could be important to my investigation. Would you mind if we had a look at it?"

The twins exchanged glances again, and then they nodded. Marcie noticed they looked very relieved.

"I think you *should* read it." Rick gave a deep sigh. "Right, Trish?"

"Me, too. If Mom was murdered, you should catch Brad and put him in jail."

Marcie bit her lip to keep from blurting out what

she was thinking. She didn't want George or Sam to read Mercedes's diary. But perhaps that was foolish. She still didn't believe that her sister had been murdered. There was certainly no proof to substantiate it. But if George's hunch was right, and Mercedes had actually been murdered, she wanted her sister's killer apprehended and brought to trial. Of course, there was no way that Brad was involved. She knew the man who had made such gentle and passionate love to her could never be a cold-blooded killer. The thought was ridiculous! But her sister's diary might contain a clue to the real culprit.

"Any objections, Marcie?" Sam turned to her. "Legally speaking, the diary belongs to you."

Marcie shook her head. "If the twins agree that you should read it, I don't have any objections."

The twins nodded soberly and Sam smiled at them. "It's settled then. And now we can get down to the serious business of eating our desserts."

Marcie picked up her fork again and tried the cheesecake. It was every bit as delicious as it looked. Now that she thought about it, she was almost as relieved as the twins. Mercedes's diary might contain a reference to the missing money, a big expense her sister had incurred right before her death, or a charitable donation she'd asked Brad to make. It was possible they could solve the mystery tonight, and then she wouldn't be in the awkward position of having to ask Brad about it when he called.

They were all in the den with a fresh pot of coffee, when Rick and Trish came in.

"Here it is." Rick handed them the diary. "You won't tell anyone what's in it, will you?"

Marcie hugged them both. "Of course not. We'll make sure to protect your mother's privacy."

"You won't tell Brad, will you, Aunt Marcie?" Trish still looked very anxious.

"No, I won't tell him." Marcie promised. "Your mother's secrets are safe with us."

"Rosa's going to let us watch a movie." Rick spoke up. "She went to the store and got our favorite monster movie. It's called . . ."

". . . *Creature from the Black Lagoon*." Trish gave Marcie a radiant smile.

Marcie looked worried. "But won't that scare you, right before bedtime?"

"Oh, it doesn't scare us." Rick laughed. "They're just movie monsters. And if you look real close at the monster . . ."

". . . you can see the zipper down its back!" Trish chimed in. "Rosa puts the picture on stop frame, so we can see it better."

Marcie laughed. "Okay. I'll see you in the morning, guys. And don't forget . . . tomorrow we're going to the zoo."

"Right." Trish nodded. "Aunt Marcie? We wanted to tell you not to get upset over some of the stuff Mom wrote about you."

"Like what?" Marcie did her best to maintain a neutral expression.

Rick looked embarrassed. "Oh, she mentioned something about how you dressed."

"You mean like a middle-aged schoolteacher?"

Trish burst into giggles. "Actually, the word she used was *frump*. But you look much prettier, now that you're not a schoolteacher anymore."

"Thank you . . . I think." Marcie laughed, and the twins hurried away to watch their monster movie. Then she turned to George and Sam. "Would either of you like some brandy with your coffee? After that warning, I might need some."

Sam got up to get the brandy bottle and poured Marcie a shot. Then he sat down next to her, slipped a casual arm around her shoulder, and they began to read Mercedes's most intimate thoughts.

It was long past midnight before they were finished. When Sam closed the diary and leaned back on the couch, Marcie picked up the brandy snifter, took the last swallow, and gave a deep sigh. Her sister had only written a couple of short paragraphs every evening, but her diary spanned two years. It was a record of her marriage to Brad, and the portrait she had painted of her husband wasn't very flattering.

"Are you all right, Marcie?" Sam turned to her with a worried look.

Marcie nodded. "I'm fine. I'm just sorry she was so unhappy. Brad told me they were having problems with their marriage, but I had no idea it was this bad."

"It might not have been." Sam slipped his arm around her shoulders again, and gave her a little squeeze. "Mercedes never expected anyone to read her diary, and we're getting a very one-sided picture. Don't forget that she wrote about the things that were *bothering* her, not the good things."

Marcie smiled at him. Sam was very understanding. "Thanks, Sam. And you're right. If anyone read my diary, they'd be convinced I was a terribly unhappy person. And I'm not."

George nodded. "Very true. And we have to take that into account. I jotted down the important things we learned. Do you want me to read you my notes?"

"Yes." Marcie and Sam spoke at once, and Marcie gave a relieved laugh. "We sound like the twins, and we're not even related. Go ahead, George. It's hard for me to be objective, but I'd like to know what you think is important."

George glanced down at his notebook. "She was worried that Brad was having an affair. That may or may not be true. And she didn't request separate bedrooms, as she told Marcie. That was Brad's idea."

"Which may or may not be true," Marcie pointed out. "Brad *told* me it was her idea."

Sam nodded. "It doesn't really matter whose idea it was. The point is, they both told different stories about it. Someone is lying."

"Maybe not." George shrugged. "It may have turned out to be a mutual decision. Perhaps Brad mentioned it first, and Mercedes thought she had to agree. So she blamed him for suggesting it."

Marcie jumped in. "Or vice versa. Mercedes may have mentioned it, and Brad agreed. Is that really important?"

"Only because it establishes a pattern of poor communication. Mercedes was sure that Brad was no longer interested in her as a woman. And Marcie told us Brad thought Mercedes was no longer interested in him as a man. They were obviously growing apart, becoming indifferent to each other."

There was a long silence, and Marcie sighed. "I guess you're right."

"Then there's the section where Mercedes writes she was worried about the way Brad was handling her money. That was why she put off revising her will. She'd told Brad she'd already done it, but she hadn't, and she wasn't about to, not while she had any doubts about Brad's management of her money."

"I can verify that." Sam nodded. "She had me draw up a new will, but she put off coming in to sign it."

Marcie began to frown. "But that's natural, isn't it? If Mercedes and Brad weren't getting along anymore, she certainly didn't want to leave all her money to him. But that doesn't give him a motive to kill her."

"Oh, but it does!" George gave Marcie a level look. "It doesn't matter whether your sister revised her will or not. The point is, Brad *thought* she had. And he thought he'd inherit everything."

Marcie turned to George with fear in her eyes. "Surely you don't think that Brad murdered Mercedes for the money he thought he'd inherit!"

"It's a possibility. I checked out Brad's alibi personally, and he was where he said he was that night. He went out to the stables and had a meeting with the horse trainer. That's confirmed. And then they went out to the track. But there are a couple of strange inconsistencies."

"Like what?" Marcie could feel her heart pound hard in her chest. George was actually suggesting the man she loved had murdered her sister!

"Brad gave Rosa money and told her to take the twins out to a movie and then for a hamburger. And Rosa said it was the first time he'd ever planned a night of entertainment for them."

"Did it ever occur to you that Brad was just being thoughtful?" Marcie stared right back at him. "That's not so unusual, is it?"

George shrugged. "Perhaps not. But the trainer said that there was a period of time when he and Brad were separated at the track. I checked that out, too. I drove from the track to the house, and then back again. Brad had time to kill Mercedes and get back to the track to pick up the horse trainer before the races were over."

Marcie shuddered. It couldn't be true! But how could she prove that to George and Sam? "How about the letters from the crazy fan? Surely *he's* a suspect!"

"I'm not discounting that. And if it makes you feel any better, I don't believe Brad killed your sister."

"Of course, he didn't!" Marcie drew a big sigh of relief. "Thank goodness you see it that way!"

"But there's always the possibility that Brad hired a hit man to murder Mercedes. That could account for the missing money."

"Oh, now wait a minute!" Marcie could feel her anger start to grow. "You're putting the cart before the horse. You're assuming that Mercedes was murdered, and you can't even prove that!"

"Not yet." George nodded. "But I'm waiting for the police lab to call me about the glove."

"What glove?" Both Marcie and Sam spoke at once, but this time neither one of them noticed. They were too astonished by what George had said.

"The gardener found a padded glove in the bushes by the side of the pool. And the leather looks like it's been soaked in chlorinated water."

Sam frowned. "It could have fallen in the pool by accident."

"Sure, and pigs could fly." George laughed. "I don't think that's what happened. You see, there are some very suspicious scratches on the surface of the glove, and I think they came from Mercedes's fingernails. Since the police M.E. took routine fingernail scrapings before he released her body, we're checking to see if any particles match the leather of the glove."

Marcie looked at Sam anxiously. "Is that enough evidence to prove that Mercedes was murdered?"

"Not really." Sam shook his head. "Of course it falls

under the heading of circumstantial evidence, but it wouldn't make for a very strong case."

"Very true, Counselor. But if my theory about the hit man is correct, everything fits. Unfortunately, we need hard evidence and there's only one way to get that."

Marcie experienced a sinking feeling in the pit of her stomach as George turned to her. He looked very serious. "I need your help to trick Brad into hiring the hit man again."

"Come on, George!" Marcie sighed in exasperation. "Brad won't hire the hit man again because he didn't do it in the first place!"

"But will you cooperate with me? I'd like to set up a trap."

Marcie frowned. George had a one-track mind. He was convinced that Brad was responsible for Mercedes's death, and she wished there was something she could do to prove him wrong.

"I think you should cooperate, Marcie." Sam looked serious, too. "Suppose for a moment that George is wrong. You'd be giving your future husband a chance to prove his innocence."

Marcie began to waver. Sam had made an excellent point. She had nothing to lose by cooperating, and everything to gain. She was sure that George's trap would be unsuccessful, and then they'd know she was right, that Brad had absolutely nothing to do with Mercedes's death.

"Yes, I'll cooperate." Marcie nodded, suddenly eager. "Just tell me what you want me to do and I'll do it!"

CHAPTER 20

Marcie listened carefully as George outlined his plan. When Brad called her tomorrow night, she was to tell him she'd made out her will and named him as the beneficiary. Sam would be on the line to confirm it, and he'd tell Brad it would be ready for Marcie to sign the next day.

"All right. I'm certainly willing to do that." Marcie nodded. "I was going to do that anyway, after we were married. Is that all?"

George shook his head. "I want you to go down to the bank on Monday morning, and transfer at least ten thousand dollars to that household account. It has to be available, if Brad wants some ready cash."

"All right." Marcie nodded again. "But Brad won't withdraw any more money. You'll see."

Sam shrugged. "I'm not so sure about that, Marcie. He certainly withdrew plenty last month."

"I know." Marcie sighed, and turned to George. "Do you want me to ask him about that?"

"No, don't mention it. We don't want him to know it's been discovered yet. But get the number of the hotel where he's staying. Tell him Sam may need to contact him, in case there's some question about the wording of your will."

Marcie nodded, and made herself a note. "All right. I'll do all that. But I still don't see why we don't just . . ."

"Let's do this my way," George interrupted. "Don't forget you agreed to help. If Brad doesn't fall into our trap, I'll owe you an apology, okay?"

"Okay." Marcie nodded, a bit reluctantly. She didn't like the idea of setting up her future husband for anything.

"Now, Sam . . ." George turned to him. "On Tuesday night, you call Brad and ask him about the missing money. Don't accuse him of anything. Just say you need a full accounting by the end of the week, so probate can settle Mercedes's estate."

"Got it." Sam jotted down the information.

"If Brad's guilty, that ought to make him very nervous." George turned to Marcie. "And if he's not, it won't bother him a bit. Now, late the same night, say about eleven, you call him, Marcie. Tell him you're very upset, that Sam just dropped by and he thinks that Brad has appropriated some of your money."

Marcie frowned. "Do I really have to do that?"

"Yes. Of course, you should reassure him. Tell him you don't believe a word of it, and you're sure he didn't do anything wrong, but Sam is urging you to make out a new will, putting all the money in trust for the twins. He's drawing up the papers now, and he wants you to sign them on Thursday."

"But he'll just tell me not to sign the will until he gets home!" Marcie frowned. "And I'll agree with him."

George shook his head. "No, you won't. Tell Brad that Sam is really pressuring you. You've got to get him off your back, and you can't see what harm it'll do to sign the new will. Promise him that when you two get married, you'll tear up the new will, and the old one will be in effect."

"Well . . . okay." Marcie nodded. "But why go through this elaborate charade? What do you think will happen?"

"It's simple, Marcie. We're giving Brad a deadline to arrange a hit on you to get the money."

"A hit on me!?" Marcie's mouth dropped open. "Don't be ridiculous! Brad loves me! Why, he'd never . . ."

"I hope you're right." George sighed. "But meanwhile, we're setting you up as a decoy."

"That's insane!" Sam put his arms around Marcie. "There's no way you're going to use Marcie as a decoy! It's much too dangerous!"

George held up his hand. "Calm down, Sam. Marcie's not *really* going to be a decoy. I'll have the bank notify me immediately *if* and *when* Brad makes a withdrawal! And the moment Marcie makes her second call, she'll rent a hotel room and stay there with the twins, until this whole thing is over."

"Wonderful." Marcie looked at George and sighed. "If I'm not home, just who is this mythical hit man supposed to kill?"

"A policewoman who'll stand in for you. And there's no way the hit man will succeed, not with all the undercover policemen we'll have staking out the house. What do you say, Marcie? Will you do it?"

Marcie sighed and then she nodded. "I'll do it. It's a perfect way to prove you're wrong. I'm going to make you eat your words, George."

"Wait a second, Marcie." Sam gave her a hug. "Are you really sure you want to do this? George seems to think his plan is foolproof, but sometimes these things go wrong."

Marcie hugged him back. "Thanks for worrying

about me, but I have to do it. And you'll help me if you're really my friend. I'm tired of hearing all these suspicions about Brad. I'll do anything to prove that he's innocent."

He crouched outside the window and watched through the glass. His love was alone, paging through the diary. He could understand the reason behind her frown.

The diary contained many secrets between its covers, and there was mention of the warning he had given her. But she had ignored that warning, and wrapped herself in a cocoon of loneliness. She had been so helpless, so needy. And she had failed to realize that the balm for her wounds, the solution to the terrible, aching void inside her, had waited for her in the magical labyrinth of her own guest cottage.

She had not known, and that guilt rested squarely on his shoulders. He had kept from her the secret of his presence. It had been a tragic error.

But that was past him now, and the future was no longer the bleak gray emptiness that he had foreseen. The impossible had become reality. She was back in the body of her twin sister. Fate had granted him another chance to prove that he was worthy of her love. Only one thing threatened his new serenity. The husband. Somehow he had to keep her from marrying him.

The night winds were sharp, and he shivered as he crept closer to the house, kneeling down on the soft, wet earth. No one knew he was about and there were many times when he felt invisible. She did not know he existed, although he had joined her at the studio, been close when they went skiing in Aspen, even watched the husband please her body. He was a cousin of the wind, a palpable presence who could wreak great destruction, and then vanish on the gentle breath of a summer breeze.

But the husband was his enemy, a clear and present danger. He must not let the husband deceive him again.

The memory of that first deception made the red mist shimmer under his feet, and he stomped it down before it could rise. He would think about it later. Not now. Now he had work to do.

The housekeeper came in, and they began talking about the children, who were tucked safe in their beds in the non-red rooms. He listened for a few moments. The children were of no interest to him. And then they said good-night, and she went up the stairs to bed.

Her light went on, a brief glimmer that pierced the darkness of the night, as she undressed and put on the beautiful green nightgown. He watched, imagining all the perfectly ordinary tasks that mortal angels were required to do before they were permitted to sleep. The teeth were brushed, the face washed, the alarm clock set, the covers turned back. And then the light clicked off, and his ally, the night, was back in command.

His legs were stiff when he got to his feet, thankful that it was safe to move without caution now. The night was peaceful, and deep, and black, but he knew the path as well as he knew the back of his hand. He smiled as he passed the rose garden and, a moment later, the tennis court. What would they say if they suddenly discovered him walking down the path in the night?

Imagining such an incident made him chuckle. They would be surprised, perhaps even shocked, but as long as he had a reasonable explanation, they would not be unduly alarmed. They had seen him many times before.

That was the beauty of the game. They all thought they
knew him, but, of course, they were wrong.

   Pappa Sutton's was crowded, even at one-thirty in
the morning. It was a fifties bar and grill, frequented
mostly by the show biz, artsy crowd, gay and straight
combined. Jerry walked in and made his way to a table
in the back, near the old-fashioned jukebox.

   "Could I get you something to drink?" An athletic-
looking waiter-wearing a white shirt open at the neck,
yellow- and green-checkered Bermuda shorts and a
leather apron-appeared at his table almost immediately. His teeth were so even, they had to be capped,
and his smile was totally engaging. There was no doubt
that he was an aspiring actor, earning his living as a
waiter until he got his first big break. Jerry had been in
Los Angeles for quite a while now, and he'd never met
a waiter who admitted to being merely a waiter. They
were always aspiring actors, or struggling screenwriters,
or would-be directors.

   "I'll have a double scotch on the rocks. Chivas, if you
have it."

   "We have it." The waiter eyed Jerry's Rolex watch, a
birthday gift from his lover. "Nice watch. You must be
in the biz."

   Jerry was about to deny it, when he remembered
that Worldwide Studios was looking for some fresh new
faces for a sitcom they were casting. This kid would be
perfect for one of the minor characters. "That's right.
And you want to be an actor?"

   "That's right." The waiter looked surprised. "How
did you know?"

   "Just a lucky guess. Can you ride a horse?"

"Sure." The waiter grinned. "I grew up on a ranch in Wyoming."

"Good enough." Jerry handed him a card. "Send me a résumé, and I'll see what I can do about getting you a couple of auditions."

"Wow! Thanks!" The waiter's smile widened until it was completely genuine. "That's really nice of you. You don't need to meet with me . . . uh . . . personally?"

Jerry caught his implied meaning and shook his head. "Ten percent of your earnings is all I expect. Just make sure I've got that résumé bright and early Monday morning."

"Yes, sir. And thanks a lot!"

Jerry sighed as he watched the waiter rush off to get his drink. He remembered being that enthusiastic once, but that was when he'd first moved here. He'd gotten a break then, too. His lover had set him up in the agency business, but he'd demanded a lot in return. Jerry was beginning to realize that the price he'd paid had been much too high. And he was still paying, with no end in sight.

Fifteen minutes later Jerry was sipping his second scotch, but it wasn't working to ease the pounding pain in his head. He was afraid tonight would be another lost night. It had become a pattern with him. He'd drink until the pain went away, and then there would be a terrifying blank period when he was bombed out of his skull. He'd always managed to get himself home, but he woke with no memory of how he'd gotten there. It was a vicious cycle he was trying to break with very little success.

"Hi, Jer." Beau LeTeure waved from across the room, and made his way through the crowd to Jerry's table. "Are you here with someone?"

Jerry shook his head. He wasn't about to admit it,

but he'd come here looking for Beau. One night, in group, Beau had mentioned that this was his favorite hangout, and Jerry had come here several nights in a row, looking for him.

"I'm alone, too." Beau looked a little uncertain. "Mind if I join you?"

Jerry shook his head. "I was hoping you would. I hate to drink alone."

"Drinking a lot, Jer?" Beau eyed the glass in his hand.

"Yeah. Too much. But it helps the pain, you know?"

Beau nodded. "Why don't I set you up with my doctor, Jer? It could be something simple that he could fix. You can trust my guy to keep his mouth zipped. He's a good guy, and he's seen everything before."

"Well . . . maybe." Jerry sighed deeply. He'd put off going to the doctor for over a year, and he'd suffered through countless pounding headaches. There were times when he felt like he had a rodent caged in his brain, scratching and biting until his mind screamed with agony.

"Don't let a little thing like fear stop you." Beau grinned at him. "Think how good you'll feel if it's nothing serious."

"But what if it is?" Jerry took another big swallow of his drink.

"Either way, you win. You're imagining the worst anyway. You might feel relieved, even if you find out it's true."

"Yeah. Maybe." Jerry sighed and nodded. "Okay, Beau. I've put it off for as long as I can. I'll go see him, I promise."

Beau grinned. "And I'll take you, to make sure you get there. I'm not working next Monday. Is that good for you? Or shall I try to make an emergency appointment?"

"I've waited this long. I guess I can wait another week."

"That's the stuff." Beau patted him on the shoulder. "You feel better already, don't you?"

Jerry blinked and then he nodded. He wasn't sure why, but he *did* feel better. Perhaps the support group really had helped. He'd agreed to let Beau take him to the doctor to find out what was causing his excruciating headaches. And he was much more comfortable with the fact that he was gay. One more week of pain and fear to get through, and he'd have an answer. And maybe after the doctor had made his diagnosis, he might even consider reclaiming his life, and calling it quits with his lover for good!

CHAPTER 21

It was Tuesday evening, and Marcie was talking to Brad on the phone. She'd asked Sam and George to come to the house to make sure she said the right things, and they were sitting on the couch, listening to her side of the conversation.

Brad had called on Sunday evening, and Marcie had told him about her new will, leaving everything to him. She'd gotten Brad's number, so Sam could contact him, and Sam had called Brad on Monday, confirming that Marcie had been in to sign the will. The first part of George's trap had been set according to plan.

Just a few minutes ago, Sam had called Brad from this same phone, saying he needed a full accounting of Brad's withdrawals by the end of the week, so that Mercedes's estate could go through probate. Now it was Marcie's turn to put the second part of the plan into effect. She'd just finished telling Brad she was changing her will again, on Sam's advice, naming the twins as her beneficiaries, until the matter of the missing funds could be resolved.

"I don't think you did anything wrong, darling. I

know you used that money to pay Mercedes's bills. But Sam is really giving me a hard time about it. He's insisting I sign that new will Thursday."

Marcie turned to give Sam a desperate look. She didn't like lying to the man she was going to marry, but there wasn't any other choice. George's friends at the police lab had given him the information he'd requested. The scrapings the medical examiner had taken from Mercedes's fingernails did contain particles from the glove. George was right. It really looked as if Mercedes had been murdered. Now Brad was a suspect in a real police investigation, and this was a chance to prove that the man she loved was innocent.

"But, Brad . . . I don't see what harm it would do to sign it. It'll get Sam off my back. And after we're married, I'll just cancel that will, and the previous one will go back into effect. As Sam pointed out, it's just an interim arrangement."

Marcie gave Sam the high sign. Brad had agreed. Sam held up a note card and Marcie read it. It said, *Make sure he stays at that number.*

"Of course. I love you, too. And one more thing, darling. If Sam needs to contact you again, you'll be at the same number, won't you?"

Sam nodded as Marcie gave him the high sign again. She was a very good actress, and everything rode on this performance.

"Yes, I wish you were here, too. But I know how important your meetings are. I'm fine, Brad . . . really. This is just one of those horrid inconveniences, that's all. And Sam is positively paranoid about that money. Oh, just a moment, darling. Rosa's calling me. Hang on for a second, will you?"

Marcie frowned and jotted a quick note to George. *He wants to know if I'll be home, in case he needs to call.*

George smiled. Brad was really sweating. If they put on enough pressure, he was sure that Brad would hire the hit man again. Then he nodded to Marcie and scrawled a reply. *We'll forward your calls to the hotel. Tell him you'll be home.*

"Sorry about that." Marcie gave a little laugh as she got back on the line. "The twins just wanted to say good-bye, before they left on that school campout."

Sam and George looked surprised. This wasn't part of the scenario.

"Oh, didn't I tell you? The whole class is going up to Arrowhead. They'll be back by the time you get home. I hope you do call, darling. I'll be here all alone, and it's going to be boring. I gave Rosa a couple of days off so she could spend some time with her sister."

Marcie winced as Brad told her he loved her and he missed her. She felt like an absolute traitor for telling him so many lies. "Yes, Brad. You know I do. Good night, darling. I'll be waiting when you get home."

"Great job, Marcie! Especially the bit about being here all alone." George jumped up from the couch to pat her on the back as she hung up the phone.

Marcie frowned. "Yes. I guess my acting classes paid off. I'm a wonderful liar."

"Hey, Marcie." Sam slipped an arm around her shoulders, and gave George a warning glance. Marcie obviously felt guilty, and they certainly didn't want her to call Brad from the hotel and tell him what they'd coerced her to do. "Brad'll thank you when this is all over. And there's even an added bonus, if you think about it."

"What do you mean?" Marcie looked puzzled.

"Let's say you're right, that Brad has absolutely nothing to do with this, and the crazy fan killed Mercedes. Since you look like Mercedes and you're finishing her part in the movie, he might just be after you, too."

Marcie frowned as she considered it. "Yes . . . I guess that's possible. But what's your point, Sam?"

"This little trap of George's might catch *him*. After all, you've told everyone you'll be here alone, haven't you?"

Marcie nodded. "Yes. Everyone thinks I'm going to spend a long, relaxing weekend here, all by myself."

"Perfect." George smiled. Sam was on the right track. If Marcie thought she was helping to catch the real killer, she wouldn't have second thoughts about lying to Brad. "Sam is right. There's no reason for the crazy fan to suspect it's a trap, and it's a perfect opportunity for him to try to kill you. If we get lucky, we could catch him."

"I never thought of it that way." Marcie gave them a small smile. "That makes me feel better."

Sam nodded. "Brad'll be very proud of you when he finds out you helped set the trap that caught the real killer."

"Do you think so?" Marcie looked a little happier as she considered it.

"I'm sure of it. If I were a suspect in a murder case, I'd be very grateful to the person who proved my innocence. Come on now. I'll help you pack and take you over to the hotel."

"Rosa did it before she left. Are you sure it's all right for the twins to stay with her, instead of at the hotel?"

"It's fine." George nodded. "You told them the house was being fumigated?"

"Yes. It was the best excuse I could think of."

George smiled at her. "It's a very good excuse. The police should be here any minute, and then we can leave. Sam'll get you all settled at the hotel, and I'll transfer your calls. Just make sure you stay in your room, so the hotel switchboard doesn't pick up."

"It's a good thing I had Rosa pack some of my books." Marcie sighed. "It'll drive me crazy if I have to watch television twenty-four hours a day."

Sam noticed that Marcie looked depressed at the thought of staying in her room, and he had a sudden inspiration. "Forget the hotel, Marcie. Why don't you stay at *my* place? I've got a guest room and a separate phone. You can use the pool and soak in the Jacuzzi all day if you'd like. And you can still get your calls."

"Oh, that sounds much nicer than being cooped up in a hotel room!" Marcie began to smile. "Would that be all right, George?"

George had to hide a grin, as he pretended to consider it. The three of them had been thrown together all week, and he'd been watching Sam and Marcie. Whether Sam realized it or not, he was in love with Marcie. And Marcie certainly seemed to be fond of Sam. With Brad out of the picture, something might develop, something that could be very good for both of them.

"I don't see a problem, Marcie. The only reason we were putting you up at a hotel is so that no one can locate you. Sam's condo complex will serve the same purpose."

For a brief moment, right after she opened her eyes, Marcie didn't know where she was. Then she remembered and smiled. Sam's guest room was very nice, with blue- and white-striped wallpaper and white curtains at the windows. She hadn't thought she'd sleep well in a strange bed, but she'd been so tired when she'd gone to bed last night, she'd fallen asleep the moment she closed her eyes.

Marcie glanced at the alarm clock on the bedside

table and gave a little cry of remorse. It was already past nine, and she'd wanted to get up early and make coffee for Sam before he went to the office. She jumped out of bed and slipped into the robe Rosa had packed for her. Then she opened the door, and walked across the hall to tap softly on Sam's bedroom door.

"Sam? Are you there?"

There was no answer, and Marcie hurried down the stairs to the kitchen. There was a thermos sitting on the counter, with a note propped up beside it. *This coffee should still be hot by the time you get up. Have a cup, and as soon as you're coherent, call me at the office.*

Marcie laughed and poured herself a cup of coffee. It was almost as good as Rosa's, and she sipped the hot liquid appreciatively. Sam had already told her that his office number was programmed on his phone. She carried her coffee over to the stool by the phone, and dialed the code he'd given her.

"Good morning. Mr. Abrams's office," a cheerful voice answered on the second ring. "This is Miss Collins. May I help you?"

"This is Marcie Calder. Mr. Abrams asked me to call."

"Yes, Miss Calder. He's expecting your call. Just a moment, and I'll buzz him."

A moment later, Sam's voice came on the line. "Hi, sleepyhead. Did you just get up?"

"I'm afraid so." Marcie giggled. "Thanks for leaving me the coffee, Sam."

"No trouble at all. I just wanted to tell you that I transferred all my calls to the office. If the phone rings, it'll be for you. Shall we try it, and see if it works?"

"That's a good idea. But do you have time?"

"Of course. My next client isn't scheduled until

eleven. Just hang up, and I'll call your number at the house."

"All right. Good-bye, Sam."

Marcie hung up and waited. A moment later Sam's phone rang. She picked it up and said hello, expecting to hear Sam's voice again.

"Miss Calder?"

A strange voice came through the receiver, and Marcie frowned. "Yes?"

"This is Bernie, down at the garage. I'm calling to tell you that your Mercedes is due for a tune-up."

"Uh . . . thank you very much, Bernie." Marcie recovered quickly. This was a call that had come in to the house number. "I could bring it in on Monday, if that's all right with you."

"That's fine. About nine? Or is that too early?"

"It's just fine. I'll be there. And thank you for calling, Bernie."

Marcie hung up, and the phone rang again. This time it was Sam.

"Hi, Marcie. I got a busy signal the first three times I dialed you."

Marcie laughed. "That's because I was on the phone. It was the garage, calling to tell me I needed a tune-up."

"And they called your house?"

"They must have. They certainly didn't know I was here at your condo."

"Great. Everything's working all right then. Just make yourself at home, and if you go out on the patio, take the phone with you."

"I will. What time are you coming home, Sam?"

"I'll try to get out of here by five-thirty. Barring complications, it's a fairly light day. We can order in pizza or Chinese for dinner."

"Why don't I cook?" Marcie smiled. "I haven't cooked for ages, and I enjoy it. Is meat loaf all right?"

"It's great. But my cupboards are pretty bare, and you can't go out shopping. George wants you to stay put."

"I'll call Von's Market. They deliver. And don't worry if you get hung up at the office, Sam. Meat loaf keeps."

"Marcie?" Sam sounded amused. "Are you sure you won't marry me?"

"What?!"

"Just kidding. But it's very unusual to find a woman who doesn't mind when you're late. See you when I get home, Marcie."

Marcie hung up the phone with a smile on her face. If she didn't love Brad, she'd be very tempted to think seriously about Sam's offer. He'd make an excellent husband, and he'd certainly be good to the twins. He already was. If Sam ever married, his wife would be a very lucky woman.

When Jerry walked into Hampton's, Beau was already there waiting for him. He made his way to the table in the back, sat down, and tried to look cheerful.

Beau looked sympathetic. "Problems, Jer?"

"Yeah." Jerry tried to steady his shaking voice, but it was apparent he couldn't control his anxiety.

"Here. Have a sip of scotch." Beau gestured toward the drink he'd ordered for Jerry. "You want to talk about it?"

Jerry nodded. "Do you know who my lover is?"

"No. You never mentioned his name."

"Any guesses?"

Beau shook his head. "Not really. All you've ever said

is that he was handsome and about your age. That fits almost everyone I know."

"Good." Jerry sounded relieved. "Look, Beau . . . can I tell you something in confidence? It's really important."

"Of course, you can! That's what our group is for. We're supposed to learn to trust each other. And we're also supposed to swear never to betray a group member's trust."

"Okay." Jerry nodded. "I need to ask you a question. Have I ever acted weird to you? Like I was spaced-out, and I didn't know what I was doing?"

"No. I don't think so. What's this about, Jer?"

"My lover says I have these lapses when I'm not all there. You know about the headaches and how I drink to get rid of the pain?"

"I know." Beau nodded. "That's why you're going to the doctor on Monday."

"Well . . . sometimes I black out, and other times I guess I keep right on functioning, except I'm not myself. My lover's noticed it a couple of times, and he's told me about the crazy things I've done."

"But you don't remember it?"

Jerry shook his head. "Not at all. It's a complete blank. He told me about one time when I picked a fight with a guy at a bar, and it turned into a regular brawl. It must have been true, because I woke up the next morning with a black eye."

"But you're not a violent guy, Jer. Picking a fight is completely out of character for you."

"I know." Jerry sighed. "That's what's so scary. I could handle it, if it was just a fight in a bar, or acting weird at a party. Everyone gets a little crazy once in a while, right?"

"That's true."

"But last week, I got out a jacket I hadn't worn in a couple of months, and I found a necklace in the pocket. I didn't recognize it, and I have no idea how it got there. And this morning, at the office, I was cleaning out some files, and I found a picture of Mercedes Calder wearing that same necklace."

Beau frowned. "Look, Jer. You were Mercedes's agent. Maybe she asked you to keep it for her."

"Maybe. But the point is, I don't remember it at all. And I'm not sure that's what happened. You see, I used to be a guest at Mercedes's house quite often. If I was there, and I went into one of my crazy periods, I could have *stolen* that necklace!"

"That may be true," Beau agreed. "But chances are you didn't. There's probably some perfectly reasonable explanation of how that necklace got in your pocket."

"Maybe, but there's no way to ask Mercedes now. And that means I'll never know what happened. I'm just not sure what I should do."

"Return it, and say she left it at your office. You stuck it in a drawer, meaning to return it the next time you saw her, but you forgot all about it. No one will be the wiser."

Jerry nodded. "That's exactly what I was planning to do . . . until I got the bank statements."

"What bank statements?"

"Hers. Since I was her business manager, the bank always sent the statements to me. I guess I'm still on their mailing list, because the statements came today. I was going to send them over to Sam Abrams's office. He's handling all that now. But I opened them to see if some checks I'd written had come in, and I noticed that almost sixty thousand dollars had been transferred to that account, and then withdrawn."

"I don't see why you're concerned, Jer." Beau frowned. "Brad probably withdrew the money to pay some outstanding bills. Or perhaps Marcie did."

"That's just it, Beau. They didn't. These were cash withdrawals, and Brad always pays the household bills by check. And I know Marcie didn't withdraw any money, because she mentioned she'd never been to the bank."

Beau nodded. "Okay. But I don't see the problem, Jer. All you have to do is to ask the bank who signed the withdrawal slips."

"I did." Jerry looked very upset. "I called the bank immediately. And they told me the withdrawals were made in Brad's name."

Beau looked puzzled. "Okay. So Brad withdrew the money. Why is that a problem?"

"Maybe he didn't. There are two other people who had the right to sign Brad's name. Sam Abrams had Brad's power of attorney. He's the family lawyer. He could have signed it."

Beau nodded. "Did he?"

"I haven't had the guts to call him and ask. You see, there was another person who had the legal right to sign Brad's name. His business manager. And that's me."

Beau looked at Jerry with sudden understanding. "You're afraid you withdrew all that money when you were in one of your blank periods, and now you don't remember it?"

"Exactly. And if I *did*, I can't find any record of where it's gone. No big deposits to my checking account, no major purchases, no cash stashed around the house. Nothing."

Beau nodded. "I can understand why you're so

upset. But you're jumping the gun, Jer. You've got to ask Sam Abrams whether he withdrew that money before you start blaming yourself."

Jerry nodded and stood up. "I will. First thing tomorrow. Thanks for listening, Beau. You've been a real friend. But now I think I'd better go home and get some sleep. I'm starting to get another headache."

"Are you sure you want to be alone tonight?" Beau stood up, too. "I can stay with you, if it'll help."

"Thanks, but I think I'd rather be alone." Jerry shook Beau's hand and made his way to the door. It was one of the hardest things he'd ever done, but he didn't trust himself around anyone right now. He could have another blank period and do something horrible.

As Jerry got into his car and pulled out into traffic, his hands were shaking. He couldn't help wondering what else happened that he didn't remember. He could be a rapist, or even a murderer!

Suddenly, Jerry's hands started to shake so violently, he had to pull over to the curb. He was sure he'd stolen Mercedes's necklace. And it looked as if he'd taken her money. He had the combination to the security system because Brad had mentioned that they were using their anniversary as a code. What if Mercedes hadn't accidentally drowned in the pool? He could have murdered her in cold blood, and he'd never even know he'd done it!

CHAPTER 22

"That was a great dinner, Marcie." Sam leaned back on the couch. "Are you sure you don't want me to help with the dishes?"

Marcie smiled as she stacked the dishes in the dishwasher. "No, thanks, Sam. I like to putter around in the kitchen. Besides, you worked all day, while I just lazed around your place."

"There's no way you lazed around today. Somebody made that delicious meat loaf, and those creamy scalloped potatoes, and that tasty spinach soufflé."

"It didn't really take all that long." Marcie's smile stretched to the limits. It was obvious that Sam had enjoyed her cooking. "The only thing that took any time was the homemade apple pie."

"Homemade apple pie?" Sam made his way to the kitchen. "How did you know that was my favorite?"

Marcie turned to grin at him. "The twins told me. They said that Rosa always made apple pie when you came over for dinner, so I grabbed her recipe before we left the house."

"Smart thinking. Did you get any ice cream?"

"French vanilla. Rosa wrote a note on her recipe card. See?"

Sam looked down at the card. It said, *A la mode French vanilla for Mr. Sam.* Then he sighed with regret. "I don't know if I can handle my usual serving tonight. I really made a pig of myself with the meat loaf."

"What's your usual serving?"

"Three pieces." Sam's eyes widened as Marcie took the pie from the oven, where it had been warming, and set it on the table. It was golden brown on top, and juice had bubbled up through the little slits she'd cut in the crust. Suddenly, the whole kitchen was filled with the mouthwatering aroma of apples and cinnamon and nutmeg, and Sam groaned as he broke off a piece of flaky crust and let it melt in his mouth. "On second thought, maybe I'll go for it. Start me with one and see what happens."

He looked at the gates in the distance with longing. He didn't like being on the outside, but he knew it was no longer safe to hide himself in the labyrinth. Something was different. Something was wrong. No cars had gone in or out since he had been here, and that was very unusual. The green panel truck was late. It always brought the fresh produce for her dinner. And the man who delivered the meat hadn't come today, either.

He moved a bit deeper into the trees, and watched the house through his binoculars. At first he had thought that she was there, but now he knew better. The little mannerisms he loved were missing. This one didn't push her hair back from her neck with her left hand, or open the kitchen door with her foot. She didn't bend from the waist when she picked up the newspaper, and she failed to tuck her feet up when she sat in the chair. This was not her. It was her stand-in, who walked through the house and pretended to read in the chair. Her stand-in postured in front of the window and ran useless water in the sink.

There were other people in the house who didn't belong there, either. He'd caught a brief glimpse of a man in the shadows when she had opened the door, and where there was one man, there would be more. The men were concealed very well, but he knew the house and where they were hiding. One by the pool; he had seen the bushes move with more than the winter wind. And another in her bedroom, behind her sea green drapes. The binoculars had shown him the tips of two shiny black shoes. A third was in the den, behind the couch. He had seen her turn to talk to him. And the fourth had a place in the hallway, behind the door. That was why she had been very careful not to open it all the way.

He knew he had to be cautious. The shadowy men and her stand-in were performing the drama of her life. This was the trap they'd planned that night in the den, the trick to catch a killer. But the husband would be smart enough to stay out of the trap. He was sure of that.

He huddled at the base of a tree, and let the binoculars drop to hang from their strap around his neck. The woods were cold and damp, and he was glad he'd worn a warm coat. He would not move until it was absolutely necessary. Only then would he let himself in through the gates, and perform his part in their scenario.

They had just finished watching *Moulin Rouge,* and Marcie dabbed at her eyes with a handkerchief. Then she smiled at Sam. "I just love that last scene. And it makes me cry every time I see it. John Huston was a great director, wasn't he?"

"Yes, he was . . . although he did do a couple of films that weren't very successful. *Freud* comes to mind."

"I've never seen that. Do you have it?"

Sam laughed and shook his head. "They ran it once, at four in the morning, but I haven't seen it since. How about watching *Prizzi's Honor?*"

"I'd love to. I missed it when it came out. But don't you have to work tomorrow?"

"I cleared the decks today, so I'm not going in. And I think I'm too jumpy to fall asleep. Let's make another batch of popcorn and watch movies all night."

"That's a wonderful idea!" Marcie smiled at him gratefully. "I know I couldn't sleep, either. I keep wondering what's happening at the house, and waiting for the phone to ring."

"You find the movie. It's in the bookcase in the den, and all the titles are arranged alphabetically. I'll get the popcorn."

Marcie glanced at the grandfather clock in the hallway as she went to get the movie. It was only ten-thirty, and she sighed deeply. She'd hoped the killer would strike by now, and everything would be over. This would be a long, sleepless night, and she was glad she was here with Sam, and not alone in a hotel room.

The movie was right where Sam had said it would be, on the shelf between David O. Selznick's The *Prisoner of Zenda,* and Hitchcock's *Psycho.* Marcie grabbed it, and then she noticed another tape with a blue cover in the P section. It was labeled *Passover Seder with Zayda and Bubbe.* She pulled that out and carried both tapes to the living room. If they were going to stay up all night, they'd need more than one movie.

A few moments later, Sam came in from the kitchen carrying a huge bowl of popcorn. He set it on the table in front of the couch and smiled at her. "Here we are. Popcorn straight from the microwave. It's one of my few culinary talents."

"It smells wonderful." Marcie took a handful and munched. "And it's absolutely delicious. Do you have any other favorite recipes?"

Sam nodded. "Absolutely. I can heat bagels in the microwave, and I'm very good at thawing those frozen burritos you buy at the grocery store. And last week I perfected my recipe for grilled cheese sandwiches. All you do is toast the bread, put two slices of cheese between the slices, and nuke it for twenty-five seconds."

"Oh, Sam." Marcie giggled. "I think you need a wife."

"I know that, honey. But you're taken."

Marcie winced. She hadn't meant to start all that again. And Sam had called her honey. Of course, it was probably a slip of the tongue, but she'd be wise to change the subject, before it turned into an uncomfortable evening.

"I brought out two tapes, Sam." Marcie picked up the tape in the blue cover, and turned to him with a bright smile. "I've never seen *Passover Seder with Zayda and Bubbe,* either."

Sam laughed so hard, he almost dropped the bowl of popcorn, and Marcie stared at him in confusion. "Did I say something funny?"

It took Sam a moment to stop laughing and then he nodded. "*Zayda* and *Bubbe* are the Yiddish words for grandfather and grandmother. It's a home movie, Marcie. My older brother filmed one of our Passover seders, and I transferred the film to video."

"Are you in it?"

Sam nodded. "David's ten years older, so I'm just a

toddler. It's not exactly a starring role. I spend the whole seder being passed from lap to lap and, at one point, I manage to get down and crawl around the table."

"I'd like to see it. Do you have any more tapes of you, when you were growing up?"

Sam nodded. "David was quite the amateur film-maker. I have videos of Sammie's first haircut, Sammie gets long pants, and Sammie in the first grade Thanks-giving pageant."

"I want to see that one first!" Marcie grinned at him. "What part did you play in the pageant?"

"I'm afraid I was cast as a turkey. I had the best gobble in the class."

"Don't feel bad about it," Marcie giggled. "I didn't even have a speaking part. I was a stalk of corn."

"But you have blond hair! That made you a natural. It was obviously typecasting."

Marcie laughed. "I wouldn't talk, Sam. After all, you were a . . ."

"I know." Sam interrupted her. "I put my foot in it that time. And some of my clients would definitely agree with you. Are you sure you want to watch all these old home movies? It could be pretty boring."

Marcie shook her head. "It won't be boring. I'd like to see you as a little boy, Sam. I bet you were cute. Why don't you get that Thanksgiving one right now and show it to me."

"Well . . . all right. As long as you sign an agreement promising never to mention it to another living soul. I was a terrible ham."

"Turkey," Marcie corrected him. "They didn't have ham at the first Thanksgiving dinner. Hurry up, Sam. I want to see it. And bring back everything else you have."

Sam sighed as he got up from the couch, but Marcie

noticed that he was smiling as he went off to the den to get the tapes. She felt a rush of affection for him, and for one brief moment, she felt a twinge of alarm. Was she being disloyal to Brad by liking Sam? But that was silly. There was no reason why they couldn't all be good friends. The twins adored Sam, and now that she'd gotten to know just how nice he was, she could easily understand why they'd wished their mother had married him.

Lisa Thomas paged through a magazine, but her eyes weren't on the pages. She was alert to any sound outside the windows. She knew the danger of getting too complacent on an assignment like this. After hours of inactivity, it was easy to relax and fail to notice the danger signs.

She got up and walked to the kitchen, intending to get a diet Coke out of the refrigerator. Then she remembered her briefing, and reached for juice instead. Marcie Calder never drank diet Coke. She wasn't engaged in the same Battle of the Bulge that Lisa was. But Marcie was fond of orange juice. Even though Lisa hated orange juice, she poured herself a big glass and forced herself to sip it with a smile on her face.

Lisa was about to go back to her chair and pretend to look through another magazine, when the beeper she carried in her pocket began to vibrate. She turned her back to the window, and spoke softly into the receiver. "Yes?"

The voice was low, little more than a whisper. "Blue Ford just went through the gates. Single white male in his mid-thirties, brown hair. He knew the combination."

"Okay. Did you alert the rest of the team?"

"Affirmative. They're in position and standing by. Good luck, babe."

Lisa felt her heart pound, and the adrenaline surged through her veins. This was it, the moment they'd all been waiting for. Even though she was nervous, she made herself turn calmly and walk toward the glass doors that led to the patio. They'd decided to stage their trap there, where the team could be concealed more easily.

Who was in the Ford? Lisa set her glass down on a nearby patio table, and positioned herself so she could see anyone approaching from the house. She pretended to be admiring the night, out for a casual stroll around the pool, but she was alert for any sound that wasn't a part of the natural night. It was difficult to pretend to be nonchalant when, at any given moment, the hired killer might strike.

Lisa took another deep breath and forced herself to stand immobile, staring calmly off at the rose garden. This type of assignment wasn't new to her. She'd been a decoy several times before. One had been a dope deal, when she'd posed as a desperate junkie looking for a fix. In another, she'd been a woman walking alone at night, a convenient target for a mugger who'd been working the area. The third decoy assignment had been for Vice, and she'd helped to catch a rapist. But her former assignments had been a walk in the park compared to this.

She moved around the shallow end of the pool, and sat down on a redwood bench. This was where she would stay until something happened. Since she could no longer see a reflection in the windows of the house, it was a blind position. She had to trust her life to her back-up team.

Lisa tried to convince herself that she was perfectly

safe. Six good men were in place, and they were all crack shots. There was even a bonus. George Williams, himself, was concealed in the bushes at the deep end of the pool. And even though Detective Williams had been retired for over ten years, whenever cops got together, they still talked about some of the amazing collars he'd made.

So why was she nervous? Lisa gave a wry smile. Detective Williams wasn't sitting out here as an unarmed decoy. She was. And her life was on the line. Lisa Thomas could lose her life tonight, and it could happen at any second. All it would take was a carelessly aimed shot, or a moment of indecision, and she would be dead. But this was why she'd become a cop. To help people and to save lives. Marcie Calder's life was at stake tonight, as well as her own. If they didn't get him now, he'd try again.

Lisa prayed for something to happen. Anything. The suspense was almost unbearable. And then, out of the corner of her eye, she caught a movement near the rose garden.

Lisa's first instinct was to dive for cover, but she forced herself to stay in place and wait. They had to catch him in the act, or they wouldn't get a conviction.

That was when something went wrong. Drastically wrong. There was a single gunshot and Lisa reacted by diving for cover behind a large potted palm.

Then pandemonium broke out, as the back-up team rushed forward. Lisa got to her feet just in time to see a man slump to the ground just steps from the rose garden.

Detective Williams motioned her over, and Lisa stared down at the man on the ground. A bullet through the head. Quick. Painless. Exactly what he'd probably planned on doing to her.

Even though she tried not to react on a personal level, Lisa couldn't help but wince. This man looked nice, not like a hired killer at all! But if a hired killer walked around looking the part, he wouldn't last long in the business.

"Lisa! Are you okay?"

Lisa nodded. The shakes would come later, when she realized how close to death she'd come. For now, she was just grateful that her ordeal was over.

The youngest member of the back-up team looked up, and Lisa saw fear in his eyes. He'd been assigned to the team at the last minute, and she was almost sure he'd been the one to fire. "Somebody'd better call for an ambulance. This guy's still alive!"

CHAPTER 23

Sam ejected the movie, and turned to Marcie. "You don't really want to watch Sammie's First Bicycle, do you?"

"I certainly do." Marcie nodded emphatically.

"But why? It's just ten boring minutes of me wobbling around and falling over."

Marcie considered it for a moment, and then she laughed. "It'll make me feel better to see someone else falling off a bike."

"Are you telling me that you're a fellow bike-faller-offer?"

"I am." Marcie laughed. "Mercedes and I got bicycles for our sixth birthday. Mercedes jumped right on and rode around the block, but it took me a week of skinned knees to learn."

"Did your father hang on to the back to steady you?"

"Of course. And the poor dear probably thought he'd be running along behind my bike for the rest of his natural life."

"But you finally learned, didn't you?"

"Oh, yes." Marcie laughed again. "I still remember the day I finally learned to ride. My dad started me off around the block, steadying me around the first corner. And then he let me go and walked back to the house."

"And you didn't know he wasn't there?"

Marcie nodded. "Exactly. I rode around the second corner just fine. And the third. But when I approached the house and saw him waiting for me on the front steps, I promptly fell over."

"I think they learn that in fathers' school. My dad did exactly the same thing to me. Did he make you get right back on and ride?"

"Oh, yes." Marcie nodded again. "He told me to pretend that he was back there every time I got on my bike. It's a funny thing, Sam. Even after he died, I still felt that Dad was right there behind me, protecting me so I wouldn't hurt myself. He was a wonderful man, Sam. He's been gone for over ten years now, but I still miss him."

"I miss my father, too."

"When did he die?"

"Oh, he's not dead. He's living in New Mexico with my mother, but it's not the same. He's getting old, and he has some serious health problems. I miss the tower of strength he used to be when I was a kid."

They sat in reflective silence for a moment, and then Marcie smiled. "Come on, Sam. We're getting what Mercedes used to call the middle-of-the-night-sads. Let's watch the bicycle episode. That'll cheer us up."

"Oh, sure." Sam got up and went to the cabinet to put it on. He was grinning as he sat back down on the couch. "That's easy for *you* to say. You're not the one falling off."

But before Sam could reach for the remote control to start the action, the telephone rang. They both stood up, nearly colliding, but Sam motioned for Marcie to sit back down.

"I'll get it, Marcie. And try to relax. It could be a client with a problem."

Relax? Marcie sat back down on the couch and crossed her fingers for luck. There was no way she could relax until Sam came back to tell her who'd called. It just had to be George. Sam had been a true friend, and watching the movies had been diverting. But Marcie knew she couldn't take much more of this waiting.

Sam was back in less than a minute, and he had a peculiar expression on his face. It was a strange combination of satisfaction and regret.

"They got him?" Marcie jumped to her feet as Sam nodded. "Thank God!"

But Sam still looked disturbed, and Marcie began to fear the worst. "What's wrong, Sam? Was it anyone we know?"

Sam nodded again, and then he sighed. "I'm afraid so. But something went wrong, and they shot him in the head. They're rushing him into surgery right now, but George says he's not expected to make it."

"Not Brad?!" Marcie felt her anxiety reach a frightening peak, as she stared into Sam's unreadable face.

"No. Not Brad. It was Jerry Palmer."

Every light in the house was ablaze as Marcie and Sam drove through the gates. They were greeted at the door by a uniformed officer, and led directly to the den, where George was waiting for them. He looked very grim.

"Sit down, Marcie. I need to talk to you. You, too, Sam."

As Marcie sat down on the leather couch, she shuddered. What if George hadn't set his trap? She could have been sitting right here when Jerry came through the gates and tried to kill her!

George turned to Marcie. "I want you to think carefully, Marcie. Jerry had a combination to the gates, and he headed straight for our decoy. But we don't have a motive. Can you think of any reason why Jerry might have wanted to kill your sister?"

"I . . . I don't know." Marcie considered it. "He might have been angry because she fired him as her agent."

George shook his head. "That's weak, but it's all we've got. Now, how about you? Can you think of any reason why Jerry wanted to kill *you?*"

"I have absolutely no idea! I thought Jerry was a . . . a friend. I can't believe he tried to kill me!"

"Sam?" George turned to him.

"Beats me." Sam looked just as confused as Marcie. "You didn't get a chance to ask him?"

"I'm afraid not. The gunshot wound rendered him unconscious. We rushed him off to the hospital, and they're operating to remove the bullet, but it doesn't look good."

"Is he going to die?" Marcie clasped her hands tightly in her lap, to keep them from trembling.

"The doc at the scene used the word *critical.* That's all I know. But he promised to keep me posted."

"At least this proves that Brad is innocent." Marcie gave a big sigh of relief. But George didn't nod, or smile, or say anything at all. He just continued to look grim. "George? Brad isn't still a suspect, is he? I mean . . . you caught Jerry red-handed!"

George frowned. "They're closing the file, Marcie.

As far as the police are concerned, Jerry's their man, even without a confession. Personally, I'm not so sure."

"You're still concerned about the missing money?" Sam raised the question.

"You bet I am! It's entirely possible Brad hired Jerry to kill Mercedes. And he could have hired him again, to get rid of Marcie."

"I don't believe it!" Marcie shook her head. "You have absolutely no basis for suspecting Brad . . . do you?"

George sighed. "No. No reason. I just do, that's all."

"Brad didn't take any more money from the account." Sam pointed out. "I checked with the bank at the close of business today."

"I know. I checked, too. But he may have promised to pay Jerry later, after Marcie was dead."

Sam nodded. "Okay. That's one possibility. But there's also the possibility that your trap didn't work at all. Jerry could have merely been an innocent bystander."

"But you said he tried to kill the decoy!" Now Marcie was confused.

"No. I didn't say that at all. I said he headed straight toward her. And he had his hand in his pocket. When he started to withdraw it, one of the SWAT team fired. It wasn't until later that we discovered Jerry wasn't carrying a weapon. All he had in his pocket was this antique diamond necklace."

George placed the necklace on the table, and Marcie gasped. "This necklace belonged to Mercedes. I recognize it."

"So do I." Sam nodded. "I was there when Brad gave it to her on their last anniversary."

Marcie looked up at George. "Maybe Jerry was keeping it for her, and he was just returning it to me."

"Then why didn't he call to tell you? And why did he

312   *Joanne Fluke*

suddenly decide to return it so late at night? It just doesn't track. The man definitely looked guilty about something."

"Perhaps he stole it, and then had second thoughts," Sam suggested. "Where was it kept, Marcie?"

"I haven't the foggiest idea. Upstairs in her jewelry box, I suppose."

"Marcie's right. She kept it in her jewelry box."

Marcie whirled to see Brad standing in the doorway, and she rushed over to hug him. "Oh, Brad! I'm so glad you're here!"

"So am I, darling." Brad hugged her back. "I never would have forgiven myself, if something had happened to you! Pour me a drink, will you, Sam? I think I need one."

Sam went to the liquor cabinet to get Brad's drink, and Marcie led him over to the couch. When they were seated again, George turned to Brad. "Did they tell you what happened?"

"Yes. Jerry Palmer! I still can't believe it! I owe you a debt of gratitude, George. If you hadn't set up that trap, he might have actually—" Brad shuddered, and pulled Marcie close to him. "I don't even want to think about what could have happened."

George nodded. "Sorry, Brad. I know this has been a shock, but I need to ask you some questions."

"Of course. I imagine you're wondering why I flew back here tonight."

George nodded again. "That'll do for starters."

Brad took the drink Sam handed him, and took a hefty swallow. "That telephone call from you threw me into a panic. I knew Marcie hadn't made any withdrawals, and I hadn't, either. Naturally, I assumed it was a banking error, so I called and had them fax me a complete record of all the transactions."

"And that was when you realized that I was right? That the money really was missing?"

"I certainly did!" Brad sighed deeply. "And it looked bad for me, especially since I had no idea where the missing money went. The whole thing had me completely stymied . . . until this morning."

"What happened this morning?" George took over the questioning again.

"I had a stockholders' meeting at WesTech. That's a company Mercedes and I invested in last year. One of the other stockholders mentioned dividend checks, and everything fell into place."

Marcie felt her anxiety begin to abate. Brad obviously had an explanation for the missing funds. "What fell into place, darling?"

"When Mercedes hired Jerry as her business manager, she gave him permission to sign her name. And since I was out of town so often, I gave him permission to sign my name, too. When the dividend checks came in, they went to Jerry's office. He signed our names and deposited them to our account. And if Jerry could sign our names to deposit funds, he could also sign our names to withdraw."

Sam turned to George and nodded. "Brad's right. Jerry could have signed either or both names to a withdrawal slip. And the bank didn't keep the original paperwork. They just made note of the name on the slip."

"So you think *Jerry* withdrew the money?" George still looked dubious.

"Of course, he did!" Marcie spoke up. "Who else could have done it?"

Sam and George exchanged glances, but neither of them spoke. Brad took another sip of his drink, and sighed deeply. "At first I didn't want to believe it. After all, Jerry's been my friend for years. But there's no other explanation that makes sense." Brad turned to Marcie and shook his head. "I could kick myself for trusting Jerry. The guy had a bad gambling habit, and he was stealing us blind!"

George still didn't look convinced. "That explains the missing funds, but it doesn't explain why Jerry would kill Mercedes."

"Or why he tried to kill Marcie," Sam added.

Brad gave a deep sigh. "I know. I was hoping I wouldn't have to go into this, but I guess I have no choice. I promised Jerry I'd never tell, but I don't think I owe him anything after what he did to Mercedes, and what he tried to do to Marcie tonight!"

"Very true." Sam nodded. "So what was Jerry's motive?"

"Jealousy. In both cases."

"What!"

George looked mystified, and Brad did his best to explain. "This is a little embarrassing, but . . . Jerry's gay. And when we were roommates in school, he had a real crush on me. Of course, I wasn't interested in anything but friendship, and I told him that."

"What was his reaction?" George frowned slightly.

"He was fine. At least, I thought he was. He never mentioned it again, and we lived together for the rest of the year. Then he went to Aspen and we lost touch."

"He contacted you again when he moved to L.A.?"

"Yes. I helped him get started here. I even sent Mercedes to him as a client." Brad took another swallow of his drink and sighed. "That was a big mistake. If I'd known then what I know now, I never would have referred Mercedes to him!"

Marcie patted his arm. "But you didn't know. You can't blame yourself for that."

"Jerry was jealous of your relationship with Mercedes?" George raised his eyebrows.

"Absolutely. I realize that now. And then Mercedes and I got married, and Jerry couldn't stand the idea of me getting married!"

George nodded. "Okay. Jealousy's a powerful motive, but there's no proof that Jerry killed Mercedes. And even though Jerry walked into our trap, there's no actual proof that he was trying to kill Marcie. As far as I'm concerned, the murder investigation is still open, and you're still a suspect."

"That's ridiculous!" Marcie turned on George angrily. "If Jerry didn't kill Mercedes, then the crazy fan did. You have no right to accuse Brad!"

Brad slipped his arm around Marcie's shoulders and gave her a little squeeze. "Calm down, darling. I know a way to settle this once and for all. I'll take a lie detector test."

"But you shouldn't have to!" Marcie was still upset. "They have no right to put you through something like that!"

Brad gave her a tender smile. "I know, but I want to do it for you."

"For me?" Marcie looked surprised. "What do you mean?"

"I never want you to wonder about whether I might be guilty."

"But I wouldn't! I've never doubted you, Brad!"

Brad hugged her and held her close. "I know that. But someday that little seed of suspicion might start to grow. And it's very important to me that you trust me completely."

"I'll arrange it." George nodded quickly. "And don't leave town."

Brad grinned at him. "Once a cop, always a cop. But I don't resent that, George. I know you and Sam were only trying to protect Marcie. That's precisely why I'm volunteering to take that lie detector test. I'm going to prove to both of you that Marcie doesn't need any protection from me."

CHAPTER 24

Marcie glanced at her watch and sighed. Brad had only been in the testing room for ten minutes, but it seemed like ten hours. She was sitting between George and Sam in the waiting room, a dismal little alcove with yellow plastic chairs, a table with old magazines, and a wall calendar from a neighborhood pharmacy which displayed the previous month.

"Nervous?" George turned to her with a smile.

"No. Not at all." Marcie didn't smile back as she shook her head. She didn't feel particularly friendly toward George right now. She knew she was being irrational. Brad had volunteered to take this test. But she still blamed George for not believing the man she loved.

"Marcie?" George reached out to touch her shoulder. "I'm sorry I'm being such a hard case, but I'm only concerned for your welfare."

Marcie forced a smile. "Welfare? That's exactly where I'll be, if I don't get back to work soon. The welfare office. The studio won't send my check until

I finish dubbing. And I promised them I'd be there in less than two hours."

"You'll make it." George looked relieved at her joke. "I'll drive you myself."

Sam, who had been silent up to this point, turned to smile at Marcie. "There's no way you can wind up on welfare, Marcie. You inherited a ton of money."

Marcie nodded. "That's true, but it's sixty thousand dollars less than a ton, thanks to Jerry. The money doesn't really matter. I never expected to have this much anyway. But I can't get over the fact that I was betrayed by someone I thought was a friend."

"Hey . . ." Sam gave her a sympathetic smile. "Just be thankful you weren't home alone when that friend showed up!"

"I'm very grateful. Did you know I sent Lisa Thomas a thank-you bouquet?"

"Everyone at the station heard about that," George said, smiling. "Five dozen roses in a real crystal vase. Lisa was thrilled. She told me to tell you she'll be your decoy anytime you want. She's never had anyone send her roses before."

"She was wonderful!" Marcie smiled a genuine smile. "I wouldn't have the nerve to do something like that."

"Lisa's a good cop. She may even get a promotion out of this." George got up and stretched. "I'm going to check to see if they're almost finished. I'll be right back."

The moment George had left, Sam turned suddenly serious. "You're not really mad at us, are you, Marcie?"

Marcie sighed and shook her head. "No. I'm not mad at you. I realize that both of you had my best interests at heart. But I do think you were picking on

Brad. You'll stop when he passes this lie detector test, won't you?"

"I promise." Sam patted her shoulder. "But you don't pass a lie detector test, Marcie."

"I know. They explained all that when we came in. The lie detector just tests for guilty knowledge by using a series of physical indices, like blood pressure and galvanic skin response. They also told us that the results aren't admissible in court in the State of California."

"But they still take themselves very seriously." Sam grinned. "Did you see the sign on the door?"

Marcie nodded. "CALIBRATED RESEARCH AND PSYCHOMETRICS. I was impressed."

"You shouldn't have been. Just think about the initials, and it'll put everything in perspective."

"Calibrated Research and Psychometrics." Marcie thought it over for a moment, and then she started to laugh. "C.R.A.P.? Oh, Sam! That's funny!"

"Somehow I don't think they intended it that way."

"Should we point it out to them?" Marcie tried to look serious.

"Oh, no. They'd probably change the name, and that would spoil the whole thing. Let's let them discover it on their own."

George came back into the room, and Sam and Marcie immediately sobered. Both of them had forgotten for a moment that this was serious business.

"It's going to be another twenty minutes. The receptionist wants to know if we want coffee."

Both Sam and Marcie shook their heads, and George gave them an approving nod. "Wise decision. I saw the coffeepot. It looks just as bad as the one we used to have at the station."

"That's bad?" Sam asked.

"It's not good. We only washed it once a year, when the chief came in for his annual visit."

The next twenty minutes passed very slowly, as they paged through old issues of *Reader's Digest* and *People Magazine,* the only offerings on the rickety table in the corner. Marcie read an article about how to save money on her year-before-last taxes, and sighed. She supposed she'd need a tax accountant, now that she was a rich woman. She'd have to remember to ask Sam for advice.

At last the inner door opened, and Brad walked out. He was grinning from ear to ear, and Marcie felt a giant weight slide off her shoulders.

"He wants to see you, George." Brad waited until George got up, and then he sat next to Marcie.

"Is everything all right?" Marcie snuggled close as Brad slipped his arm around her shoulders.

"Just fine. The examiner told me that there was no way I had anything to do with Mercedes's death. The test proved it."

"Congratulations, Brad." Sam reached out to shake his hand. "That took a lot of guts."

"Hey. I didn't do anything courageous. All I did was take a lie detector test to prove I was telling the truth."

Another moment passed, and George joined them again. "Okay, Brad. You're definitely in the clear. And I apologize for suspecting you."

"No problem." Brad smiled at him. "I know you were only concerned about Marcie. And I appreciate you guys taking care of her while I was out of town. Now that I'm back, I can take over, and you two can get back to your own lives."

Sam stood up. "That's our cue. Come on, George. Let's give Brad and Marcie some time alone."

"Do you need a ride to the studio, Marcie?" George turned to Marcie.

"She doesn't need a ride." Brad got up and held out his hand for Marcie. "I'll drive her to the studio, and stay with her until the dubbing's finished."

George gave a little wave as he went out the door. Sam hung behind a step and looked at Marcie. "Call me if you need me. You've got the number."

The moment the door closed behind George and Sam, Brad turned to Marcie. "Why would you need to call *him?*"

Marcie shrugged. She was grateful that Sam had given her his private number, but Brad looked a little jealous. It would be wise of her to downplay the friendly relationship she'd shared with Sam.

"I'm not sure." Marcie smiled up at Brad. "I guess he means for questions about the estate. Come on, darling. Let's get out of here. If we go straight to the studio, we might even have time for lunch."

Brad nodded. "Okay. But first I have a question. Will you marry me, Marcie?"

"Of course. I already told you I will."

"Not eventually. I mean now. Like tomorrow. Or maybe the day after. I really don't want to wait, Marcie. When I thought I'd lost you, I almost died. And I realized that every moment we have together is precious. I want to be your husband now, not six months from now."

Marcie felt tears well up in her eyes. It was true. And if every moment they had together was precious, why did she have to wait to marry Brad? The twins would adjust. Marcie knew they wanted her to be happy. There was no reason in the world to wait, now that the police had caught Mercedes's killer.

"Well?"

Brad was looking down at her with an anxious expression, and Marcie smiled happily. "You're right, Brad. I don't want to wait, either. Let's get married tomorrow."

George and Sam walked down the hospital corridor. When they'd left Marcie and Brad after the lie detector test, they'd decided to stop by to see how Jerry Palmer was doing.

"I hate hospitals!" George frowned.

"I'm not exactly fond of them myself. My former partner died in here. Ruptured appendix. The doctors said the operation was a success, but he died anyway."

George nodded, but he was silent. He didn't really want to go into his reasons for hating hospitals. Over ten years had passed, but he still felt lousy when he walked down this corridor. His wife, Adene, had spent months in this hospital, in the room at the end of this corridor. His daily visits to her had been agony. It had been almost impossible for him to pretend to be cheerful and optimistic, when he'd known that her condition was terminal. George didn't believe that anyone should have to watch the person they loved waste away day after day in such a foreign, sterile environment. That was why he'd mortgaged the house, hired round-the-clock nurses, and taken her home for the last month. Adene had died in her own bed one sunny summer afternoon, surrounded by her friends and family. It had taken him ten years to pay off that debt, but he knew he'd done the right thing.

As they passed an open door, someone called out, "George? George Williams?"

"Yeah?" George stopped and peered into the room. "Keith! What the hell are you doing here?"

"I'm just sitting here, enjoying the peace and quiet of this lovely place. Come on in. I'm not contagious."

George motioned to Sam, and they entered the room. "Sam? This is Keith Lucas. I worked with him in my last year on the force. Keith? This is Sam Abrams. He's a lawyer."

"Sam smiled. "Glad to meet you, Keith. What happened to you?"

Keith attempted to shrug, but it was difficult because his left arm was in a cast, from his wrist to his shoulder. "Dope deal gone sour. I took three hits in the arm."

"How long are you going to be in here?" George pulled over two chairs, and they sat down.

"As long as I can. It's safer in here than it is out on the street."

"You said it!" George sighed. "Are they going to bump you upstairs for a while?"

"Not if I can help it. It's even more dangerous up there. In case you haven't heard the rumors, I'm not very popular with the big brass."

"I wasn't, either. That's one of the reasons I took my early retirement."

Keith nodded. "Smart move. Lisa Thomas was in to see me today. She told me about that trap you set. It sounded like a nice piece of work."

"Maybe." George frowned. "But I'd feel a lot better if we had a confession."

"You got doubts?"

"Yeah. Everything points to Jerry Palmer, but it's all circumstantial evidence. Right, Sam?"

"That's right."

"And you don't think he did it?" Keith raised his eyebrows.

"Nope." George shook his head. "I've got a gut-level feeling that he's innocent."

"Then you're right. I know you, George. You always had great hunches. I'll put my money on you any day of the week."

"Thanks, but I'm not so sure. My chief suspect just took a lie detector test, and he turned out as clean as a whistle. Maybe I'm just losing my touch."

"You?" Keith laughed. "Impossible! Go with your hunch, George, and stay with your suspect. If you think he's guilty, he is. Say . . . I don't suppose you could smuggle me in a pizza, could you? That's the only problem with this place. The nurses are cute, and they got fifty channels on cable TV, but the food really sucks. I'm dying for a pizza."

"Do you still like sausage, pepperoni, and extra cheese?"

"That sounds like heaven! But you gotta figure out how to get it past that dragon lady at the desk. They don't allow anybody to bring food in here."

Sam started to grin. "That's an example of cost effectiveness. Eating their food makes you so sick, they can keep you here and charge you for an extra couple of days."

"It's true." Keith nodded. "If you don't believe me, just take a look at that lunch on the tray."

George reached out and lifted the lid off the tray on the bedside table. "What is it?"

"I don't know." Keith tried to shrug again. "It looks like oatmeal, but it's green. The nurse that brought it said something about broccoli, but it smells like old tennis shoes to me."

Sam frowned. "Put the cover back on, before we all get sick, and I'll get you a pizza. Do they have officers guarding Jerry's room?"

"Yeah." George nodded. "Two rookies. But what does that have to do with . . ."

"Just watch." Sam interrupted him. "I didn't go to law school for nothing."

George and Keith watched as Sam picked up the telephone by the side of Keith's bed and dialed. "Hi, Tony? This is Sam Abrams. I'd like to order a large pizza with pepperoni, sausage, and extra cheese. I know you don't usually deliver, but a friend of mine is in the hospital, and he's dying from the food in here. Do you suppose you could . . . Thanks, Tony. I really appreciate it. Add on a nice tip, and I'll give you my credit card number."

While Sam repeated his credit card number and gave directions to the hospital, Keith turned to George. "It's a great idea, but I still don't see how he's going to get it past the dragon lady."

"Yeah, Tony." Sam winked at Keith. "Now, delivering this pizza is going to take a little finesse. When your guy gets here, have him tell the desk that it's for the officers on guard duty on the third floor. That'll get him up here. Then he should deliver it to . . . what's the room number?"

"Three-eighteen." Keith grinned and turned to George. "Sam's right. He didn't go to law school for nothing."

Sam hung up the phone and turned to Keith with a smile. "Your pizza'll be here in less than an hour."

"Thanks." Keith was obviously impressed. "If one of you guys will hand me my wallet, I'll pay you back for . . ."

Sam held up his hand. "That's not necessary. Consider it payment for services rendered."

"What services?" Keith was puzzled.

"For helping a former officer to trust his hunches. You see, I don't think Jerry Palmer's our man, either. And I'm counting on George to prove it."

Marcie was in her room with the twins, and it wasn't a comfortable moment. She'd just finished explaining the trap that George and the police had set for their mother's killer, and how Jerry Palmer had been shot.

"Are they sure Jerry killed Mom?" Trish turned to her with absolute amazement. "I thought . . ."

". . . Jerry was our friend." Rick broke in. "And he always seemed to really . . ."

". . . like Mom." Trish finished the thought.

"I know it's hard to accept, but that's what happened." Marcie put her arms around them. "Jerry was headed straight for the policewoman when they shot him."

"Poor Jerry." Rick looked upset. "Is he going to die?"

Marcie frowned. "No one knows, Rick. He came through the operation, but he's still in a coma."

"Well, I hope he doesn't die!" Trish looked very worried. "They've got to ask him . . ."

". . . why he did it," Rick broke in. "We won't believe it, unless he confesses."

Marcie nodded. "I feel the same way. I want to know why. We'll all keep our fingers crossed, okay?"

"Okay." Rick and Trish spoke at once and solemnly crossed their fingers. Then Trish giggled. "Does this mean we don't have to do our homework? We can't write with our fingers crossed."

Marcie laughed. "Oh, no, you don't! I didn't mean it literally. You both have to do your homework, especially next week. You see, that's the other thing I wanted to talk to you about. I'm going on a little vacation, and you have to promise to be good for Rosa."

"Where are you going?" Trish started to look anxious. "And when are you coming back?"

"I'm leaving tomorrow, and I'll be back next Saturday. It's only for a week."

"Are you going back to Minnesota to get your stuff?" Rick looked curious.

"No, I'm . . . Brad and I are getting married tomorrow, and we're going on our honeymoon. That's why I can't tell you where I'm going. Honeymoons are supposed to be a secret, and I don't even know myself. Brad said he wants to surprise me."

"You're getting married *tomorrow*?" Trish was clearly shocked. "But you can't! That's absolutely . . ."

". . . impossible!" Rick interrupted her. "Mom spent six months planning her wedding, and the studio did most of it. There's the reception, and the church, and the flowers, and . . ."

". . . the wedding gown and the cake." Trish shook her head. "Nobody can arrange a wedding for the next day!"

Marcie smiled. "Of course, they can. Especially if they go down to city hall to get married, and they only invite their closest friends. Like you two, and Rosa, and one other person."

"Sam?" Rick looked anxious. "You're going to invite Sam, aren't you?"

Marcie winced. She really didn't want to invite Sam. Even though Brad hadn't actually said anything about it, she knew he was upset that she'd spent the night in

Sam's guest room. "Sam's very busy. So I thought we'd invite Jolene Edwards. You like her, don't you?"

"Sure we do." Trish nodded. "And I think you're right, Aunt Marcie. You shouldn't invite Sam. Uncle Brad would just . . ."

". . . get jealous." Rick finished the thought for her. "He really doesn't like Sam that much."

Marcie nodded. It was impossible to keep anything form the twins. They were just too perceptive. "It's not that he doesn't like Sam. It's just that they . . . uh . . . had a difference of opinion. I'm sure they'll work it out."

"Maybe." Trish gave a deep sigh. "But I doubt it. It's just like the movie we watched about the love triangle."

Rick nodded. "I wish you'd waited, Aunt Marcie. I think Sam was almost ready to ask you to marry him."

"Oh, I don't think so." Marcie did her best to keep a straight face. "Sam and I are friends. That's all."

Trish frowned. "But friendship sometimes develops . . ."

". . . into a deeper relationship." Rick looked very adult. "Oh, well. I guess we're stuck with Brad."

"I thought you liked him." Marcie frowned.

"Oh, we do!" Trish threw her arms around Marcie's neck. "He's much better now than he used to be. Honest!"

Rick nodded. "And he makes you happy. That's the most important thing."

Marcie smiled, but she knew the twins were saying what she wanted to hear. They loved her, and they weren't about to criticize her choice of a husband.

"Okay." Marcie gave them both a hug. "Now I'm going to need a lot of help picking just the right dress to wear. Any suggestions?"

Marcie kept a smile on her face as the twins raced to

the closet and began to discuss the pros and cons of various dresses. Were they right? Should she wait to marry Brad? She was rushing into this whole thing. But then she thought of the expression on Brad's face when he asked her to move up their wedding date, and she felt reassured. The man she loved needed her, and she would be there for him.

CHAPTER 25

"Beau!" George was surprised to see Beau LeTeure sitting in a chair by the side of Jerry's bed. "What are *you* doing here?"

Beau looked anxious. "Since I'm a relative, they're letting me stay with my brother Jerry."

"Oh. Of course." George nodded, and shut the door. Then he laughed. "I guess the guys outside aren't very swift. They didn't even check your I.D.?"

"No. They just told me that I couldn't go in unless I was a member of the immediate family, so I said I was Jerry's brother. And then I asked them why they were guarding his door." George rolled his eyes skyward. "I suppose they told you?"

"Sure. They said Jerry was going to be charged with Mercedes's murder, and he'd been caught trying to kill Marcie. That isn't true, is it?"

George looked very serious as he pulled up two more chairs and gestured for Sam to sit down. Then he leaned close to Beau and lowered his voice. "I'm going to tell you something, Beau, and I don't want it to leave this room."

"Okay." Beau nodded.

"I don't believe Jerry tried to hurt Marcie, and I'm almost certain he didn't kill Mercedes. But I don't have a shred of evidence to back it up."

"Maybe I can help." Beau looked anxious. "You see, Jerry belongs to my therapy group, and he told me things he didn't tell anyone else."

"Therapy group?" Sam was curious.

Beau nodded. "It's for gays who are involved with abusive lovers."

"You?" George looked surprised.

"Not anymore. I managed to break off that relationship. But I still belong to the therapy group."

"Do you know Jerry's lover?" George leaned forward.

Beau shook his head. "Jerry never divulged his name, but I know he's physically violent. Jerry told us about some of the things he did."

"How's Jerry doing?" Sam felt a wave of sympathy as he stared down at Jerry's unconscious face.

"The doctor was here this morning. And he told me that Jerry was doing a lot better than anyone expected. When they did the CAT scan to locate the bullet, they found out that Jerry had a cerebral aneurysm."

"That's very serious." Sam looked worried.

Beau nodded. "I know. Since they had to open him up to take out the bullet, they removed the aneurysm. Jerry's lucky to be alive. They caught it just in time. That's why Jerry was having those awful headaches."

"Hold it." George frowned. "What headaches?"

"The bad ones that made him black out. The doctor said they were petit mal seizures."

"He actually lost consciousness?" Sam was intrigued. A friend of his had experienced petit mal seizures, but she hadn't blacked out, and her condition had been cured with drugs.

"Jerry said he used to pass out every couple of weeks

or so, right after one of his headaches. I finally talked him into seeing my doctor, but he didn't have an appointment until Monday."

"Why did he wait so long?" George frowned. "He must have been in a lot of pain."

"Because he was afraid he had a brain tumor. That's how his father died. But there's something else I have to tell you, something even more important. I know why Jerry went to see Marcie last night. He was just returning Mercedes's necklace."

Sam and George listened as Beau told them about Jerry's lapses of memory, how he was afraid he'd stolen Mercedes's necklace, and made large withdrawals from Brad and Marcie's account when he was in one of his blank periods.

"But what made him suspect he'd done something like that?" Sam was confused.

"He found the necklace in his jacket pocket, and he didn't know how it got there. And his lover told him that he did crazy things when he got one of his headaches. Jerry believed him, because he couldn't remember anything he'd done when he woke up."

George nodded, but he wasn't convinced. "Were you ever with Jerry, when he got one of these headaches?"

"Yes. He got one in group one night, and I drove him home. He was in a lot of pain, but he seemed perfectly rational to me."

"Did you mention this to the doctor?" George's frown deepened.

"Yes. Normally, I wouldn't divulge a confidence like that, but . . ." Beau stopped speaking and sighed deeply. "I thought maybe it would help Jerry."

George nodded again. "Jerry needs all the help we

can give him. What did the doctor say when you told him about the crazy things Jerry's lover alleged he did?"

"He said that would be inconsistent with the symptoms of a cerebral aneurysm. He told me that Jerry would have lost consciousness and slept until his body recovered. There was no way Jerry would have been physically capable of going anywhere or doing anything."

Sam glanced at George. "So Jerry's lover was gaslighting him?"

"Could be. It's certainly a good possibility."

"Of course!" Beau looked excited. "I saw that movie. Why didn't *I* think of that? Jerry's lover might have been blaming Jerry for the things he'd done himself. Maybe he even . . . Do you supposed he might have even . . . ?"

Beau stopped, unsure if he should go on. ". . . killed Mercedes?" Sam provided the words that Beau was hesitant to say. "Anything's possible, Beau."

"Yes, but we don't know who Jerry's lover is! And Jerry can't tell us until he comes out of his coma."

Sam nodded. He didn't want to say what was on his mind, that Jerry might never come out of his coma. It was possible that Jerry could die right here in this hospital bed without ever regaining consciousness.

George got out his notebook and pen. "I need to know everything that Jerry told you about his lover. I know it's confidential, but I believe that Jerry would tell us if he were conscious. Maybe we can put the pieces together. Do you know where his lover lives?"

"Jerry told me he saw him when he went to Aspen with Marcie and the twins."

"I was there at the same time." Sam spoke up. "We

all had dinner together. But I didn't see Jerry with anyone except Brad."

Sam stopped cold and stared at George. Brad wasn't gay. He'd married Mercedes, and he was about to marry Marcie. He'd volunteered to take the lie detector test, and the examiner had staked his reputation on the fact that Brad hadn't killed Mercedes. As much as Sam disliked the guy, he *had* to be in the clear.

George seemed to read Sam's mind, because he raised his eyebrows and jotted another line in his notebook. Then he turned to Beau. "We need more information. Did you get the impression Jerry's lover *lived* in Aspen?"

"No. I assumed he lived in L.A."

"Why was that?"

"Because Jerry saw him so often. But I guess he could have flown in from Aspen every couple of days. He had plenty of money."

"How do you know that?" Sam asked.

"Because he bought a new car last year. Jerry told me that the car cost more than Jerry had paid for his condo."

"What kind of car?" George asked.

"I don't know. Jerry didn't say. But I know the color. Will that help?"

"Anything you can remember might help. What color was it?"

"British racing green. Jerry said his lover was an impatient person, and he got a lot of speeding tickets. That's why he bought a dark green car. Since it's less visible than a brighter color, he thought he'd get less tickets."

George and Sam exchanged glances. Brad had a dark green Jaguar. And he drove fast. But British racing green was a popular color, and almost everyone in L.A. had an expensive car. Still, the evidence was mounting up.

Sam took over the questioning. "Was Jerry's lover single?"

"No, he was married . . . or maybe he was divorced. Jerry said something about his lover's family once, and how they had to be careful that the kids didn't find out about Jerry."

"How many kids?" George took over questioning.

"Two of them. A boy and girl. I know Jerry met them, because he told me how hard it was to pretend to be just a family friend."

Sam and George exchanged glances again. A boy and a girl. Trish and Rick?

"Do you think Jerry's lover is in the biz?" George made another note.

"I don't know. But Jerry said he was a whiz at the stock market. He told me about a killing he made with a small electronics company a couple of . . . Hey! Wait a second!"

"What is it?" Both Sam and George leaned forward. Beau looked very excited.

"I just remembered something. Jerry said he handled some of his lover's business affairs. That means all we have to do is go over Jerry's client list, and we can figure out who he is!"

Marcie was radiant in a white linen suit and white high-heeled sandals. It wasn't the traditional wedding gown she'd dreamed of wearing when she was a teenager, but she knew she looked good. Rhea had put her hair up in a shining gold twist, and Jolene had brought pink tea roses for her bridal bouquet. Brad was wearing a dark blue suit with a white shirt and tie.

Marcie thought he looked very handsome. Everyone was dressed in their best, and they would have made a charming picture, if they hadn't been sitting on orange plastic chairs in the cavernous waiting room at city hall.

A baby cried, and Marcie looked around with a frown. The other couples were younger. Much younger. She knew she was the oldest bride there. And she was the only woman waiting to be married who wasn't obviously pregnant!

"Next?" A bored-looking clerk opened the door to an inner office, and motioned to their small bridal party. They were only seven. Marcie and Brad, the twins, Rosa, Jolene, and Jolene's boyfriend, Kurt, who was serving as Brad's best man.

The clerk, an older woman with frizzy, salt and pepper hair, wore the unhealthy pallor and sour demeanor of a career civil servant. "This way. Mrs. Chavez is waiting for you in the conference room. English? Or Spanish?"

"Excuse me?" Marcie was totally confused.

"The ceremony. Do you want it in English? Or Spanish?"

"English, please."

Brad turned to wink at Marcie as they walked down the long hallway. She winked back, and did her best to keep a smile on her face. Weddings were supposed to be romantic. This wasn't turning out at all like she'd expected.

"In here." The clerk opened a door and ushered them into a bare room with bright fluorescent lights and brown mini blinds on the windows. An official-looking Hispanic woman sat behind a desk at the front of the room. She rose as they entered.

"My name is Marta Chavez, and I'm a Clerk of the

Court, City of Los Angeles. The State of California has endowed me with the authority to perform a civil marriage ceremony. Will the wedding couple please step forward? The rest of you wait back there."

Brad took Marcie's hand and they stepped forward. Somehow, Marcie managed not to look as distressed as she felt. She'd known that a civil ceremony wouldn't be as nice as a church wedding, but surely their surroundings could have been a bit more traditional. She missed the little touches. A vase of flowers on the desk would have helped, or even curtains on the windows, instead of those awful institutional blinds.

She barely listened as Mrs. Chavez read the required ceremony from a clipboard she held in her hand. Brad looked serious as he repeated his vows, but Marcie couldn't help feeling as if she were a child in school, parroting the teacher, as she promised to be Brad's wife.

"By the authority vested in me by the State of California, I now pronounce you man and wife. Congratulations. You may kiss the bride."

Brad kissed her, and Marcie felt a little better. Then Jolene and Kurt signed the marriage certificate as witnesses. That reminded Marcie of the promise she'd made to Sam. She'd agreed that she wouldn't change her will until she married Brad, but now that she was Brad's wife, there was no reason to wait any longer. She pulled the will out of her purse, and handed it to Mrs. Chavez.

"I know this is unusual, but could you witness my signature?"

Mrs. Chavez glanced down at the will and frowned. "My fee for notarizing a legal document signed by two witnesses is fifteen dollars."

"That's fine. You can keep the change." Marcie handed her a twenty-dollar bill. Then she signed the will and passed it to Jolene and Kurt, for their signatures as witnesses. Mrs. Chavez notarized it, and Marcie handed the document to Rosa. "Take this home with you, Rosa. Please put it in my center dresser drawer."

"What's that?" Brad was clearly puzzled.

"My will."

Brad still looked puzzled. "But why did you sign it *now?*"

"I promised Sam I wouldn't change my will until we were married. And we are." Marcie turned to Mrs. Chavez. "Aren't we?"

Mrs. Chavez nodded. "You are. The ceremony I performed is legal and binding. Is there anything else you want me to notarize while you're here?"

"No, I think that's . . . Wait." Marcie pulled out the pink slip for her old Volkswagen Beetle and signed it over to Shirley Whitford. Then she handed Mrs. Chavez another twenty-dollar bill to have that notarized.

"What's that?" Brad was beginning to look amused.

"The pink slip for Miss Ladybug. I don't need it anymore, so I signed it over to Shirley Whitford. Send it to her, will you, Rosa? Her address is on the slip."

Brad laughed. "Are you through now? Or would you like to sign the house over to someone?"

"We're through." Marcie took his arm, and they walked out of the room as man and wife. It hardly seemed possible that they were married. Marcie felt more like she'd just appeared in court to pay a traffic ticket!

Everyone congratulated her as they walked through the waiting room and out to the parking lot. Marcie stopped by the only tree in sight, and Rosa took their picture. Then the new bride tossed her bouquet to

Trish as she'd promised, and Kurt opened his trunk and took out a bottle of champagne, one of sparkling apple juice, and seven glasses. There were several short toasts, lots of hugs and kisses for the twins, and before Marcie knew it, she was sitting in the back seat of Kurt's car, heading for the airport.

"That wasn't so bad, was it?" Brad turned to smile at her as they hopped on the freeway.

"Not really." Marcie sighed. "But I don't feel married. Maybe we should have asked for the ceremony in Spanish. Mrs. Chavez might have given it more *oomph*."

Brad laughed and put his arm around her. That helped a little. She shut her eyes and told herself that the ceremony didn't matter. She was Brad's wife. That was the only thing that really counted.

In less than fifteen minutes, they were at the airport, and Kurt unloaded their luggage at curbside. Marcie felt a jolt of loneliness as they drove away. This wasn't right. There should have been rice, and a reception, and lots of friends to wish them well. She wasn't regretting the fact that she'd married Brad, but she couldn't help feeling as if their actual wedding ceremony had been a giant mistake.

"Stay right here, honey." Brad smiled at her. "I'm going to get a skycap."

Marcie watched as he hurried inside the terminal. There must have been a baggage handler waiting just inside, because Brad was back almost immediately.

"Come on, darling. He'll make sure our luggage gets on the plane. Let's go."

Marcie nodded and took Brad's arm. But they passed the entrance to the terminal, and Brad kept on walking down the sidewalk. Marcie tugged at his arm. "Brad? Where are we going?"

"To the right terminal." Brad grinned at her. "I

didn't want anyone to know where we were going, so I had Kurt drop us off here. That'll throw them off the track."

"But why?"

"Because I want to be alone with my lovely wife. And if no one knows where we're spending our honeymoon, no one can bother us."

Marcie laughed. She was beginning to feel a lot better. "That was pretty sneaky. When are you going to tell me where we're going?"

"Not until we board the plane." Brad glanced at his watch. "And that should be in less than fifteen minutes. We board first, because we're flying first-class."

"At least I know we're not going overseas." Marcie glanced at the signs as they walked past. "We just passed the international terminal."

Brad grinned. "Maybe that's true, and maybe it isn't. International flights leave from other terminals, too. Close your eyes, honey. And hang on tight. I want this to be a total surprise."

Marcie laughed and closed her eyes obediently. She loved surprises. She heard the *whoosh* of a door opening, and then she felt her stomach drop down to her toes. "An elevator?"

"That's right. Okay. You'll have to open your eyes now. We're going through the security check."

It only took a moment to walk through the archway metal detector. Then Brad took her arm again, and led her to a door at the end of a long concourse.

"The V.I.P. lounge." He opened the door and ushered her inside. "I reserved a table by the window."

The moment they entered, a flight attendant greeted them with a smile. Brad handed her their tickets and she nodded. "Please follow me. They're boarding the first-class passengers now."

Marcie and Brad followed her out another door and into the tunnel-like boarding ramp. Marcie had never experienced this kind of courtesy before. She'd always waited at a crowded gate, and joined a long line of passengers waiting to board the plane. Flying first class was very different, and she liked it much better.

"Congratulations!" The flight attendant who greeted them at the door to the plane was smiling. "Welcome to Island Air. We're very glad you're flying with us. We've arranged the first-class section for you."

Marcie was thoroughly mystified. What did that mean? She glanced at Brad, but he just raised his eyebrows and smiled. Then the flight attendant pulled back the first-class curtain, and Marcie gasped. There were only two seats in the whole section, and they weren't like any airline seats she'd ever seen before!

"Come on, darling." Brad led her into what looked like a small living room. "Which seat would you like?"

"I . . . uh . . . does it really matter?" Marcie giggled. Both seats were identical leather swivel chairs, flanking a round wooden table.

Brad shook his head. "I guess not. Here. Let me buckle you in."

Marcie sat down and Brad clasped her seat belt. Then he sat down and buckled himself in.

"We're on the plane." Marcie swiveled around to smile at him. "Can you tell me where we're going for our honeymoon *now*?"

Brad nodded. "Hawaii. You said you'd never been there, and I wanted to be the first to take you. Is it all right? It was the most romantic place I could think of."

"It's perfect!" Marcie gave a happy little sigh as she envisioned white sandy beaches, and romantic nights under the sparkling stars of a tropical sky. "Are we staying in a big hotel?"

Brad shook his head. "I reserved a lovely little condo, where we can be completely alone. I want you all to myself."

Just then the flight attendant pulled back the curtain and entered their section. She was carrying champagne in a silver bucket. "Would you like me to open it?"

"I'll do it."

The stewardess left, and Brad took out the bottle of champagne. Just as he was preparing to uncork it, she came in again, carrying a tray with a silver domed cover. "Here's everything you ordered, sir. Will there be anything else?"

"Not right now." Brad smiled at her. "We'll ring for you if we need you."

The moment the flight attendant left, Marcie reached out to lift the silver cover. She gasped as she saw the crystal dish of caviar, and the basket of toast tips. "Oh, my! I always wanted to taste caviar."

"You've never had it before?"

"No. They don't have it in St. Cloud, Minnesota." Marcie started to grin. "Or if they do, they call it bait."

Brad threw back his head and laughed. "That's one of the things I love about you, darling. You have a great sense of humor."

Marcie watched while he poured two flutes of champagne. She recognized the name on the bottle. It was Dom Pérignon. Marcie had come out to visit when the twins were born, and Mike had opened a bottle to toast Mercedes that night in her private hospital room. When Marcie had asked, he'd told her it was the best champagne for a joyous occasion.

Brad poured two glasses and handed her one. Then

he raised his glass in a toast. "To my wife. I love you, Marcie."

"And I love you." Marcie smiled at him. Her wedding had been disappointing, but her honeymoon was turning out to be wonderful. As she looked up into her husband's handsome face, Marcie was sure that this was the most joyous occasion of her life.

CHAPTER 26

Getting into Jerry's office was easy. The nurse had put his personal effects in the top drawer, and Beau had remembered that all Jerry's keys were color coded. Jerry had used a blue key for his condo, a gold key for his storage locker, and a red key for his office door. It hadn't taken long to drive to Jerry's office. It was only a few blocks from the hospital, and less than twenty minutes later, all three men were sitting around Jerry's desk, going through his client list.

"Sorry, guys. I didn't know there'd be so many clients." Beau frowned as he paged through the list. "There must be a hundred names here, and I only know a few of them."

"Tell me about the ones you know." George took out his notebook again.

"Well . . . here's Robert Erne. He's a screenwriter. But I'm sure he's not Jerry's lover."

"Why not?" Sam asked.

"He's not gay and he's single. No kids."

"Put a check by his name." George instructed him. "And tell us about the others you know."

Beau put a check mark in front of Robert Erne's

name and went down the list. "Harry Workman. He's been in the hospital for the past two months. There's no way he met Jerry in Aspen. Ira Levinson's at least seventy years old, and I know Jerry's lover was approximately his age, so he's out, too."

One by one they went through the names, eliminating the ones who didn't fit, and copying others on another list of possibles. They were halfway through when Beau started to frown. "Here's Brad. But it couldn't be him. You said he passed that lie detector test. And I don't know any of the rest of these people, except for Leslie Alcan. And she's a woman."

"Hold it." George interrupted him. "My cell phone's ringing."

George took out his phone and stared down at the number on the screen. He frowned, and then he said, "It's the hospital. I told them to page me if there was any change in Jerry's condition."

Beau's face turned white as George answered the call, and Sam patted him on the shoulder. Both men stared at George's tense face, as he listened to the voice on the other end of the line. It was impossible to tell what the message was by his monosyllabic replies. It could be bad news or good news. They had no way of knowing. But they both breathed a sigh of relief as George hung up and turned to them with a smile.

"Let's get over to the hospital." George stood up and grabbed the list. "The nurse says Jerry's beginning to come out of his coma."

Marcie was impressed as she walked through Brad's time-share condo. There was a lovely view of the ocean from the living room window, and the condo had its own stretch of private beach. They'd just finished unpacking their suitcases, and Brad had left to pick up some groceries.

The bedroom was in the rear of the building, and Marcie pulled open the sliding glass doors to the balcony. Their unit was on the ninth floor, and the large bedroom balcony overlooked a beautiful golf course. That gave Marcie an idea, and she hurried to the phone. She wanted to give Brad a wedding present, and she knew he was an avid golfer.

Ten minutes later, it was done. Marcie smiled as she imagined how surprised Brad would be when she gave him her present. Since Brad hadn't brought his golf clubs, she'd ordered a deluxe set for him with the advice of the club pro. She'd also reserved time for him on the course tomorrow, and the golf pro had promised to put together a foursome that he said would be challenging and fun.

Marcie picked up the notes she'd made, and stuck them into her purse. Brad would be delighted by her little surprise, especially since the golf pro had told her that this was one of the finest golf courses in the world. She was about to put the pencil she'd used into her purse as well, when she noticed that it was personalized.

Naturally, Marcie had assumed the pencil belonged to Brad. She'd picked it up from the floor in the bedroom, near the spot where he'd unpacked his suitcase. But now that she looked at it closely, she saw that this particular pencil was the kind teachers gave to their students in grade school. It was green, and it had a name stamped on the side in gold letters. Obviously, another person who'd used the time-share had dropped it. There was no way to know who that former occupant had been, since all she had was the first name. And a pencil certainly wasn't valuable enough to try to trace it back to its original owner.

Marcie shrugged and slipped it into her purse. You never knew when you might need a pencil. Then she walked back out onto the balcony, watched the golfers play on the lovely course below, and smiled happily as she thought of how delighted Brad would be with his wedding present.

Rosa frowned, as she told Rick to stop wiggling his foot for the fourth time in less than five minutes. When he was younger, he'd always wiggled his foot when he was nervous, but he hadn't done it for years. She turned to him with concern. "Something's bothering you, Rick. What is it?"

"He's worried about Aunt Marcie," Trish explained. "I think it's because we don't know where she is."

"And she hasn't called." Rick nodded.

"I'm sure she'll call soon." Rosa gave them a comforting smile. "She's probably gone out to dinner with Brad."

Rick nodded. "I know, Rosa. But that's what we're worried about. You see, the only person with Aunt Marcie is Brad. What if he tries to hurt her? Sam's not there, and she wouldn't know . . ."

". . . who to call." Trish's voice was shaking. "We're scared, Rosa. We don't want anything bad to happen to Aunt Marcie!"

Rosa put her arms around both of them. "Uncle Brad won't hurt your aunt Marcie. He loves her. I think you're both just missing her, and imagining all sorts of bad things that'll never happen. How about some popcorn and some hot chocolate? And then we can watch that movie you wanted to see."

"*Attack of the Killer Tomatoes?*" Rick looked hopeful. "But I thought you . . ."

". . . didn't like that movie." Trish began to grin. "You always said it was . . ."

". . . totally ridiculous nonsense." Rick finished the thought for her.

"Well, it is!" Rosa nodded and turned to Rick. "You put the popcorn in the microwave, and I'll make the hot chocolate. Trish can get the movie and put it in the machine. I think that a good dose of *Attack of the Killer Tomatoes* is just what we need to get our minds off our troubles. It's impossible to worry, if we're busy watching all that totally silly nonsense."

Sam, Beau, and George were sitting in a booth at Harry's Haven, a twenty-four-hour coffee shop across the street from the hospital. All three of them looked glum as they sipped the coffee the waitress had brought them. Jerry had been so agitated when he'd come out of his coma, the doctor had given him a sedative. By the time they'd arrived at the hospital, Jerry had been sleeping, and the doctor had told them he wouldn't wake up for at least six hours.

"Is anybody hungry?" Sam passed Beau and George the menus that had been stashed behind the ketchup bottle on the table.

George nodded. "Yes, but I don't want to risk it. A coffee shop with coffee this bad can't have any good food."

"Look on the bright side." Beau attempted a smile. "If you come down with a case of food poisoning, you're just across the street from the hospital."

George nodded. "I think that's why Harry built his restaurant here."

"More coffee?" The waitress, a dyed redhead wearing bright pink lipstick and an orange uniform that was two sizes too small for her, approached their table with a coffeepot.

"No! Please!" Sam grinned at her. "Tell me . . . is there anything here that's safe to eat?"

The waitress shrugged. "Don't ask me. I bring my lunch from home. But the cook just cleaned the grill, and we got in eggs this morning, so I'd recommend the breakfast."

"Ham and eggs?" Beau looked interested.

"No way." The waitress shook her head and leaned a little closer. "The ham's awful. Harry buys that processed kind in the can, and the regulars don't order it, so it's been sitting in the cooler for at least three weeks. Don't get the sausage, either. The grease that cooks out of that stuff is orange."

"How about the steak? You've got steak and eggs on the menu." George pointed to the number-five breakfast.

"Uh-uh. I don't know what kind of animal they use for the steak, but it's sure not beef."

Sam laughed. "Maybe we should take a tip from the regulars. What do they eat?"

"Cheese omelets with toast, and a side of hash browns. I've got a couple of guys that come in every morning, so I guess it must be okay."

"That's what we'll have." George decided for all three of them. "Do you have any strawberry jam?"

"Nope. All we got is berry. And it doesn't say what kind of berry it is. You want to try it?"

"Sure." George nodded. "They can't mess up jam, can they?"

The waitress laughed. "I think they can. The regulars won't touch it. They order honey because it comes in those little packets, and it doesn't spoil."

"Okay." Sam nodded. "Honey for all of us. I don't suppose you have any decent coffee?"

"I can make a fresh pot and use two packets, but you'll have to pay double price. Harry figured it out one day. A packet of coffee with one refill for each cup serves five."

"Harry counts the cups of coffee on the ticket?" Sam looked surprised. He'd heard of cutting costs, but that was going a bit too far.

"You bet." The waitress nodded. "And if that doesn't match with the packets left, he docks us."

"Don't worry. We'll pay double." George nodded. "We wouldn't want you to get docked on our account."

The waitress smiled. "Thanks. I wouldn't want to get fired over something like that. This is a real good job."

"A real good job?" Beau looked at her in utter amazement.

"You bet! Harry's only hung up on the coffee. The last boss I had counted the french fries, too."

As soon as the waitress left, Beau turned to Sam. "What time is it?"

"Ten-thirty. We've still got five and a half hours to go."

"After we eat, maybe we should all go home and try to get some sleep." George suggested.

Beau shook his head. "I couldn't sleep anyway. I'll stay at the hospital in Jerry's room. And I'll stop them if they try to give him another sedative. A brother's got that right, doesn't he?"

Sam shook his head. "Not unless you have his medical power of attorney. But I'll sack out in the waiting room, and you can call me. I'll snow them with some legalese."

"I guess I might as well stay in the waiting room, too." George sighed. "I have a feeling Jerry knows who murdered Mercedes, and I'm going to be right there when he wakes up."

"Oh, I couldn't!" Marcie turned to Brad with a smile. They'd just finished dinner at a marvelous restaurant overlooking the ocean, and the waitress had wheeled the dessert cart to their table.

"Not even the cheesecake?"

"Well . . ." Marcie looked longingly at the chocolate cheesecake, dribbled with raspberry sauce. "Could we split a piece?"

Brad nodded. "I was hoping you'd say that."

The cheesecake was just as delicious as it looked, and they ended up ordering another piece with two cups of espresso. Brad had a brandy, while Marcie sipped the last of her wine. Then Brad called for the check.

"What time is it?" Marcie asked. She hadn't worn her watch.

"It's early. Only nine o'clock. Are you tired?"

"Not exactly." Marcie began to blush. "But I thought you might want to get back to the condo."

Brad began to grin as he opened the folder the waitress had brought with his credit card slip. "That's the best idea I've heard all day. We'll open a bottle of champagne, toast each other and . . . damn!"

"What's the matter?"

"Our waitress forgot to bring a pen. And I didn't bring one with me."

"I've got a pencil," Marcie offered. She opened her

purse, pulled out the personalized pencil, and held it up for him to see.

"Where did you get *that!?*"

"I found it. Someone named Jimmy must have stayed in the condo, because his name is stamped on the side in gold letters. At first I thought I'd call the time-share company and offer to return it, but I figured that since it's just a . . ." Marcie's voice trailed off. Brad looked very strange. His face had turned white, his hands were trembling, and his eyes were cold as he stared at her. "What's the matter, darling?"

"It's mine!" Brad grabbed the pencil and stuck it in his pocket. "Where did you find it?"

Marcie felt a twinge of alarm. Brad looked very upset. "On the floor by the dresser. I'm sorry, Brad. I would have asked you, but I had no idea it was yours."

Marcie watched as Brad struggled for control. Some of the color came back to his face, and he gave an apologetic smile.

"I'm sorry, Marcie. It's just that . . . uh . . . this is my good luck pencil. I use it to sign all my big deals, and I never go anywhere without it. I know it's silly, but I panicked when I saw that you had it."

Marcie was still confused, and more than a little frightened. Brad had seemed like a different person when he'd grabbed for the pencil. She knew that some people were very attached to their good luck charms. Shirley Whitford carried a rabbit's foot on her key ring, and Harriet Scharf had once admitted she burned green candles for luck. But she'd had no idea that Brad was so superstitious.

"I'm certainly glad I found it, if it means that much to you." Marcie gave him a smile. "But, Brad . . . why do you have a pencil with someone else's name on it?"

Brad smiled, and Marcie breathed a sigh of relief. It was his old, familiar smile.

"This pencil belonged to my best friend Jimmy. We went to grade school together, and we were so close we were practically brothers. When his mother died, they sent him to an orphanage, and before he left, he gave me his pencil."

Marcie nodded. "I understand now. Do you know what happened to Jimmy?"

"He was adopted." Brad picked up the pencil and signed the credit card slip. "Let's finish our coffee and go back to the condo."

Brad looked depressed and Marcie sighed. Talking about his friend had upset him. She wanted to cheer him up, so she decided to tell him about her surprise.

"Let's have one more cup of coffee." Marcie smiled at him. "I want to tell you about your wedding present."

"My wedding present?"

Brad looked surprised, and Marcie laughed. "It's an old custom I just invented. A new bride gives her groom a present the first night of their honeymoon."

"I know all about that." Brad gave her a knowing grin. "And that's exactly the kind of present I'd like."

Marcie blushed. "Uh . . . I'm sure you'll get that present, too. But this is different."

Brad looked absolutely astonished as Marcie told him about the set of new golf clubs she'd ordered, and the foursome she'd arranged with the golf pro. "I've always wanted to try this golf course, but I could never get a reservation before. How did you do it?"

"I pulled a few strings." Marcie grinned at him. "I just told the golf pro that we were honeymooners, and this was my wedding present for you. And I also promised to tip him two hundred dollars."

Brad laughed. "No wonder! Thank you, Marcie. Do you know that I love you?"

"I know." Marcie nodded. "I love you, too. Maybe we should forget about the last cup of coffee. I want plenty of time to give you the kind of wedding present you really expected."

CHAPTER 27

George woke up as Beau tapped him on the shoulder. His years on the force had enabled him to instantly assess a situation, and he was on his feet immediately. "Thanks, Beau. He's awake?"

"Almost." Beau nodded. "Hurry. As soon as the doctor finds out, he might give him another shot."

"What time is it?" Sam sounded groggy as he got to his feet.

Beau glanced at his watch. "Eight-fifteen. He slept longer than they thought he would."

"Is he rational?" George asked.

"Absolutely. When I told him you two were sleeping in the waiting room, he said that was good, because he needed to see you right away."

Jerry was sitting up in bed as they entered the room. Except for the thick bandage around his skull, he looked remarkably like his old self.

"Jerry!" Sam hurried to the bedside. "We're so glad you . . ."

"I know," Jerry interrupted him. "Save it for later, okay? Is Marcie all right?"

George nodded "She's fine."

"Thank God!" Jerry winced as he turned to look at George. "Could you all come closer? It's hard to turn my head."

All three men pulled up chairs and sat by the side of Jerry's bed. It was clear that Jerry was in pain, because he winced again.

"Do you want me to ring for the doctor?" Beau asked.

"No. He'll just give me another shot, and I'll be out cold again. I heard what you guys were saying last night."

Sam frowned. "But you were in a coma."

"I know. I couldn't even blink my eyes, but I heard every word you said. You were right. I'm sure Brad killed Mercedes."

"*Brad* was your lover?" Beau looked shocked.

"Yes. We met in college. He's the one who convinced me to move out here. Did the police get him?"

"Not yet." George shook his head. "We don't have enough evidence, and he passed his lie detector test."

"The lie detector test is wrong. I'm positive Brad killed Mercedes. I just got the bill for a dozen red bathing suits."

Sam, Beau, and George exchanged worried glances. Was Jerry in his right mind? But then Jerry laughed.

"I know how it sounds, but I'm not crazy. I figured it all out. That's why I went to see Marcie. Somebody's got to warn her!"

"I think you'd better start from the beginning." George opened his notebook. "The red bathing suits threw me."

"Okay. I didn't make those withdrawals from the bank. I think Brad did it to pay his gambling debts."

"Gambling debts?" Sam frowned. "I didn't know that Brad gambled."

"I went to the track with him a couple of times. And I saw him drop several thousand. I also know he was in hock to some pretty dangerous guys."

"That figures." George nodded. "Go on."

"The bill for the red bathing suits came in, and it was so unusual, I called the designer. You see, Mercedes only wore white. The designer told me that Brad had called to change the color to red."

"I don't get it." Beau looked confused. "What's so significant about red?"

"Brad hates the color red. It makes him crazy. I wore a red shirt once, when we were in college. When Brad saw it, he flipped out and attacked me. He said all sorts of weird things about the Red Lady, and some kind of red room, and how red was the color of blood."

George and Sam exchanged worried glances. They remembered the words that the crazy fan had written. *Red is the color of blood.* It was too accurate to be a coincidence.

"So what happened?" Beau looked anxious. "Were you hurt when Brad attacked you?"

"Not seriously. I finally managed to subdue him, but it really scared me. It was as if the Brad I'd known had disappeared, and a violent stranger had taken over his body. Naturally, I never wore red around him again."

"Wait a second." George frowned. "There was a case twenty-some years ago. We called it the Red Murder. A prostitute was murdered in her red bedroom, and she was wearing a red negligee."

Sam raised his eyebrows. "Brad?"

"Maybe." George got up and headed for the door.

"I just remembered who handled that case, and I hope he's still here."

As the door closed behind George, Sam explained to Beau and Jerry. "Keith Lucas is in a room just down the hall. George knows him from the force."

In just a few moments George was back, and he had Keith Lucas in tow. He introduced him all around and Keith sat on the edge of Jerry's bed to tell them about the Red Murder.

"It was my first case working homicide, and I remember it like it was yesterday. Bernice Adams. That was her name. I went down to Family Services to interview her foster son. The poor kid was so upset, he could barely speak. I felt really sorry for him. Of course, living with a prostitute couldn't have been the best environment, but at least he'd had a home of sorts. I asked the people in charge what would happen to him, and they weren't very encouraging. They said his chances of being adopted were pretty slim, that no one would want a ten-year-old boy who'd witnessed his foster mother's murder. It was bound to leave dreadful emotional scars, and the kid would be hard to handle."

"Did he know anything about her murder?" Sam asked.

Keith frowned. "Hard to tell. The kid wasn't very communicative. We wrote it off as a sex thing gone wrong, but I'm pretty sure they never made a collar."

"What was the kid's name?" Jerry asked the question that was in all their minds.

"Jimmy." Keith stared off in space and tried to concentrate. "I remember I typed out the report. Jimmy . . . uh . . . Bradley! The last name was Bradley."

Sam gasped. "Are you sure?"

"I'm positive. It was my first report for homicide,

and I must have gone over it ten times, to make sure it was right. The kid's name was James Bradley."

"James Bradley. Brad James." Sam turned to George. "It's the same guy! The name's just reversed. Two different personalities in the same body."

"Like Jekyll and Hyde?" George looked dubious.

"Exactly!" Jerry looked excited. "I told you he turned into someone I didn't know!"

Suddenly, George was a model of efficiency as he gave the orders. "Sam? Call the lie detector expert, and explain it to him. Then ask if Brad James could have passed that test if James Bradley committed the murder. Beau? Go out in the hall and use your cell phone to call Marcie. Don't alarm her, but get her to meet you at that awful coffee shop across the street."

"I shouldn't tell her?" Beau looked confused.

"No. Brad might listen in on the call. Just tell her you have to see her right away. Make up some excuse."

Keith watched as Sam dialed the lie detector office, and Beau raced out to the hall. Then he turned to George with interest. "What can I do?"

"You've got a major in psychology, don't you?"

Keith nodded. "Sure. It's always fascinated me."

"Then take a look at these letters." George reached in his pocket and pulled out the three letters from the crazy fan. "Tell me if you think they were written by the same person."

Keith scanned the letters, and frowned. "I'm not exactly an expert, but I'd say they were written by two different people."

"What makes you think that?"

"The first letter sounds like it was written by a younger person, a disturbed person who's very frightened. The second and third letters are much more rational. They contain a definite threat, while the first one doesn't."

"Okay. That fits." George explained. "The kid you interviewed, Jimmy Bradley, wrote the first one. And I think Brad James wrote the others, trying to get money from Mercedes. When that didn't succeed, he ordered the red bathing suits, and set Mercedes up for a hit. He figured that if he couldn't *scare* her into giving him the money, he'd have her killed and *inherit* it. Brad hired a killer, just as I suspected. But the killer-for-hire was his own alter ego, James Bradley."

Sam hung up the phone with a frown. "You're right, George. If Jimmy Bradley killed Mercedes, Brad James could have passed the lie detector test. The expert said he had a case like that once, with a classic split personality."

"Okay. All we have to do now is . . ."

George stopped talking as Beau raced into the room. His face was white, and he looked ready to drop. "She's gone!"

"Gone where?" Sam felt the sweat break out on his forehead. He had a terrible feeling he knew the answer.

"Rosa doesn't know! Marcie married Brad yesterday afternoon, and they've gone on their honeymoon!"

"Are you sure you don't want to come with me?" Brad slipped an arm around Marcie's shoulders and gave her a little squeeze. "I'd love to teach you to play golf. It's something we could do together."

Marcie smiled and shook her head. "No, thanks, darling. You can teach me when we get back to California. I'd just slow you down today."

"But won't you be bored, all alone?"

"How could I be bored in Hawaii?" Marcie laughed. "There's a beach right outside our condo, and wonderful little shops to explore. I can even take a sightseeing tour of the island. Don't worry about me, Brad. I'll find plenty of things to do."

"Well . . . if you're sure . . ."

"I'm sure," Marcie insisted. "Go ahead, Brad. Have fun. That's what I intended when I arranged this."

Brad pulled her into his arms and kissed her. Then he headed for the door. "I'd better hurry or I'll be late for my reservation. We'll have a nice romantic dinner when I get back. And then we'll continue right where we left off last night."

Marcie gave a happy smile as Brad went out the door. Last night had been wonderful. Perhaps it had been a mistake to arrange a full day of golf for Brad. They could have spent the entire day in bed. But that was selfish, and they had a whole life of love and passion to look forward to.

After a leisurely shower, Marcie dressed in shorts and a blouse. It was ten past eight in the morning, and the shops probably wouldn't open until nine. She'd stop at one of the little cafés and have coffee. And then she'd go shopping for the perfect dress to wear tonight.

Marcie left the condo and rode the elevator down to the lobby. It was a lovely day, and the warm sun and blue skies matched her happy mood. She had plenty of cash for shopping, but perhaps she'd use the credit card Brad had given her last night. She could hardly wait to sign her new name: Mrs. Brad James.

Rosa's face was white as she poured cups of freshly made coffee for George, Sam, and Beau. "I told you on the phone. I don't know where they went."

"We have to find them!" Sam was clearly worried. "Think carefully, Rosa. Did Marcie give you any clues to where she might be going?"

"She told the twins she didn't know. Brad wanted to surprise her. But"—Rosa stopped and frowned—"Mr. Brad told me to pack summer clothes for her, and I know she didn't take a coat. Does that help?"

George nodded. "That means they didn't go back East. They wouldn't travel to a cold climate without coats."

"Did you pack a bathing suit?" Sam looked worried. Marcie mentioned that she wore Mercedes's swimsuits.

"No. All I could find were red ones, like the kind Miss Mercedes was wearing the night she died. I guess it was superstitious of me, but I lied and said I couldn't find one. Did I do wrong, Mr. Sam?"

Sam gave a sigh of relief as he smiled at her. "No, Rosa. You did exactly right."

"How about Marcie's passport?" Beau suggested. "Did she take it?"

Rosa shook her head. "It's still in that little leather folder in her top dresser drawer. I did some cleaning in her room yesterday, and I saw it."

"Great!" George took charge again. "That means they took a domestic flight. Wake up the twins, Rosa. Maybe Brad said something to them."

It didn't take long to wake the twins. In just a few moments, Trish and Rick came down the stairs in matching pajamas and robes.

"What's going on?" Rick asked.

George smiled at him. There was no sense in alarming the twins. "We have to talk to your aunt Marcie. Do you have any idea where she went on her honeymoon?"

"She wouldn't tell us." Trish looked betrayed.

"But that's only because she didn't know," Rick corrected her. "Brad said it was a secret."

Sam nodded. "Did he say anything to you? Maybe give you a clue to where they were going?"

"Well . . . yeah." Rick looked at Trish and she nodded. "You first."

"Brad said he'd bring me back a shell for my collection. So we know they went to a place with a beach."

Rick nodded. "And he asked me if they had any Hawaiian baseball players. Trish and I think they went . . ."

". . . to the time-share condo." Trish finished the sentence for him.

"You guys are great detectives." George smiled. "I suppose you've got the condo telephone number around here somewhere?"

Rick reached in his robe pocket and pulled out a slip of paper. "Mom left it for us the last time she went to Hawaii with Brad. Trish and I were going to . . ."

". . . call Aunt Marcie today." Trish nodded. "And then when she answered, we were going to hang up quick."

Rick looked very guilty. "We know that's not nice, but we just wanted to see if she was there."

Sam took the number, and dialed the phone. He frowned as he listened to empty ringing, and finally he put the receiver down. "What time is it in Hawaii?"

"There's a two-hour difference." Beau glanced at his watch. "That would make it eight-thirty in the morning."

"Well, they're not answering the phone. And we don't even know for sure if they're at the condo."

"Call the time-share company and ask," George suggested. "You know the name, don't you?"

"Dream West. I remember it from the will." Sam nodded and picked up the phone.

"Is Aunt Marcie in trouble?" Trish looked very worried.

"No." George tried to lie reassuringly. "We just need to talk to her."

"Are you sure Brad isn't going to hurt her?" Rick looked just as worried as his sister.

George frowned and avoided the question with one of his own. "Why do you think he'd do something like that?"

"Because he acts crazy sometimes." Trish glanced at Rick. "I think we'd better tell them."

Rick looked hesitant, but then he nodded. "We're going to get in trouble for this, but . . ."

". . . we peeked in the guest house window one time, when Brad was supposed to be gone on a business trip." Trish interrupted her brother. "And he was in there behind some boxes, acting very weird."

"In the guest cottage?" George frowned as both twins nodded. "What was he doing in there?"

Rick shrugged. "Cutting up magazines . . ."

". . . and pasting letters on a piece of paper." Trish finished up for him. "We couldn't see what the paper said, but he looked very weird."

"You didn't tell your mother about it?"

"No way!" Both twins spoke at once.

"Because you didn't want to get in trouble?"

Rick nodded. "That's part of it. Mom told us never to go in the guest house. She said it was . . ."

". . . dangerous, because everything was piled up in there." Trish finished the sentence for him. "And we were scared to rat on Brad."

Sam hung up the phone with a frown on his face. "I just talked to the booking agent, and she said a Mr. Al

Coplin from Chicago was using the condo this week. Do you want me to start calling hotels?"

"They're at the condo." Rick sounded very positive. "You can switch reservations, and you don't even have to tell the company."

Trish nodded. "That's what Mom and Brad did once. They called this guy and offered him free airplane tickets if he'd switch weeks with them. Why don't you call Mr. Coplin in Chicago and ask him if that's what they did?"

A few moments later, Sam had Mrs. Al Coplin on the phone. Everyone listened to his one-sided conversation, and it was very clear that the twins had been right. Brad had switched weeks with the Coplins, and promised to buy them two first-class, round-trip tickets to Hawaii in return.

"What now?" Sam turned to George as he hung up the phone. "Shall I try the condo again?"

George nodded. "Keep trying until you get Marcie on the phone. If they went out to breakfast, she's bound to be back soon."

He had never liked to play golf, so he stayed inside the labyrinth of his mind. Golf was a boring game. Businessmen were forced to play to make deals, but he wasn't a businessman, and there was no reason for him to play.

Most of the men on the golf course were old, and they wore Hawaiian shirts, and shorts that exposed their skinny white legs. It was not a game for spectators. One easily tired of watching the small white ball as it traveled over the immaculately kept grass, to finally drop into a hole marked with a pole and a flag. The holes were all the same. As were the balls. And the clubs.

There was no provision for creativity in the game of golf. Perhaps that was why the husband enjoyed it. He was not a creative person. Everything he did was programmed, from the way he combed his hair, to the way he made love to his bride. And when she had served her purpose, she would go the way of the other.

That thought made him feel anxious, and he was glad the husband was here, and not in the condo with her. He liked her. She was different from the other one, but still the same. It reminded him of his relationship with the husband. They were different, but they were the same.

Was there some way that he could warn her? He would never try the letter again. That had been a terrible mistake. She had refused to believe him. And then she had shown the letter to the husband, and he had set the wheels in motion that had resulted in her death.

No. It was better to watch and wait, and guard her against the red. He would stomp it out before it could reach her, render it harmless so that it couldn't hurt her. If he succeeded in rescuing her, he would be saving himself as well. But the husband had plans for her. He could tell. The husband wanted her money, and he couldn't get it unless she was dead.

Dimly, he heard them calling the husband. They were waiting, and it was his turn to play the silly game. That meant he had to go back into hiding and let the husband talk and smile, and go on with his plan. At first it had been just him, Jimmy, the boy alone. Then Brad had joined him, and he had grown so powerful that Jimmy was barely there. Jimmy had been a faint shadow, a mere flicker, a feeble specter obscured behind Brad's dominant presence. Only one thing possessed the power to make Jimmy strong. Red. Jimmy's whole purpose for being was to fight the evil red. Brad knew it. And he would use Jimmy when the time was right, to destroy her.

Marcie tossed her packages on the couch and raced for the phone. It had been ringing when she unlocked the condo door, and she'd almost dropped her keys in her rush to get inside to answer it.

"Hello?" Marcie answered, expecting to hear a click and then a dial tone. It seemed that whenever she rushed for the phone, the person on the other end of the line would hang up just as she answered.

"Marcie. It's Sam."

"Sam?!" Marcie's mouth opened in surprise. "How did you find me?"

"Never mind that. Is Brad there?"

"No." Marcie frowned. "Brad's playing golf, and he won't be back until this evening."

"Thank God! Now listen, Marcie. Jerry came out of his coma this morning, and what he told us means that you're in terrible danger! You didn't sign that will yet, did you?"

Marcie sighed. She knew what was coming. More accusations against Brad. "I signed it yesterday, at city hall, right after we were married. It's witnessed, notarized, and completely legal."

"Does Brad know that?"

"Of course. He was there."

"Just hear me out, Marcie. Don't say a word until I'm finished. And promise me you won't hang up."

Marcie sighed. She supposed she owed Sam that much. "All right. I won't hang up until you're finished."

"Thank you."

As Marcie listened, her frown deepened to a dark scowl. Brad was having an affair with Jerry? Never! And he stole money from Mercedes to pay his gambling debts? Absurd! Brad was the crazy fan? Totally ridiculous! And now that she'd signed her will leaving everything to him, he would use his alter personality, James Bradley, to kill her!?

"Marcie? Are you still there?"

Sam sounded anxious, and Marcie had all she could do to contain herself. She felt like slamming the phone down and never speaking to him again.

"Look, Sam." Marcie took a deep breath and did her best to calm down. "I really think you need professional help. What you've told me is utterly ridiculous, and I don't believe a word of it. Brad's a wonderful man, and he's also my husband. I don't want to hear another negative word about him from you or anyone else. And don't bother trying to call me back, because I'm not going to answer!"

CHAPTER 28

Marcie had been as good as her word. George and Sam had taken turns calling for a solid half hour, before they'd given up and rushed for the airport. Sam had decided that if Marcie wouldn't answer the phone, he'd break into the condo and drag her out of danger by her hair, if necessary. George had insisted on going along. His stateside police connections might help. And now they were standing at gate twenty-eight, hoping to buy two tickets from passengers who'd booked in advance on a sold-out chartered flight.

"Are you sure this is the only flight to Hawaii?" George scowled at the boisterous college students sprawled out on every available chair.

"This is it." Sam sighed deeply. "The only other flight leaves later and doesn't arrive until after nine Hawaiian time."

"Okay. I guess we're stuck with a bunch of college students on Spring Break. At least they always need money. How about the blonde in the pink shorts and the redhead in the jeans?" George motioned toward two girls who were sitting on their luggage near the check-in desk.

"Okay. Do you want to approach them? Or shall I?"

"Count me out. You're the lawyer. It's your job to be convincing."

Sam sighed as he approached the two girls. They didn't look like good candidates to him, but George could be right. "Excuse me . . . girls? Would you be interested in selling your tickets for double their purchase price?"

"No way!" The blonde shook her head. "We'd never get on another flight tonight, and our boyfriends are already in Hawaii."

The redhead nodded. "She's right. There's no way we're going to give them the chance for a night alone in Hawaii!"

"But think of all the money you'd have to spend, once you got there."

The blonde laughed. "And think of all the girls Phil and Ray might pick up if we're not there to keep an eye on them. No thanks, mister. Try somebody else."

"You bombed out?" George raised his eyebrows as Sam came back.

"Completely. They're afraid to leave their boyfriends alone for the night in Hawaii. Maybe we'd get better results if you tried two guys."

"Me, huh?" George shrugged. "Okay. I'll give it a whirl. Those two football player-types by the window might do it."

Sam watched as George approached the two guys in jogging suits. They seemed to be listening. One even looked tempted, but the other said something, and then they both shook their heads. When George came back, he had a frown on his face.

"I was right. They're football players. But they won't do it, either. They don't want to give the rest of the team a head start."

"I don't understand it." Sam frowned. "When I was in college, I would have jumped at the chance to sell my ticket for a profit."

"Maybe their parents are rich, and they don't need the money. Or maybe spending the night in Hawaii with their girlfriend or boyfriend is more important than cash."

"Okay." Sam nodded. "Let's pick a couple in love, and try to get *their* tickets. How about that skinny brunette with the frizzy hair, and the guy with the John Lennon glasses?"

"Good choice. They look like hungry students. Throw in the money for a meal at the airport restaurant, and they might go for it."

Sam put a smile on his face as he approached the young couple. "Hi. My friend and I are trying to buy two tickets to Hawaii. Would you sell yours for double price, plus a free meal in the airport restaurant?"

"Can we, Pete?" The frizzy-haired brunette looked excited.

"Well . . . I don't know." Her boyfriend frowned. "Are we talking hamburgers? Or steak?"

"Anything you like. They've got a full menu. I'll spring for fifty dollars' worth of any entree you like. For each of you."

"Well . . . maybe." The young man looked interested, but not convinced. "With wine?"

Sam tried not to grin. "With a twenty-dollar bottle of wine. Will that do?"

"It's sounding a lot better. But we might not be able to get another flight tonight. And that'd cause us real emotional suffering."

"Of course, it would," Sam agreed. "But I imagine, if I put you up at the Hyatt, you'd forget about your emotional suffering."

"Could be. Let's see . . . two eighty apiece for the tickets. That's what it'll cost us to book another flight. A hundred for the meal, and another twenty for the wine. And a hundred sixty for the Hyatt. That comes to eight hundred forty. Let's call it an even nine hundred. I'm giving you a real break on the tickets. We'll fly coach."

"It's a deal." Sam opened his wallet and counted out the cash.

"Give him the tickets, Sara."

The frizzy-haired brunette was all smiles as she handed over their tickets. "Thanks, mister. You just gave us enough money for next semester."

"Good." Sam smiled back. Then he turned to the young man. "What's your major?"

"Pre-law."

"That's what I thought." Sam reached in his pocket and pulled out a card. "When you graduate, come and see me. Maybe we can work out an internship."

The young man glanced down at the card, and when he faced Sam again, he looked dismayed. "Sorry, Mr. Abrams. If I'd known who you were, I wouldn't have given you such a hard time. We'll be glad to give you our tickets at cost."

"Absolutely not." Sam shook his head. "You drove a hard bargain, and you stuck to it. I've got a couple of young lawyers in my office who could learn a thing or two from you."

"Are you sure?"

"I'm positive. Law school's expensive, and my firm is setting up a scholarship fund. What's your name?"

"Mark Adler."

"Okay, Mark." Sam shook the young man's hand.

"Don't forget about that scholarship fund. Make sure you send me your application."

"I won't forget. Thank you, sir."

Sam felt good as he headed back to the spot where George was waiting. Mark Adler would make a fine lawyer someday.

George grinned as he saw the tickets. "You got them?"

"I got the tickets, but I think the kids got me. They drove a hard bargain. Come on, George. The sign at the desk said we leave in twenty minutes."

"Students?" An amplified voice came over the loud-speaker. "Students? Please listen to me!"

It took several more calls from the loudspeaker before the crowd of students was quiet. Sam spotted a heavyset woman wearing a purple pantsuit, holding a microphone. She looked more like a harassed elementary schoolteacher than a flight attendant or ticket agent.

"My name is Miss Ripley, and I'm your tour director. Are we all ready for a nice vacation?"

Several students cheered, but the rest looked bored.

"That's wonderful! Now, I want you to all sit quietly and relax. Our flight has been delayed just a tiny bit, but we should be . . ."

There were groans so loud, the rest of her sentence was drowned out, and Sam and George exchanged glances. One of the football player-types that George had approached stood up and shouted, "What's 'a tiny bit'?"

"No more than thirty minutes, I promise you. And I know you're all adult enough to wait for thirty minutes."

"Can we board now and wait in the plane?" The football player's buddy spoke up.

"No, dear. You see, the plane isn't here yet. They're

still getting it nice and clean for you. You wouldn't want to get on a plane that hadn't been cleaned, would you?"

"Yes!"

Several students shouted in unison, and the tour director looked even more harassed. "To pass the time while we're waiting, let's all sing a song. What's your very favorite song?"

There was absolute silence, and the tour director put on a forced smile. "All right. I'll choose one."

Sam and George exchanged glances as the tour director started to sing "Puff the Magic Dragon" in a quavering soprano. No one joined in, and her voice trailed off. Even if they boarded in thirty minutes, as she'd promised, it was going to be a very long flight.

It was three in the afternoon when the doorbell rang, and Marcie hurried to answer it. Perhaps Brad was home early. But it was a deliveryman from a boutique.

"Are you sure this is for me?" Marcie was puzzled.

"Yes, ma'am. If your name is Marcie James, it's for you."

Marcie began to smile as she tipped the deliveryman and took the package inside. There was only one person in Hawaii who would call her Marcie James. She wasn't sure when he'd had time to shop, but this was a gift from Brad.

The package was wrapped in gold paper, and Marcie looked down at it for a moment, enjoying the suspense. Then, when she couldn't stand it any longer, she ripped off the paper and lifted the lid of the box inside.

Marcie gasped as she lifted out a lovely red silk negligee with delicate lace trim. It was so sheer, it was

almost transparent. A perfect gift from a new husband
to a new wife.

There was a card in the bottom of the box, and
Marcie pulled it out eagerly. It was in Brad's handwriting, and she could almost hear him saying the
words. *My darling. Please wear this for me when we're alone
tonight.* Then the handwriting seemed to change
slightly. Perhaps Brad had written the last line with a
different pen. *I love you more than life itself.*

Marcie felt tears of happiness fill her eyes. How
sweet! How romantic! And how very sexy! She ran her
fingers over the smooth fabric, and imagined how it
would feel when Brad touched her skin through the
material. But then an unpleasant thought intruded on
her happiness, and she frowned as she folded the
negligee carefully and put it back in the box. The crazy
fan had written, *Red is the color of blood.* And Brad had
given her a red negligee!

Even though she tried to push the thought out of
her mind, Marcie shivered. Sam had insisted that Brad
was the crazy fan, and that his alternate personality was
triggered into a killing rage by the color red. Of course,
that was impossible. She had to trust her new husband.
She would hurt Brad's feelings if she didn't wear the
negligee he'd chosen for her, and there was no reason
in the world not to wear it. She was just overwrought
from Sam's call, but she was determined not to let his
insane suspicions spoil the lovely night Brad had
planned for them.

Sam buckled his seat belt, and turned to George. "At
last! I thought we'd never get off the ground!"

"My mother used to tell me not to count my chickens
before they were hatched. We're not off the ground yet."

Unfortunately, George was right. There was another delay, and then another. The tour flight had a low priority, and several other commercial jets were allowed to take off first. When they finally lifted off, George glanced at his watch. "It's almost six-thirty. We might have been better off if we'd caught the commercial flight."

"You're probably right, but at least we're finally on our way. Five hours from now we'll be in Hawaii."

"Students? Excuse me!" The tour director stood in the front of the plane, using the flight attendant's microphone. "Quiet down, please. I have an important announcement."

There were several groans, but the plane full of vacationing students quieted somewhat. George grinned at Sam. "I hope she's not going to sing again."

"Me, too!" The pretty young redhead sitting next to George gave him a smile, and George smiled back. Several students had asked them if they were chaperones, and they'd been more friendly when they'd found out that George and Sam were just on the plane as passengers.

"Students?" The tour director tapped the microphone until she got everyone's attention. It was impossible to ignore a squealing microphone. "Our pilot has just told me that we'll be slightly delayed by head winds. Our E.T.A. is now ten P.M., Hawaiian time."

The redhead sitting next to George gave a deep sigh. "Personally, I think we'll be lucky to get there by midnight. I took this flight last year, and it was five hours late! We circled the airport in Honolulu for an hour and a half, waiting to land!"

Sam glanced at George and frowned. Marcie was in terrible danger, and they were stuck with a hundred boisterous college students on a flight that might arrive hours too late. And there wasn't one single thing they could do about it!

Marcie had just finished dressing in the lovely white cocktail dress she'd purchased that morning, when she heard the key in the lock. She glanced at the clock and smiled. Brad was home early. It was only six-thirty.

"Marcie? Where are you, darling?"

"I'll be right out." Marcie gave one final pat to her hair, and walked out into the living room. "Did you have fun?"

Brad nodded. "It was great! And you look fantastic! Is that new?"

"I just bought it this morning. But it's not as beautiful as the wonderful present you sent."

"The negligee." Brad pulled her into his arms and kissed her. "There's a boutique at the club, and I saw it in the window when we broke for lunch. Do you like it?"

"It's absolutely gorgeous."

"Will you model it for me?"

Brad wiggled his eyebrows and Marcie laughed. "I'd love to. But you'll have to wait until later. I don't think that's the kind of outfit they let you wear in a restaurant."

"You're probably right." Brad grinned. "It'll keep. But you will wear it tonight, won't you?"

Marcie hesitated, and then she nodded. "Of course. Where are we going for dinner?"

"A little French place called Le Chêne."

"The dog?" Marcie frowned slightly.

"No, the Oak. Unless you speak French, they sound the same. The golf pro told me all about it. They have a crispy duck with apricot sauce that's supposed to be the absolute best anywhere."

"It sounds wonderful." Marcie smiled happily. She loved duck. "What time do we have to be there?"

"Not until seven." Brad glanced at his watch and whistled. "I'd better shower and get dressed. I didn't realize it was so late."

The words made him cringe inside the labyrinth of his mind. The husband had given her a red negligee. And she had promised to wear it tonight. But he would be strong this time. He would not let his fear push him into the vortex of insanity.

He let the husband climb into the shower, soap his body, and stand under the hot spray of water. He preferred cold showers, but this time he did not feel the heat of the water. If he could triumph over the water, he could also triumph over the red. He would not let it affect him.

The husband had made a mistake by warning him, and now he had the upper hand. He knew what his trial would be, and he had ample time to prepare for his battle with the red. He would win by convincing himself that she was wearing a negligee of a different color. White. Blue. Black. Green. Anything but the evil red. He would change the color of her negligee by employing the power of the mind.

He knew that this was the right course, the honorable course. The essayist Carlyle had said that foolish men mistook transitory semblance for eternal fact. That meant that things were not always as they seemed. He could use this bit of knowledge to save her.

The husband got out of the shower and began to dry his body. This did not take much thought, and he was free to use the unoccupied portion of their mind to formulate his plan. Color consisted of varying wavelengths of light. It was a reaction in the mind, an individual perception. He could alter that perception and transform the evil red to an acceptable hue. Thus, he would alleviate the necessity for her destruction.

As the husband chose clothing to wear, he felt his power fade. More brain cells were being utilized, leaving less for him. But he would save the portion of brain he needed. He had reached a decision, and he would do this for her. She was his lost love. He would not let the husband kill her through him.

"What's the matter, darling?" Marcie frowned. Several times during the excellent meal, Brad had seemed preoccupied.

"What? Oh . . . nothing. Just tired, I guess. It's been a long day."

"That's exactly what I was afraid of." Marcie gave him a tender smile. "How about a quick nap on the couch when we get back to the condo? I can always wake you later."

Brad grinned at her and shook his head. "No way! I've been thinking of you in that blue negligee all day."

"It's red." Marcie looked puzzled. "You sent me a red negligee, Brad."

"Oh. Of course. I meant to say red. For just a second there, I remembered it as blue. I must have looked at a blue one, too."

Marcie breathed a sigh of relief. There went Sam's theory. Brad hadn't chosen the red negligee for any ulterior purpose. He'd also considered a blue one.

The waiter appeared at their table with a silver pot of coffee, but Marcie shook her head. "No more for me, thank you."

"Could I interest you in our dessert tray? We have excellent French pastries."

"Darling?" Marcie glanced at Brad, but he looked preoccupied again. "Not tonight, thank you. I think we're ready for the check."

Brad seemed to rally a bit when the check arrived. He added the tip, signed it, and smiled at Marcie. "Ready to go?"

Marcie nodded and followed him out of the restaurant. It took at least fifteen minutes to get a taxi, but the fresh night air seemed to perk Brad up. When they finally climbed out of the taxi at the entrance to the condo, he was as energetic and talkative as usual.

"Would you like to take a walk on the beach?" Marcie suggested. "It's a beautiful, warm night."

Brad nodded. "Good idea. Let me run in and get you a sweater."

"But it's warm, Brad. I don't think I need a sweater."

Brad shook his head. "No, Marcie. I insist. It seems warm now, but the ocean breeze can be chilly. I don't want my lovely bride to catch a cold."

Marcie frowned as she watched Brad rush inside. He was so suddenly solicitous, it made her feel uncomfortable. He actually reminded her of the husband in *Summer Heat*. He was bending over backward to please her and allay any suspicions she might have about him.

That was ridiculous! Marcie pushed the thought from her mind. Brad was just being sweet. Comparing him to the husband in *Summer Heat* was grossly unfair. Brad was only concerned about her welfare because he loved her.

"Here, darling . . . put it on."

Brad appeared at her side so suddenly, Marcie jumped. Then she gave a nervous little laugh. "You startled me. I guess I was daydreaming."

"About me, I hope." Brad smiled at her lovingly, and slipped his arm around her shoulders. "Careful, darling. The path's slippery, and you could twist your ankle in those sandals."

The walk on the beach lost some of its magic as Brad warned her of every loose pebble. By the time they finally reached the edge of the water, Marcie felt as fragile as a basket of eggs. She'd always thought she wanted someone to take care of her, but Brad was being overly protective.

"It's all right, Brad." Marcie turned to him with what she hoped was a convincing smile. "I'm not *that* breakable."

Brad looked dismayed. "I'm sorry, darling. It's just that I don't want you to hurt yourself. You're the most important person in my life."

"And you're the most important person in mine." Marcie slipped her arm around his waist and snuggled close, forgetting how irritated she had been only moments before.

They watched the waves for a while, lapping at the shore gently and swirling back out again to be lost in the depths of the sea. Marcie felt the tensions of the day disappear with each passing moment. The moon glistened on the surface of the water, creating a shining, mirrored surface that stretched out to the horizon.

"Shall we go in now?" Brad turned to her with a smile. "I've got champagne on ice."

Marcie nodded, and they climbed the path to the condo again. As they passed a bed of night-blooming jasmine, she suddenly thought of the day Sam had met her at the airport, and how kind and gentle he had been, not the least bit fawning or overprotective as Brad had been tonight, but genuinely concerned about her welfare.

Thinking about Sam made her sad, and she forced that memory back. Sam was no longer a friend. He'd insulted her husband, and caused her to doubt him.

Marcie shivered as the reality struck her. She *did* doubt Brad. Sam had made her doubt him. It wasn't right, and it wasn't loyal, but she no longer completely trusted the man she loved.

"What's the matter, darling? Are you cold?"

"No, I'm fine." Marcie shook her head, but Brad held her a little tighter as he escorted her into the elevator. He was being overprotective again, just like the murderer in *Summer Heat.* Sam had planted these seeds of doubt in her mind. She had to ignore them, or they would ruin her whole honeymoon!

CHAPTER 29

Sam ignored the flight attendant's standard warning and raced for the exit as the plane touched down. George was right behind him. They were the first two off the plane, and they ran through the terminal, dodging people and baggage.

"What time is it?" Sam was puffing as he reached the door to the street.

"Almost ten." George pointed to the lighted kiosk in the distance. "There's the rental car counter down there."

"Okay. Good luck."

"Same to you, buddy."

George headed to the taxi stand at a dead run, while Sam hurried off in the opposite direction. They'd worked out a game plan on the plane. Sam would rent a car and drive straight to the condo. George would take a taxi to police headquarters, and pull every string he could to get them rolling. The first one to arrive at the condo would get Marcie out.

"May I help you, sir?" The girl at the rental stand gave Sam a friendly smile.

"Here's my card. I need a rental fast."

"Certainly, sir. Would you like a compact, a subcompact, a sedan, a sports car, a luxury car, a sports-utility vehicle, or a passenger van?"

"I don't care. Just give me whatever's gassed up and ready to go."

The girl punched a few numbers in her computer and studied the display. "How about a luxury Lincoln?"

"That's fine. How fast can I get it?"

"In less than five minutes, sir. They had it all prepped, but the customer decided he wanted a van instead. All I have to do is call, and they'll bring it around right now."

"Make the call. If it's here in less than five minutes, I'll give you a nice tip."

"Yes, sir!"

As soon as the girl had called for the car, Sam took out his driver's license and pushed it through the window of the kiosk. "Make a copy of this. All the information's correct. Give me a copy of the rental agreement, and I'll sign now. You can fill in the details later."

"Whatever you say, sir." The girl ran his driver's license through the copier and filled out a credit slip. Sam signed the slip and the rental agreement, and the transaction was done.

"Is that my car?" Sam gestured toward the white car that had just pulled up to the curb.

"Yes, sir. All of us here at Island Rental hope you have a wonderful vacation."

"What time is it?"

"Five minutes after ten, sir."

"Thanks. This is for you." Sam pushed a fifty-dollar bill through the window, gave a quick smile as he noticed the girl's astonished expression, and raced off toward the car. A moment later, he was speeding away from the airport, heading for the condo. He'd checked with one of the flight attendants on the plane, and she'd told him that the condo was forty minutes from the airport. He just prayed he'd get there in time to save Marcie!

"What time is it?" Marcie smiled as Brad handed her a glass of champagne.

"Five after ten. Why? Do you have a pressing appointment?"

Marcie giggled. Brad was teasing. "Only with my husband. But he looks very tired tonight. I don't suppose you'd be willing to stand in for him?"

"Thank you, my love. Nothing would please me more."

Marcie had been about to take a sip of champagne, but Brad sounded so strange, she stopped, the glass halfway to her lips. She glanced up at him and frowned slightly. He was wearing a very bemused expression, one she'd never seen before. But when he saw that she was puzzled, he smiled.

Even though she was still a bit confused by his rapid change of expression. Marcie smiled back. "You startled me, darling. You sounded almost like a different person."

"Perhaps I am a different person." Brad reached out to take her hand. "The love of a good woman can change a man for the better. Lord Byron made that observation back in the seventeenth century."

Marcie raised her eyebrows. She'd never heard Brad quote Byron before. Now that she thought about it, she'd never heard him quote anyone. There was a lot she had to learn about her new husband. But then he pulled her into his arms and kissed her, and Marcie sighed in pleasure. There was a new gentleness in his kiss. The almost insincere, overly solicitous Brad had disappeared. In his place was a man who truly cared about her.

As the kiss ended, Marcie opened her eyes. Brad was wincing, as if in pain, and Marcie sensed an internal struggle. Just as she was about to ask him what was wrong, he smiled his old, familiar smile again.

"You really threw off my golf game today."

"I did?"

"You did." Brad grinned down at her. "I kept imagining how beautiful you'd look in that red negligee. Go put it on, darling. I want to see you."

Marcie smiled, although she was still disturbed. Brad had switched moods again. For one brief instant, she thought about Sam and his crazy theory of alter egos, but she pushed the thought firmly from her mind. If Brad wanted her to wear the red negligee, she would. She'd do anything to make him happy.

"Wait here and have another glass of champagne. I'll be right back." Marcie gave him a quick kiss. Then she walked into the bedroom and closed the door. She knew she was acting like the proverbial blushing bride, but she was still a bit shy about undressing in front of her new husband.

Just as she was about to slip the new negligee over her head, the phone rang. Marcie waited for Brad to answer, but then she remembered that she'd unplugged the phone in the living room, right after Sam had called her. She had a good notion to let the bedroom phone ring, but it might disturb Brad and she certainly didn't want him to come in the bedroom to answer it.

"Marcie? Thank God I got you!"

Marcie frowned as she recognized Sam's voice. "Forget it, Sam. I refuse to listen to any more of your . . ."

"I'm calling from my rental car, and I'm ten minutes away. Please, Marcie. Don't let Brad in. Lock the door and wait for me to get there."

"I don't want you to come here." Marcie started to get angry. Sam was being a pest. "Turn right around and go back to the airport. Brad and I were just going to go to bed, and . . ."

"He's there?!"

"Of course, he's here. He's my husband. Look, Sam . . . I've had enough of . . ."

"Please believe me, Marcie. I'm trying to save your life!"

Marcie frowned. Sam seemed sincere, but he was terribly mistaken. "Look, Sam . . . you're wrong about Brad. I'd stake my life on it!"

"That's exactly what you're doing." Sam sounded very definite. "Stall Brad somehow, and I'll call the police. And whatever you do, don't wear red!"

"But I'm about to put on . . . Sam? Are you there?" The phone crackled with static, and then there was nothing but a dial tone. They'd lost contact. Marcie frowned and put the receiver back in its cradle. There was no doubt in her mind that Sam was wrong, but Brad *had* acted very strange tonight.

Marcie glanced down at the red negligee in her hand, and shuddered. She realized that Sam was being totally ridiculous, but it wouldn't hurt to wear the lovely white lace peignoir set that Rosa had given her for a wedding present. She'd tell Brad that the red negligee hadn't fit. He might be disappointed, but he would understand. After all, he'd almost given her a blue one, instead.

* * *

He was locked in a deadly struggle for the life of the woman he loved. The gods had given him a second chance to save her, and this time he was determined to triumph. At any moment she would appear, and she would be wearing the red negligee. He must not react to the evil red. It was a snare the husband had set for him. He would change the color in his mind, and thus avoid the trap.

He could feel the husband grow stronger as her footsteps approached. He fought to hang on to his small share of consciousness, and he succeeded. Another trap avoided. Another strategy rendered useless. The husband had planned to shut him out until the precise time had come to destroy her, but he was too strong to recede. He would remain here, fully cognizant, for all that transpired. He would not let the husband shock him into action, as he had done in the past.

The husband smiled at her as she opened the door. But then, as their eyes saw her, the husband made their face fall into lines of disappointment. "Marcie, I thought you were going to wear the red negligee."

He exulted in her perceptiveness. She had aided him in saving her life. But he was not dominant, and their face looked angry.

"I'm sorry, darling. I hope you're not too upset, but it's the wrong size. Can we exchange it tomorrow?"

"No! Put it on anyway! I want to see it!"

Her face turned white. She realized that the husband was very angry, and she hurried to placate him. He could have told her that it would be a losing battle. The husband was never placated.

"But . . . if I wear it, we can't exchange it."

"I don't care!" The husband made their face glower fiercely. Since frightened prey avoided the web, he made their face smile an embarrassed, sheepish smile. "I'm sorry, darling. I didn't mean to shout. It's just that I've been imagining you in that negligee all day, and I'm terribly disappointed. Won't you please wear it for me, even if it's the wrong size?"

He wanted to tell her to refuse, to make up another excuse, but the husband was too dominant to let him speak. He watched with dismay as her beautiful face reflected her emotions. Love. Fear. Suspicion. But love won out, as she smiled and nodded. "Whatever you want, darling. I'll put it on right now."

She turned and went back to the bedroom, closing the door behind her. He listened, but he did not hear the lock snap in place. Love had made her foolish, as it was wont to do. She trusted the husband, when she should have put her trust solely in him.

The husband was not observant. He poured himself a glass of champagne and drank it down in one gulp. There was a smile on their face; he saw the reflection in the mirror hanging over the fireplace. It was the smile of a predator.

But the alcohol had dulled the husband's perceptions, and he failed to hear the slight clicking sound as she locked the bedroom door. She had sensed the danger, and she was acting accordingly. But the husband was strong, and the lock on the bedroom door could be easily broken. If his love delayed too long, the husband would not be denied. He would smash through the door and dress her in the red negligee himself.

* * *

Marcie's hands were trembling as she took off the white peignoir set. Could Sam be right? The expression on Brad's face had been frightening. Of course, he'd said all the right things to reassure her, but something was terribly wrong. She had to delay as long as possible. Sam had said he'd call the police, and they could be here any minute.

"Marcie? Are you almost ready?"

Marcie jumped as she heard Brad's voice. He sounded anxious, and there was an undercurrent of something else in his voice, something that made her shiver. Did the voice belong to Brad James? Or James Bradley?

"I'll be there in just a minute." Marcie did her best to sound eager and loving. It was difficult when she was so frightened.

Suddenly, she thought of the phone and she picked it up. Thank God there was a dial tone! She punched out 9-1-1, and shivered as she waited for someone to answer. If he heard her, he might crash through the door and rip the phone out of the wall.

A woman's voice answered, but before Marcie could say a word, the line went dead. She was sure Brad had done something to disconnect it. Marcie glanced frantically around the room. She knew the lock on the bedroom door wouldn't stop him for long, and there was nowhere for her to run except . . .

Quickly, Marcie pulled on her jeans and a sweatshirt. Then she inched open the balcony door. Perhaps there was some way to climb down to a lower floor. She tiptoed out and glanced over the rail. No handholds. No footholds. It was a sheer drop, straight down to the golf course below.

The rail moved slightly as she brushed it with her hand, and Marcie frowned as she looked at it closely.

She'd seen this type of construction before. Her parents had owned a lake cottage with a balcony just like this one. Six holes were drilled in the wood, and six long metal pins held the railing in place. But the pins were missing on this railing. There was nothing to keep it from falling!

Marcie shuddered. If she'd leaned against the railing to look over, as most people did, she would have fallen nine floors to the ground!

Suddenly, Marcie understood. Brad had insisted they have wine with dinner. He'd even ordered a second bottle. And when they'd come back to the condo, he'd opened champagne. He would have claimed she was drunk, just like he'd done with Mercedes, and her death would have been listed as a terrible accident.

But when had Brad removed the pins? Marcie thought back to the morning, when she'd awakened very early and found Brad standing on the balcony. He'd told her he'd been admiring the view, but now she knew he'd been lying. That was when he'd removed the pins. And this was to be her fate. He planned to push her over the balcony, and then play the part of the grief-stricken husband again.

"Marcie? Let me in!"

Marcie shuddered. The dangerous undercurrent in Brad's voice had grown. Now he sounded very ominous. She tiptoed back in and rushed into the bathroom, calling out to him. "Just a second, darling. I'm going to take a quick shower."

There was another lock on the bathroom door. Marcie clicked it shut, and leaned against the door, trembling with fear. The walls were thin, and she could hear him pacing the floor, like a caged animal, outside the bedroom door. How long would he wait, before he broke down the doors to kill her?!

CHAPTER 30

"Okay, okay. Calm down." Captain Ted Oukalani rolled his eyes toward the ceiling. "I believe you. You think your friend's in danger, but you can't give me any proof. And your buddy thinks she's in danger, too. He's called three times from his car phone. I'm sorry, Mr. Williams, but we can't just send out a . . ."

"Captain?" A policewoman knocked on the open door. "Somebody just called in an emergency from that new time-share condo complex on Ocean Boulevard."

George jumped to his feet. "Which unit?"

"Nine-seventeen. But they hung up before our operator could ask any questions."

"That's Marcie! I told you she was in nine-seventeen. Are you going to roll now, or would you rather wait until you've got a murder on your hands?"

Captain Oukalani turned to the policewoman and began barking out orders. Then he turned to George with an apologetic expression on his face. "Sorry I didn't believe you before, Detective Williams. Your description of Mr. James sounded crazy."

"That's because he *is* crazy. But he's smart, too. He's already killed two women we know of."

Captain Oukalani got up from his desk. "Come on, Detective Williams. You can ride with me."

As they hurried out to the captain's cruiser, George realized that the captain had spent the previous half hour calling him mister, but now he was addressing him as Detective Williams. Normally, this show of respect would have delighted George, but he was too worried about Marcie to even smile.

Marcie tried to scream as the bathroom door clicked open, but she was too terrified to utter a sound. Her startled mind registered the small piece of metal he held in his hand. An Allen wrench, the proper tool for opening a door when someone had locked himself in the bathroom by mistake. And then he was bending over her, lifting her to her feet from her huddled position near the shower.

"You lied, darling. You never intended to take a shower. You were hiding from me."

The expression on his face was chilling. He wasn't angry, or upset, or even annoyed. Instead, he was smiling at her dispassionately. It was the kind of smile one would give to someone else's recalcitrant child. She opened her mouth about to say something, anything, to try to stall him. The police would be here any moment. "No, Brad. I . . . I wasn't . . ."

But opening her mouth was a terrible mistake. Before she could say another word, he had shoved a washcloth into her mouth, gagging her so she couldn't talk, or scream, or beg him to let her go. And then he was carrying her to the bed, and placing her gently on the mattress.

"Now, where is that lovely red negligee I gave you?" He smiled his chilling smile again, as he gazed into her terrified eyes. "I know you'd like me to take off that gag, so you could tell me, but it's really not necessary. I'll find it."

In some small corner of her terrified mind, Marcie blessed her mother's training. She'd never been allowed to leave clothing draped on chairs or scattered in piles on the floor. Her mother had believed that there was a place for everything, and everything should be in its place. It was a lesson Marcie had remembered to this day. When she'd taken off the red negligee, she'd folded it carefully and put it back in its box. And that box was now sitting on the top shelf in the closet.

"Of course." Brad smiled at her again. "Mercedes was the same way, you know. She always put everything away. But if I leave you to look for it, you'll run away again, won't you, darling?"

Marcie tried to shake her head. Here was her chance! But Brad gave an amused chuckle.

"Of course, you will. You have a very strong survival instinct. So you see, I have absolutely no choice in the matter."

Marcie watched in terror as he picked up the heavy glass vase from the night table. Her mind screamed out for Sam to hurry, to save her from the monster who was her husband. She'd been so wrong, so terribly wrong. And now he was going to kill her, just like he'd killed Mercedes!

But she could still move. He hadn't tied her hands and feet. Marcie kicked, and scratched, and twisted. But Brad was too strong, and he subdued her quickly. He gave an amused chuckle as he held her with one arm, and raised the vase with the other.

And then his arm swung in a wide arc, and came down toward her with horrendous force. She had time for only one short prayer for Sam to hurry, before everything went black.

The speedometer on Sam's rental car hovered at eighty as he barreled down the road, passing everything in sight. He saw flashing red lights behind him, but instead of slowing, he tromped harder on the accelerator. If the police stopped him for speeding, he'd convince them to escort him to the time-share condo. A speeding ticket didn't matter when Marcie's life was at stake.

But the police cruiser didn't stop. It just passed him and kept on going. There was a second cruiser behind it. And then a third and a fourth. George must have convinced them down at headquarters. Sam held the accelerator to the floor, and fell into line behind them.

A road sign flickered by at an incredible speed. One mile to go to the turnoff. Sam moved behind the fourth cruiser. There was no need for signaling. There was absolutely no traffic behind them. They'd passed every car on the road.

And then they were turning. And speeding down a city street. Sirens blared deafeningly in the quiet night. Other cars swerved quickly to the curb, to give them access. And the few lone pedestrians who were out this time of night stared as they screeched to a halt in front of the entrance to the condo.

"What the hell do you think you're doing?" Two men jumped out of the lead cruiser and confronted Sam angrily.

But Sam was prepared. Before he'd left Los Angeles, Keith Lucas had given him his badge, to use in an emergency like this. "Keith Lucas, L.A.P.D. Let's go! I know Brad James, and they sent me to help you talk him down."

The officers didn't bother to examine Sam's badge. They were in too much of a hurry. They just motioned him to follow as they rushed for the entrance.

He used every ounce of his will, but he could not control the husband. The husband's power had grown strong with the act of violence, and he used their hands to dress her in the red negligee. Then he stepped back and waited.

He knew the husband expected him to explode with rage at the sight of the evil red. He had done it before. But with the small awareness he had left, he fought the husband's plan.

Mind over matter. He stared at the evil red and altered it in his mind. It was blue. As blue as a summer sky on a perfect day, as blue as the calm waters of a lake, as blue as Jerry's startled eyes, when they'd shot him with the bullet that should have killed the husband. Their hands did not reach out to grab her. Their arms did not lift her and carry her to the balcony. Their eyes saw the blue, instead of the red, and nothing happened. Nothing at all.

The husband used their throat to give a frenzied cry of frustration. And then the struggle began. It was a classic struggle of right versus wrong, of good against evil. And he, Jimmy, could feel his power ebb.

Too strong. The husband was too strong to control, and he took the upper hand. Greed made him pick her up in their arms, and evil made their feet step closer and closer to the balcony door. Out into the night air the husband carried her, to the very edge of the balcony. And then they both heard a sound, one that filled the husband with despair and Jimmy with hope. The police were breaking in the door.

Sam rushed in and stopped as he saw the open balcony door. Brad had her in his arms, and he was about to throw her over the balcony. He shouted. Brad turned. And then he called out the name. "Jimmy! Stop him, Jimmy! If you love her, stop him!"

That was the boost he needed the extra push to give him enough control. She was his love, and the strength of that love made their feet pause. And stumble. And their arms tremble with the effort of carrying her. Their knees buckled, and his love dropped heavily to the floor. Evil would not triumph this time.

And then he found the courage to do what he should have done long ago, when the husband had first appeared. He would drive out the demon, even if it meant his own death. He had written that last line in the husband's note, and it was true. He loved her more than life itself. And now his love was safe. The lawyer would take good care of her.

He made their body turn, and leap, and crash through the rail. There was an instant of euphoria as he fell. The deed was done. The battle was won. Good had truly triumphed over evil. The ground rushed up with a mighty force, and he met it with an exultant cry.

EPILOGUE

She opened her eyes to the blinding whiteness. At first she didn't understand; her mind was floating from place to place, and it was difficult to think. Then she remembered, and she felt a chill creep over her body. She must be dead, and in the center of the white light everyone talked of when they'd had a near-death experience. She'd always thought those stories were ridiculous, but now it appeared that they were true, after all.

There was a haze in front of her eyes that she couldn't blink away. Everything shimmered and swam in a white sea. Brad had killed her, pushed her over the balcony, just as he'd planned. But this time he wouldn't get away with it. Sam knew. And George knew. All they had to do was prove it to the police, and Brad would get the punishment he deserved.

She felt tears gather in her eyes as she thought of Sam. Poor, dear Sam. How guilty he must feel that he hadn't gotten there in time to save her. He'd been right all along, and she'd ridiculed him and told him he was crazy. She wished she could tell him how sorry she was. She should have put her trust in Sam instead of Brad.

Too little, too late. The cliché rushed through her mind with startling clarity. She'd put too little faith in the one man she should have trusted. And now it was too late. How happy she'd been the night she'd stayed at his town house, watching glimpses of his family, and admiring the closeness that had surrounded him as a child. If she'd only known then what she knew now.

Sam had asked her to marry him. How different things would have been, if she'd agreed to be his wife. She'd fought that closeness, that love she'd felt for Sam, and she'd chosen Brad instead. She knew now that she'd made a terrible mistake. Sam would have loved the twins as his own. And Trish and Rick had already loved Sam.

Trish and Rick. What would happen to them, now that she was gone? There was Rosa, of course. Rosa would love them and care for them. But was Rosa's love enough? They'd been so brave, but now they had to endure another tragedy. Their whole family had been wiped out by one man, one monster. The twins had warned her. From the mouths of babes. And she hadn't listened to them.

Thank God they had Sam! He would love and comfort them at this terrible time. Without Sam they would have been lost.

The room revolved as she turned her head. It was an illusion, of course. She couldn't really turn her head. The light was blinding, but she managed to make out a huddled figure near her. Who could it be? An angel? A fellow traveler in the great beyond?

There was another illusion. Her eyes seemed to blink. And then she saw the dear features of the man she had come to love. Sam. He was here by her side. But how could he be here, unless Brad had killed him, too?

It was simply too horrible to contemplate, and her eyes snapped shut. It was just another illusion. But when she opened them again, Sam was still there. Tears streamed down her face. No! It couldn't be! The twins needed Sam!

Then he was leaning over her, brushing the tears from her cheeks. And she could feel his hands on her face. She opened her mouth and cried out, "Sam! Oh, no, Sam!"

"Easy, Marcie. You're going to be just fine. Just hang on a second, and I'll call the doctor."

What doctor? A dead doctor? But that was . . .

She blinked again and the room swam into focus. She was in bed. In a white room. With white sheets and a white blanket. She wasn't dead! Brad hadn't killed her. She was in a hospital room, and the blinking white light was only the sun shining through the blinds at the window!

"Well, well." A man in a white coat approached her bed. "It's about time you opened your eyes. You have a nasty gash on your head, but you're going to be just fine."

"Sam?" Marcie felt panic sweep through her. Had Sam really been there? Or had it been merely a dream?

"I'm here, Marcie." Sam appeared beside the doctor. "Let the doctor check you over. And if he says it's okay, I'll bring in Rosa and the twins."

Marcie winced as she turned her head so she could see him better. "They're here?"

"They caught the six A.M. flight. I told them you were going to be all right, but they insisted on coming to see for themselves."

Marcie smiled. "They just wanted an excuse to miss school. But I'm so glad they're here, Sam. They were right about . . . Sam! Did they catch him?"

"It's all right, Marcie." Sam saw the terror that flooded her face. "He's dead. He can't hurt anyone now. Just stay quiet, and let the doctor examine you. I'll go out and tell them you're awake."

Marcie's mind was whirling as the doctor probed and prodded. She hardly felt it as he examined her wound and re-bandaged it. It seemed to take forever but when he was through, he nodded. "I want you to stay overnight, just to make sure. We'll release you tomorrow."

"Oh, thank you!" Marcie smiled at him. "Could you ask Sam to come in? There's something I want to tell him."

A moment later, Sam was at her bedside. "What is it, Marcie?"

"I just wanted to say . . ." Marcie blinked back tears. "I'm sorry, Sam. I should have believed you. When I woke up, I thought I was dead. And I realized how different things would have been if I'd married you instead of Brad."

Sam smiled at her tenderly. And then he said something that made Marcie smile through her tears.

"I'll tell you a secret, Marcie. It's not too late."

BY REASON OF INSANITY . . .

Ten years ago, a jury found Michael Hart guilty of
murdering his wife. Confined to a state hospital for
the criminally insane, Michael has never stopped
insisting on his innocence—even though his
memories of the trial are murky and his nights are
plagued by bad dreams and sleepwalking.
After years of being tormented by doctors who
believe he is guilty, Michael finally gets his chance
to prove them wrong—by escaping.
Hiding in a safehouse, Michael must rely
on two allies to find an alibi.
One is a beautiful woman who believes his story
and is willing to gamble her life to help him.
The other is Michael's brother, an attorney at law
who's at risk of losing everything.
But all the evidence in the world won't be
enough to overturn twelve guilty verdicts . . .

Not when the members of Michael's jury
begin to get brutally murdered.
One . . . by one . . . by one . . .

**Please turn the page for an exciting sneak peek of
Joanne Fluke's
FINAL APPEAL
coming in August 2015
wherever print and e-books are sold!**

PROLOGUE

Hollywood, California

Carole Hart knew that her marriage was dead, but she wasn't the type to mourn. She'd already shed her tears, many of them during the years she'd been married, and her resolve was firm. She still loved Michael, she'd never stop loving him, but divorcing him was her only chance to have a normal life. Her new husband, the one she'd marry after her divorce was final, would be a wonderful provider. And even if the passion she'd shared with Michael was missing, she realized that she was probably much better off without it.

Despite her resolve, tears threatened to fall as she folded her designer silk blouse, the only quality item of clothing she owned, and placed it carefully in her old red suitcase. The blouse had been a birthday present from Amy Weston, her best friend at work.

Amy and the other secretaries who worked at World-Star Studios owned such extensive wardrobes that they were often mistaken for glamorous actresses. Carole was the only exception. In the years that she had worked at the studio, no tourist had ever mistaken her for anyone. Her skirts, blouses, and dresses were relics left over from her single days, shortened and altered in a desperate attempt to keep up with the styles but never quite achieving that fashionable look. Carole hadn't purchased a single new item of clothing since she'd married Michael. Most of her salary had gone for necessities: the rent, the food, the utility bills. And since maintaining Michael's career was so expensive, any extra money was quickly allocated for his acting classes. And his SAG dues. And the glossy photographs he had to provide for casting directors. No matter how carefully Carole had economized, it had never seemed to make a real difference in their financial status.

Once, when the bills had piled up and Carole feared she'd never be able to pay them all, Michael had made a joke of it. He said that if they won just one major sweepstakes, they could get their heads above water. Carole had thought it was the funniest thing she'd ever heard. Back then.

Six years ago, when she'd married Michael, the couples in their Hollywood apartment building had formed an informal support group. They'd all been young and poor and on the brink of that first big break. They'd met for potluck dinners and either commiserated or celebrated, depending on their circumstances. Back then Carole had been known for her cabbage salad. Cabbage was cheaper than lettuce, because it wasn't seasonal. She'd chopped it and mixed it with grated carrots and onions, then dressed it with an economical mixture of vinegar, sugar, salt, and black pepper. If Michael had worked that week, she occasionally splurged on red and yellow bell peppers to decorate the top. The first time she'd made her coleslaw, Michael had quipped about their salad days. Carole had laughed along with everyone else, but she hadn't understood the joke. Later she'd asked, and Michael had told her it was a quote from Shakespeare's *Antony and Cleopatra.*

Looking back on those days now, Carole realized that she'd never had much in common with Michael. He was a college graduate, and she'd gone right to work as an entry-level secretary at World-Star the moment she'd finished high school. They'd met at an audition, where Carole had fallen in love with his voice and his handsome face. When Michael had landed the part, he had taken her out for dinner to celebrate.

There had been many dinners when Michael was working. And even more lunches at hot dog stands when he was between roles. There had also been long, romantic evenings spent in his tiny apartment—the same apartment she was now leaving—listening to music and making love.

All the other secretaries, Amy included, had warned her not to get involved with an actor. She hadn't listened. And then, before she'd really thought about how terribly insecure their life together would be, she'd become Mrs. Michael Hart, the shoestring gourmet, bringing cabbage salad to potluck dinners where the men talked about artistic integrity, and the women sat next to them and dreamed of all the things they couldn't afford.

At first it had been exciting, being married to an actor. Carole had experienced a rush of pure pleasure every time she'd seen her husband's image on the screen. But show business was fickle, and it always took time for an actor to get established. Gradually, over the years, the other couples had traded their dreams for financial security. Most of them had decided the odds were against them, and they'd sacrificed their integrity to climb up corporate ladders. Couple by couple, they'd deserted their cramped apartments to make down payments on small houses in the valley where they could start their families. And then, one day during their fourth year of marriage, Carole and Michael had looked around and realized that they were the only holdouts from the original group.

Michael had never criticized their friends for giving up. The life-style of a dedicated artist was a tough one, and not everyone could endure the hardships it entailed. They'd kept in touch, and every time Carole and Michael had driven out to one of the rambling homes in the valley for a housewarming or a baby shower, the men had slapped Michael on the back and told him that they admired his perseverance. But their wives had gazed at Carole with eyes full of pity and offered to share their wealth. Here was the color television set that Tina's husband had replaced with a big-screen model. Since it was just sitting in the garage taking up space, they'd regard it as a real favor if Carole and Michael would take it off their hands. And Ellen's old Cuisinart, the old set of china that didn't go with Patricia's new wallpaper, the glassware that didn't fit in Yvonne's new dishwasher, and the answering machine that Tom no longer needed since he now subscribed to a service.

Carole had accepted the castoffs gratefully, even though she sometimes felt like their friends' favorite charity. She'd done her best not to envy the new, bigger houses, the prestige cars, and the vacations in Europe. She told herself she'd have all those things someday. She had faith in Michael's talents, and she could wait. But then she'd held her friends' babies, and her resentment had started to grow. They'd agreed not to have children until they were financially secure, but how much longer would she have to wait?

Three months ago, on the morning of her thirtieth birthday, Carole had awakened to take stock of her life. Michael was an excellent character actor, and when he worked, he was paid very well. But there were those frightening dry periods between roles when Carole was forced to sit back and worry, watching helplessly as their savings dwindled. The stress of not knowing when her husband would land his next part had turned her into a nervous wreck. Their whole life was a series of ups and downs, regulated by the crazy whims of casting directors and studio executives. There were no guarantees in show biz, none at all. Carole had known this from the beginning. And on the morning of her thirtieth birthday, she'd finally realized that they'd never have the security she craved, not even if Michael made it big. He could be a huge success one year and box office poison the next. She'd seen it happen just that way.

Michael had arranged a surprise party with the old crowd, even though they'd been smack in the middle of one of their down periods with creditors calling and the rent two weeks overdue. That night, when Carole had arrived home from work, she'd found everyone waiting for her, armed with food and champagne.

After a toast to her birthday with expensive champagne, Daryl Forrester pulled both of them over for a little talk in the corner of the kitchen. Daryl had been a struggling young artist when they'd met, but now he was a corporate executive with a wife and a family and a big home in the valley. He told Michael that Amcorp needed someone to host daily motivational seminars for their salesmen, and he'd recommended Michael for the job. They'd pay thirty-thousand-a-year in base salary plus a percentage of the increased sales. Michael could pull in fifty or sixty grand annually, maybe more.

Carole shut her eyes and prayed. It would solve all their financial problems if Michael took the job. Then they could pay off their bills and think seriously about a house and a decent car and the baby Carole so desperately wanted. But Michael thanked Daryl for thinking of him and turned it down flat.

After everyone had left, Michael tried to explain. He was sorry that Carole was disappointed, but couldn't she see that hosting promotional seminars for a big corporation was the ultimate in selling out? He was an actor, not a company puppet. A job like that would kill him.

They'd gone to bed and tried to resolve their differences by making love, but the old magic didn't work. After Michael had fallen asleep, Carole had stared up into the darkness and realized that there was no future with Michael. As painful as it might be, she had to leave him if she ever wanted to live a normal life. But where could she go? And what would she do? She'd begun to make her plans.

With a start, Carole came back to the present. It was already eight o'clock, time to load the car and drive to Amy's. The bedroom was stifling, not a breath of air even though she'd opened the window as wide as it would go. Their air conditioner had gone on the blink two months ago, and they hadn't been able to spare the money to pay a repairman.

Her old red suitcase had a broken latch. As Carole tied it shut with a belt she promised herself that the moment she was remarried she'd march into Gucci and pick out a whole set of expensive matched luggage. Her lover had been shocked when she'd told him that she was pregnant, but she knew he'd come around. Her voice had held just the right tone of injured outrage when she'd said that of course the baby was his. And no, she hadn't confided in anyone. She'd kept their relationship a total secret, because she'd known how important it was to protect him from the slightest scandal. Her only concern was to provide a normal family life for the baby, with a mother and a father and nice surroundings. His son or daughter deserved the best, didn't he agree?

He was an intelligent man, and he'd quickly realized that she had him over a barrel. One word to the wrong person and he could kiss his career goodbye. So they'd made a date for lunch tomorrow, and Carole was sure he was sitting in his office right now, figuring out the best way to preserve his reputation and meet her demands at the same time.

Carole picked up the phone and dialed Amy's number to tell her that she was on the way. Amy must have been sitting right by the phone, because she picked up the receiver on the first ring.

"Carole!" Amy sounded worried. "Is something wrong? I thought you'd be here by now."

"I would have been, but Michael came in while I was packing."

"My God!" Amy gasped. "Are you all right? I can be there in twenty minutes if you need me."

"Thanks, but that's not necessary. He's gone now."

"Was it awful?"

Carole sighed. "That's the understatement of the year! I'll tell you all about it later. Right now, I want to get out of here before—"

Carole paused as she heard a key in the lock.

"He's back! Hold on, Amy. I'll find out what he wants."

Carole put down the phone and stood up. She was surprised to find that her knees were shaking, and she took a deep, calming breath. It was ridiculous to be afraid of the man she'd lived with for the past six years. Michael had a volatile temper, but he usually kept it under tight control. He'd probably thought it all over, replayed that ugly scene in his mind, and now he'd come back to apologize.

"Michael? I'm in here." Carole sighed as she headed for the door. There would be another scene. He'd tell her he loved her and beg her to stay. Maybe he'd even promise to call Daryl Forrester to see if that job with Amcorp was still open. She'd just have to tell him all over again that it was too late. Their marriage was over. He had no choice but to accept it.